MW00849860

FOREVER REIGN

THE ELEMENTALS OF IONA

V.B. LACEY

Forever Reign: The Elementals of Iona Book Two

Copyright © 2024 by V.B. Lacey

All rights reserved.

No part of this publication may be reproduced, distributed, or transmitted in any form or by any means, including photocopying, recording, or other electronic or mechanical methods, without the prior written permission of the publisher, except as permitted by U.S. copyright law. For permission requests, contact vblacey.books@gmail.com.

The story, all names, characters, and incidents portrayed in this production are fictitious. No identification with actual persons (living or deceased), places, buildings, and products is intended or should be inferred.

ISBN 979-8-9877211-3-1 (paperback); ISBN 979-8-9877211-4-8 (hardback); ISBN 979-8-9877211-5-5 (ebook)

Cover designed by Maria Spada; Instagram: @mspremades

Map illustration by Andrés Aguirre; Instagram: @aaguirreart

Editing by Amanda Chaperone; Instagram: @achaperonwrites

Fiction & Fate Press LLC

www.vblaceybooks.com

For you, dear reader,
because we're all a little bit broken—
but that doesn't mean we're not whole.

PRAISE FOR FOREVER REIGN

"Forever Reign is the perfect ending to this duology! Full of heart-warming romance, laugh-out-loud banter, and characters willing to do anything for those they love, this is a story I'll be thinking of for a long time."
Nicole Platania, author of *The Curse of Ophelia*

"A heartfelt story featuring swoony romance, a found family you'll wish you were a part of, and the power of overcoming the darkness of your past."
Rachel L. Schade, author of the *Fae of Brytwilde* books

"Bold, sweeping, and heart-wrenchingly romantic, Forever Reign provides a gloriously epic conclusion to what is by far one of my favorite romantic fantasy duologies. Driven by a cast of beautiful, flawed characters and held together by stunning prose, V.B. Lacey has created a world and a story I would be happy to get lost in, again and again."
Tay Rose, author of *Threaded*

Author's Note

This book has scenes depicting anxiety, violence, grief, mentions of sexual assault, sexual harassment, unwanted physical touch, claustrophobia, traumatic flashbacks, and derealization. Please be mindful of these and other possible triggers.

PROLOGUE

Once, there was a fierce huntress.

A young woman with a simple life among those she loved.

Now, only a wraith remains.

Isolated from the world in a realm that is not her own, elevated above all who came before her, exists a being more powerful than even the gods. A being who evaded death itself, who calls grief her companion, who sees all. Knows all.

Ripped from her home and placed among the stars, there is a scorching, aching ember within her that yearns for peace she once knew. For another life under the night sky. For freedom, joy, and comfort.

Instead, fate has given her this.

Nothing.

Everything.

Forever.

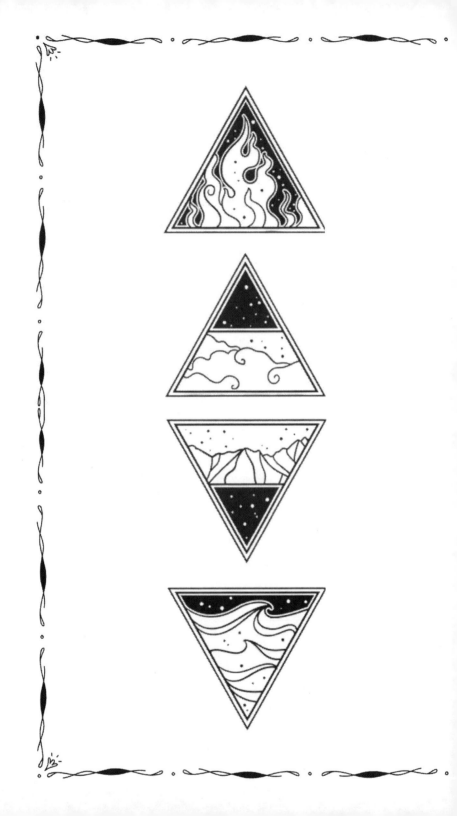

PART ONE:

BREATHE

CHAPTER ONE

Sebastian

The king lounged on his throne, one leg propped atop the other, a glass of whiskey resting lazily in his hand. It was his second—or third?—and almost empty; he could practically feel the judgment and condescension radiating from the lords convening before him. He wanted to see how quickly he could make the buzzing inside his head drown out the buzzing of their empty words—that didn't seem like too much to ask for. Not after he'd sat through four hours of middle-aged men droning on about which type of *bean* should be planted later in the spring and what color to paint the new wing.

Obviously, all important things that required his *utmost* attention.

"Your Majesty?" A familiar feminine voice broke him from his musings.

Well, he supposed not *all* of the council in attendance were middle-aged men.

If he hadn't known the owner of that voice so well, he might not have noticed the hint of exasperation that laced her use of his title. Sebastian shifted in his seat and raised his eyes from his glass to meet those of dark green, his jaw twitching involuntarily.

These weren't the same green eyes that haunted his dreams. No, he hadn't looked into *those* green eyes for three months now.

Annalise Dalgard, his royal advisor and best friend, quirked an eyebrow. "Your thoughts, sir?"

This palace needs better whiskey.

"Whatever Lord Perrin recommends for crop rotation is fine. Be sure we send half the goods in the upcoming shipments to the southern territories that were hit hardest in the storm. And for the love of the gods, I do *not* care what color the shelter is painted—just get it up and running, yes?" He uncrossed his legs and tapped his ring twice on the armrest of his throne, the heavy crest creating a reverberating *clang*.

The lords of his council nodded and rose swiftly from the long table at his dismissal. It had been months since Sebastian had returned to the council meetings, but the men were still stiff and hesitant in his presence, as if they expected the cruel tyrant of the last two years to rear his ugly head again.

Sebastian didn't blame them.

Annalise remained behind as the councilmen exited the throne room. She was one of the only people who had accepted Sebastian's miraculous return without fanfare. She'd taken it in stride: a curt nod, a slight wrinkle across her brow, and a "took you long enough."

He wished the rest of the kingdom were so easy to convince. When he'd returned from Iona, once again a free man, he hadn't known what to tell his people. He and Annalise had come up with some tale of grief and trauma related to his father's passing that had affected his mental health, and that he'd sought help and was improving, ready to enter society again as the king they once knew. Yet his council, his guards, his staff...they all treated him like an explosive that could go off at any moment. Nobody trusted him, and for good reason.

Gods, he'd made a mess of things. He could spend the rest of his reign trying to undo all his terrible deeds, the alliances he'd ruined, the people he'd let down. *His* people. The unfair taxes that had been penned by his own hand, the unjust punishments that had left his very mouth. Letters written to his royal guard to hunt down innocent merchants still littered his desk, signed with *his* name. People who had lost their livelihood for being unable to pay their dues to the crown still lined the streets of Karstos. Surely, countless bodies had piled up over the years because of his actions.

The kingdom that had praised him and welcomed his reign now whispered curses under bated breath. And they didn't even know the worst of it.

Sebastian inhaled sharply and released a deep sigh. He needed another drink.

"Well, that went better than last time," Annalise said as he stood and sauntered down the gold-lined steps of his throne. She turned on her heel when he approached her, their footsteps falling into sync as they exited the room.

He threw her a glance out of the corner of his eye. "None of them would even look at me, Anna. Please tell me how that's any better."

"At least Lord Everett didn't say a prayer of protection when you spoke to him."

"It's the little things, I suppose."

Annalise stopped walking and briefly touched his arm, the only sign she was breaking from her normal polished and official demeanor as his advisor. "Honestly, Seb, you're doing what you can. You're making a difference. The rest will come with time."

Only his closest companion and childhood friend was able to tell when his sarcasm veiled the hidden well of insecurity and self-doubt. He swallowed thickly and nodded, needing to break through his uneasiness.

"You know how I feel about that nickname. *Seb.* It's a rather informal way to address your king, no?" he taunted weakly. "Doesn't show much respect."

Her dark green eyes shifted from comforting friend to serious royal advisor. "And you know how *I* feel about you drinking at the council meetings," she quipped, grasping the golden handle of the throne room door and pulling it open. "I'm not picking you up if you fall face-first off your little throne."

He let out a huff of a laugh, following her down the massive hallway and to his office. There weren't many people he would let lead him, but he trusted Annalise Dalgard with his life. He owed her all of the respect he jokingly demanded. She was thirty-two, only a year older than him, and they had grown up in the palace together, her own father being the royal advisor to his—the late King Ryder. The entire capital had the two of them betrothed at birth, marveling at the striking couple they would undoubtedly make as King and Queen of Karstos.

But their relationship had never gone down that path. Perhaps it was because of the pressure of a kingdom, the weighted expectation on their every move, or the fact that they'd seen each other covered in pig feces after a particularly daring prank in their teens. They were simply too comfortable with each other, too different, too...familial. Neither one had ever expressed any interest in romance.

Except for that one night.

Annalise had been jilted by a potential suitor on the eve of her eighteenth birthday, and Sebastian had found her hiding away in a maid's cupboard. Her floor-length mahogany dress, the exact color of her hair, had pooled around her feet, streaks of kohl running down her tawny cheeks. Sebastian had seen the pain in her eyes, the humiliation and rejection written across her face, and had just...kissed her. He'd hoped it would take away whatever scars the foolish suitor had left on her. Instead, it had left them both utterly embarrassed and unable to look at the other for a week.

But at least he'd been able to give her *that* uncomfortable yet humorous memory to replace the one of young heartache.

Sebastian had known long before he ascended the throne that he would accept no one else as his royal advisor. Despite Annalise's youth, she was wise beyond her years and knew him better than anyone. Even more importantly—and only slightly annoyingly—she disagreed with him quite often and wasn't afraid to voice her opinions.

The fact that she had never lost faith in him, even in the two years when the darkness had ravaged his soul, was a gift he could never repay.

They entered his office, a large but simple space filled with only a few items. A rich brown desk built of sturdy oak sat against the center of the wall to the right of the entrance, with two matching bookshelves on either side. Across the desk was a couch with navy velvet cushioning and a cart of drinking glasses holding various decanters of liquor.

Which were looking rather low.

A floor-to-ceiling window took up the wall directly opposite the door, allowing a view of the gardens beyond. On the floor in front of the window rested a golden telescope. It had been a gift to Sebastian from his father when he was a boy and had been his most treasured possession throughout the years, especially as he grew older and had more responsibilities placed on his shoulders.

When his world felt overwhelming, he would look through the lens to the magnificence of the sky and remember that no matter what he was going through, the stars were watching over him.

The newest addition to the office resided on the wall behind his desk: a massive landscape of the night sky, with deep hues of blue, purple, and black washing over the canvas, blending together in delicate swirls. Bright silver flecks were scattered across the scene, a mass of twinkling stars that loomed over him as he worked. Sometimes, if he stood close enough, he could imagine he was among them.

Annalise walked to his desk and dropped a stack of papers on top of the already overflowing pile. She looked down at it, paused, then rolled her neck to eye Sebastian. "You have to go through these at some point. And no, I'm not doing it for you."

He sank onto his couch and eased back against the cushions, crossing one leg over the other. "I'm pretty sure I can make you do anything I ask. I *am* the king."

"Oh, is that what this means?" she deadpanned, pointing to the gold crown resting on the corner of his desk. "Good gods, how many times a day do you work that into a conversation? Really, Seb, I'm beginning to think you're overcompensating."

He let out an involuntary chuckle and leaned his head against the back of the couch, closing his eyes. "Ah, Anna, I missed you."

The sentiment slipped out without his permission. It had been three months, but any confession or acknowledgement of his time *before* was still like throwing ice over his body.

Annalise cleared her throat. "Look—"

He cut her off. "How is the storm relief coming along? Of all the topics of conversation in that ridiculous council meeting, nobody bothered to brief me on this."

"It was mentioned twice."

Ah, well.

"But you tell it so much better," he said, offering a meek smile as an apology. He knew he was distant, knew he needed to do better. *Be* better. Everything was simply...harder now.

Annalise let out her usual sigh—a sigh he was far too familiar with—but gave in. "The architects are almost finished with the new wing. Once it's painted and furnished, it'll be open to those whose homes were taken out by the storm. Priority will be given to families with children and the elderly, but we're hoping to accommodate"—she glanced down at one of the pieces of paper she'd put on the desk—"eight hundred displaced citizens."

"Is that enough?" Sebastian asked.

She waited a moment before responding. "The latest report came back showing numbers closer to two thousand without adequate shelter."

Not enough. It was never enough.

Sebastian ran his hand through his hair, the rings on his forefinger and pinky catching and pulling a couple of blonde strands with a sting. "We need to move funds to erect a shelter in the southern region. The one we have here will help some, but there's plenty of people who won't be able to travel the long distance. And send a messenger to the staff at Grenleigh House. Tell them to convert it to a refuge site for the foreseeable future. We'll make sure people know they can go there for temporary relief and a hot meal when needed."

Somewhere during his speech, Annalise had taken a pencil and began scribbling down his instructions. When he mentioned Grenleigh House, she'd paused and waited for him to finish.

"Are you sure? The manor has only ever been used by the royal family."

"Yes, Anna, I'm aware of that, given it's my house. Make sure it's done, please."

Grenleigh House was a lavish mansion located on the southeastern coast of Karstos. It had been in his family for generations, a secluded haven where they could get away for a period of time and enjoy the seaside. Anna was right, though: it had never been open to the public before.

But, desperate times, and all.

Three weeks previously, an enormous and unnatural storm had decimated the entire central and southern regions of Karstos. Buildings and homes were destroyed, crops were ruined, and much of the wildlife had been killed or endangered. The record keepers across the kingdom swore there had never been an instance like it in the history of the realm. Of course, they'd experienced bad thunderstorms—it rained often, which was how the land stayed so fertile and green—and the coastal cities had their fair share of hurricanes. But this storm was unprecedented.

It was a blizzard.

Karstos had never seen so much as a single *speck* of snow. Its climate was far too tropical. Yet overnight, the temperature had plummeted and the skies had opened, a torrential flood of freezing rain and ice chunks the size of saucers descending upon an unsuspecting and unprepared kingdom.

And this wasn't the only anomaly Sebastian had heard of gracing the realm. There had been reports from Ara Mir, the desert land, of people drowning in the middle of sand dunes. Lightning strikes in Evonlea that caused small avalanches up and down the Aataran Mountain Range, burying villages in snow and debris. Animals across all three kingdoms dropping dead from poison, crops catching fire and flames blazing through entire farms.

It was as if nature itself were rebelling.

Sebastian had thrown palace resources into caring for as many of his people as he could, but he feared it wouldn't be enough. Not if these natural disasters kept bludgeoning them. He knew they were no random acts of nature. There was only one reason the elements would be lashing out at humanity.

The sharp sound of Annalise creasing her paper brought him back to the present. "It will get done." She walked toward the door but hesitated before leaving. Sebastian watched as she brushed her hair away from her eyes and turned toward him. He could tell whatever she was about to say was from Anna, the friend, not Annalise, the advisor.

"You *are* doing a good job, Seb. I want those words to get through that thick head of yours. I'm proud, and your parents would be proud. And look, if this is about what happened on Iona, or about the girl...you can talk to me. You know that, right?"

Sebastian stiffened at her words, his clothing suddenly too tight. He hadn't told Anna much of anything that had happened during the last two years. She knew he hadn't been himself, but he'd shut her out too much for her to figure out what was going on. She had, however, seen his drawings: the ones he kept tucked away in his desk. Drawing had been one of the only times he felt his mind was his own—each careful stroke of the brush, each vivid image taking form, was from *his* hand. Nobody else's.

He'd drawn the coast of Karstos against a fading sunset, landscapes of all the places he'd traveled, faceless people on nameless streets. If there was something pressing on his mind, such as when he was searching for the Dagger of Volnus, he drew it over and over. He painted the monsters from his nightmares, giving life to the shadows that haunted him.

But mostly, he drew *her.*

Isla.

When Annalise had first seen the drawings, he'd offered that single name in answer—and Annalise hadn't questioned him again. His best friend could put two and two together. One look, and she'd known what Isla meant to him.

He put a finger to his temple. He needed a drink.

As Annalise wrapped her fingers around the handle of the door, it suddenly swung open. Sebastian jerked in surprise as she jumped backward to avoid being hit.

"Explain yours—"

"I apologize, Your Majesty," a short, plump man with a red face and sweat dripping from his forehead said as he panted, looking anxiously between Sebastian and Annalise. "We have news from another kingdom." He swiftly held out an envelope.

"And why didn't you find the ambassador for that kingdom and give him the news? We have protocols in place. You can't just barge into—" Annalise started, but the messenger interrupted again.

"It's not from Ara Mir or Evonlea, ma'am." The man pinched his brow. "It's from Iona."

CHAPTER TWO

Sebastian

U nease crept down his spine, his heart pumping erratically.

Iona. Murky memories swam in his head, images he usually repressed until he was alone in his room without the eyes of a kingdom upon him.

Purple shadows sliced through his mind.

The crack of a neck.

Green eyes, crimson hair, wet blood on his fingers.

Regret. So much regret.

"Give me that," Sebastian said as he lurched toward the messenger, whipping the envelope from the man's hand.

Why was Iona writing to him? The kingdom the world had once believed to be lost had only recently exposed itself again. The Chamber, the group of elected leaders on the island, had decided it was time to embrace the truth and open their borders to the other nations for trade and communication.

There had been no pomp and circumstance, merely a sealed letter delivered to the three rulers: King Adrik and Queen Melanora Kegameth of Evonlea, the Triad clan of Ara Mir, and Sebastian himself. He'd already known of its secret existence, of course, but receiving the news had still sent him reeling. Iona was supposed to *stay* a secret. There were...things the world couldn't know about. Things he hadn't told anyone.

The letter had been concise and to the point, briefly explaining Iona's history and why the people had gone into hiding. It included a list of resources the island had to offer and expressed interest in trade discussions with the kingdoms. The writers had emphasized their desire for peace and harmony among all people, and ended with: *We are here. We are not going anywhere.*

A bold claim to stake from a small island community. Evonlea and Ara Mir had seen it as a confident bout of pride from the prodigal kingdom. Sebastian, however, had seen it as a threat.

Logically, he knew that Iona itself wasn't guilty of anything. Those people had no hand in what had happened to him or the events of three months ago. But he couldn't seem to separate those white sands from the darkness that plagued him. It was a constant reminder of what he'd done.

Sebastian opened the envelope and pulled out the thick, crisp parchment inside. Lifting his eyebrows to the messenger, who was still standing at the door with a look of mild curiosity, Sebastian gave a flick of his wrist. Annalise ushered the man out of the office and shut the door with a soft *snick*.

"Well? What does it say?" she asked.

He flipped the envelope, showing his name and title in swooping, cursive letters, so she could read it. "I believe this is addressed to *me*, Anna."

"Oh, give it to me, Your *Arrogancy*." She swiped the paper from his hand. A smirk twitched at the corner of his mouth until he saw Annalise's face sour, then his lips fell.

"Just tell me," he said, throwing himself back onto the couch and pouring three fingers of amber liquid into a glass from the cart beside him.

"It's nothing bad. They're inviting the rulers of each kingdom to Iona for a 'time of celebration, to unite under a canopy of peace and conformity.' Who writes this stuff?" She shook her head. "It's in a month's time," she finished, tossing the paper onto his lap.

Sebastian quickly scanned the contents. *Here* was the pomp and circumstance he'd expected. A week-long political rendezvous with all of the highest-ranking people in the realm. What would they do all day, sit there and posture at one another?

Or, perhaps there was another reason for the invitation.

"This is ridiculous," Sebastian said, leaning back. He couldn't give off any hint of his trepidation or suspicion, any clues to the worries he had. Not until he was sure.

"Yes," Annalise sighed. "I suppose it's a show of partnership and good faith, and it *has* been a long time since all of you were in one place—Iona excluded, of course. But an entire *week*? That seems a bit frivolous."

"I completely agree."

"I assume that means you want to go."

Sebastian nodded. "Oh, absolutely."

Annalise rolled her eyes. "You lot just leaving your kingdoms completely unattended to throw a party on an island while the rest of us—"

"I want you to come with me, Anna."

She stopped mid sentence, shutting her mouth with a click of her teeth. Sebastian had to fight a smile at the childlike spark that momentarily lit in her eyes.

"Well, I suppose if I *have* to," she said, tucking a curl of auburn hair behind her ear.

"Ever the dutiful advisor, making such sacrifices for me," he said with a chuckle.

She smiled and tapped his foot with the tip of her boot before sitting next to him, exhaling loudly. "You aren't buying this is simply some big welcoming party, are you?" she asked.

His brow creased as he swirled the contents of his glass. "I don't know, Anna. They seem to want to make their mark on the world. Isn't that all any of us hope to do? I don't want to assume some nefarious agenda before even meeting these people."

"So you didn't meet any of their leaders when you...when you were..." Annalise trailed off, as if unsure how to bring up any mention of *that* time.

"No, Anna, can't say I had the honor," he snapped, then scrubbed a hand over his face. She didn't deserve his ire—she didn't even know what had *happened*, but it seemed those were the two responses closest to his surface these days: antagonism or sarcasm. Or antagonistic sarcasm.

"That's enough of that for now," she said matter-of-factly as she took the glass of whiskey from his hand and set it back on the cart, then rested her head on his shoulder. He knew it was her silent show of forgiveness for when his sharp tongue lashed out. Her way of offering comfort. Solidarity.

"Are you going to be alright going back there? Truly?" she asked quietly.

Sebastian fidgeted with the ring on his pinky, mulling over her question and the depth of answer he should give.

No, he wouldn't be alright. He hadn't been alright for two years and three months. How could anyone be after what he'd been through? Having one's mind, one's free will, one's spirit massacred and shoved to the side to make space for a power hungry, morally misguided immortal's whims—that wasn't something he could easily bounce back from. All the secrets he harbored, the aching regret he carried...he didn't know if he'd ever be alright.

But he had to be for his kingdom. For the people who once looked up to him and now despised him, for the families that had lost their loved ones because of him, for the legacy he had to recreate from the ground up. If he was going to be the great king he'd always wanted to be, he had to be alright.

If he was going to find *her* again, he had to be.

"It'll be fine, Anna. We'll have a few evenings of well-mannered preening and spend our mornings exploring a mysterious island. No malevolent forces at work this time," he said lightheartedly, although his chest constricted.

He felt more than heard Annalise sigh next to him, her shoulders rising and falling dramatically. "Let me know when the real Sebastian wants someone to talk to, Your Majesty," she said as she lifted from the couch.

He knew he was in trouble when she used his title correctly.

"Anna, wait," he groaned, reaching out and grabbing her sleeve. She turned back to him with eyes raised in expectation. "I don't know how to do this. Please...be patient with me, yes?"

She sank back to her seat. "Don't know how to do what, Seb? Talk to me?"

"Talk to you, talk to anyone, *live*...I just—" He stopped and made an involuntary noise in the back of his throat as he pinched the bridge of his nose between his fingers. He needed that glass back in his hand for this.

"I'm not the person I was before, Anna. I'm not the Sebastian from three years ago, nor am I the same king from the past two. I have pieces of both of them inside of me, and I've got to figure out who that makes me *now*."

Annalise leaned back against the couch cushions. He expected her to give some grand speech or cliche adage of comfort, but instead, they sat in silence. After a few moments, he looked at her.

"What, no words of wisdom from my advisor?"

"Sorry, I was too busy thinking about what I'm going to wear on Iona."

Sebastian threw his head back and laughed. "You should be more concerned with what *I'm* going to wear. I am the one they actually invited, after all."

She looked at him out of the corner of her eye. "That's four times now."

He gaped and clutched his chest. "I didn't even say anything!"

"I'm counting it anyway."

Sebastian let his head roll back on his shoulders and propped his leg on her lap. "You'll be the death of me, Annalise Dalgard."

She shoved his leg off of her and snorted. "No, I'm pretty sure the whiskey is what will do you in."

"I can think of much worse ways to meet my end," Sebastian retorted, then suddenly felt the world stop. His chest tightened, and his mind whirled with a memory so real and strong, he thought she was in the very room with him.

"You wouldn't want me on a throne, Sebastian," she said, her bright green eyes dancing tauntingly between his.

He leaned in, letting her scent wash over him. Evergreen and apples. "And why is that?"

"Because I would make wretched men like you kneel at my feet as I cut them down."

Did she not understand these threats did nothing but ignite a fire within him? It was moments like this where he felt almost like his old self, with the banter and excitement and anticipation.

He smiled wickedly, letting a bit of the dark god through. "I can think of much worse ways to meet my end than on my knees before you."

Sebastian could still see the shock on her face and the following heat that blazed in her gaze. His fingers fluttered at his side in an attempt to reach out to her, touch her...but she wasn't there. He gritted his teeth and tried to control his breathing, working to return his heart rate to normal. The tightness in his chest wouldn't ease, and the air around him was stifling. Black spots danced in his vision.

Episodes like this happened to him often, where he would get so lost in a memory that he couldn't break himself free. Or worse, his mind would convince him he was back under Celesine's control, and he'd find himself alone in his bed for hours trying to shake the darkness closing in on him from all sides, suffocating him.

He stood abruptly and strode across the room, kneading his knuckles into his forehead. He wished he could stop seeing her, even for a *moment*—

"Seb, what's wrong?" Annalise's voice broke through the cloud. He'd forgotten she was there.

Turning to face her, he pasted on a weak smirk. "Sorry. Do you need assistance planning for the trip?"

She crossed her arms. "I'm not some mindless lord on the council, Sebastian. I've known you our entire lives. Where did you just go?" When he didn't respond, she cleared her throat. "You can't keep your demons to yourself forever. I know what it's like when they come back to terrorize you. I'm here for you, okay?"

Sebastian nodded curtly and crossed the room to his liquor cart, every step sending a pang of guilt through his heart at his dismissal of her concern.

What's wrong with you?

Why won't you talk to her?

She's the only one who loves you anymore.

He pulled the stopper off a bottle of whiskey with a slight *pop*. As he poured them both a small portion, she began talking behind him.

"So, who all do you think will be going to Iona?"

Thankful for the change in conversation, his shoulders relaxed an inch. "Adrik and Melanora will bring their children and their lap dog guards, no doubt. And the Triad won't leave their palace without those doting priests. Who knows who else might have gotten an invitation? Anybody the Ionans consider powerful and influential, I suppose."

"Hmm," Annalise mused, accepting the glass he handed her. "There aren't many others I can think of who'd be more powerful than you lot."

Sebastian raised his glass in a toast to her and smiled. He could think of a person more powerful than him and his fellow rulers.

Four, in fact.

CHAPTER THREE

Kai

"Here, you have to make sure you wrap the cloth tighter around the gauze," Kai said gently, taking the bandage from the little girl and pulling the fabric to apply more pressure to the wounded man's arm. "Now you try." She handed the end back to the girl.

The little one's small fingers captured the cloth and continued wrapping it like Kai had shown her, her tongue sticking out the corner of her chapped lips. When she finished, she looked back at Kai with a proud grin plastered across her face.

"Thanks, miss!" she said, the words whistling through the wide gaps in her front teeth.

Kai couldn't help but smile when the girl ran off to find the head healer, Zephania. Glancing around, her grin faltered as she took in the sight of the injured men and women who had been steadily pouring into the healer's tent for the last hour. A large section of one of the jewel caves had collapsed that morning, bringing in more patients than she'd seen in almost three months of working there. Teams were still out searching for miners stuck under the earth, and Kai had glimpsed numerous stretchers passing by with white sheets covering unfortunate victims.

The death toll would grow for days if what Zephania had told her of cave collapses was true.

It was the first disaster of this scale Kai had witnessed since she and Aidan had moved to Ara Mir three months previously. She'd heard stories of even stranger things happening across the desert kingdom in recent weeks. A man in the far north region of Xitol had gotten half of his body stuck in a sinkhole and drowned to death when a sudden rainstorm overtook the stretch of land.

Drowned. In the *desert.*

Once upon a time, Kai could have helped.

Now, without her powers, without Isla...nobody could.

She forced the thought from her mind, refusing to let more worries and wild theories about what could have happened to Isla and Celesine when they disappeared from that beach distract her from her duties. Almost every night during their first month in Ara Mir, she and Aidan had driven themselves crazy repeatedly going over the details, wondering where Isla might be, if she was even *alive*, and whether Celesine would come back to finish the job. Kai had practically made herself sick imagining every worst case scenario.

She was turning into Isla, with all of this worrying.

Gods, she missed that girl.

"Mrs. Fyredrake, could you come here for a minute?" The sound of Zephania's voice, the head healer in Ta'aveen, pierced through the grunts and moans of the men surrounding her.

Kai tried not to roll her eyes at the fabricated last name. Shockingly enough, Aidan had been the one to choose it. They'd needed a family name to assume when starting their new life in Ara Mir. She swore it was the last time she'd agree to a bet with that man.

"Coming!" Kai called, rushing to the opposite end of the tent where Zephania stood beside shelves piled high with various medical supplies. Boxes of gauze and cloth bandages, burn salve, bottled herbs and oils for pain and other ailments. A few tourniquets and a bone saw for the truly desperate situations rested on the top shelf. Glass tankards of white liquor were hidden below, also for said situations. Although, Kai saw Zephania sneaking sips of it for herself after particularly long days—like this one.

"We need some more beds for these fellows. I'm about to start having to make them wait outside if more keep coming." Zephania shook her head, her flow of tight, black braids brushing against her white shirt. The colorful beads adorning the ends of the braids danced and clacked together at the movement.

Kai nodded. She didn't want to have to turn away anyone who needed medical attention, if they could help it. "I'll see what I can find in the storage bunker."

"Thanks, dear." Zephania's wrinkled hands found Kai's as she was about to walk out the back exit, her brown eyes shifting as concern flitted across her dark face. "Your Aidan? Was he down there?"

Kai offered a small smile. "No, he wasn't assigned to that sector today. Thank you for checking."

"Well, thank the gods for that," Zephania said matter-of-factly, and turned back to her newest patient.

I'm not sure who to thank, but it won't be the gods, Kai thought bitterly before walking out the back flap of the healer's tent into the wooden storage unit that neighbored it.

She *was* thankful Aidan hadn't been in the collapse, of course. It was still a strange feeling to be worried over such mundane things. She wasn't used to the sudden lightness in her chest every time Aidan walked back through the doors of their little hut, hating the idea that he could be hurt during his hours mining beneath the earth. His safety and strength had always been such a surety. She'd had to reprimand him because of his recklessness more times than she could count in the last three months. Aidan hadn't quite seemed to grasp that he was no longer an immortal who could withstand any bodily harm. Kai had almost had a heart attack when he'd come home in the second week with blood covering his dirty clothes, the tip of his middle finger sliced off because he'd gotten into a knife-throwing contest with a fellow miner.

At least he'd had the foresight to keep the bit of finger that had been cut off, and Zephania had been able to sew it back on.

But he was still an idiot.

Kai chuckled to herself as she looted through the storage unit for more blankets and pillows, then dragged a couple of cots to the door.

She sometimes couldn't believe the life they now lived. So...domesticated. They'd decided to move to Ara Mir because they'd needed a change of scenery, and the desert kingdom had always intrigued her. She and Aidan had no problem with the heat. The people in the northern town of Ta'aveen had taken one look at Aidan, his broad shoulders and muscled frame, and immediately offered him a job mining for jewels in the local underground caverns. It had been a relief to find a way to make a living so quickly, since they'd had nothing but the clothes on their backs when August and the crew of the *Mekaisa* had dropped them off after the events on Iona.

Kai hadn't known *what* she wanted to do with her life. She'd dreamed of being human with Aidan for millennia, but those dreams had become a reality faster than she could process. The first few weeks had felt like swimming against the tide; she'd constantly tried to reconcile the fact that she was getting everything she'd ever wanted with losing a piece of her spirit. Her movements had been sluggish and forced, like her mind was in a fog and it took too much energy to clear. She hadn't even bathed for the first two weeks. Being near any type of water made her acutely aware of the gaping hole that now existed.

It wasn't *her* water anymore.

Aidan had seemed to adjust a little better than her. Perhaps it was because he'd found something to occupy his time and attention, whereas Kai stayed in their little hut day after day, trying to make the house a *home*. They were lucky to have even found lodging so easily; Aidan's new boss let them rent his extra living space for a small percentage of Aidan's monthly earnings. It had a broken door, a spider infestation, and lacked the running pipes Kai had grown to love over their time since awakening from their thousand-year slumber, but it was a roof over their heads nonetheless.

On the same day Zephania had sewed the tip of Aidan's finger back on, she'd asked if Kai wanted to be her apprentice. The older woman must've seen how lost Kai was. Grateful for something to take her mind off the ever-darkening thoughts that plagued her, Kai had accepted. She'd done her fair share of medical work over the centuries, helping the people learn new remedies to aid the sick and dying.

She enjoyed what she was doing, and felt a small sense of fulfillment in the care she could provide the town. Even if days like this one were more difficult to bear.

It took Kai several trips, but she eventually made it back to the healer's tent with all of her findings. The tent was a large, rectangular structure with wooden poles spaced evenly to hold up the thick, white fabric. There were two flap openings: one in the front and one in the back. The inside was surprisingly spacious, with enough room for twenty cots and open floor space that could be used for overflow beds when needed, as well as a smaller section in the back with shelves of extra supplies.

The scent of sweat, blood, and peppermint from the burn salve stung Kai's nose as she entered the tent, making her already sensitive stomach turn. Yet another thing she'd had to get used to as a human—being much more susceptible to normal bodily ailments. Stomach pains, fatigue, tender muscles, head colds. Although, she'd been strangely excited when she'd had her first—and so far, only—bleeding. As an immortal, her body hadn't operated the same way humans did. She'd never experienced a woman's cycle, but she'd heard about the various side effects and painful discomfort.

And *gods*, did she understand now.

Thankfully, it looked like no new patients had arrived, which she hoped meant they'd finished clearing out the mines and had found no more casualties. The atmosphere had lightened considerably in the twenty minutes it had taken Kai to gather cots and blankets; low murmurings of chatter and even a few chuckles filled the air, the men and women now sitting upright or walking around.

As she set the last pillow down, warm hands circled her waist.

"I think I may need some one-on-one time with a certain healer," a deep voice rumbled in her ear, sending a wave of heat over her skin.

She turned in his arms to glance up and down his body. "You, sir, do not look injured in the slightest," she responded with a grin. "I'll see if I have time after I handle some other patients."

"Don't you dare," he growled, pulling her closer and nuzzling his nose into the crook of her neck. "I'm the only one you get to handle, Mrs. Fyredrake."

"Gods, Aidan." She laughed and slapped him away. "You always ruin it with that ridiculous name."

"Get used to it, sweetheart. You're stuck with it. Till death do us part, remember?" Aidan's hands stayed firmly planted on her waist.

"Oh, Aidan! I'm glad you're alright," Zephania exclaimed, appearing in front of them with a bundle of dirty towels. "And thank goodness for this one," she added, jerking her head toward Kai. "She's been a lifesaver today. I still can't believe you're so new to this. It's like you've been doing it for years!"

"Imagine that," Kai said, smirking lightly at Aidan as she stepped out of his grasp and held out her hands to take the dirty towels from Zephania. His eyes gleamed when she caught them again, still able to ignite her even without the flames that once simmered in his veins.

"Newlyweds," Zephania tittered and shook her head fondly. "If only I could be as young as you two again." Kai and Aidan exchanged hidden smiles, looking away quickly. "I wish I could give your lady over to you for the evening, Aidan, but I'll need her here for a little longer."

"No need to apologize, Zeph—I know how useful those pretty little hands can be," Aidan said, winking at Kai and waving at Zephania as she retreated, her shoulders bobbing up and down with laughter.

"Aidan!" Kai scolded, but couldn't repress the snort that escaped her. "For the love of the gods, read the room." She nodded toward the beds of injured men, dirt and blood still covering their bodies.

"I can't help that I missed my wife today," he said while he took an armful of towels from her. Amusement clung to his words, but a sense of worry had crept into his tone. He sobered quickly and lowered his voice as Kai led him to the back, where they sorted the laundry.

"We heard the crash from all the way down the tunnels. Scared us half to death. It's one of the first times I've ever thought..." He shook his head and set his pile down, then clapped his hands together as the crease in his dark brows disappeared.

"So! Put me to work, my beautiful sea temptress. How can I be of service?"

CHAPTER FOUR

Jade

Three months and four days.

Three months and four days of a mortal body.

Three months and four days of silence from her earth.

"Jade, you know what I have said about moving the bucket for the well too high."

Three months and four days of *that voice*.

Jade let out a slow breath. "And you know what *I've* said about you going to the well." She tromped back through the open door into their little cottage, the bell she had placed above it tinkling as it swung inward. "If we're out of water, tell Emilee or myself, but don't go try to do it on your own, Rynn."

She turned the corner into the kitchen and saw Rynn reaching for the top of their storage shelves, searching blindly for the large wooden bucket, their only method of collecting water from the well half a mile from the cottage. One hand was stretched high, the corded muscles of his forearm bulging, while the other gripped his wooden cane so tightly, his knuckles were turning white.

"For the love of—stop that, you're going to knock everything off." She crossed the space to him in three strides, slapped his hand away, and grabbed a step stool from underneath the hanging shelves. After retrieving the bucket, she returned Rynn's glower with a glare of her own.

"Don't give me that look. It's for your own good, you stubborn man," she grumbled under her breath as she headed to the front door.

Never in her thousands of years on the earth would Jade have thought she'd be in this position. Living in dreary, frigid Evonlea with the *one* being she'd spent her entire existence at odds with. And not a single drop of power in her veins to quell the aching in her soul.

How the gods had made fools of them all.

As she balanced the bucket on her hip and pulled the handle to open the door, she almost collided with a frazzled, young blonde woman whose wool cap was pulled low over her ears, her nose bright pink from the cold wind.

"Oh! Sorry, Miss Jade!" The girl held her hands up. "And I'm so sorry I'm late. A tree fell in our front yard last night during the storm, and I had to—"

Jade sidestepped the girl. "It's fine, Emilee. It's probably best you didn't show up any earlier—he's in quite a mood this morning."

"I heard that."

Emilee's cheeks burned even brighter at the sound of the low voice coming from inside the cottage. "I'm sure it won't be a problem, Miss Jade. Do you need me to take that?" She gestured to the bucket.

"Actually, yes, thank you," Jade said, handing it to Emilee. "That way, I can go run an errand before more bad weather strikes." Even for Evonlea, the number of blizzards raging this late in the winter was astonishing.

Emilee curtsied—an action Jade had told her a dozen times to stop doing—before hurrying off to the well. Jade yelled a quick goodbye to Rynn, telling him Emilee would be right back if he could *please* avoid doing anything foolish, and shut the front door. She turned left on their street, heading toward the town square, and caught the swinging, blonde braid of Emilee up ahead. The girl had grown on Jade over the last two months since they'd hired her. She was thankful to not have to deal with Rynn all on her own.

He had fought hard against hiring anyone for those first few weeks after they had arrived in Evonlea. He was strong-willed and belligerent, and had never required someone to care for him before. But the injury he'd received to his leg on Iona—that *Jade* had given him—changed everything. He'd almost died of blood loss on those white sands, and again from infection on the precarious journey back to the western kingdoms. Jade wasn't sure how he had survived without his immortality and quick healing to aid him.

The voyage across the Wyndsor Sea as they left Iona three months ago was still a blur to Jade. Even thinking back to those initial days without her powers made it difficult to draw breath. The emptiness, the stillness, the loss. It was like the earth had been ripped from beneath her feet, and she'd been falling through darkness with nothing to guide her and nothing to hold onto.

What was she supposed to do with her life? Who was she supposed to *be*? Without her earth, she was left a bitter husk with a cracked and dead heart.

As they had neared the shores of Evonlea, where they would be forced to figure out what came next, Jade had wanted to disappear and waste away into nothing.

But then, something happened.

Rynn had walked.

The ship's best healer, along with Kai and Aidan, had spent days at sea treating Rynn's fever and infection, not knowing if he would even *live*, much less walk again. Watching him take that first trembling step onto the gangway in Vyros had been like watching a tree take root and break through the earth's surface into the sunlight. The only explanation Jade could think of was that for the brief time he'd still held his immortal abilities after the injury, his body had healed *just* enough to allow him a miraculous recovery.

Jade had felt a spark of purpose. And perhaps the heaviness of guilt; it had been *her* vine that ripped a hole in his leg, after all. Whether or not she'd been in control didn't take the shame away. In that single moment of clarity, her decision had been made.

To Kai and Aidan's surprise, Jade had charged right up to Rynn as they exited the ship and said, "Come with me. We're getting you a cane."

She had not left his side since.

Well, figuratively speaking. If she truly spent every second with that man, she was bound to willingly jump off the cliffs of Aataran.

Which was why she was thankful for Emilee. After several shouting matches and one broken cane later, Rynn had agreed to hire the young healer with the stash of gold he'd taken from Iona before they went down for the long slumber. Jade was grateful for the girl's abounding patience in helping him complete day-to-day tasks that now irritated his leg and his attitude.

The infection had flared up again a month and a half later. Jade had returned from her weekly trip to the market to find Rynn unconscious on their living room floor. Sheer panic arose in her at the blue tinge to his skin, the breaths barely fluttering in through his nose, the lifelessness of his cold features. If Emilee hadn't arrived minutes later, Jade wasn't sure what would have happened. The healer explained that since it hadn't been properly treated immediately after the wound was inflicted, the infection had never been killed, and had therefore spread through his blood and into the vital organs of his body.

But, he was now recovering and finally letting others take care of him for once.

Sometimes, Jade wished she had someone to take care of her, as well.

Rynn was not the only one who she had taken upon herself to watch over after the events on Iona. They left the beach with more questions and fear than ever before. For one, they didn't know where the Dagger of Volnus had vanished to. Such a powerful weapon, a weapon that had altered her life forever—*gone*. Along with Isla and—

Even thinking the name of her old mentor made Jade's insides freeze and shatter. She refused to let her mind linger too long on the betrayal that ran as deep as her mountains were tall.

Jade and Rynn had no idea where *she* and Isla had disappeared to after Isla had been stabbed, but it made sense that the dagger would be with them—if they were even alive—or potentially commandeered by the Primeval gods. No matter where it was or who had it, the blade still required Vasileia blood to work properly. And the only living person of the ancient bloodline they knew of was currently residing in Lockhurt, Isla's home village in northern Evonlea.

This was ultimately why Jade and Rynn had decided to follow Luca Vasileia and Brielle Harvish after they'd disembarked in Vyros, burdened by heavy loss and grief. Someone needed to look out for them, to make sure history didn't repeat itself, and that Luca's children's deaths did not lead to his own early grave, as well.

Jade winced at the thought. She found it difficult to stop thinking of Isla as dead; she'd seen the mortal wound with her own eyes, had seen the sharp sword drive through Isla's chest. It seemed impossible the girl could still be alive.

Yet Rynn was convinced Isla *had* survived, that she'd been granted immortality by the Dagger of Volnus when she took their elemental powers. He also swore he saw the girl take Sebastian's blood and consume it, thereby giving her powers of the Aether—if that was truly what ran through Sebastian's blood.

Jade wasn't as easily convinced.

She *wanted* to believe the best, truly, but she couldn't overlook the fact that Rynn was speaking not only with logic, but also with a scorned lover's hope—a curious brand that ignited his resolve, given the other option was to drown in emotions he wasn't yet ready to face.

She would love nothing more than for them to discover Isla was still alive somewhere, perhaps scattered among the stars on the spirit plane, but *hope* was a luxury she didn't have in this new life.

After several minutes of walking, Jade came upon the town square and headed directly to the Bear's Head, the most popular tavern of Lockhurt.

While Jade didn't particularly enjoy participating in the nighttime revelry of the citizens, she found it was the best time to check on Brielle and see how the girl was faring. Jade would sometimes catch Luca in attendance too, but more often than not, he stayed home.

When she did manage to spot the two of them, they always avoided her.

Jade made her way to the tavern, already full and raucous despite the sun still hovering above the horizon. Pulling the door open, she was greeted by the sour scent of warm ale and sweat from the crowds of men and women recently returned from a day of hunting. Their chatter rang in her ears, the pounding of boots on the floor and fists against wood giving her pause to take a few deep breaths of clean air before letting the door swing shut behind her.

"Can I get you anything?" a tan, middle-aged woman called from the bar as she whipped her towel around the dirty countertop.

"Just a cup of tea is fine," Jade responded.

The bartender squinted, looked down Jade's body and back up again, then shrugged. "Suit yourself," she said, walking through a door that led to the kitchens.

Jade scanned the large room. There was a group of men playing a game of darts, a couple of servers walking with trays of empty glasses, and several tables occupied by loud hunters. By the way their stories all seemed to be followed by obnoxious rounds of laughter, Jade concluded they were probably multiple drinks in. But there was no sign of the familiar short, glossy black curls. Perhaps Brielle had not come tonight, although Jade knew the girl's routine fairly well by now.

No sooner had the thought passed through her mind when the front door opened and Brielle charged in, two burly men on her heels. Jade quickly averted her gaze to the tea cup that had been placed before her, knowing the girl wanted nothing to do with her or Rynn at this point. But Jade couldn't force away the sense of duty she felt, the need to ensure both Brielle and Luca were out of harm's way and moving on with their lives, as much as they could.

Perhaps it was the fact that Jade couldn't move on with *her* own life, couldn't mourn *her* loss, but this small act could bring her a sense of fulfillment.

Jade let her eyes wander over to Brielle sitting with her friends, one of whom she now recognized as Hamil—the man who had come after Isla all those months ago. The two of them chatted and laughed with their companions, but when the others looked away, Jade saw the haunted looks in both Brielle and Hamil's eyes.

Jade knew those ghosts well.

After spending another half hour drinking her tea, listening to the sounds of small village life around her, and comforting herself that Brielle and Luca were safe, Jade paid her tab and shrugged on her heavy coat, making her way out the front door. She'd only traveled a few steps down the road when a soft hand grabbed her elbow.

Jade instantly flicked her fingers to summon her vines, before the emptiness smashed into her like a boulder.

Every time. It felt like losing her earth all over again.

"Why do you keep coming back here?" Brielle hissed as Jade whirled to face her.

"They have good tea," she replied coolly.

The girl rolled her eyes. "Don't you think you all have caused enough problems? Just leave us alone."

Jade swallowed. This wasn't the first time they'd had this conversation. "I'm not trying to bother you, Brielle. We only want to keep you and Luca safe. We can't be sure he's not a target, what with the dagger still missing—you know this."

"And what good would you be if we *were* in danger, hmm? You can't do anything to protect us anymore," Brielle sneered. Jade could see her anger for what it truly was: a mask for her heartache.

Jade sighed. "You may be right, but it's what Isla would have wanted—"

"Don't talk about her to me," Brielle said, suddenly mere inches from Jade's face, her dark eyes flashing. "You don't get to care what she would want. *You're* the reason she's gone. If *you* and your *friends* hadn't dragged her into this mess in the first place, she would—" Brielle stopped herself, her voice shaky and eyes glistening. "Please, just go away."

Clenching her fingers into fists, Jade watched as Brielle turned on her heel and stomped away, her words cutting deep. She wasn't wrong, of course. In the end, it may not have been *entirely* their fault, but they weren't innocent. They never were. When those with power failed to protect others, partial blame could always be set on their shoulders.

Jade felt the weight of it like a second skin.

As Jade walked, she tried not to let Brielle's indignation eat at her, tried not to imagine the "what ifs" and the ways they could have prevented the events of three months ago. If only Jade had *seen* the betrayal coming, had convinced Isla to not get involved, had taken out the king before he got as far as he did—

But no, it was never the king's fault. Not in the end.

She padded back to the cottage, the fresh-fallen snow crunching and giving way beneath her boots. According to the townspeople, it *should* be the last snow of the season, as they were quickly approaching spring. But over the course of the last few months, they had learned nothing was predictable anymore.

She'd seen entire streets buried in piles of snow within mere *minutes*, people trapped in their houses until the town rallied forces to dig them out. Citizens told her that while Evonlea always had a couple of fearsome blizzards every winter, the severity of these was like nothing they'd ever experienced before.

Paired with the gossip and murmurings of what was happening in the other two kingdoms, Jade had no choice but to speculate if the elements were punishing them, seeking retribution for the way they had been treated. Rynn claimed that was foolish, of course—he was more inclined to believe it had something to do with the fact that magic had been severely damaged when Isla took their elements, and they were now suffering the consequences of nature in its most chaotic form.

Brielle's words whispered through her. *"You can't do anything to protect us anymore."*

She was right. They couldn't stop these wild acts of nature, they couldn't find Isla, and they couldn't prevent Celesine or any attack against them she may one day plan, if she was alive. What *good* were they anymore?

Pausing in her tracks a short distance from the cottage, Jade caught sight of a small tendril of green pushing its way through the white blanket ensnaring it. She calmed her mind and knelt, her fingers gently brushing the tiny leaves that waved in the wind as if to say "hello."

When she glanced back up to the end of her street, she cocked her head at the sight of a horse and its rider turning away from her cottage and cantering off down the lane. *Interesting.* They didn't often have visitors.

Jade hurried to the front door and took off her soggy, snow-ridden boots. She set them beside the large clay pot housing a bundle of snowdrops, their petals looking less than lively after the storm from the night before. How her fingers and soul itched to give them life.

"Emilee?" she called as she opened the door. "Was someone just here?"

"Oh, yes!" Emilee's soft voice came from the kitchen, followed by her slight frame as she turned the corner and wiped flour onto her apron. Rynn had become so spoiled—the young healer insisted on baking sweets, minced pies, and other treats on a weekly basis. Jade wanted to roll her eyes, except she'd grown fond of the chocolate and cherry pastry that mysteriously appeared in her room from time to time.

"He left right before you got here, actually. It was a messenger. He said to give a note to the master or mistress of the house."

"So where is this note?" Jade inquired.

"Oh, well—I already gave it to Mr. Rynn," Emilee replied sheepishly, giving Jade an apologetic smile.

Hmm. Jade pursed her lips. "Alright, thank you."

Walking further down the hallway, she passed barren, cream colored walls that were beginning to fade and chip at the ceiling. As she entered their larger living space, Jade found Rynn sitting on their worn leather couch—a lucky find from a secondhand furniture shop—with his bad leg propped on top of several plush pillows. The book he had been reading was discarded on the floor, his normally stoic face pale and anxious. A thick piece of parchment rested between the fingers of one hand as he scratched at the beard he'd been slowly growing the last several weeks.

"What is it?"

His hard, gray gaze met hers, and he answered her question with a flick of his wrist. The back of the parchment now faced Jade, and she instantly stiffened.

An insignia of a mountain with two arrows striking the center. The image that once made her chest swell with pride and nostalgia now had the hair on her neck raising in apprehension.

"What does Iona want with us?" she asked, trying to keep her voice steady. The once-lost kingdom had recently made itself known to the rest of the world, but Rynn and Jade had kept their distance from news regarding its return. It was far too painful.

"Our presence, it seems." When she leveled him with a stare, Rynn sighed. "It is an invitation. Iona wants to welcome the world leaders to their shores for the first time in over a millennium."

"What?" Jade snapped, crossing the gray rug and plucking the paper from his hands. Suspicion, dread, and a bit of curiosity pricked her as she read its contents.

The Chamber of the Kingdom of Iona cordially invites the rulers of the realm to the Reign of Dawn, a six day event commemorating the rebirth of newfound harmony among the four kingdoms, culminating in a feast on the eve of the Spring Equinox.

It is a time of celebration, to unite under a canopy of peace and conformity. The Chamber hopes you will join us as we usher in a new era under the light of the rising season.

Long Live,
Stefan Rigaldi III
Nor Noxen
Ezeretta Bannock
Mariana de Faye

"This sounds like a bunch of puffed-up nonsense," Jade said, but the way her fingers clutched at the paper belied her dismissal.

"I agree."

"I don't know why they would invite us. We're not 'rulers of the realm.'" *Not anymore.*

"I agree. It's most peculiar."

"Stop doing that. You know it sets me on edge."

Rynn raised an eyebrow. "Doing what?"

"Agreeing with me."

He let out an exasperated sigh as he brought his leg to the ground and reached for the cane resting against the couch. "I don't think we should go."

"I...well, yes, I agree," Jade mumbled, her fingers absentmindedly roaming the indentations of the crest of Iona.

"Wonderful." He rose and headed toward the hallway on the right, the cane tapping against the wood floor with each step.

"Where are you going?" Jade asked.

"My room. Is that allowed?" he deadpanned, not even turning back to face her.

Gods save me. "This is fairly important news, and that's all you have to say about it?"

Rynn twisted his neck to look at her out of the corner of his eye. "If you must know, I'm going to write a couple of letters."

"To whom?"

"One to Kai and Aidan. It would be wise to see if they received an invitation too, and what they make of it. I cannot think of a single *innocent* reason why this—this Chamber would invite us. Does that not concern you?"

It *was* suspicious, extending this invitation to four seemingly normal, inconspicuous mortals. It made Jade wonder what this Chamber might know.

Nodding in agreement, she said, "Alright, and the other letter?"

"The second is to King Sebastian."

"*What?*" Jade's eyebrows flew into her forehead. That was the last thing she expected him to say.

He pivoted to face her fully and pointed to the parchment still in her grip. "I do not trust these people. And who else do we know who would also have a reason not to trust them, who will more than likely be in attendance at this event?"

She could always count on Rynn to use mistrust and secrecy to his advantage.

"What do you think writing to him will accomplish? You *hate* him. Why would he listen to us, anyway?"

"I do not *hate* the king," he said, bristling. "We must do what we can to keep our enemies close, Jade."

Always so dramatic. "We don't know that Iona is our enemy."

He gave her a pointed look before turning away. "I certainly do not think they're looking for friends."

CHAPTER FIVE

Isla

*I*n the darkness, she saw...everything.

Five familiar figures, cloaked in the power of the gods, molded from nothing as they rose with the dawn of a new world. First confusion, then wonder, beauty, purpose, and pride. They brought water for life and earth for growth, fire to forge and air to move forward.

And finally, the spirit that dwells within all. The promise of an everlasting kingdom, a forever reign of prosperity and peace.

They built the first kingdom from the ground up.

With their hands, they carved the rivers and plains, mountain passes and harvest fields. They provided food, water, protection, and warmth. The humans needed their strength and power, needed their help when storms arose and washed out their lands, when their crops died and their people starved.

Decades passed.

Centuries.

Millennia.

Visions flew through her mind like shadows, some hard to grasp, others playing out before her in vivid detail.

She was in a forest. Canopies of decaying trees expanded above her, golden light from the fading sun gilding the branches and dying greenery. A bronze hand ran through deadened leaves, ruby red fruit appearing in its wake like magic. The giver of life.

The forest disappeared, only to be replaced by the depths of the sea. Swirls of angry water rushed against the shore, the sky darkening and crackling with lightning. People screamed in the distance—"save our land!" Against the shadows of the waves, a blonde goddess appeared, hands held wide and determination in her eyes. The savior.

Blinking, she was transported to a cave, tendrils of steam rising from bubbling, boiling water. There they were—dark hands in blonde hair, wild hearts beating as one. He thought she was so beautiful. Eyes like sapphires, a smile like the sun, fingers that promised his undoing. He had loved her since the first moment they were formed by the gods. The lover.

Another instant, and she was atop a mountain. Gray eyes circled with blue stared into the heavens, whispers on the wind circling his thoughts—pleas from the hopeless, prayers from the helpless, pain from the heartless. He would go where he was called. The fighter.

One thing the four had in common: the strength and resolve that filled their souls.

There was so much they had left to do in this world.

More centuries passed.

Sunrises and sunsets and midnight skies bled across her eyelids like paint dripping down a canvas.

The world became darker.

The four became forgotten.

"How could these people think they are anything without us?"

"We are their gods."

"We are their deliverers."

"We are the reason they have food in their bellies, land to stand on, kingdoms to rule."

Their anger and need for praise ran together and overflowed, a boiling mass of pride feeding their claim on this world. They watched the people turn from them, watched as the humans gave themselves the glory for creating such a perfect world. The kingdoms left the four behind and carved new idols from the ashes of their ancestors.

But they would make them remember.

Blood runs free when there is nothing to quell the wounds of war.

She gazed in horror as the kingdom fell into ruins, as the humans fought for something they didn't understand. They thought they knew what they wanted; some desired freedom, some yearned for their old gods. But it was pointless. She could see that now. The people wanted someone—anyone—to guide them.

The four higher powers simply wanted bodies kneeling at their feet.

Is that all power was good for?

The clash of steel. The wails of men. The wet smell of rot and waste, of copper and salt. Fields bathed in a blood orange sun as it set over corpses of kindred men and women.

They were tearing themselves apart. But the four had not forgotten.

She feared she would never forget, either.

And then, she was falling.

CHAPTER SIX

Sebastian

*P*ain lanced across his back, dark shadows slicing in an arc, the sting echoing through him and throbbing with every heartbeat. Sharp claws dug into his mind as the familiar blackness closed in. From the corner of his eye, he saw a lithe figure cloaked in purple smoke, a sneer contorting her red lips and olive-toned face.

Her voice rang through his head. *"Don't fight it, darling. It will be so much easier this way..."*

Sebastian woke from the nightmare in a panic, silk sheets sticking to his sweaty skin. He couldn't move his limbs; while in his mind he was thrashing and fighting to get loose, his body stayed still, immobilized by fear.

His eyes were wide and unblinking as he gazed up at the ceiling, the moonlight filtering in through the small crack in the curtains of the window. A weight crushed his chest, but he couldn't move it, could barely breathe as it caved in on him and wrapped him in shadows, his entire body encased by the Aether's words as his heart hammered faster and faster until—

His arms jerked and he sat abruptly, his limbs finally obeying. Shallow gasps escaped his lips, his whole body shaking beneath the sweat-stained sheets. He lifted his hands to his head and gripped his hair, willing his heartbeat to slow.

It wasn't real. Celesine wasn't here. It was only a dream.

The night terrors had been happening for months. He couldn't rid himself of her, no matter how hard he tried. It was as if she'd left behind tendrils of her shadows, embedded in his mind to torture him for the rest of his life. Every night was the same: he would wake up with fear coursing through his veins, only to find that he couldn't move, like he was still locked in her web. It would take several moments for his body to calm down and tell his brain he was safe.

And then he would lie awake for the rest of the night, too shaken to fall back asleep.

With a groan, he eased himself off the bed and crossed to the bathing chamber attached to his suite. He stared in the mirror at the deep purple circles beneath his eyes, then met his own clear, bright blue gaze. He remembered the black pools they'd once been, the strange and vile power they'd held.

His hand was still shaking as he ran it through his disheveled hair before turning on the faucet. After rinsing his face with cold water and trying to wash away the dread of the night, he grabbed a towel and patted his skin dry.

When he looked back into the mirror, he was not alone.

Sebastian froze, his breath caught in his throat. Everything disappeared except for a flash of red hair.

He slowly lowered the towel, knowing it was a figment of his imagination. He'd been picturing her everywhere, wishing he could reach out and touch her.

But when he turned to go to his bed, she didn't disappear.

His breath returned in a rush. She simply stood there with her back to him in the doorway of his bathing chamber, clothed in a soft, navy dress that shimmered slightly in the moonlight. Red hair cascaded down her back in waves, shifting as she turned her head.

Gathering his strength, he stepped forward and slowly reached out a hand. He didn't want to ruin this vision; it was the clearest image his mind had ever formed. Maybe it would also conjure an imprint of her on his fingertips, let him remember for a moment what it felt like to brush his hand against her skin.

The moment his fingers grazed her shoulder, he sucked in a breath. He could *feel* her. Her dress was soft and smooth, and her scent, like sweet apples, filled his nostrils. *Gods*, his mind was good. He didn't think he'd ever imagined a more lifelike vision.

"Sebastian?" she whispered, her back still to him as her head angled to where his hand rested on her shoulder. He saw her bright freckles, the side of her full lips, her long eyelashes brushing against the top of her cheek.

"Yes, love?" he breathed, shifting his hand to run his fingers through her hair. She inhaled at his touch, and he thought if he'd had to live in his own personal hell for the past three months, this single moment of peace made it worth it.

She suddenly turned to him, her gaze running up his body until it landed on his face. Her lips parted slightly, her cheeks flushed, and her eyes...

Sebastian stumbled, his hand falling away.

Her eyes glowed violet.

Hundreds of memories rushed through him. He still saw those purple eyes in his nightmares, still felt the shadows snaking around his mind and squeezing. *It can't be...*

"Isla?" he whispered tentatively, unsure now whether this was truly an illusion.

Eyes widening, she said, "Sebastian, I—I don't know how I got here."

He couldn't believe it. Three months of silence, no hint of whether she had survived the attack on the beach...and here she was. *How?* How could she be here? And *why*?

Wetting his lips and swallowing the lump in his throat, he asked, "Is this real?"

She took a few steps away, into his bedchamber. "Yes. I think so." Pausing, she looked around and said, "But I don't know how I'm here."

Shock finally loosened its hold on him, and he snapped. Crossing the distance to her in a single stride, one hand came to her waist and pushed her against the closest wall, the other hand planting itself on the wood behind her. His forehead met hers, his entire body buzzing where they touched.

"I never thought I'd see you again," he whispered, closing his eyes as he breathed her in. She trembled beneath him, her hands pushing firmly against the wall as if she was trying to distance herself from him.

He was scaring her.

He shouldn't be surprised. For almost the entire time she'd known him, he'd been the enemy. The cruel, selfish king who had used her and caused her pain. She barely knew the *real* him. Sure, she'd seen glimpses, and perhaps had felt the same unexpected, burning temptation he had, but this version of him was still a stranger to her.

He couldn't help the fact that he'd known her for years...had watched her and admired her from the hidden pockets of his mind, even while under Celesine's control. She'd brought him the smallest amounts of peace in those times, a ray of sunshine breaking through an eternal storm.

She felt like home.

He didn't want to let go.

Pulling his forehead from hers, he used all of his self control to release his grip on her waist and take a step back. Every part of him screamed to close the distance between them, but he didn't want to frighten her even more. He searched her eyes, his muscles once again locking at their violet glow.

Just like Celesine's.

But it was still *her*, wasn't it? His Isla?

His brow furrowed. "Where have you been? What happened to you?"

Her eyes flitted around the room. "I don't know. I can't—I can't figure out how I got here. I was somewhere else, somewhere...gods, I don't know.

They—they keep showing me things—" She cut herself off with a shudder, almost choking on her words.

"You're here now. With me." He brushed a thumb against her cheek. "It'll be alright, Isla."

She shook her head. "No, I don't—I don't think I have much time."

His chest tightened. "What do you mean?"

"I feel like I'm being...pulled back somehow." She rubbed the palm of her hand against her forehead, then met his eyes, pleading. "Look, Sebastian, I don't know what's happening. But—Papa," she forced out, as if it took all her energy to keep her mind focused. "I need you to make sure my papa is safe. Please."

A swirl of dark smoke began pooling at her feet, and panic rose up his throat.

"No—no, stay with me, love. We can fix this," he said, his voice strained and frantic as he grasped the back of her neck. He finally had her—she was *right here*—

Her purple eyes glistened, her breaths coming faster. "I can't. I don't know how. I don't—just promise me!"

He wanted to refuse, because this request meant she was giving up—but he nodded tightly, taking in her features, memorizing every inch of her. The smoke curled to her waist now, and he knew what that meant. He'd seen it happen when Celesine would appear to him, before her power gave out and she had to go back to the spirit plane.

The same place Isla had spent the last three months, it seemed.

"Find me again, alright?" he whispered as her form began to pulsate and fade before him.

"I promise," she said, then the shadows engulfed her, and she vanished from sight.

Sebastian tumbled into the wall, her scent of apples and evergreen trees washing over him as he turned and slumped to the ground. His mind raced.

A pit formed in his chest, his skin still tingling where he had touched her. Gripping his head in his hands, he wanted to rage. Wanted to scream and throw anything he could get his hands on, to rip his curtains and shatter every window.

He'd been *so close.*

But he didn't break down. He didn't explode. Instead, he breathed deeply. Settled his mind. Focused on what he'd learned. Because he knew now, without a shadow of a doubt, that Isla had not died on that beach.

She'd become the *Aether.*

Was it possible to bring her back?

CHAPTER SEVEN

Aidan

"They're not going," Kai said, looking up from the letter in her hands. It had just arrived by the early morning messenger, and it must've been at least two weeks old. With how long it took any form of correspondence to be delivered across the ocean and then through the villages on land, they were lucky to get news quicker than that.

"Color me shocked. Jade and Rynn, not wanting to attend a party? I would've never guessed," Aidan said with a raised eyebrow, moving to stand behind his wife so he could tuck her under his chin and read the letter for himself.

His eyes skimmed the words, and he let out a bark of laughter. "Gods, this has Rynn written all over it. 'It would be in your best interest to let the mortals deal with their own agenda.' He realizes *we* are mortals now too, right?"

Kai folded the parchment and put it on the small kitchen table, only a couple of feet away from their front door. The house his employer let them use—if one could call it a "house"—was basically the size of the cave they'd stayed in during those weeks at the Aataran Mountain Range. The front door led straight into the kitchen, which consisted of a single table, a couple of shelves, a bucket for water, and a fireplace they used to cook food. Several steps from that was the bedroom. They had an old mattress and some pillows and blankets Zephania let them take. Off to the side of the "bedroom" was a curtain covering a hole in the ground that served as their bathing facility.

It was certainly not a palace, but it was *their* home. The Fyredrakes.

He chuckled. *Never gets old.*

"I get that they're suspicious—we are too, of course. Why would these people invite *us* to their world leadership meeting? But we're never going to find out if we stay here." Kai sighed. "I wish they'd go. I'm sure even *they* could have fun on a week-long vacation," she said with a laugh, then paused before adding quietly, "I miss them."

Aidan took a step and held out his arms, her body melting into him as she wrapped her arms around his back. "I know you do, sweetheart," he murmured into her ear, running his fingers through her blonde hair. "Maybe we can make a trip to Evonlea after the festival. What are they calling this thing again?"

"The Reign of Dawn," Kai answered, her voice muffled against his chest.

"Right. Knew it was something like that. These people better know how to have a good time, because by the sound of that invitation they sent, they have sticks shoved so far up—"

"Aidan!" Kai broke out into laughter and smacked his chest. "You don't have any right to make fun of what they named it, *Mr. Fyredrake.*"

He rolled his eyes. "Ah, not this again. Remember what I said would happen last time you made fun of it?" he asked, his voice lowering as he pulled her closer and kissed her neck, nipping sharply at the bottom of her ear.

She hummed, and he could feel the vibration in his chest. "You may have to remind me."

"Gladly."

His mouth captured hers, the taste of salt and citrus rolling across his tongue as he parted her lips. He would never get tired of this, how she lit him up from the inside and made him forget his fire had ever left him. Because it hadn't, not truly. She carried enough flames on her own. His little wildfire.

He'd believed, once upon a time, that losing his element would ruin him. That he wouldn't be able to overcome that sort of void in his soul. And while he still felt the bitter burn of its absence, there was also...*freedom*. Freedom to live a new life on his own terms, with the woman he'd loved for an eternity.

Nothing could take that away from him.

Her arms circled his neck, tugging him further into her. A slight rumble left his throat as she broke their kiss and trailed her lips down his neck, her teeth suddenly biting down on the sensitive skin.

"Impatient, much?" he asked.

"You were taking too long."

His lips quirked up. "Never been a problem before, sweetheart. But, if you insist..." He swiftly removed her arms and gripped her wrists in one hand, the other moving to her waist, pushing her backward until they reached the mattress. The backs of her legs hit the edge and she fell onto it with a giggle, which he cut off as his mouth crashed into hers. His fingers found the bottom of her white tunic and then met warm skin, his heart beating wildly when she let out a soft noise.

Gods, that noise.

A loud knock sounded on their front door, and Kai stiffened beneath him.

"C'mon, Aidan, we're going to be late."

Aidan's forehead fell against Kai's, his fingers still grazing along her lower stomach. "Not a good time, brother."

Another knock. "I'm not getting my pay docked because I waited for you!"

Aidan groaned while Kai shook with laughter. "I'm glad this is funny to you," he said before kissing her once more and pushing himself off the bed. She gave him a teasing smile.

"This isn't over," he growled, pointing at her.

"Have a good day at work, *sweetheart*," she called out in a melodic tone as Aidan grabbed his work boots and pickaxe from beside the door. He narrowed his eyes at her mischievous grin.

This is going to be a long day.

Aidan and his friend Elwan made their way down the sandy streets, passing the numerous tan limestone huts that speckled their small village. Women hung laundry out on lines to dry while kids ran shoeless down the dirt path, waving to parents who were off to start their day in the blistering morning sun.

Aidan had never lived in a land as flat as Ara Mir; there were no trees visible for miles, nothing but sand dunes dotting the horizon beyond the village, and rocky, reddish-brown spires protruding from the landscape. While vastly different from their home on Iona, Ara Mir held a certain beauty. The sunrises and sunsets over the beige expanse were bright and vivid, sometimes hitting the sand just right so it shone an iridescent red.

The two men neared the entrance of their assigned work area. There were three large underground mines in their village of Ta'aveen and several in the surrounding cities that the men alternated between. They all had official names, but the three in Ta'aveen were always referred to by their nicknames: Q, Castle Rock, and the Banger.

Aidan still hadn't asked why. Some stories were better left a mystery.

Every week, his employer—the wealthiest jewel miner in northern Ara Mir—hung a list outside his office of each man's assigned sector. Within his first month, Aidan had worked in all three of the Ta'aveen mines, and had even been assigned to some of the outlying cities from time to time. This week, he and Elwan were headed to Castle Rock.

"You hear about that storm up in Evonlea a couple weeks ago?" Elwan asked, wiping sweat from his tan forehead, which was already pink from the heat. His nasally voice seemed more obnoxious than normal. The man was friendly enough, Aidan supposed—when he wasn't interrupting his and Kai's morning activities. Aidan often enjoyed spending time with him, as long as Elwan kept his entitled upbringing and condescension shoved down.

Today did not seem to be one of those days.

"Can't say that I have," Aidan responded gruffly, swinging his pick at his side as they walked.

"It was a bad one. Brought trees down all over the place, even buried several neighborhoods. Thousands of houses were ruined. And so soon after the disaster in Karstos too. Crazy weather, huh?"

Aidan nodded but stayed silent. He and Kai had talked at length about this; the unnatural phenomena happening all over the kingdoms set both of them on edge. They were sure it had something to do with their elemental powers being taken away. It was a fear of Kai's ever since she dreamed of becoming human—what would happen to the world if they lost their powers? He'd told her not to worry about it, that the world could sustain itself perfectly fine without them.

Now, well...he wasn't so sure.

He should've known better than to dismiss his wife's concerns. All of these wild events had started taking place shortly after the showdown on the beach three months ago. Hardly a coincidence.

But what were they supposed to do about it? What *could* they do about it? He had no power. No control. He was simply a man, trying to love his woman.

He wished that were enough, but the unbearable weight of the world he once carried didn't seem to want to let him go.

Elwan continued. "I just hope the king and queen up there actually do something to help their people." He snorted. "I don't know what that peacock of a king over in Karstos is doing ever since he took away those tax laws, but he needs to get his act together."

Defensive anger bubbled to the surface of Aidan's skin. He slapped a hand onto Elwan's shoulder, a bit harder than necessary. "Almost to the mine. See you there," he said between gritted teeth, then sped down the small sand dune to the entrance of the mine.

He wasn't sure why he got so defensive of Sebastian. For most of the time he'd known the king, they'd been enemies. And it wasn't like they'd had much contact since that day on Iona. They had exchanged a couple of letters, mostly so the king knew where he and Kai were in case he ever needed them. But Aidan felt connected to Sebastian somehow. He'd been as much a victim as they were. Aidan had seen the moment of relief when Celesine's influence left him, had seen the look of agony on his face when Isla vanished from his grip.

He couldn't help but feel sorry for the man. Nobody deserved to be used as a pawn in a game among gods. From what Aidan and Kai could tell, Sebastian was doing the best he could.

Whatever that was worth these days.

Aidan nodded to his fellow workers, making his way to the racks of protective gear lining the inside of a tent next to the Castle Rock entrance. After grabbing a helmet, he looked around to find the section supervisor.

Seeing the familiar dark-haired man across the tent, Aidan waved as his supervisor called out, "Fyredrake! Follow Zayne over there, he's your leader for today. You'll be in level seven."

Level seven. He'd never been assigned that far down before. Most of the mines, whether they held jewels or other precious resources the kingdoms needed, were split into nine levels. The deeper levels hadn't been explored as much and were still ripe with untouched riches. Several hundred years ago, people weren't even able to go past the first couple of levels, but recent advancements allowed them to dig deeper and deeper into the earth. He couldn't help but be excited about the prospect.

A few minutes later, the rest of his team arrived, and they followed Zayne into the opening of the cavern. His team leader was a dark-skinned man with long, black locks weaving down his back, hints of blonde dye intertwined in the braids. A lantern and several small, sharp tools hung from a huge belt around the man's waist, a protective jacket covering a pair of dark blue overalls.

"Alright, whose first time down to level seven?" he asked as their small group entered the square-shaped shaft that would carry them into the dark depths of the cave. Aidan raised his pick a few inches in response, along with two other men. He looked around to see Elwan standing next to him and forced back a sigh.

"Just stick to the lit paths. Don't try to show off or go any further. We've already got blocks at various points to stabilize the ceiling," Zayne said, slamming a helmet on his head as the rickety shaft began its descent. "Don't be stupid and you won't die, yeah?"

Aidan chuckled. He liked this team leader.

As their shaft came to a shaky halt at level seven, the man operating the lift gave them all a tired nod as their group took their first few steps into the cavern. The pulley system for the shaft could be operated from above if needed, but there was often someone manning each level until the end of the day, when they'd be hauled back up with the last team to leave.

Enclosed torches were lit every few yards down the center of the cave and illuminated most of the space. This section was fairly wide, probably three times larger than his and Kai's little hut. The rough ceiling was so low, Aidan could lift a hand and set his palm flat against the rock. Bricks were piled from bottom to top along the edges to support the roof. Paths led in all directions into the abyss beyond their light.

The rotten, dusty smell Aidan had unfortunately grown used to was even more overpowering further in the mines. He coughed and brought his shirt up to his nose to try and block the fumes. Following Zayne's instructions, he joined Elwan against one of the closer walls and began chipping away with his small rock pick.

The old Aidan would've been completely opposed to this work. He wasn't used to answering to others, to following instructions and being cautious with his actions. But the *new* Aidan was learning to be comfortable without the same control he once had; the new Aidan felt a small sense of pride in the mundane work, the dirt behind his ears, the calluses on his fingertips. The way he was providing a life for his wife, however tedious and *normal* that may be, gave him purpose.

Besides, they could use a bit of normal for a change.

He paused his work, a gentle vibration making its way beneath the rock at his fingers. Aidan glanced around to see if anyone else felt it. Most of the men kept going, but a couple swiveled their heads, brows furrowed.

The vibrations grew, and with it came a low *whooshing* noise from the north side of the cavern.

"Zayne?" Aidan called, trying to keep his voice calm. It was probably nothing.

"Yeah, I hear it, we're fine—sometimes the nearby underground well shifts around. Just keep—"

Suddenly, an enormous *boom* sounded to Aidan's right, from one of the darkened tunnels. He dropped his tools and pulled on Elwan's shirt, tugging him back toward the shaft. The floor started to shake as the rest of the men abandoned their positions, cries of confusion echoing off the stone walls.

One brave—or foolish—man took a few steps in the direction of the ominous tunnel. Peering down it, he called, "I don't see anyth—"

In the next breath, a torrential wave of water burst through the darkness and enveloped the man. His strangled cry was silenced as he flew backward from the force of the water, his head hitting a sharp rock jutting from the ground. Blood poured from the wound and as he slid down into the oncoming flood, bits of bone and flesh stuck to the rock.

Adrenaline and fear coated Aidan's throat. Water continued to come. Shouts of terror rang in his ears, along with a thunderous splashing of waves on stone. It had already filled the cave and risen to Aidan's calves, climbing steadily higher with each passing moment.

They were hundreds of feet below the surface with nothing but an ancient, wooden shaft able to lift them to freedom.

Heart dropping to his feet, his pulse pounded erratically, making it hard to catch a breath. The shock of cold water through his pants made his legs numb, even as his mind screamed at him to *move*. He wasn't used to this raw terror—this dread that tore his organs apart and ripped the air from his lungs.

The splashing of men trudging through water and the rumbling of the cave as pressure built and built drowned out the worries screaming in his mind. He had to get out of this.

Aidan shook off the fear and clenched his teeth. He may not be an elemental anymore, but his soul was still made of fire—and his heart, water.

He would not die down here.

Most of their small group clambered to the wooden shaft, but a couple of men closer to the tunnels struggled to regain their balance and get their heads above water. Cursing, Aidan stumbled back to them, sputtering and blinking through mouthfuls of water as he waded against the flow. He pulled one man up by his overalls and yelled, "Get back to the shaft!"

Another head floated closer to the opening of the tunnel, even further from his reach. *Gods, Kai is going to kill me*, he thought as he sloshed forward.

"Aidan, c'mon! We've gotta move!" Zayne called over the roar.

"Yeah, yeah," he muttered under his breath, grabbing the thrashing man. His face came out of the water, but something tugged against Aidan's hold.

"I'm stuck!" the man shouted frantically, gasping for breath as his fingers clawed beneath the water.

"Just calm down! Give me a second," Aidan said, feeling for whatever was snagging the man's clothing. His fingers brushed against the edge of a pickaxe and he quickly dislodged the fabric from the blade, the man springing to the surface. They both turned toward the shaft and began wading through, occasionally shoved against the wall by the force of the rapidly climbing water.

He saw Zayne had already rung the emergency bell by the shaft, signaling to the operator at the top that they needed quick evacuation, but it didn't look like the platform was moving yet. Zayne anxiously slammed his hand against the stone wall.

"What's wrong?" Aidan shouted.

"The water must be messing with the cables—I can't get a response from the surface!" He cursed as he yanked on the end of the bell.

"Is there any other way to get the lift up?"

Zayne took several breaths, then rubbed his hand across his mouth. Anticipation snaked through Aidan's veins as Zayne said, "It can be operated manually. From down here."

Aidan blinked. "So...someone would have to stay."

Closing his eyes, Zayne nodded swiftly. "Get on the shaft."

"What? What about you? We're not leaving you down here—"

"I'm team leader, and this is my call, Fyredrake." The resignation in Zayne's voice cut Aidan like a knife.

"If we could figure out a way to engage the pulley system without somebody being there, maybe—"

Zayne grabbed Aidan roughly by the collar, cutting him off. "We don't have *time*. Get. On. The. Shaft." He shoved Aidan toward the others, and Aidan grabbed the wooden beams of the platform to keep from falling into the water, which was now almost to his chest.

There had to be something they could do. It wasn't fair—the man before him looked barely thirty. He had so much life ahead of him. Every inch of

Aidan screamed it should be *him* standing there, preparing to sacrifice himself to save these men. He'd lived *thousands* of lifetimes, more than any one person should get. He'd gone millennia with all the power, riches, and control he could ever want. What kind of a man had that made him, though?

Perhaps it took him losing it all to become the "good man" Kai always called him. And a good man would not leave someone down here to die.

The shaft shook precariously as it slowly started to rise. Aidan jerked his head to see Zayne pushing down on the operation lever. It groaned under the exertion of all the bodies plus the water, which circled viciously around their waists as it fought for somewhere to move.

Spying a long cord with a buckle attached hanging from one of the beams of the shaft, Aidan lunged for it, wrapped his fingers around the buckle, and launched himself at Zayne. With a shout from the team leader, Aidan hooked the buckle around the man's overalls and snapped it shut around his waistband.

"Pull him up!" Aidan shouted to the men aboard the shaft, who looked at him with uncertainty. A yelp left Zayne's throat when he was snatched backward. The men moved to grab him before his body banged into the shaft.

Aidan took his position at the lever, which had stopped moving in Zayne's absence. The platform hung several feet from the hole in the ceiling that led to the surface.

Zayne cursed at him, the pleas of the other men mixing with his furious commands when they realized what Aidan planned to do. Their shouts were cut off by the creaking and shifting of gears as the platform raised higher and higher, the water running off of it in waves.

Aidan took a deep breath. The water was nearing his neck now, but he had to hold on long enough to get them to the surface. The mechanism only worked if the lever was held down; once released, all movement stopped. He had to make sure they got to the top.

A chuckle escaped his lips. How ironic that *this* was how he would go—surrounded by water. He glanced up at the ceiling and to the Primeval gods beyond. *Cheeky little bastards.*

Shuffling to get a better grip on the lever, his leg brushed against something under the water. It felt...long. Rope-like.

His head jerked down, a plan beginning to form in his mind. He held his breath and with one hand, reached into the cold depths and felt at his calf for the object. After several tortuous seconds, his fingers closed around the end of the rope. It took a few tries, but he was eventually able to make his numb hands tie the end tight enough around the lever so it didn't pull free when he tugged it.

Now he just needed something to attach it to.

And then find a way out of this gods-forsaken pit.

Should be easy.

The shaft was probably only halfway to the top. He didn't think he'd have time to wait it out before the water overtook him. But if he secured the rope and kept the lever pushed down, he could get to the opening and try to—what, ride the water all the way to the top?

Wasn't the worst idea. Wasn't the best, either, but he'd cross that bridge when he got there.

He scoured what was still visible of the cave wall beside him. The lanterns were barely above water, and even those were beginning to dim as the flood submerged them. Soon, he wouldn't be able to see anything at all.

A pile of bricks supporting the ceiling caught his eye. He took several deep breaths before plunging into the icy water, letting go of the lever briefly so he could wrap the other end of the rope around the base of the bricks. Using only his sense of touch, he swam toward the lever to make sure the rope was keeping it down, relief flooding his body when he felt it was secure. He kicked his feet and broke the surface with a gasp, needing to stand on the tips of his toes to avoid taking in mouthfuls of water.

His heartbeat pounded in his ears. He was so close, *so close*, but the sudden reality of dying down here began to overtake him. Panic rose up his throat, his arms locking into place from cold and fear. Swallowing down bile, he closed his eyes. An image of beautiful blonde hair, dazzling blue eyes, and full lips curved into his favorite smirk met the back of his eyelids.

Gods, she was going to be so pissed at him.

Clenching his fist, he shoved off the ground and swam to the center of the cave, where the hole in the ceiling leading back to the surface was located. Could he simply wait for the water to carry him higher? The flow had to stop at some point, surely. He didn't know how much water the underground well held, but chances were it would reach its limit soon. So, he could stay down there, in the cold and dark, and wait for someone to come for him.

Which could be hours. Days. He was impressive, but even he doubted he could tread water for that long.

He growled. There had to be *something*—

Suddenly, the last remaining lantern flickered, and he spotted a piece of metal hanging from the vertical tunnel. He kicked as fast as he could to the edge, his eyes widening as he drew closer.

A ladder.

Laughter shook his shoulders, his relief so tangible he could feel it fluttering through every muscle of his body. Grabbing the end of the rusted metal frame, he hoisted himself up to the first rung.

Let's hope this doesn't break.

CHAPTER EIGHT

Kai

K ai fumbled with the glass vial in her hand, her entire body shaking and tensing and twitching with each sound. Every time the healer's tent flap rustled, her neck jerked to the side to see who was entering.

Not him.

Not him.

Not him.

Gods, where is *he?*

Zephania came up behind her and gently set a hand on Kai's shoulder, then took the vial of ointment from her. "Go," the woman said kindly, nodding to the back of the tent. "Rest. I'll do this." Zephania turned to the injured man before her and began applying the thick ointment to the cuts on his arm.

Kai murmured her thanks before walking to the back. Slumping against a small wooden table, her feet slid out from under her and she slipped down until she slammed against the rough floor.

There had been another accident in the mines today—a *flooding.*

As always, her ears had perked when the worker ran into the healer's tent to inform them of potential injuries, waiting for him to say which mine. It had never been Aidan's, but every time, her heart still squeezed with painful anticipation, her breath catching until an answer was given, and then she would always sigh and chide herself for being so worked up over nothing.

But not today.

"It's Castle Rock, Miss."

Aidan's section. She'd tried to maintain composure as the words settled over her like a fog, but inside, her thoughts were a maelstrom of questions and anxiety.

A *flood?* How had that even happened? The panicked man delivering the news didn't have any more details, as the crew who had been in level seven had only just arrived back to the surface. They were still trying to assess the damage.

Aidan hadn't been among the crew to resurface.

Kai sat against the desk, replaying the last hour in her mind. She put her head between her shaking knees to calm her breathing. Did humans always live with this fear? Did the idea that their loved ones could be so easily broken and ripped away from them constantly pull at their minds?

Kai's skin tingled and her stomach twisted into knots. Gods, she was going to be sick. She'd *never* been sick.

Someone crouched beside her, and a hand began rubbing circles on her back.

"Just breathe in, girl. That's it, deep breaths. Slower, slower...there you go," Zephania said quietly, and Kai obeyed. Her breaths became stronger and the panic cleared her mind ever so slightly, but the nausea remained.

"Thank you," she said with a sniff, lifting her head and leaning it against the desk. Her fear was still there, lurking and rippling beneath the waves, but she could hold it at bay.

"Team leader from Castle Rock's here. He's got news about your Aidan," the healer said, offering Kai a hand.

Kai leapt to her feet, her head rushing and vision going gray as her body swayed. Pushing against the dizziness, she bolted to the front of the tent, where a dark man with long braids and soaking overalls sat by the opening.

"Where is he?" she demanded, noting the weary look on the man's face. "Where is my husband?"

He stood. "Ma'am, my name is Zayne Daya, and I'm an extraction coordinator over at Castle Rock. I was leading your husband's team today—"

Kai put a hand up to stop him. "Cut the formalities and tell me where he is," she said through clenched teeth.

Swallowing, Zayne said, "He—he's still down there, ma'am."

Kai blinked and narrowed her eyes. She curled her fingers at her side, wishing desperately for the water that used to thrum through her veins. "I'm sorry, he's *what*?"

"Well, he"—the man rubbed at the back of his neck nervously—"he insisted on staying down there to make sure we got—"

"Aren't *you* the team leader? Why in the gods' names did you let *him* stay there?" she exploded, barging toward him with her finger jutting into his chest until he backed up against the tent wall. "Is he alive? Did you leave my husband down there to die?"

Her rage boiled over, both at this sad excuse for a leader and at her irrational, over-confident husband. *Of course* he willingly chose to stay down there to help the others.

He was going to be the death of her.

"I tried to stop him! I was supposed to be the one down there. I made him get on the platform while I manned the controls, but he tricked me onto the shaft and took my place. We're sending some men down there as soon as we can get the shaft operational again."

"Kai, come here. Let the man go," Zephania urged, tugging on Kai's arm to lead her away. "He was just doing his job."

"If he was doing his job, *he'd* be the one down there, not Aidan," Kai snarled and jerked out of the healer's hold. She stormed from the tent, trying to subdue the storm swirling inside her. Anger, fear, desperation, and hopelessness pushed at every inch of her skin. She marched further down the sandy road, toward the open market residing not far from the healer's tent.

"Where are you going?" Zephania's voice called from behind her.

"Which way is Castle Rock?" was all she said in response. If these idiots wouldn't go down into the mine to find her husband, then she would.

"I'll take you, just follow me," Zayne said in resignation, his waterlogged overalls sloshing as he made his way to her. Kai gritted her teeth but nodded, following him down the sandy terrain.

He had to be alive. She'd feel it if he wasn't, wouldn't she? Jade would scoff at the romantic notion, but Kai clung to it. Aidan was strong; he would figure out a way to stay alive, to wait for someone to rescue him. The alternative was too much for her to think about.

Kai had been so lost in thought that she hadn't noticed Zayne was talking to her.

"...thing we can think of is the underground barriers holding the well must've broken or eroded so much that it wasn't strong enough anymore. People have been doing this for forever, and nothing like it has ever happened before." He paused and looked over at her sheepishly. "I'm sorry about Aidan. I didn't want this to happen. It's my duty to protect my men, and I failed them today."

She balled her hand into a fist at her side. "He's going to be fine," she responded.

Something he said nagged at her. How had the barrier holding the water broken? If it really had eroded or weakened, what had caused that to happen? All of the bizarre natural disasters happening across the kingdoms concerned her, and this was another tally to add to the growing list of suspicious events.

She couldn't help but think if he died down there, it would be partially *her* fault. All of it was their fault, for giving up the elements. This was a warning.

Those thoughts fled her mind as they crested a sand dune and came upon the entrance to what Kai assumed was the Castle Rock mine. A rather large gathering of people congregated around a tent outside the caverns, made up of both men and women angrily shouting at two men standing before them. Exchanging a wary look with Zayne, Kai picked up speed.

"That's two accidents in less than a month!"

"You said our families would be safe down there!"

"We're not paid enough for these conditions."

One of the men addressing the crowd stretched his hands out placatingly. "Look, we hear you, and we understand you're scared. This is completely unprecedented, and we're working as hard as we can to find the problem and address it so this never happens again. If you would all please go back to your homes, we will—"

"My husband died down there today!" one woman wailed, pushing her way through the throng until she was inches from the men in charge. "It's just a bunch of empty words. How many more have to die before you *do* something? What does the Triad have to say about this?"

At the mention of the rulers of Ara Mir, the people's chatter picked up. The man at the front wrung his hands nervously. "Ma'am, I'm very sorry for your loss. But he knew the risks of the job, and—"

The entire crowd erupted at his words. Incoherent shouts and threats echoed all around, and beside Kai, Zayne let out a long breath.

"Gods, this is a mess."

"Well, it's *your* mess. Yours and the Triad's. I'm just here to find my husband." Kai hurried past the angry mob and made her way to the entrance of the caves.

"What do you think you're going to do, climb the whole way? You can't get down there right now, and even if you could, it's flooded. You'll drown," Zayne said frantically as he ran in front of her to block her path.

Oh, the irony.

She tried to shove past him, but he put a hand out.

"Listen, I don't care if you weren't enough of a man to go back down there yourself, but *nothing* is going to stop me from getting to him. Now, *get out of my way*," Kai seethed, nostrils flaring.

A deep, tired chuckle reached her ears. "I forgot how sexy you are when you get angry, sweetheart."

Zayne whipped his head around, and Kai's heart jumped to her throat. Right behind Zayne, at the entrance of the cavern, was Aidan.

He slumped against the cave wall, his clothes dripping wet and his knees shaking as he fell to the dirt floor. Zayne's mouth dropped. Kai rushed forward, a strangled yell leaving her lips as she sank to the ground beside him. Her fingers cupped his face while her eyes trailed his body, looking for any sign of injury.

"Are you hurt?"

"How did you get out of there?"

Kai's and Zayne's questions overlapped, and Aidan's eyes fluttered as he leaned against Kai. She'd never seen him so exhausted, and his labored breaths had spikes of worry replacing her relief.

"I'm alright—just tired." Slow breath. "Found a ladder and climbed up the side."

Zayne cursed next to her. "You climbed up *seven levels*? Gods, that's—"

"Hard? Yes, it is. I could use some help," Aidan said, and Zayne scrambled to get his arm beneath Aidan.

Kai kept her hands on Aidan's chest as they hoisted him up. "But you're not hurt? Nothing broken or bleeding?" she asked, feeling around for wounds.

"Not that I know of, but keep checking all you like," he said, and she glanced up to see his usual cocky smirk spread across a tired face.

She slapped his chest. "Don't you *dare* pull something like this again. What were you thinking, staying down there? That's not your job, Aidan! You scared me to death!" she shouted, her voice on the verge of breaking as she slapped him again. "We've talked about this over and over. You *have* to be careful! What would I do if you'd—if you—"

"Sweetheart, hey, I'm alright—I'm here, it's okay," he said gently, using his free hand to tug her toward him and tuck her body under his arm. "I'm so sorry I scared you, Kai. I promise it'll never happen again." He kissed the top of her head, and her frenzied heart began to calm.

Zayne snorted. "I'm glad you're alive, but you're right—that will never happen again. You'll be lucky if I don't have you fired for that stunt," he said, but the relief in his voice betrayed his threat.

"No, he'll be lucky if I ever let him leave the house again after that *stunt*," Kai muttered.

With a chuckle she could feel rumble all the way through her, Aidan said, "Now, that doesn't sound so bad."

She rolled her eyes, her anxiety slowly dripping away. Aidan recounted his story of the minutes he'd spent in the dark, flooded mine, and how he'd spent the last couple of hours slowly climbing up the old ladder. She had to stop him when he started to tell them about almost falling off—her stomach couldn't take any more worry.

The rest of his crew broke into applause and gasps of shock when they entered the work tent beside the cavern. Despite Aidan's reassurances he was fine and simply needed rest, Kai hovered over him like a hawk and insisted they go see Zephania. There was no way his body would've been able to climb hundreds of feet under normal circumstances, and the adrenaline and shock that must have coursed through him would be wearing off soon. He'd be lucky to not have any strains or tears in his muscles.

One of the men brought a cart around and urged Aidan and Kai to let him take them back to Zephania's. They accepted, and the second Aidan collapsed in the back of the cart, he let out a groan.

"I *knew* you weren't as fine as you kept saying," Kai said, pulling his head into her lap. "I'm still mad at you, you know."

"I know, and I'm sorry, Kai." He sighed as she massaged his scalp. "All I could think was if a man had to give his life for the rest of the group, why should it be someone who'd barely lived to begin with? How is it fair that *I* would get to be saved, after my millennia of memories, while someone else's time is cut too short?" Grunting, he shifted and looked up at her. "At least it would've been my decision. But I'm here, and I'm not going anywhere, alright, sweetheart?"

She looked down at him, finding it harder and harder to hold onto her anger. "I think I liked it better when you didn't want to be the hero all the time," she grumbled. When he gave her a tired smile, she leaned over and pressed a kiss to his lips. "Thank you for coming back to me."

"Always," he said. "Did they tell you what happened?"

"Just that one of the underground barriers holding the big well must have broken, and that's why it flooded the mines."

Aidan nodded. "Things are getting bad, Kai. There's no way that well would've busted unless the earth caved in. You were right: something happened when we gave up our powers."

Kai twisted her lips. "I know. But we can't reverse it; we don't have the dagger, and the gods only know where Celesine and Isla are. *If* they're still alive."

"We've gone over this again and again. She's *got* to be alive."

"Then why hasn't she tried to contact us?" Kai bit down on a nail. "I miss her, and I know you do, too...but the more I think about it, the more I wonder if all of these unnatural disasters are happening because she's gone. For good. And maybe the elements left with her."

"*Or* it could mean she's on the spirit plane."

Kai's eyes snapped to Aidan's. "What are you saying? That Isla became the *Aether*?"

He shrugged. "Crazier things have happened."

"No, they haven't," Kai said with a snort.

"Rynn thinks he saw her take Sebastian's blood, meaning she took the Aether's power, *meaning* she would have to go to the spirit plane."

"Rynn was also barely standing and had lost buckets of his own blood," Kai pointed out. "I wouldn't trust everything he thinks he saw."

"Let's just say he's right, and she didn't die on the beach. If she can get back to the physical plane, maybe it would resolve everything with the storms. Get the earth back to normal, so to speak."

Kai let out a breath. It was a very large *if*, but she had to admit, the idea that their friend might still be alive sparked hope in her chest. "Alright, I'll bite. How do we get her back from the spirit plane? And even if we did, you know it's only temporary. There wouldn't be a way to get her to stay permanently."

"What if we had the Dagger of Volnus back? Or maybe there's something that could help us in that Vasileia book of hers. Where'd that go, anyway?"

"I'm pretty sure Bri left the ship with it. So it's probably with her or Luca in Evonlea. And as for the dagger...none of us know where it went."

Aidan nodded and rubbed at the stubble on his jaw before closing his eyes, a slight grimace on his weary features.

"Gods, it would be so much easier to figure it all out if we had Rynn and Jade too," he said. "But there's one thing in all of this I'm fairly certain of."

"Oh, and what's that?" Kai asked, humoring him as she began to knead the muscles at his shoulder.

"Where was the last place we saw Isla, Celesine, *and* the dagger?" He cracked one eye open. "This all started on Iona. I bet you that's where it'll end."

"What did I say about making more bets with you?" Kai sighed. "If you're right, then I guess it's a good thing we're going back."

CHAPTER NINE

Isla

G rief is a selfish demon.

It demanded attention, demanded to be seen, demanded to take. It's not satisfied to lie dormant in the background, like a single, glimmering star in the cosmic universe. No, it must be the entire sun, burning and pulling and shaping the worlds around it.

Grief is also an insatiable monster.

Even when one had given it months—*years*—of time, it always came back for more.

Isla thought she knew grief. She'd called it a close companion for years as the loss of her mother and Waylan became a part of her.

But then, she'd watched her brother fall.

Crack.

And she'd felt herself die.

Blink.

And she'd been lost in a world she had no understanding of, completely alone.

Well, that wasn't entirely true.

Her elements pulsed beneath her skin, providing a small comfort when she felt her own mind caving in. They clung to her and wrapped themselves around her heart, coils of power that reminded her, ever so briefly, of home. Of rushing water and warmth and the kiss of wind and sand between her toes.

The only one she still couldn't feel running through her veins was the Aether. The spirit element seemed...unimpressed. Could an element have feelings? Opinions? Isla wouldn't have thought so before, but the spirit liked to test her. Taunt her. Especially at the beginning.

Do you want to see the world?

I can show you everything.

Can you handle it, little queen? Can you handle the weight of thousands of years of humanity thrust upon your shoulders?

It will crush you.

But Isla hadn't cared. What else was there to possibly crush—her heart? Her mind? Her life? It was all ashes on the wind, anyway.

Yes, she had responded. *Show me everything.*

Isla didn't know how much time had passed since that day on the beach, or since she'd been flung back to the physical plane and into Sebastian's bedchamber. Time was meaningless. It was everywhere and nowhere all at once. It could've been weeks, months, years—it didn't make a difference. Time floated through and around her like a strand of starlight dancing across her skin. She could rake her fingers over it and watch it shatter and disperse before weaving back together.

She'd tried to feel her grief, in the beginning. When she'd woken up in the darkness, with that ethereal whisper clogging her senses and her elements bursting within her, she'd relived the moments on that beach a thousand times over. Heard the snap of Arden's neck, felt her knees hit the sand, saw the burning hatred in Celesine's eyes.

How was she supposed to overcome that? Loss never got any easier. It was never the same, never constant. One couldn't pick up where they left off the last time and get through it faster like the pages of a book. She had to claw her way through the all-encompassing suffocation, the denial, the memories that rose unbidden to her mind.

Arden was dead.

She would never see her twin again.

Would she ever see *anyone* again?

And then *that* thought, that panic and fear, would burst in and vye for her attention. Where was she? Was she even alive? How would she get back to her world, her friends, her papa?

Such a mortal way of thinking, the ethereal voice would whisper. Isla didn't have the motivation to snap back. Perhaps she should've been grateful for another voice besides her own, something else to distract her from the anguish, but she only wanted it to stop. How was it possible that she could want to both suffer alone and also feel the warmth of an embrace, hear the soothing sound of a heart beating next to hers?

She felt so isolated. So chaotic. So...broken.

When that voice had offered to show her everything, she'd taken it.

And gods, it had shown her *everything.*

Isla saw vision after vision, moment after moment in the history of the realm. The creation of the world and the elementals, the rise of kingdoms. It passed over her like hundreds of sunrises and sunsets in the blink of an eye, the land spread out before her, bathed in the glow of a thousand new dawns.

She'd watched the earth grow and flourish, centuries of work and innovation and passion flitting by. The elementals—her heart had stuttered the first time she'd seen them, looking almost exactly the same as the beings she knew now, except not quite as hardened—had worked with the people to start civilizations and build kingdoms that could withstand the passing of time. They'd stopped wars, saved entire cities from disaster, altered the earth itself to bend to their needs. Their power was as beautiful as their compassion was strong. It took Isla's breath away to see how seamlessly the elementals worked with the humans, how perfect the Primeval gods' plan for them was.

Until it wasn't.

Isla knew bits and pieces of the elementals' past; they hadn't kept their eventual corruption a secret. She remembered the night Jade had talked to her by the hot springs in Aataran, confessing her need for the people to worship her, and how the earth elemental had lost herself in that desire. And Isla could still hear her conversation on the ship with Rynn as he spoke of assassinating the King of Iona as revenge for his friend's brutal murder.

But none of that prepared her for watching their fall from grace unfold before her eyes.

It wasn't a cataclysmic collapse. It wasn't a burning inferno of chaos and destruction. It was step by step, year by year, a slow-growing malignancy. Like small, barely noticeable cracks in a foundation of a house that kept spreading until, eventually, the entire structure caved in.

Isla tried to find that initial crack in each of them. Tried to pinpoint what could have started the elementals she'd come to know down that terrible spiral, what could have caused them to start an entire *war* simply to appease their pride. She watched it over and over again: their ego, their need for control, their contempt toward the humans, their rage. They all had moments that planted a kernel of darkness inside of them, twisting and deepening until it was so ingrained in their spirits they became willing to do whatever it took to command the kind of respect and control they'd once had.

Isla hated it. She'd grown to love the elementals. She'd trusted them and laughed with them and given up *everything* to save them. It was like watching four complete strangers force the humans of the world to bow to them. She tried to turn away, tried to wall herself off from the visions, but she couldn't.

Keep watching, the voice hissed.

Scenes of the civil war on Iona slashed through her mind with vicious strokes.

Rynn stood over King Elrich's body, a blood-stained sword in his grip and a wicked smile on his lips as he thrust the blade once more into the king's chest, then sliced it across his neck, blood spraying his face like war paint.

Aidan under a canopy of trees, his entire body lit with angry flames. Red and orange flickered across his dark eyes, the rage in his features mirroring his fire's blaze. Strangled cries of humans pleading for their lives ripped through Isla. His lips twisted in a sneer as he stalked toward them.

Kai—her sweet, bubbly friend—with a cold, determined gaze, looking down on a group of rebels as they knelt in shackles before the Vasileia throne. *"These are the traitors,"* she whispered to the king. *"Shall I have them executed?"* he asked in response. A blink of sapphire eyes, a nod, a raise of a sword.

Jade's fixed gaze staring out a tower window, signs of her seclusion evident in her sallow skin, the room around her overgrown with vines, cobwebs clinging to the doorframe. *"Please, you must help us!"* the people begged her. She saw them slaughtering one another in her name—in *their* names. Heard their helplessness and cries of mercy. *"I'm done helping this world,"* she said, and let them sink in defeat.

With each vision, each moment in history, Isla's heart hardened. Her once wide eyes and refusal to believe what she'd seen soon morphed into a clenched jaw and bitter resentment. How could they have done those things? How could they have let so many people die?

All those millennia of watching the elementals twist and gnarl into spiteful, vengeful beings...Isla didn't know how Celesine had put up with it.

And then a frightening thought popped into Isla's mind.

What if the spirit elemental had been...right?

Careful, little queen, the voice purred.

Gods, she couldn't believe she was even *thinking* that. Of course, the spirit elemental hadn't been right. There was no excuse for the vile deeds she'd done; taking Sebastian's mind prisoner, orchestrating Isla's family's kidnapping, killing her broth—

The pain tore through her heart so fast, like she was watching it happen all over again.

Crack.

Isla gripped her head and took a gasping breath to fight against the feeling of being strangled. It was as if someone had punched her in the gut, the way her chest caved in on itself as she doubled over, trying to make herself smaller so the grief wouldn't have as much space to consume.

It didn't work. It never worked.

But then...

Get up, little queen, the voice suddenly urged. *They are coming.*

CHAPTER TEN

Isla

Who is coming? Isla asked in her mind. When the voice went silent, she gritted her teeth. "Who is coming?" she repeated, aloud this time, and her voice came out scratchy and raw from disuse.

There was a shift in the air. The black void surrounding her—nothingness, stretching on forever—rippled. A silken fabric fanned out before her, a prism in shades of black, gray, and deep purple ebbing and flowing like waves on the sea. She'd never seen anything like it during her time on the spirit plane. It was only ever an unending blackness, unless she was being shown visions of the past, which were then spread all around her, like she was walking through those moments in time.

"Who are you?" she asked, anticipation mounting in her bones. *Something* was coming.

Isla's core tugged at her, the elements pulling taut as a bowstring. It was almost painful, the way the very air around her stretched, plucking at her body from every direction. Her chest tightened, the darkness falling and cresting with increasing speed as a buzzing started low in her ears, when suddenly—

It stopped.

They are here.

Isla's head jerked to the side at the voice, but still, she was alone. And yet, she felt...*something*. Her elements called to it, this unseen force that seemed to command the entire plane.

"We have been watching you, daughter of the island."

Isla sucked in a breath to hold back a cry of surprise. That voice...it was like a dozen voices blended into one: melodic and grating, guttural and honeyed, deep and ringing. The words echoed around her, bouncing off invisible walls and grazing against her skin.

"Where are you?" she asked.

As if in response, five dim lights appeared in the black expanse above her, twinkling and growing until they took the form of five bright, glowing stars.

"We are the Primeval gods. We are everywhere," it—*they*—answered, and as Isla heard the words, the stars pulsed.

"Are you—" Isla stopped herself, her mouth hanging open. She wasn't even sure what she was about to ask. *Are you those big stars in the sky talking to me?* Her time on the spirit plane had finally made her go insane.

Instead, she settled on, "Why are you...up there?"

Well, that wasn't much better.

A pause, and then, *"We take the form you give to us. If you worship us as the stars, then that is what we shall be for you."* The words rang out and fused together, and her mind almost couldn't focus on them all at once. It was like trying to pinpoint a single voice in a crowd full of people. The all-encompassing power radiating from the stars rolled across her, her entire body and the elements inside prickling with awareness.

"What do you want?" she yelled into the void.

A deep rumbling shook her feet, and the stars twinkled. Were they...*laughing* at her?

"So brave, daughter of the island," they said. *"We desire the same as you."*

Her pulse quickened. "And what is that?"

"Balance restored. Nature at peace. The world as it should be," the voices resonated around her. *"Have you not seen how your world once existed? We have shown you how it was meant to be, time and time again."*

Isla bit at her lower lip. "Yes, I've seen it. But—I don't know what any of that has to do with me."

"The world has shifted. Our plan for nature has been tarnished and perverted over time, and now, the earth has been left void of its base needs. This cannot happen."

A wave of frustration rushed through Isla. She welcomed it; it had been so long since she'd felt something other than grief and loneliness.

"You act as if that isn't something *you* could've prevented. What were you doing up here while the elementals became corrupted all those years ago? What were you doing while Celesine plotted to kill them and take their power? What about when she—"

"Do not reprimand us, daughter," they commanded, the voices rising as their power slammed into her body. *"We have no control over the actions of the elementals we created, nor do we interfere with the workings of men. Would you have us take away their free will?"*

Isla's nostrils flared. "No, but what Celesine did caused this whole problem! She's the reason your precious balance of nature has been upset. Why didn't you even try to stop her?"

"Hmm," the stars thundered, and the ground at her feet shook again. *"And yet, she is not the one standing before us."*

Isla blinked. "What's *that* supposed to mean?"

"You are the one who took the powers of the elementals as your own."

Her mouth dropped open. *Are they serious?* "Do you think I *wanted* any of this to—"

"Were you forced into this position against your will? Or did you choose, with full knowledge of what would transpire, to take their power?"

Isla's mouth snapped shut and she clenched her teeth together to prevent the onslaught of fury boiling within her. How *dare* they blame her for this.

Everything that happened had been Celesine's fault. Did they honestly believe she would've chosen this path if she'd been given a choice at all?

"Ah, but you did have a choice, daughter. And we do not fault you for it. But these transgressions must be resolved."

Transgressions? Gods, what a bunch of—

Isla quickly shoved away those thoughts; she had an inkling these stars—the Primeval gods—could see inside her mind. "What am I supposed to do about it now, then?"

The stars sparkled brighter. *"Since the elemental power has been taken from the earth, it has begun to rebel against the people."*

As they spoke, visions played before Isla's eyes. She saw avalanches on what she recognized as the Aataran Mountains, heavy piles of rock and snow decimating towns at the base of the range. Floods, earthquakes, massive cyclones washing ashore in Karstos and wreaking havoc on countless villages. Blizzards and dust storms, poisoned water and crumbling islands. Tens of thousands of lives upended.

It was...a nightmare. It looked like the end of the world.

Isla brought a shaky hand to cover her mouth as her eyes scanned the scenes. When a blazing forest fire took a small cottage captive and she heard the screams of a child, she slammed her eyes shut.

"Stop!" she shouted. "I get it—I don't need to see any more."

The visions ceased at her cry, but she didn't think she'd ever forget what she saw. The destruction and loss at the hands of—of *her* elements, as she now thought of them. They were a part of her. And they were destroying the earth.

"You see, daughter of the island, what occurs when that power has been ripped from the world."

"How do I fix it?" she whispered, tears threatening to overwhelm her.

"You must restore the elements to their rightful place. Locate the Dagger of Volnus once again. It is the only way you will be able to transfer your elemental power to bring peace back to the nature of this world."

Isla pursed her lips. None of what they said made sense. "What am I supposed to do with the power? How do I restore balance?"

The blanket of darkness danced around her again, its power tugging at her like strings on a puppet. *"There is only so much information we can give you. The time will come for all to be revealed."*

She held back a growl. Weren't they the "almighty gods"? The literal creators of the world? They should be able to do whatever they wanted.

"You do not see as we see, daughter. You do not know as we know. Do not ask for that which you do not understand."

Her hands curled at her sides. She was tired of their cryptic nonsense. "Fine. But how exactly do you expect me to find the dagger when I'm stuck up here? I don't even know how to get off the spirit plane," she admitted, thinking of that quick encounter with Sebastian in his bedchamber. She hadn't been thinking of him when it happened—at least, she didn't *remember* thinking of him. But her time on the spirit plane had become a jumbled mess of memories in her mind, and every time she closed her eyes, she saw those she'd left behind. Maybe the Aether had sensed her despair and sent her where she needed to be.

The stars took a long pause before finally responding. She felt the air pulse around her sporadically, as if they were communicating without her hearing.

"There is a way we can help you to remain on the physical plane for an extended period of time."

Her neck snapped toward them at those words, her heartbeat quickening. "Show me."

CHAPTER ELEVEN

Sebastian

There were only nine days left until they were to leave for Iona, and Sebastian knew there was still far too much to get done. Or rather, for *Annalise* to get done. He'd tried for days to get her to delegate more to the staff—or, gods forbid, to *him*, as he was more than capable of running a kingdom—but his royal advisor was set in her ways.

Truth be told, he was thankful; the idea of dealing with his council any more than he already had to made him want to bash his head against a wall.

Still, he wished she would pass off some of her ever-growing list of tasks to her subordinates. Annalise's face had grown paler and the shadows under her eyes darker in the weeks leading up to the Reign of Dawn. Sebastian had to start force-feeding her meals once he realized she'd been getting by with a single orange and a block of chocolate a day as sustenance.

There was an enormous amount of work to do to prepare for their absence. Anna, Lord Everett, who was the head of his council, and several of Sebastian's guards would accompany him to Iona. They had to set up protocols for the chain of command in an emergency, work with the commander to modify the schedule for the royal guard, and appoint someone to hold court in Delarossi in Sebastian's place. And, of course, to fill every role Annalise presided over.

Which, to Sebastian's shameful shock, was...an incredible amount. Gods, how did one woman *do* everything she did?

"I still need to check that Rogers can visit Grenleigh House to see how the refugee site is coming along," Annalise started as they walked back to

Sebastian's office following an *obscenely* long council meeting. "We need to make sure Lord Perrin follows through on your instructions to send some of the goods from the upcoming shipment to the southern territories. Oh, and I need to find someone to oversee the new shelters. They're nearly finished and should be ready for people to move in starting the week we're gone, of course. *That* will be a nightmare. And—"

Sebastian turned on his heel. "Anna," he said, and she skidded to a halt before smacking into his chest. "When was the last time you slept? Or...breathed?"

She let out an amused huff, pushing a lock of auburn hair out of her face. "Those things are overrated."

"You're working yourself into the ground. If you don't start taking care of yourself, I might have to let you go."

Rolling her eyes, she shoved past him. "I think you would forget your own *name* if I weren't around."

"Of course, I wouldn't," he scoffed, matching her steps as they neared his office. "It's Rolfe."

That earned him an actual laugh, which he wished he could pluck from the air and keep forever. He didn't hear true laughter in the castle very often.

"Oh, I almost forgot," Annalise said slowly. "We've got to remind the nurses caring for your mother that we'll be gone for the week." Her voice softened, as it always did when she mentioned his mother. "Were you planning to visit her before we left? Tell her about the festival?"

His eyes fell to the floor, his stomach twisting into knots. It's not as if his mother would remember, if he did tell her. The former Queen Carissa Avax had been bedridden for years, plagued with a degenerating mind and body, unable to remember so much as her own son's name. Every time he visited her, every time he looked into those deep blue eyes that mirrored his own and did not see a single spark of recognition, it chipped away at him.

But she was his mother. One of the only people he had left.

"Yes, I was going to see her this afternoon or tomorrow, and again before we leave. I'd like to take her some of the hyacinths from the south garden—they're blooming early this year, and you know they're her favorite."

"I'll have someone put together a bouquet."

He reached for the handle of his office door and pushed it open. "No, Anna, it's fine. I'd rather—"

Sebastian suddenly stopped at what was waiting inside, almost tripping over his feet as his breath caught in his throat. Quickly shutting the door, he turned and pressed his back against the handle.

That was the last thing he expected to see.

"What's wrong?" Annalise asked, her eyes on high alert.

"I just—ah, I need a moment," he answered, his heart thumping wildly. "There's something I forgot to take care of. I'll come find you later, yes?" She scrunched her forehead at him, confusion written on her face, and he sighed. "I'm fine, Anna. I promise."

She tapped against the side of her leg before shrugging. "Alright. I have things to do, anyway." She pointed a finger at him. "But you better stop acting so bizarre before the trip. I can't have you embarrassing me."

"Wouldn't dream of it."

He watched Annalise stride back down the hallway and took a deep breath, turning to the door and slowly pulling down on the handle. The faint scent of apples and evergreen reached his nose at the same time as he saw a flash of red hair.

"I'm surprised to see you here," he said, closing the door and leaning against its frame, shoving away his shock. "Although I must say, I'm disappointed it's not my bedchamber this time."

Isla's head jolted up at his words, dropping the piece of parchment she'd been holding over his desk. Her eyes widened at first, then she schooled her features.

"Back to the cocky king routine, I guess?" she said with a tilt of her head, her fingers running across the edge of the desk.

"I prefer to think of it as confidence." He made his way to her, a smirk playing on his lips. "But trust me, I can be cocky, as well."

Isla let out a huff of laughter and rolled her eyes, but he was relieved to see the contempt she'd once held for him as the *dark god* had completely left her gaze. Still, a shadow fell over her face, ghosts dampening her bright purple eyes—eyes that still sent a wave of unease through him.

"How are you here, Isla?" he asked softly, dropping his arrogant pretense. It was easy to fall into, easy to be the self-important king who could charm his way out of—or into—any situation. But that's not what she needed, and that's not who he wanted to be with her. Not anymore.

She sighed and slumped against the edge of the desk. "I have...a lot to explain," she began. "How long has it been since I—since I visited you?"

"Eight days."

She quirked an eyebrow, that little spark of playfulness appearing behind her walls. "That was quick."

"It was a memorable night." He meant the words to be coy, but the moment he said them, a trail of ice snaked down his back. The memory of the night terror he'd had came roaring back to life, along with the vision of different violet eyes, her claws of power digging into his flesh and ripping, tearing, shredding—

Isla must have noticed the change in his demeanor, for she took a concerned step forward. "I'm sorry. I shouldn't have just shown up like that, but I didn't even know what I was doing. I couldn't control it."

"Don't apologize, love," he said, reaching out a hand then dropping it instantly. What was he about to do, touch her arm? Tuck that loose curl behind her ear? Those were all things the old Sebastian would have done, the corrupted one, the possessed one—he didn't want her to remember him that way. No matter how much he longed to seek comfort in her or feel her skin against his, he couldn't push those boundaries. Not after the way he'd treated her all those months ago.

He continued his thought. "I wasn't trying to imply it was an unwanted visit. You're welcome"—*with me, at all times, whenever you want*—"here anytime."

Sebastian cleared his throat. Gods, what was this woman doing to him?

Her lips twitched as if fighting a smile before her eyes fell back to the piece of parchment she'd been holding when he walked in. "This is the festival Iona is hosting, right?"

"How did you know about that?" She simply gave him a look out of the corner of her eye, and he nodded. "Ah, yes. 'The Aether sees all.' I remember that bit."

"I don't see as much as I'd like," Isla said, looking out the window to the sun setting beyond the trees of the garden. "There are still things they won't tell me. It's incredibly annoying."

"What do you mean, 'they'?"

"The Primeval gods."

Now *that* surprised him. "They're truly up there? You met them?" His voice was laced with awe; Celesine had mentioned the gods before, but it was strange to envision them walking around with Isla, carrying on mundane conversations.

The room heated a few degrees as she ground her teeth together. "Oh, they're up there, alright. And they're a bunch of pretentious, manipulative—" She took a deep breath and held her hands out as if to stop herself. "They want me to help them fix everything. All the wild natural disasters are happening because the elements are no longer living on the earth, if I understand correctly."

This was more like the Isla he knew. A beautiful temper and sharp tongue beneath that layer of uncertainty. Sebastian's feet moved toward her of their own accord. "How do they expect you to do that?"

"They said I need to find the Dagger of Volnus again. It's the only way to put the elements back into someone—or some*thing*. That part is still a little unclear." She rolled her eyes, then paused and bit her lip. "But I've seen what's happening here. All the people who've died, all the cities destroyed...I want to help them, Sebastian. I *need* to."

Ah, yes. Isla's propensity for carrying the weight of the world—he'd seen it in so many ways, so many times as he watched her the last two years. Whether helping a family in Lockhurt or killing a band of thieves single-handedly, her heart beat for those in need. And yet, the way she wouldn't look him in the eyes and fidgeted her hands in her dress as she spoke made him believe that wasn't the entire reason for her altruism.

Approaching her tentatively, as if she might spook if he moved too fast, he put his hand next to hers on the desk. "Isla, love, none of this is your fault."

Her lips twisted and she looked down at their hands, mere inches apart on the shining wood. "You don't know that," she whispered.

It physically pained him to see her this way. The self-imposed burden of blame crushing her slowly, the light in her eyes replaced by a haunted stare of someone who had lost far too much.

"Look at me," he murmured, bringing his thumb and forefinger to her chin and lightly drawing her eyes to his. Just that simple act, the barest of touches, made his body relax and yet crave more at the same time. Her watery, violet eyes flicked to his and then down again, as if she was too ashamed to meet his gaze. The effect was still jarring—how similar they looked to Celesine's.

But he kept reminding himself it wasn't her. This was *Isla*. Familiar freckles dotted her nose and cheeks, the darkened scar under her left eye that, for some reason, had not healed when she became an immortal.

So beautiful.

"Why are you blaming yourself for this?" he asked. If this was something she needed to work through, he would let her.

She swallowed. "I could have done so many things differently that day. If I'd figured out what was going on with you sooner"—she glanced up at him—"I could've used the dagger on you immediately instead of taking all of the elementals' powers. We could have faced Celesine *together*, instead of fighting each other."

When she paused, he opened his mouth to counter her argument, but words continued to spill from her lips as if a dam had broken.

"Even if I'd just left *one* of them with their powers, we might've been able to match her. But no, I had to take them all; the dagger made me greedy. Or I could've given it all over when Celesine threatened to hurt—when she—" She took a deep breath. "Maybe then *he* wouldn't be gone." A single tear spilled from beneath her closed lids. "But I didn't. And then, at the end, when I took *her* powers and was forced to the spirit plane...that's why all of this is happening. That's why I blame myself, Sebastian. I was selfish, and I didn't want to die. And because of that, countless people have lost their homes and lives in these storms."

"Isla..." Gods, what he would give to take away her pain. To bear it himself. What was one more person's guilt added to his own growing pile? He'd be dealing with it for the rest of his life, anyway. His hands were forever stained red. "You were faced with insurmountable odds. If you had given the dagger and power over to her, what do you think would have happened? It would be *infinitely* worse. You kept that from her—you kept the world safe from her."

He rested his hand on her forearm, waiting for any sign that she would shy away from his touch, but she didn't.

"Nothing I say is going to take away from what you lost that day," he continued. "I've thought about it countless times, too. How I should have gotten to your brother faster, or fought against her harder. I don't know if we could have done anything differently, Isla, but there's one thing I'm absolutely sure of." He moved his hand to the back of her neck, angling it gently so she had to look into his eyes. "Do not, for one second, blame yourself for wanting to live. For doing everything you could to survive."

The sorrow on her face as she stared up at him felt like a blow to his chest. He wanted to kiss away each perfect tear that fell from her eye, wanted to hide her from the monsters whose teeth tore into her. But he knew the monsters lived *within* her, and he couldn't save her from them. She had to do that herself.

"Will you stay with me this time?" he asked. He wasn't sure what made him say it, only that he feared the moment her power would take her from him again, their time together limited by the spirit element in her veins. There was so much he wanted to ask her, so much he wanted to say.

"I can't," she answered quietly. "I came to talk to you about the festival, but I can't hold myself here for long. I'm not that powerful yet."

He nodded and released his grip on her neck, taking a step back. The absence of his skin on hers felt like a chasm dividing them. "What do you need?"

"I still don't know, exactly. The gods weren't very forthcoming with their *advice*. But I know one thing—the dagger is on Iona."

"Are they sure? We saw it disappear when you and Celesine did."

"According to the gods, it sent itself back someplace on the island—almost like it was protecting itself. There must be some specific spot it knows to magick itself to when it senses danger."

"You talk of it as if it's sentient."

Isla gave him a bemused look before sitting down at his desk chair. "You haven't felt it the way I have. I swear, that thing is alive. The way it got inside my head..." She shuddered. "I have to go back to Iona to find it. The gods told me about this festival the people are throwing, and it seems like the perfect opportunity to search."

"What do you plan to do once you find it?"

"Well, that's where you come in," she said, glancing up at him through her lashes.

His heart faltered. If she kept looking at him like that, he'd *crawl* to Iona.

"Oh?" was all he said.

"I'm assuming you're going to this?" she asked, gesturing to the invitation. He nodded. "Do you think there's a way you could get the elementals—all four of them—to come with you? I think we'll need them, too."

He hummed. The reason for this gathering already gave him pause, even if he refused to admit it to anyone; he didn't want to bring others into it if there was any chance of danger. Choosing his words carefully, he said, "They were actually all invited to attend by the Ionan Chamber. I've kept in touch with them over the past couple of months, and Kai and Aidan wrote to me from Ara Mir that they plan to go." He'd tried to convince them not to but had never heard back.

Her face brightened. "Really? That's—"

Sebastian held up a hand. "Don't get too excited. Rynn and Jade refuse to go. They don't trust Iona, and they'd rather stay isolated in their little cottage."

Isla's brow immediately furrowed. "They—are they...together?"

Her question hinted at something deeper than mere curiosity. Sebastian remembered the times he'd been forced to spy on her when she was with the air elemental, the churning, sickening feeling in his gut that would light up every time he saw the way Isla looked at Rynn. And then the day on the beach, when he'd seen the bruise...

Sebastian's fists clenched at his side. "From the very few letters they've sent, they're living together in Evonlea because Rynn needed assistance after the injury."

Isla's eyes widened. "That's right. Gods, I forgot about his leg."

"You truly don't know where the four of them are? Or what's been going on these last few months? I thought you would be able to see things from—" Sebastian motioned to the sky. Celesine had always known where her little pawns were, had always seen events play out on the physical plane like pieces of a chess match.

Isla's cheeks reddened. "I haven't figured out how to use the powers of the Aether. It's like they're fighting against me, or holding back somehow. I could barely even come here to visit you."

She must be incredibly lonely. He didn't know how she could stand it, isolated in the stars, unable to so much as check on her loved ones while time passed below.

"Will you get Rynn and Jade to come with you?" she asked again.

He rubbed a finger along his lip. "Why do you need to make sure they're all there?"

"It's just a hunch. Something the Primeval gods said made me think I'm supposed to use the dagger to take the elemental powers from myself and put them *back* inside the original carriers. And then everything would be in balance again."

Sebastian considered his options. While part of him wanted to keep everyone safe, he couldn't be sure the ominous feeling in his gut was based on anything but unresolved anxiety. They might all be perfectly fine. And if this was their chance at putting things to rest, at stopping the violent acts of nature from destroying his people, then he could cast aside his fears.

"I'll try my best to convince them," he promised. "And if they still refuse, I'll have them tied up and thrown onto the ship with me." He smirked, the image of Rynn chained to the mast of his ship giving him an unreasonable amount of pleasure.

Although, Annalise would most definitely kill him when he told her they had to leave even *earlier* to make a detour through Evonlea.

"Thank you, Sebastian," Isla said. "Oh, there was one more thing—do you know what happened to my ancestor's book? The one that helped us figure out how to use the dagger?"

"I never saw who ended up taking it with them. I can find out, if you need it."

"At this point, anything would be helpful. It may have more information about the dagger, or something we missed."

Nodding, he said, "I'll find it for you."

She smiled and opened her mouth to reply, then faltered, her expression falling. "I don't think I can stay much longer." She rose from the chair. "I can feel it starting to—"

Before she could finish her sentence, the ground beneath them shook violently. Isla lost her balance and slammed into Sebastian, who caught her by the waist.

"What was that?" she asked.

Another tremor rocked the castle walls, this time causing books to fall from his shelf and the windows to rattle dangerously. A pounding on the door was soon followed by the sound of Annalise's concerned voice.

"Seb, come on! We need to get you away from outer walls." The door flew open and Annalise strode in, promptly stopping in her tracks. She looked at Isla in Sebastian's arms, then at him, then back at the door. "Wha—who is this? Was she in here the whole time? Is this the thing you *forgot to take care of?*"

Sebastian blinked and tightened his grip on Isla as the earth beneath their feet rolled again. "It's not what it looks like. I'll explain later, Anna. Let's get to the safe room."

"Would someone like to tell me what's going on?" Isla hissed, her eyes darting to the shaking walls.

"I'm wondering the same thing," Annalise said, eyeing Isla with suspicion.

"It's an earthquake, Isla." Recognition dawned on Annalise's face as Sebastian said the name. "They've been happening more frequently. We need to stay away from windows and anything that could fall on us."

"An earthquake? But...why couldn't I feel it coming?" Isla mumbled to herself, confusion sweeping across her features.

"I don't know, but we need to go," he insisted as he pulled her toward the door.

Isla tugged out of his arms. "No, *you* go—I can stop this. I don't want anyone to get hurt."

"Isla, wait—"

But she was already gone, darting down the hallway and turning the corner before he could stop her.

Annalise's eyebrow lifted. "Does she even know where she's going?"

Sighing, Sebastian said, "Just get everyone else to the safe room. I'll be back."

"Are you joking? As you so often remind me, you're my *king*. I can't let you go out in the middle of this!" Annalise cried exasperatedly, then clutched at his arm when the ground shook again, harder this time. He stumbled into the wall and groaned as a portrait almost toppled onto his head.

"Anna, with all due respect, I believe I'm much safer in the hands of that woman than any bunker we could design." He righted her before adding, "And I'd rather look at her than any of the lords in that room." With a quick wink, he took off after Isla.

Racing through the halls, he dodged falling pieces of decor and avoided tripping over his own feet as the earth continued to quake. It was lasting longer than the other ones had. He wondered how far the damage extended. How were the cities faring? How many of his people were in danger? Not all of his subjects had the safety and support his castle provided.

He caught sight of Isla slipping through the tall front doors of the castle, her crimson hair and navy gown flowing behind her. When he burst outside, his heart constricted at the sight.

It wasn't just an earthquake.

Above him, the sky was a churning expanse of charcoal gray and ominous green, dust and clouds mingling together and whipping into a frenzy. The wind howled like a banshee across the earth. In the distance, beyond the property of the castle, was a massive, swirling cyclone, bits of debris flying through the air in its wake.

The enormous wrought iron gates that marked the entrance had been wrenched out of the ground, some rails twisted and flung dozens of yards away. Trees had been uprooted, branches lodged into broken windows lining the front of the castle. He couldn't see much beyond the gates, but the cyclone wasn't far from the center of Delarossi.

Thousands of his people lived there, with nothing to protect them.

Except her.

In the center of the courtyard stood Isla, hair lashing around her face in the wind. Her back was to him, but when a streak of lightning burst from the sky, it cast the world around her in shadows while illuminating her body.

She was...breathtaking.

Her arms flew out to her sides, and it was like everything—the air, the trees, even his own body—was pulled toward her. Tree limbs reached out to feel her power, lightning rained down like falling stars at her feet, and Sebastian's jaw dropped when the gray shadow of the cyclone began to twist and twine away from the city—and toward her body.

It traveled quickly over the broken land to wrap itself around her, encompassing her in flashes of light and darkness. Sebastian couldn't see her through the haze, and a pang of fear sliced through him.

"Isla!" he shouted, but he barely heard his own voice through the rumbling wind and booming claps of thunder. A second later, her silhouette peeked through the shadows as she brought her hands down and collapsed to the ground, her fists pounding the earth. She let out a roar, the wind siphoning down her body and into the dirt like she was forcing it out of the air. With a blast of energy that made Sebastian stagger back, the wind and clouds disappeared, and the earth ceased its shuddering.

Isla crumpled to her side.

Shouting, Sebastian sprinted forward and dropped down beside her, tucking an arm under her neck. He searched her body for injury, relief flooding him when she opened her eyes, blinking slowly up at him.

"That was—gods, you are..." His mouth opened and closed, unable to convey in words what she had done. He'd never seen anything like it.

"Didn't think someone could make you speechless," she rasped with a faint laugh, her eyes fluttering weakly.

"Only you, love." He smoothed the hair away from her face. "Are you going to be alright?"

Wisps of purple smoke began to gather at the edges of her body, signaling her loss of power and foothold in this world. His grip on her tightened, as if he could keep her with him by sheer force of will.

She gazed at him with a knowing expression. "I'll be fine." Grabbing his hand, she placed a featherlight kiss on his palm. "See you soon," she whispered, before the shadows swallowed her whole.

CHAPTER TWELVE

Rynn

This was the slowest form of torture. He would rather be anywhere else. Sweat trickled down his back like drops of blood, piercing cries filled the air, and bodies pressed in closer, closer, closer. And his *leg*. Rynn clenched his jaw, preparing for the wave of pain emanating from the gash in his shin.

"Would you like two or three chocolate rolls, miss?" the vendor asked Jade.

Jade looked at Rynn, who simply glared at her, and she rolled her eyes. "Three, please," she answered and handed the baker three coins.

Passing one of the chocolate rolls to Emilee and one to Rynn, Jade said to him, "Don't give me that look. You say you don't want one *every* time, but I know Emilee gives you half of hers behind my back."

Emilee smiled sheepishly, wisps of blonde hair escaping the blue scarf around her head as she bit into the flaky roll.

"Thank you," he said begrudgingly, taking the warm pastry and nodding at the baker behind the table.

He could have sworn he heard Jade mumble "stubborn man" in response as she continued down the row of vendors. Her burgundy cloak billowed toward him on the frigid wind and caught underneath his cane. Rynn stumbled as he tried to right it, another shooting pain spreading from the wound.

He cursed, and Emilee appeared at his side, her gentle hands holding his elbow steady as he corrected himself. Jerking his arm away, he muttered "I'm fine" and continued on down the uneven terrain after Jade.

Guilt gnawed at him. The girl was simply doing what was expected of her. But he did not take well to being another person's *job*.

He did not want to be here, in this overcrowded, clamorous market. People at every turn, shoving their wares into his face; so many scents that, when mingled together in the open air, ended up smelling like sugary sweat; children shrieking and weaving underfoot, threatening to trip him—*where are their parents?* Did humans let their offspring run amuck now?

Insufferable. Every single one of them.

Another bout of pain sliced through his leg when he stepped on a dislodged stone, and he gritted his teeth. The sensation was quick, at least, but it occurred so often he had begun living his life by the seconds of reprieve before the burning heat inevitably pulled him back.

Jade and Emilee insisted he accompany them to the market twice a month. They claimed it was "good for his healing" to be in the fresh air, putting weight on his leg, strengthening the muscles that had been lost after the injury.

That may be true, but he knew it was not the only reason. They wanted to get him out of the cottage, to enter him back into society and prevent him from falling into his reclusive ways. Why was everyone so concerned with how he chose to spend his days? The pitying way they looked at him was infuriating. Even Jade, as much as she tried to placate him with their usual bickering and flippant coolness. They were so desperate for him to heal. To hope. To live.

Perhaps he did not want any of those things.

He clutched the top of his cane as he walked, bracing for the next misstep and pinch of staggering pain.

If *this* was what a human life entailed, he did not want it. The relentless ache, the trite condolences, the monotony of day after day spent in the care of another, unable to so much as relieve himself without fear of collapsing.

A part of him was curious to learn what it was like for Jade and the others after losing their elements and immortality. He and Jade rarely spoke of it.

What little she had divulged was the idea of a void within her where her earth used to be, and he knew she felt its colossal loss. Occasionally, when she was particularly angry, he'd see the flash in her eyes and her fingers curl at her sides, like she expected her vines to appear before her. He'd catch her gazing at the dead, snow-covered branches of trees outside their cottage, an expression upon her face that he could only describe as *maternal.* Nurturing.

And yet...he was not quite sure he was experiencing loss in the same way. He did not *miss* his wind, his air—not the physical element, that is. The wind had always been his to command, to fashion into his will. He grieved its absence, yes, but more so because he grieved the control he had over it. The stability it gave him, the knowledge that, when wielded, he could be strong. Could provide for himself and others.

Without it, he was left an injured mortal, dependent on those around him. Weak. Incapable.

He often found himself wishing Isla had finished the gods-forsaken job when she had the chance.

Thoughts of her left a bitter tang in his mouth. He had always known it would end in one of three ways: Isla hurt, dead, or hating him. How devastatingly ironic that it was all three; even if she was not dead, she was still *gone.*

And she was not the only one. A part of him died that day too, and the gods only knew how deeply he now despised himself. For the way he had hurt her, and that he could do nothing but watch as she gave her life to prevent power from falling into the wrong hands.

He had been useless. Worthless. Powerless. And that had not changed in almost four months.

"One more stop, then we can head back," Jade called over her shoulder to Rynn and Emilee. They made their way through the masses and tables, Rynn's eye twitching at the woman who sprayed a puff of perfume in the air, beckoning him to her booth. Another table featured buckets of bright flowers, their leaves beginning to droop from a day spent in the sun. The red-headed young woman tending to the booth turned as they walked by, and he had to forcibly command his heart from jolting. It was exhausting, the way his infernal emotions tried to kindle hope in the barren wasteland of his soul.

Jade stopped in front of one of the last booths. The wooden table was covered in a clean, white cloth, with a myriad of leather-bound books topping the surface. Rynn could not help but lean closer. Crisp sheets of parchment were organized in rows along the back of the table, varying shades of cream or white with delicate faded designs bordering the edges.

"I'll take a stack of these." Jade pointed to a small pile of cream parchment squares. "And that black journal," she finished, gesturing to one of the pocket-sized leather books and smiling at the elderly man behind the table.

"What are these for?" Rynn asked, surprised to have found a booth with items that interested him in any way.

"You," she snapped, the kind smile she'd given the leatherworker now gone. "You finished off your last piece of parchment last week."

She had...noticed.

He cleared his throat. "That was kind. Thank you." It was easier for him to accept tokens and thoughtful offerings such as this when she hid them behind that scowling mask of hers.

The old man handed Jade her goods and took her payment. "You've got a good wife here, mister," he chortled. "She's at my booth at least once a month getting supplies for you."

Rynn's mouth dropped open. "We are definitely not—"

"Wife? That's absolutely—"

He and Jade both stopped mid sentence and turned to the sound of someone choking. Emilee clutched at her chest, a huge grin plastered on her face.

"Sorry," she gasped, "I—uh, choked on my chocolate roll." She coughed again, a snort escaping her lips.

Jade sighed. "For the love of—thank you, sir, but this is my brother. *Not* my husband."

Rynn hid a smile. As much as the idea of being married to her revolted him, he rather enjoyed seeing her flustered. It had been far too long since he'd smiled. Despite their constant irritation toward one another, Rynn found he had grown to...tolerate his companion.

"Ah, that's too bad. I always thought you two would make a handsome couple."

Rynn's spine went rigid at the familiar cocky, condescending voice. His heart raced as he schooled his features into a look of indifference. Turning slowly on his heel, he faced the man leaning casually against a nearby brick building, his feet crossed at the ankles, his navy cloak adorned with the emblem of Karstos. That insolent smirk was spread across his too-handsome face.

"To what do we owe the pleasure, Your Majesty?" Rynn said through his teeth.

King Sebastian kicked off from the wall. "Come now, I thought you'd be happier to see me. And who is this lovely lady?" he asked, gesturing to Emilee and reaching for her hand. When he placed a kiss atop her knuckles, a blush crept into her cheeks.

"A friend," Rynn cut in before Emilee could respond. "What do you want?"

"A friend?" Sebastian brought his hands together. "Well, now I'm curious. If you're being held against your will, blink twice," he said to Emilee, winking.

Rynn's fingers twitched. *This man.*

The girl laughed, still blushing scarlet. "Of—of course not. I am Mr. Rynn's—"

"Why are you here, Sebastian?" Rynn cut in again. Emilee rocked back on her heels, and shame burrowed its way through him. He would apologize and explain later, but the idea of admitting his weaknesses—his incapabilities—in front of *him*, of all people, made Rynn want to rip the air from their lungs.

Sebastian *tsk*ed. "Not even going to invite me over for tea first?" At the glares on Rynn's and Jade's faces, Sebastian smirked again and continued. "Fair enough. Straight to business. It's about the upcoming festival on Ion—"

"Hush!" Jade stepped forward, looking around the crowd. "You can't just talk about that out in the open. It's not public knowledge."

"Well, I *did* suggest inviting me over first."

Jade closed her eyes and let out a long sigh. Rynn knew that sigh well. "Alright, fine," she conceded. "You can come back to our house. We'll talk there."

"Wonderful." Sebastian turned back to the treeline he had appeared from and raised two fingers. A moment later, a sleek, black carriage drawn by two horses came into view. The hordes of people bustling around the market stopped to stare, whispers careening through the masses.

"So much for subtlety," Jade muttered.

"I never said anything about subtlety. Here we are, in you go," Sebastian said, leading them to the carriage.

"You want us to ride in that?" Rynn asked, not trying to hide his displeasure at being toted around like an arrogant king.

"Yes. Thus the 'in you go.'" Sebastian motioned toward the open door with both hands.

Jade and Rynn shared a glance. She pursed her lips, but followed, saying, "Come on, Emilee. You first."

"This will be fun," the king said, assisting Emilee up the steps of the carriage.

"I doubt it," Rynn mumbled.

"Doesn't your driver need directions to our cottage?" Jade asked, ignoring Sebastian's outstretched hand as she hoisted herself into a seat.

"He knows the way."

Rynn tried not to dwell on that disconcerting fact. He should not be surprised the king had been keeping an eye on them.

The four of them settled into the carriage, Rynn and Jade sitting side-by-side across from Sebastian and Emilee. Sebastian had not even batted an eye at Rynn's humiliating attempt at climbing up the steps. He also did not acknowledge the large wooden cane resting between Rynn's knees. Pain radiated up his leg and into his hip from the exertion, but he kept his fists clenched and his face impassive.

"Alright, you have our attention. What's so important about this festival that you had to come all the way to Evonlea to talk with us?" Jade asked exasperatedly, crossing her arms.

Sebastian glanced at Emilee, whose eyes were wide, lips parted. The inexplicable urge to chuckle swept over Rynn. This girl did not have the faintest idea what she had gotten into.

"You can speak in front of her," Rynn said.

Sebastian nodded. "In one of your previous letters, you wrote that the two of you would not be attending the Reign of Dawn. I understand—it must be difficult to go back there. Unfortunately"—he shuffled in his seat, putting one knee on top of the other—"I'm going to kindly request you change your mind."

"Why? You did not argue when we gave you our response the first time," Rynn said.

"Things have changed."

"No, they haven't," Jade argued. "They're still pretentious bastards. We're still not going. Nothing has changed."

Sebastian sighed. "You don't know that. This Chamber, or whatever they're calling themselves, could be perfectly respectable people. Who knows, you might even *enjoy* yourselves." His statement was lighthearted, but his tone was forced. Rynn was not sure if the king believed his own words.

"Get to your point," Rynn said with a glare. Sebastian was deflecting, which meant he was nervous. The confident facade could only last for so long.

Sebastian ran a finger along his bottom lip. "I need the two of you to come to Iona with me."

"That's not a good enough reason," Jade said.

"Fine." The king cleared his throat. "*Isla* needs you to go."

Shock passed over Rynn, clenching his stomach.

"*What?*" Jade screeched.

"She's alive, Jade, and she needs us all on Iona. She asked me to convince you to come."

It was like the air had been ripped from Rynn's lungs, and then rushed back in a torrential wave of emotion. *Isla.* She was alive. And she needed them.

He thought he had lost all desire to persevere, the ability to be useful, to be able to help. He had forgotten what this tempestuous longing felt like—not for *Isla* specifically, but to be *needed*. And of course, no matter how they had parted, he would still do anything for her, as she had done for them.

"When do we leave?" Rynn asked before he could stop himself.

Sebastian raised his eyebrows, and Jade scoffed. "Of course, mention *her* and he shows more signs of life than the last four months combined. *Men,*" she muttered.

A hardness passed over the king's eyes, but he cocked his head and smiled. "Yes, well, that was easier than I expected. We need to leave as soon as possible. One more thing: do you happen to have the Vasileia book?"

Rynn shook his head. "I believe her friend still has it. Brielle."

"Hmm. That's going to be a problem," Sebastian said, tapping his chin. "Isla thinks it could be useful. What are the chances her friend will hand it over?"

Rynn gave a soft snort. The thought of that fiery girl acquiescing to their request was laughable. "She will more likely demand to join than freely give you that artifact."

Jade broke her glowering silence. "You're not dragging that girl into this. Didn't we learn our lesson last time we brought humans into our affairs?" she hissed. "And besides, we're *not* going."

"I thought you might say that," Sebastian responded. Leaning forward and resting his elbows on his knees, he fixed Jade with a piercing stare. "Isla is looking for the dagger. She believes there may be a way to fix things. And that means"—his eyes darted between Jade and Rynn—"you might be able to get your powers back."

Jade sucked in a breath, her hands trembling as they gripped the edges of her cloak. Silence permeated the air.

"Are Kai and Aidan aware of the situation?" Rynn asked.

Nodding, Sebastian said, "They had already planned on going, but I explained these developments in a letter anyway, as well as helped them find passage to the island."

Well, the king truly had taken care of everything. Sharing a look with Jade, he knew their minds had been made up.

Rynn supposed they had better begin packing.

PART TWO:

QUAKE

CHAPTER THIRTEEN

Rynn

T he day dawned bright and clear. After four days at sea with the King of
Karstos and his crew, the familiar Ionan shoreline approached against
the backdrop of a cloudless sky. The great Mount Elani rose in the distance,
and crystal waters lapped at the side of the boat. Such a sight might have
been beautiful to some, but to Rynn and Jade, it symbolized betrayal and
loss—both of their beloved kingdom so long ago, and the elements that once
lived in their veins. A bitter cloud hung over him as he stood against the railing,
his cane leaning on his hip.

"Captain said we'll be there in another hour or two," Sebastian called from
his left, the king's voice more distant than normal, as if he, too, shared the
emotions that shoreline conjured in Rynn.

"Thank the gods. This ship is *not* agreeing with me," a voice grumbled
behind Rynn. Turning, he saw Brielle's eyes scrunching in discomfort as she
slumped against the mast of the ship. While still not happy about the fact that
the girl had joined them on the voyage, he and Jade could do nothing about
it now. After the two of them had agreed to attend the festival, Sebastian
had insisted they needed the ancient Vasileia book. They had tracked down
Brielle and, to nobody's surprise, the second Isla's name was mentioned, she
had forced an invitation to Iona.

Jade tried to convince her not to come. They had spent hours arguing and
raging. In the end, Brielle would not take no for an answer; she said she would

chain herself to the ship if they tried to remove her. The girl was as dramatic as Rynn remembered.

Brielle had made it all too clear this was *not* a friendly visit. She was there to help Isla, and that was it.

"I think that would be the whiskey, not the ship," another feminine voice, this one more clipped, sounded from the main deck. Annalise, Sebastian's royal advisor, came into view, pencil and paper glued to her hands. Rynn's eyes followed her against his will. He had been intrigued by the advisor, so young for her position yet wise beyond her years.

"Whiskey? It's barely morning," Jade interjected.

"That's what I said." Annalise sighed. "Unfortunately, Brielle here seems to be about as good at making decisions as my dear king."

"Oh, I think you're a dear too, Anna," Sebastian replied, slinging an arm around his advisor. "I was surprised Bri could keep up."

The two of them had become fast companions during the days at sea. It should not have come as a surprise—Brielle did not have the same memories of Sebastian the rest of them did, had no reason to feel the same flicker of panic and hatred at the sight of him that Rynn had to hide.

He imagined Brielle was still avoiding him and Jade, for she spent much of her time in close quarters with the king, Annalise, and the crew. Jade seemed content to burrow away in her cabin, her mortal body unused to the ebb and flow of the ocean and causing her to be sick if she was on her feet for too long. In an effort to return the kindness she had shown him over the months, Rynn took it upon himself to bring her daily meals and tea, along with a special concoction recommended by the ship's healer to fight seasickness.

Rynn's own days consisted of pacing the main deck in solitude, his cane rapping against the wooden planks as he mulled through the unexpected events of the last few weeks. The number of questions he had was growing, and until they reached the festival, they would remain unanswered.

Why had they been invited in the first place? Did this Chamber know who they once were? And then, there was Isla. Where had she been all this time? What did she need their help with that could possibly result in the reclaiming of their magic?

Rynn despised ignorance, and felt like a fool for blindly walking into this mess. His frustration must have been apparent, for two days into the journey, Annalise had approached him on the main deck.

"Here," she had said simply, holding out a small stack of books. "You're going to wear a hole in the wood if you keep this up."

His immediate response had been to reject her offer. After becoming accustomed to others doing things for him out of pity, he had developed a habit of shielding himself from any semblance of sympathy. But he had learned quickly this royal advisor would not be fooled by his masks.

She had raised her eyebrows in a terse expression. "It's just a book, Rynn. Take it. Trust me, you'll be sparing the rest of us the sound of that cane every two seconds." The gleam of humor in her green eyes had taken him aback, and so, he had accepted.

He had observed Annalise closely over the following days, often without even knowing he was doing so. She appeared to be a loyal and kind—if somewhat brusque—figurehead who was willing to put aside her own needs for those of her king. Rynn wondered if Sebastian knew exactly how much his advisor sacrificed for him. Most would not notice, in such a short amount of time in her presence, but Rynn could see a darkness sneaking behind Annalise's own walls. The way she would take charge of a conversation with confidence, then lurk in the shadows of a hidden alcove, inhaling shaky breaths as if fighting some internal battle. How she was always the first to rise and the last to bed, making sure the crewmembers were doing their duties, so concerned with others she would forget to eat or rest. Or how, in her rare moments of relaxation, slight panic would enter her eyes when unexpected sounds or footsteps drew near. As if she were afraid of someone. Some*thing*.

And yet...she never complained. By the end of their voyage, Rynn found himself thinking Annalise Dalgard deserved more than to be silently holding the reins of a kingdom when she had the power and strength to crush it in the palm of her hand.

That was not to say Sebastian was not a worthy king. Rynn would never admit it aloud, but he might have been wrong about the man. From news over the past four months and his own limited interactions with him, Rynn had discovered that upon Sebastian's return to the throne, he had swiftly redacted the heinous taxes, released those who had been imprisoned, rounded up the corrupted guards, and returned possessions tenfold to the families who had suffered his injustices. If the gossip in Evonlea was true, he had also apportioned sections of his own palace for those in his kingdom who had been affected by recent natural disasters.

He had come a long way from the possessed dark god Rynn had once known, and even from the boy king mourning his heroic father.

The looming shore and two large ships docked at the port of Iona caught Rynn's attention. The people of the island must have built the port recently; it had not been there four months ago. Rolling his shoulders and clearing his mind for what was to come, Rynn gathered his belongings on the main deck and waited for the crewmembers to lower the gangway.

He glanced at the steep decline of the wooden plank and ground his teeth together. These instances were the worst of them all, when he knew he would be unable to overcome an obstacle, but his pride prevented him from seeking assistance. He tucked his bag under his arm and clutched at his cane, reaching with his free hand to the ropes serving as a handrail. Slowly, he lowered himself down the gangway.

A warm hand on his wrist made him flinch, but he paused when he saw Annalise.

"You never told me how you liked those books, you know," she said, her tone conversational while her hand tightened around his, steadying him against the rocking of the unstable plank of wood.

"I was surprised to find you carry texts on ancient Karstosian philosophers and politicians around with you. Is that your idea of light reading, Miss Dalgard?"

A smirk appeared on her tawny features. "If you find them too difficult, I'm sure I have something better suited."

"By all means. I love a good challenge," he said, catching her sparkling eyes. Before he knew it, they were stepping onto the solid ground of the dock, and she released her grip.

A gasp and the sound of something heavy hitting wood made Rynn turn away from Annalise, a flash of blonde appearing in his vision as a body barreled into Jade.

"Gods, I've missed you, Kai!" Jade cried into the mane of blonde hair.

"We've gone a thousand years without seeing each other. What's four months?" Kai said with a giggle, and squeezed Jade tighter.

A deep chuckle reached Rynn's ears. "And what about me?"

Jade released a grinning Kai and turned to Aidan. "She should've left you in Ara Mir," she deadpanned, before her lips quirked up and Aidan swept her into an embrace.

"Oh, do I have some stories to tell you about this one," Kai started, shaking her finger at Aidan. "He's scared me half to death so many times. Within the first couple of weeks, he cut off his finger, and two weeks ago almost *drowned*—"

"Hey now, do you see any missing fingers?" Aidan waved ten fully intact fingers in Rynn and Jade's faces. "And the key word there is 'almost,' sweetheart."

Kai scoffed, then let out a squeal before throwing herself into Rynn's arms. His shoulders loosened, and he hugged her tightly with one arm, a current of compassion coursing through him at the sight of his friends.

"Come here, brother," Aidan boomed, clapping Rynn on the back with a chuckle. "How have you been?"

"I think you can see how I have been," he responded, holding out his cane.

"Much better than last time we saw you, at least."

That was definitely true. "How did you two find passage all the way from Ara Mir?" Rynn asked.

Pointing at the massive ship docked next to the one Rynn and Jade had just disembarked, Aidan replied, "Sebastian pulled some strings and got us onto the Triad's ship. If anyone asks, we're official ambassadors for Karstos, who just so happened to be vacationing in Ara Mir when our presence was requested elsewhere." Aidan winked at him. "Traveling on a king's coin isn't so bad."

Rynn hummed. "I can imagine."

"Ah, and who do we have here?" Aidan eyed Annalise, who had stepped back from beside Rynn during their reunion.

"This," a voice rang from across the deck, "is my dutiful and woefully unappreciated royal advisor, Annalise Dalgard." Sebastian came to a stop halfway down the gangway. He and Aidan seemed to size one another up before Aidan broke into a grin and stuck his hand out.

"It's good to see you, Your Majesty," Aidan said sincerely.

"I'm glad you and Kai made it here safely. And I've told you before, call me Sebastian. I think we've been through enough to warrant first names, yes?"

"Maybe one day you'll be lucky enough to call him *Seb*," Annalise chimed in flatly, a smirk peeking onto the corners of her lips.

"Let's not get ahead of ourselves, Anna."

Kai slipped up behind Aidan. "You look good, Sebastian. How are you doing?"

"I'm fine, Kai. I'll be much better once we get this soiree onto solid ground. Where are the guards and Everett? And Bri?" Sebastian asked, looking over his shoulder.

Kai's mouth dropped open. "Did you just say *Bri*?"

"Ah, yes. Our adventurous girl weaseled her way on another one of these fun trips yet again." Sebastian shook his head disapprovingly, but his eyes twinkled with amusement when Brielle appeared behind him.

Aidan's eyes widened. "Well, how about that? I didn't think we'd ever see you again!" He made to move toward the girl, but stopped in his tracks at the guarded expression on her face.

"Aidan, Kai. Hope you're doing well," she said formally, her eyes flitting to their faces before hardening and looking away. "Come on, Seb, I need to sleep this whiskey off." Brielle brushed past them with her bags and made her way onto the port.

"Have I—did we miss something?" Kai asked, tracking Brielle as she walked away. Four days in close quarters with Rynn and Jade had not softened the girl's heart toward any of the elementals, it seemed.

Jade sighed. "I'll explain later."

"Well, then. I'll round everyone up. You go mingle with all of the other"—Annalise wiggled her fingers at Sebastian—"important people in frilly outfits."

Sebastian grabbed her outstretched hand. "Stop it, Anna. You are far more important than any of them. Even in your drab clothing."

Annalise rolled her eyes before slipping back to the boat. Aidan picked up Kai's bags and the two of them charged forward, leaving Rynn and Jade with Sebastian.

Rynn allowed Sebastian to accompany him the rest of the way along the dock. He did not know what possessed him to say it, but as soon as Jade was out of earshot, Rynn muttered, "You do not deserve that woman's loyalty, you know. Annalise, that is."

Sebastian's reply spoke volumes of both the king and his advisor. "I don't think anybody could."

Their rather large crew was led to Palace Noctem by horse and carriage. As they drew closer, nerves broke out beneath Rynn's skin. He had not been this close to the structure in ages—a thousand years, to be exact. And the last time he had stood in its presence, it had been under the shadows of war, full of human soldiers readying to give their lives on a battlefield of a broken kingdom.

Gray walls loomed above them, the stone pristine and shining under the sun. He could tell some of it was the same ancient architecture from their time on the island long ago, but much of it had been rebuilt. Beautiful marble statues depicting various animals flanked the gardens, large columns lined the west and east courtyards, and the steps leading to the sweeping grand entrance were no longer crumbling and cracked. Looking up, the gleaming, gilded dome that marked the center of the capital city and the landmark of Iona greeted them.

A handful of servants met them in the front courtyard when their carriages dropped them off. Rynn distinctly remembered these courtyards and gardens always full of courtiers, lords, ladies, servants, even children scampering about or reading on the stone benches, tending to the flowers, or walking through the beautiful scenery. It was also not uncommon to find animals lounging in the fresh air, mingling with the people. Iona had always opened their streets to the wildlife of the island. Humans and beasts had lived in peace together for millennia in the kingdom, perhaps because the elementals made their coexistence possible.

Now, however, the gardens were empty. No maids enjoying their free time, no members of the court basking in the sunshine, no prowling wildcats or monkeys whisking by underfoot. It felt...stiff. Unnatural.

The servants led them through the garden pathways and into the majestic palace beyond. A domed archway separated the courtyard from the entrance steps, which echoed slightly as the group climbed. Aidan had stationed himself next to Rynn, ready to offer a hand if needed.

"Will we be meeting the, ah, Chamber today?" Aidan asked, breaking the uncomfortable silence.

A maid with brown hair and darting eyes shook her head at Aidan, seeming almost fearful that anyone would address her directly.

"You will meet them tonight at the welcome feast. This way, my lord," an older woman stated, ushering them through the main wing and to the right.

Aidan's dark eyebrows shot up. "It's been a long time since anyone has called me 'lord.'" He leaned his head toward Kai, but Rynn was close enough to hear him murmur, "Are you taking notes, sweetheart?"

"For the love of—" Jade rolled her eyes and swatted his arm. "We can all hear you."

"Well, you're welcome to call me lord too, Jade, but that might get weird."

Rynn tuned them out and looked ahead, where Annalise and Sebastian were speaking with the maids.

"Where will we be staying, exactly?" Annalise asked.

"We have a guest wing for each of the invited kingdoms. We are taking you to the Karstos wing now." The maid glanced at them. "You are all here to represent the kingdom of Karstos, correct?"

Jade, Rynn, Kai, and Aidan shared a glance. "Why not?" Aidan finally replied. The maid looked at them suspiciously before turning back around. "I don't think the Triad will particularly miss us."

Letting out a groan, Kai rested her head on Jade's shoulder as they walked. "I'm exhausted. And starving. I hope we can sleep before whatever is planned tonight."

Annalise rushed forward, retrieving a pencil from her ear. "I'd like to get an idea of the layout of the palace before..." Her voice trailed off as she caught up with the servants, one of the Karstos guards swiftly following behind.

It was wise, Rynn mused as they made their way to their assigned chambers, that Annalise wanted to set up security measures for the week. One could never be too careful. As much as the Chamber of Iona proclaimed a mission of peace and serenity, Rynn's paranoia was certain it was a facade. He could not help but wonder if they had stepped off the boat and straight into the jaws of a beast.

CHAPTER FOURTEEN

Sebastian

W ell, they had made it to Iona in one piece, and without anyone managing to jump ship at the last second, no less. That was the easy part. He wasn't sure how he was going to survive the entire festival surrounded by people who either wanted to kill him or take his throne. After the past two years, even the thought of convening with the other monarchs made him want to bury his head in the sand. Why had he agreed to come again?

Ah, yes. *Saving the world*, and all that. Truthfully, he would have circled the world ten times over if Isla had asked.

He could portray an image of a confident, established king all he wanted, but part of him was terrified to be on this island with leaders of the world who had watched him sink into the depths of darkness then crawl his way out on his hands and knees. To them, this was the *best* time to make a move. Kick a man while he was already down. Uncover his secrets and let him burn. And there was no telling what Iona might know about him, what they may want from him.

"Anna, are you almost ready?" he called out the door of his bedchamber to the one across the hall, where Annalise was staying. The entire west wing of Palace Noctem had been reserved for those accompanying him from Karstos—and the strays they picked up along the way. All of the rooms were now filled, save for an empty suite adjoining his own. The corridor extended to the right and opened to a massive common room with couches, several desks, a chess board, and an entire wall full of books. They were told by the maids they could request breakfast and lunch be served to them in the common room if they preferred, but their presence was required in the main dining hall every evening for a formal dinner.

Sebastian had donned his deep blue dinner jacket, affixed with gold buttons and the symbol of Karstos on his breast pocket, over a white button-down and black pants. Nerves began to creep in again, despite the very late—practically morning—nightcap he'd shared with Bri on the boat. He was anxious about the festival, yes, but also the fact that he hadn't heard from Isla since the earthquake. He didn't know when she would show up, or if perhaps something had gone wrong. What if she'd used too much power to stop the cyclone that day and hadn't recovered? What if the Primeval gods changed their mind about allowing her to come?

He needed to see her again, to know she was alright.

Heels tapped on wood outside his chamber door a moment before Annalise said, "Yes, I'm ready. Let's get this dinner over with."

Sebastian turned to find her striding toward him, her mahogany hair falling down one side of her face in thick curls as she looked down, struggling to button the clasp on her small black clutch. She wore a floor-length, forest green ball gown made of soft satin. The sleeves slipped down her light brown shoulders, and he spotted a slit extending up her thigh, revealing delicate black sandals. A belt looped snug around her waist, the buckle accentuated with black and silver designs.

He shook his head and pointed at her. "Absolutely not. You need to turn around and change right now."

Her head snapped up to him, her brow crinkling in confusion.

"I can't have you showing me up in this." He crossed the hall to her and reached for her hand. "You look astonishing, Anna, truly," he said, giving her a quick kiss on the cheek, which promptly deepened in color.

"Such a flirt," she responded with an eye roll. "Does it really look fine?" she asked shyly, her gaze dropping down to examine her shoes.

"Are you kidding me? I'm going to have to fight to keep these foreigners off of you. Unless you want them on you, in which case, I'll happily step aside."

Annalise smacked him on the shoulder before looping her arm through his and guiding him toward the banquet hall. "That won't be necessary, thank you."

He pinched her forearm. "Probably for the best. The whole lot of them are a bunch of peacocks."

"Who are you calling a peacock, there?" a deep voice sounded from behind them, and Sebastian and Annalise turned as Aidan and Kai traipsed out of their room, dressed in the latest and flashiest Aramian garb. Aidan's tan jacket and matching pants were lined with gold down the sides, numerous jewels adorning the arms and collar. Kai wore a two-piece dress that was a rich, varnished brown at the neckline and slowly lightened to a soft cream at the feet. The sleeves were sheer and flowed down her arms like liquid, where they tapered at the wrist. An inch of her tan stomach was on display before meeting the skirt that trailed behind her, a hint of gold heels peeking out.

"Where did you get these outfits?" Sebastian asked.

"Ah, well, I suppose we have you to thank for that," Aidan said, scratching his nose. "The Triad generously provided us with clothing for the trip to be added to the running Karstos tab. You know, since we're your ambassadors, and all."

Sebastian smirked. "In that case, I have excellent taste." He looked around the corridor, spotting his three guards in conversation with Lord Everett, waiting to leave. "Where are the others?"

"I think Jade and Rynn went ahead. They didn't need time to 'dress up like dolls,'" Kai responded with a laugh.

"And Bri?"

Down the hallway, a heavy door banged shut. "I'm here, I'm here. Couldn't get this dress laced up."

Bri appeared in a strapless, smoky gray gown with matching gloves coming to her elbows. The fabric hugged her dark skin tightly until it reached her hips, where it loosened and pooled at her feet. Silver jewels dotted her short black ringlets, and a dainty silver necklace hung low down her chest.

"What do you think?" she asked with a confident smile, twirling in place so they could see the extravagant laces up the back of the dress.

Aidan whistled. "Are you trying to stop hearts tonight, friend?" He took her hand and spun her before placing a chaste kiss atop her knuckles. "I've got half a mind to ask you to join Kai and me later tonight."

"I've got half a mind to agree," Kai chimed in.

"Let's see how dinner goes first," Bri said with a laugh, her eyes twinkling before suddenly, her face fell. She glanced between Kai and Aidan and took a step back.

Sebastian had ample opportunity to talk with Bri as they got to know each other on the ship. The fiery girl was still learning how to cope with her best friend missing and new knowledge of this world. She was one of the most loyal, passionate people Sebastian had ever met, and it seemed like she struggled to reconcile that with her grief and anger. She told him she blamed the elementals for their problems, claiming if they hadn't shown up in Isla's life, none of this would have happened. Bri simply needed an outlet for the emotions blazing within her, and the four would-be immortals were the perfect targets.

Sebastian worried carrying this grudge against them would soon burn her out. He didn't think she *truly* believed it was their fault—but who else was there to take her anger out on? All he could do was be a buffer between them and hope Bri realized holding them at arms-length wouldn't solve her problems. It wouldn't bring Isla back.

But working *with* them could. And if he had learned one thing about Bri in the past week, it was that she would do anything for her best friend.

"You look incredible, Bri. But I think you already know that," Sebastian said as he held his free arm out to her. "I'll be the envy of every man and woman with you two at my side."

Bri took his arm. "Gods, no wonder you're still single. Does anyone fall for those lines?"

Sebastian snorted. "That hasn't exactly been my priority lately."

Her hold on him tightened and her voice softened. "You're right, I don't know what I was thinking—I shouldn't have said that."

"It's alright, Bri. You don't have to walk on pins and needles around me. It was just a joke, yes?"

She nodded and twisted her lips. "I miss her too, you know," she whispered after a moment, their footsteps echoing down the wooden floors as they made their way to the banquet hall, the sound of voices growing louder.

He gave her a smile and a nod, afraid of saying much more. At his other side, Annalise tilted her head, assessing their quiet conversation with curious eyes.

The group approached a grand staircase leading down to the main banquet hall. Sebastian could barely make out the end of a huge wooden table and the swishing skirts and formal pants of guests as they passed by the open doors below them.

"Well," Sebastian started, looking at the women on his arms and Kai and Aidan behind them. "This is your last chance to back out."

"And miss the free food?" Aidan guided Kai down the staircase, throwing a wink over his shoulder. "Is His Majesty scared?"

"Oh, you have no idea," Sebastian muttered, then began his descent.

As the view to the banquet hall unfolded before him, even Sebastian was impressed. An enormous wooden table sat in the center of the room, chairs with tall backs upholstered in black surrounding it. A strand of thick, lush greenery ran down the middle of the table, decorated with candles and flower petals from end to end. Gold-rimmed plates and goblets sat at each place. Strings of tiny candles encased in gold spheres were connected by delicate yarn across the columns framing the outside of the hall. Looking up, Sebastian saw a transparent glass ceiling—they were standing beneath the stars, the moon and clouds on full display.

The most magnificent feature of the entire room was at the furthest end from the staircase: a beautiful tree, stretching from floor to ceiling, its branches dotted with candles and garlands of flowers. Sebastian had no idea how they kept the giant thing alive. Directly in front of the tree was the head of the table, where four wing-backed chairs sat, overlooking the rest of the room—the Chamber's place of honor, no doubt.

His crew was one of the last to arrive. With Annalise and Bri still at his side, Sebastian spotted the Triad from Ara Mir and their loyal priests, the white and gold robes blinding in a sea of muted colors and jewel tones.

"You know, I was born in Ara Mir, but I never got to see them," Bri whispered to him. "That's Ayana, right?" She pointed to the oldest member of the Triad, whose dimples appeared on tan, wrinkled cheeks as she smiled in conversation with another guest. Her gray hair was in a long braid down her back, a gold circlet centered on her forehead.

Sebastian nodded. "And beside her is Xavion. I believe both of them were elected around the time you were born."

"Oh, I remember him. Does he really not have—you know—" Bri stopped, eyes wide, and pointed at her mouth.

Chuckling, Sebastian said, "His tongue, you mean? Yes, those rumors are true." The middle-aged man had had his tongue removed decades ago out of a desire to deepen his spiritual connection with the gods. Sebastian had been fascinated with him as a child—he'd constantly asked the man to teach him new words in his sign language.

"And I assure you, he still has quite the colorful vocabulary," Sebastian added, and Annalise snorted at his side.

"Who's the younger one?" Bri asked, motioning to the third member of the Triad.

Sebastian bristled when his eyes met with the man in question: Ottorius Rejev, a short, pale man no older than Sebastian himself, with jet black hair and gold jewelry adorning his lips, nose, and ears. Sebastian was the least familiar with him, as he was the most recently elected member and had only attended a handful of meetings among the rulers—but the reports Sebastian had heard made his lip curl. Selfish, hypocritical, and far too comfortable using his position to get what he wanted—especially young women eager to prove themselves. He made a mental note to keep an eye on that one during the week.

"That's Ottorius," Annalise answered with a hiss. She was also not particularly fond of the man. "He's a snake. Always finds a way to start an argument with anyone close enough to engage."

Sebastian patted the top of her hand. "And what have we learned about dealing with snakes?"

"Go for the head. It's easier to crush."

"Well, I was going to say stay quiet and out of the way, but I like yours better."

The three of them burst into laughter right as something small and furry brushed between their legs, followed by a giggling young boy. Bri cursed and jumped into the air, but Sebastian merely laughed harder, recognizing the young Prince of Evonlea and his energetic dog.

"Trystan, sweetheart, what did I say about bringing him to dinner?" Melanora, the Queen of Evonlea, called exasperatedly after her son as he and the creature continued to zip through the banquet hall.

Adrik and Melanora Kegameth had developed an alliance with Sebastian's own parents early on in their reign, forming a trust based on mutually beneficial trade agreements. He'd accompanied his parents on trips to Evonlea countless times as a child. The Kegameths may be stuffy and pretentious, but they had always kept up their end of the treaties, and Sebastian had been thankful to have them as allies when he took the crown after his father's passing five years ago.

Smiling at the scene, Sebastian remembered when Trystan was born seven years previously—quite a shock to the kingdoms, considering Adrik and Melanora already had two adult children. Their oldest son, Klaus, was thirty, only a year younger than Sebastian and one of his oldest childhood friends.

Well, "friends" may be too strong of a word, as Sebastian had quickly grown tired of the way Klaus tossed his money and title around as one tossed feed to chickens. But they had been the only heirs of the royal families for several years—that is, until Klaus's sister, Jessenia, came along.

Sebastian caught sight of her silky blonde hair, almost silver under the glow of the moon, seconds before Jessenia appeared in front of him.

"Sebastian," she purred, dragging long, red nails along her collar, drawing his eyes to her low cut gown. "It's been a while."

"Jessenia." He tilted his head to her, then released Bri and Annalise from his arms. "I'll catch up with you later," he said to both of them with a tight smile.

Bri wandered off to the closest table of sparkling wine, but Annalise pursed her lips. "How lovely to see you, Jessenia."

Jessenia's light blue eyes trailed up Annalise's figure. "Annalise Dalgard, is that *you*? I never would have recognized you like this!" She waved her hand at Annalise's green dress. "I didn't think we'd be seeing someone like you here."

Annalise bristled. "Yes, well, as royal adviser, I do whatever Sebastian needs me to."

Eyeing Sebastian with a smirk, Jessenia hummed. "Believe me, I remember what that's like."

Behind Jessenia, Annalise pretended to gag. "Your Majesty, let me know if my assistance is needed. I'd be happy to dispose of anything for you." And with that, she turned on her heel, her mahogany curls bouncing against her back.

Sebastian pressed his lips together to hold back his chuckle as Jessenia grimaced.

"I don't know why you still have her employed," she said with a flip of her silvery hair. "Anyway, I've missed you, Sebastian. What happened to you these last two years? I was beginning to think you'd forgotten about me," she pouted, bringing the glass to her lips and stepping into him.

His fingers clenched at his side. While he was good at playing these games, he'd grown to hate this charade. Hated acting like one of *them*, when all they did was throw underhanded remarks to one another while plotting how to get what they wanted. Years ago, he'd gotten caught up in it all—the title, the wealth, the women. Getting anything he desired with a flick of his wrist. Including the woman before him—a wolf in sheep's clothing if there ever was one.

Younger than Klaus by six years, she'd been a nuisance to the two boisterous boys as they grew up. Always following them around, always giggling or crying or asking them to play with her. She'd been sent off to school before reaching maturity, and Sebastian hadn't seen her again until she was nineteen. Beautiful, young, fresh-faced...it had been impossible for twenty-six year old Sebastian to resist her advances.

Their affair had begun around the time his father passed. Sebastian was thrust into a new role while working through his grief, and there she was, poisonous temptation and desire wrapped in sultry words of comfort. They spent years in a carnal cycle of using and discarding one another like old garments. When he was in Evonlea on official—or unofficial—business, it didn't take long to find himself in her bed again.

He'd hated himself, yet he couldn't stop.

He was under no impression she'd expected anything more from him—she used him just as much as he did her. She gathered secrets and people like stones in her pocket, and inevitably hoped to add the title "Queen of Karstos" to her neverending list of accomplishments. Many thought Karstos and Evonlea would arrange a marriage of convenience between the two to unite their kingdoms.

But his time under Celesine's thumb had changed him. He was no longer the same king, and the idea of going back to those days made him sick. He didn't want to be a part of the game anymore.

"I apologize, Jessenia. Life has been rather busy as of late." A waiter passed by carrying a tray of flutes, and Sebastian plucked one off. "Excuse me," he said brusquely, giving her a nod before heading off to find Annalise. Jessenia's disgruntled scoff followed him.

The echo of metal striking wood rumbled through the hall, and all heads turned to the top of the staircase. A heavyset man with a gray mustache stood at attention, a metal scepter in his hand.

"Please take your seats. The Chamber will be arriving shortly," his voice boomed across the room.

Curious whispers reached Sebastian as the small crowd moved to find their seats. Each of their names were written in cursive lettering across golden placards. The Evonlean group was positioned to the back of the table, closest to the Chamber's seats. Sebastian and his party were assigned to the center, and the Aramian citizens were at the other end, by the entrance. Someone had even managed to change Jade, Rynn, Kai, and Aidan to sit at the Karstos section, and added Bri.

Sebastian took his seat, noticing Jade and Rynn had already found their spots across the table from him. When Annalise approached Rynn's right, he hastily stood and pulled out the chair for her, and Jade gave him a funny look out of the corner of her eye. Sebastian tucked the curious exchange away before facing the entrance, waiting for their mysterious hosts to reveal themselves.

A trumpet blared behind the staircase, followed by a steady drumroll. The crowd hushed.

"Gods, they spared no expense, did they?" Bri whispered. Sebastian turned to reply, when movement in the back of the hall caught his eye. Behind the rows of guards stationed at the columns stood a tall figure in a billowing gray cloak, an auburn beard mixed with gray reaching to his chest. Recognition flickered in Sebastian's mind. Why did he know this man?

Ah. It was *Akir*. The Ionan man who had kept Bri safe when Isla and the elementals had met him on the beach four months ago. Sebastian had only seen him briefly when they collected Bri and headed back to their respective kingdoms, but there had been something so familiar in the older man's demeanor.

The trumpet finished its obnoxious tune, and silence blanketed the hall.

"All rise," the mustached man bellowed. "Presenting the Chamber of Iona: Stefan Rigaldi the Third," he called, and then paused as a handsome, tan man in a black suit appeared on the staircase. Probably ten or fifteen years Sebastian's senior, the man's dark hair was beginning to gray at the edges, and his short-cropped beard was flecked with silver. He descended the staircase with confidence and poise, fastening the cufflink at his wrist as he walked, a gold crown perched atop his head. All around the hall, servants who had been silent up to this point murmured in unison, "Long live."

"Nor Noxen," the same man called out, and Sebastian's eyes flicked from Stefan Rigaldi to a larger, younger man in a similar black suit and matching crown walking down the stairs. His muscles bulged against black sleeves, his olive-toned skin gleaming under the candlelight. Nor Noxen was rough around the edges, his brown hair untamed as it curled at his ears, his beard full and rich. Light gray eyes scanned the room as he made his way to the end of the table. The same echo of "*long live*" sounded off the walls.

"Ezeretta Bannock."

A shockingly pale woman in a tight black dress glided toward them as if walking on a cloud. She couldn't have been older than Sebastian. White locks flowed down her back and curled at her waist, contrasting with the rose gold tiara nestled in her hair. When she passed closer to Sebastian, two different colored eyes stared back at him, one the lightest shade of blue, the other a soft brown. Her pink lips curved upward, as if they shared a secret, before she looked away and took her place by Stefan and Nox. Again, the servants muttered their mantra.

"Mariana de Faye."

The final and oldest member of the Chamber stalked down the steps, her red heels clicking against the hard floor. Steely eyes captured the room, a gold nose ring glinting against brown skin. Gray hair sprang like coils from her head and around her crown. She assessed the crowd as a predator would eye its prey, and a shiver rolled down Sebastian's spine when her gaze lingered on him.

"Long live the Chamber, and may they forever reign," the staff around them rang out. A soft peal of thunder sounded in the distance, and Sebastian looked up at the ceiling to see dark clouds rolling in to cover the stars.

"You may be seated," the announcer proclaimed, and chairs scuffed against the floor. The four Chamber members remained standing in front of the large tree.

"Greetings, friends," Mariana began in a smooth, deep voice. "We are truly delighted to welcome you all to our beautiful home of Iona. We hope this week will be a productive time of camaraderie, where we can reacquaint ourselves with one another after our kingdom has spent so many years in the shadows.

"One thousand years ago, this land was torn apart by a cruel civil war. Oppression and violence stripped away our ancestors' lives, leaving the island broken. But"—her eyes flashed as she extended her arm before her—"we are fragile no more. We have risen from the past of tyrants who sought to crush us beneath their feet, and we stand before you whole once again, ready to enter the world like a phoenix rising from the ashes."

Sebastian glanced at Rynn and Jade, whose jaws were both clenched tight, and at Aidan and Kai, the latter of which squirmed in her seat. Mariana was speaking of *them*, he supposed—the beings who had caused the war. Again, Sebastian couldn't help but wonder *why* the Chamber had invited them, or if they even knew who sat in their midst.

More thunder came from the sky, closer this time, as if the storm was drawing nearer. On the table, the delicate glass flutes shook.

"Tomorrow, we will begin forging a new path between your kingdoms and ours. But tonight, we—"

A faint tapping started behind Sebastian, growing louder from the direction of the stairs. Even Mariana stopped her speech at the sound. Anticipation and unease crawled up Sebastian's back, goosebumps breaking out across his neck. As the tapping came closer, the thunder gave a loud *boom*, making the guests jump in their seats as they craned their necks toward the staircase.

A pair of silver heels came into view. Sebastian caught a glimpse of a long, blood red gown before suddenly, the candles in the banquet hall were snuffed out. Gasps and squeals filled the air, mixing with the rolling thunder. His skin prickled with awareness.

A tremendous crash and a brilliant bolt of lightning lit the night sky, illuminating a figure in red descending the staircase. Suddenly, the flames flickered back to life.

Bri gripped Sebastian's shoulder.

Crimson curls. Scarred cheek. Violet eyes.

"Sorry to interrupt." Lightning flashed again, and she smiled, all white teeth and red lips. "I hope you saved me a seat."

CHAPTER FIFTEEN

Sebastian

If a dress could kill, he would surely be buried at her feet by now. Gods, she was stunning.

It was as if all the air had been sucked from the banquet hall as she sauntered toward them, her velvet red dress clinging to smooth skin and curves. The neckline came to her collarbone and hung off the shoulders, soft fabric hugging her body and revealing a slit on the side as she walked, exposing one toned leg. Every single person in the room had their eyes glued to her, Sebastian included. As she passed him and made her way toward the Chamber, he searched her face for any hint of the emotions she so often wore on her sleeve.

All he saw was cunning resolve.

Her eyes slid and locked onto his for the briefest of moments. He couldn't stop his neck from turning to follow her, couldn't help swallowing hard at the sight of the dress scooping low to her backside, leaving bare skin on display. Glancing at the Evonlean end of the table, Sebastian saw Klaus raise an appreciative eyebrow.

Hmm. That pretty prince would look even better at the end of his sword.

A murmuring began among the crowd when Isla approached the four members of the Chamber, who had recovered from their initial shock and now stared impassively at her.

"Did you know she was going to show up like this?" Kai hissed from his left. "And what's wrong with her *eyes*?"

Sebastian was as dumbfounded by Isla's entrance as the rest of them. He had no idea what her plan was; the last time he'd seen her, all they'd discussed was searching for the dagger. He assumed she would do so in secret, without alerting the Chamber to her existence, while they had the festival to keep them distracted.

That was obviously *not* her plan.

Bri's nails dug into his shoulder. She knew Isla was alive from their conversations in Evonlea and on the boat, but he imagined nothing could've prepared her for the shock of seeing her best friend again after months of believing her to be dead.

"Welcome to Iona, child," Mariana de Faye said. Her voice held the same amicable yet commanding tone as before, but Sebastian saw her stiff jaw, her raised shoulders. He wondered how she truly felt about losing her carefully curated moment of control.

"Your Grace," Isla responded, dipping her head toward the four members. "I apologize for showing up so late—the weather tonight doesn't seem to be cooperating." As she spoke, another clap of thunder rang out, practically shaking the palace walls.

"Not to worry. You are welcome here. Please provide your name, invitation, and kingdom affiliation so we may place you in the appropriate guest wing."

Sebastian leaned back in his chair. *This should be good.*

"Of course." Isla bowed her head, red curls dropping over her shoulder. "My name is Isla, and unfortunately, I seem to have misplaced my invitation." Her words were smooth like honey, with a bit of a bite.

Mariana hummed. "Surname, Isla?"

Sebastian held his breath and stared daggers at the side of Isla's head. *Don't do it, love...*

"Vasileia."

Well, here we go.

Whispers broke out among the servants and guards surrounding them. Most of the guests sitting around the banquet table seemed unperturbed, as the Vasileia name meant nothing to them, but the four Chamber members stiffened. Out of the corner of his eye, Sebastian saw Akir smile from the shadows.

"She really is just going all-in with this, isn't she?" Aidan muttered behind him.

Stefan Rigaldi surveyed the room, the servants ceasing their chatter when his gaze landed on them. "And you claim to have no invitation? What kingdom are you visiting with?" he asked, his voice low and gravelly.

Isla curved her body ever so slightly to face Sebastian's side of the table, and her eyes traveled to his, giving him the briefest hint of a wink. A coy smile played on her lips.

This was where he came in, he supposed.

He picked up his wine. "She's with me, actually," he said, bringing the glass to his lips and taking a casual sip. "Apologies for the late notice, Your Grace." He tipped his glass at Isla with a smirk.

Stefan looked back and forth between the two of them. Sebastian couldn't read any of the Chamber members' faces. Surely, a Vasileia showing up at their doorstep wasn't what they'd expected. What would they do with this turn of events? Would they feel threatened by the return of the royal bloodline? Would Isla be safe here?

"Very well," Mariana said. "We shall have her placed in the Karstos wing. I'm afraid we do not have a seat for you tonight, Miss Vasileia"—her voice cracked slightly on the name—"as we did not expect another guest."

Isla smiled. "Perfectly understandable, Your Grace. I'll just go make myself at home."

As a maid escorted Isla from the banquet hall, Jade closed her eyes and put a finger to her temple in exasperation. Sebastian had to cover his mouth to hide the smile that crept onto his face. He wasn't sure where this feisty Isla had come from, but she was magnificent.

"We're all going to be dead by tomorrow, aren't we?" Aidan asked under his breath.

Kai snorted lightly. "If I had to choose anyone to be on my side right now, it's her."

The trumpet and drum roll started back up, and the same man who had introduced the Chamber announced that dinner was served. Servants appeared from the side of the hall with huge trays of gold plates, silently placing them before each of the guests. As they lifted the lids, the mouthwatering scent of smoked meats, potatoes, and savory spices filled the air. Sebastian's stomach growled.

"Thank you," he said to the young man serving him. The man's eyes widened and he rushed back to his station by the columns without uttering a word.

"These Ionans are weird," Bri acknowledged as she poured thick gravy from a pitcher onto her lamb and garlic potatoes. It was the first time she'd spoken since Isla's arrival, and Sebastian couldn't tell how she was taking it.

"Are you alright?" he asked quietly.

Bri sighed. "I'm...shocked. I thought my best friend *died* four months ago, and now she waltzes in here like she owns the place. Well, maybe she kind of does. I don't know how all of that works." She waved her fork in the air before dipping it into the mashed potatoes. "She just seems different. And are her eyes *purple*? Gods, I'm still trying to fully understand what happened, and why she never told me she was alive. She could've at least visited, or...sent a message or something." A moan escaped her lips as she took her first bite, drawing the attention of several guests nearby. "I take it back, their weirdness is forgiven. This is the best food I've ever had."

Sebastian chuckled. Once Bri started talking, it was often difficult to get her to stop.

He moved to pour gravy on his own plate when a soft, familiar voice drifted through his mind, almost making him drop the pitcher.

"You should tell Bri to keep it down. She's going to have people lined up outside her door tonight with those sounds she's making."

Isla. Sebastian whipped his head around, frantically searching for her, but saw nobody except the servants and seated guests.

What was that? Had he imagined her voice?

A shiver ran down his spine. Celesine used to be able to communicate with him like this, speaking to him with her thoughts. The memories brought back the same chills to his body, the same fear and wariness. His breathing sped up as he tried to force the sensation away.

"I can hear your racing heart from a mile away. Relax, Your Majesty. If I can't be there, at least listening in can provide some entertainment." There was a pause, then, *"You should be careful not to leave your expensive jewelry lying around, you know. Anyone could break in and take it."*

His knee banged on the wood underneath the table. Glancing down at his empty fingers, he realized he'd left his rings on his dresser, and pieces of the puzzle started to fit together in his mind.

"You okay?" Bri asked, nudging his shoulder.

Schooling his features, he nodded. "Yes, fine. Sorry." He cleared his throat. "I'm sure she would've visited you if she could, but as the Aether, she's limited in how often she can come to our world. The couple of times she came to me, she was barely able to control her powers at all."

"Yes, but why come to *you*? I mean, no offense, I'm just surprised she wouldn't choose to see her father or even me. Luca doesn't even know she's alive," Bri said, her tone hushed and hurt. "I didn't want to tell him and get his hopes up. He's barely functioning. I'm lucky if I can get him out of the house to keep his business going."

"I wanted to see him," Isla said, once again making Sebastian jerk in his chair. *"But I didn't know how. I don't know what I would've said. How do I explain everything that happened? How do I watch him grieve both Arden and me, and not be able to give him peace? I couldn't make promises of returning when I don't even know if that's possible."*

Bri waved her hand in his face. "Sebastian?"

"You can't hear that, can you?" he asked.

"Hear what?"

His body relaxed slightly, remembering how Rynn used to be able to perform the same tricks—hearing things on the wind, sending messages to someone if he had a personal object of theirs. And Isla now had a personal object—his ring. *Clever girl,* he thought. His own phantom.

"Seb, what's wrong with you? I've asked you to pass the gravy three times now," Annalise called from across the table, breaking his thoughts. He blinked and apologized as he handed her the small pitcher, a smile ghosting his lips.

This was going to be an interesting week.

CHAPTER SIXTEEN

Kai

The food was divine. The music was enchanting. The banquet hall was unbelievable. But the twisting, churning sensation in Kai's stomach wouldn't go away. After Isla sprung that entrance on them—she really had learned her sense for the dramatic from Aidan and Rynn—Kai hadn't been able to settle her mind.

She'd known Isla was alive ever since Sebastian sent the letter explaining how she'd appeared to him and needed their help. It had given Kai plenty of time to prepare herself for seeing Isla again. But watching her walk down those steps, those purple eyes so similar to Celesine's, *knowing* she had their elements—*Kai's* element—in the palm of her hands...it was difficult not to feel a smidge of resentment and the sting of loss.

Guilt tugged at her, swirling uneasily in her gut. *Of course* she was glad Isla was here. Her friend was alive and healthy. It was selfish of Kai to still carry these feelings—*she* was the one who'd wanted to be human, anyway. Her emotions were being pulled in so many different directions, the longing for both her past and future at complete odds with one another.

Kai pushed the food around the plate with her fork, her appetite leaving her even while her stomach rumbled. She hadn't quite recovered from the voyage to Iona. The sea had always been her comfort, her solace, her very soul...but when she was on that ship in the middle of the Wyndsor Sea, not only was her connection to the water *missing*, it had actually made her *sick*. The motion of the waves and rocking of wood beneath her feet that had once felt like a beautiful dance now forced her to empty her stomach every hour.

This idea that her home, the deepest part of her spirit, had rejected her...it was too painful to think about.

A conversation taking place next to her between Aidan and Ottorius, her least favorite of the Aramian Triad, shook her from her thoughts.

"I never got the chance to ask: how did you come to know King Sebastian?" Ottorius asked her husband, his tongue flicking against the golden hoop on his lip. Kai tried not to bristle; her jaw automatically clenched whenever the man spoke. There was something about him that annoyed her to no end, and after several days on a ship with him, she wanted to avoid him like the plague.

"You already know we're his ambassadors, Otto," Aidan replied. His casual use of the nickname had Kai hiding a smile.

"Yes, yes, but *how* did you come into that position? Your accent doesn't sound like that of Karstos, so I assume you didn't grow up there. I'm simply curious how you found yourself at the feet of someone like *him*," Ottorius said with a sneer.

"First of all"—Aidan clapped a hand onto Ottorius's shoulder—"I would be careful what you assume about one's origins. And second, King Sebastian found himself in need of someone who could travel freely between the kingdoms and facilitate trade under his new agreements. My wife and I offered our services."

Kai raised an eyebrow, and Aidan slipped her a wink. *Someone's been practicing.*

"Well, I suppose he *would* need assistance putting out fires from the last several years," Ottorius replied.

"Perhaps it wouldn't be so difficult for him if you all would actually cooperate with his efforts instead of waiting for him to fail."

Kai's neck snapped up at those words, surprised to find a flushed Annalise sipping from her glass, fire in her eyes after her outburst.

Ottorius leaned forward. "Ah, yes, the king's faithful lap dog. Tell me, who am I supposed to cooperate with? The boy prince who lived in daddy's shadow? The king who ignored his people for two years? Oh, how about this supposed 'reformed man' playing the saint?" He spat across the table. "I don't have to wait for him to fail, girl. He already has."

They were beginning to receive curious stares and hushed whispers from the surrounding partygoers. Kai placed a hand on Aidan's arm when he moved to respond. This was not a fight they needed to get involved in.

"Better a reformed man who acknowledges his sins than a coward who hides under a title, taking credit for the work done by those beneath him," Annalise countered angrily.

Ottorius slammed his hands on the table and jumped to his feet. "How dare you, you little—"

"I do not think you want to finish that sentence."

A long cane appeared at Ottorius's chest, its tip digging into his gaudy white robe. Rynn stared the Triad member down from the other side of the table, his rigid, icy features filled with a challenge.

The air was stifling, the tension tightening like a bowstring as Ottorius seethed at both Annalise and Rynn.

"While this is quite entertaining, I believe you're interrupting a rather lovely meal. Sit down, Ottorius—you're embarrassing yourself," Sebastian said calmly from beside Kai. Slowly, Rynn removed his cane and took his seat, followed by the other two.

Leaning forward to meet Ottorius's eyes over Aidan and Kai, Sebastian said, "Insult my advisor again, and you'll find yourself at the end of something much worse than a wooden cane."

Ottorius clenched his jaw. "Threatening your equals. What a wonderful way to promote diplomacy, Your Majesty. After the last two years, I can't say I'm surprised."

"I see many people whom I consider my equal or far superior to myself, but you, Ottorius, are not one of them," Sebastian said coolly, taking a sip of his sparkling wine. "Diplomacy went out the window when you spoke ill of those I call mine."

Before Ottorius could respond, the four Chamber members stood at the opposite end of the table, drawing everyone's attention. Ezeretta Bannock, the white-haired, pale beauty, spoke.

"We will take our leave and bid you all a good night. Please enjoy the rest of your meal and have a wonderful evening. The itinerary for the week shall be sent to your chambers, and we hope to see you in the morning." Her willowy, hypnotizing voice echoed in the hall as the four of them gracefully made their way to the front and exited up the staircase.

"They give me the creeps," Bri said.

"I think I've enjoyed my meal enough. I'll see everyone back in the Karstos wing," Annalise said coldly, setting her napkin on the table and pushing out of her seat.

"It has been rather eventful, hasn't it?" Sebastian asked. "I'll walk back with you, Anna. But"—he paused and grabbed the bottle of wine off the table—"I'm bringing this with us."

"Then we'll need these," Annalise said as she collected both of their glasses.

"Ah, I knew I kept you around for a reason."

"Well, if we're taking this back to our chambers, I'm in." Aidan stood and held out his hand to Kai.

"Why not? I'm still exhausted," she said with a shrug, looking across the table to Rynn and Jade. "Are you two coming?"

"Yes, we are," Jade said, then glanced down at Rynn, who pursed his lips at her. "Oh, don't give me that look. You know you don't want to stay. It's too many people for you."

"I know. But I did not need you to speak for me," he grumbled, bringing his cane around to help him stand.

Jade rolled her eyes. "Do you see what I've put up with for the past four months?"

Turning to hide her face, Kai smiled. The most unlikely pair, and yet, she could see how comfortable they'd grown around one another. It gave her a bit of peace to know they'd had each other, however disgruntled they may act.

Their group made their way through the grand halls and back to the Karstos wing, Sebastian's guards and single council member flanking them. As they walked, Kai took in the sights of the palace. It was different in some ways than a thousand years ago, of course, with new decor, fresh rugs covering the hard floor, shinier windows. But these were superficial differences. Kai would know these walls in her sleep, no matter what art adorned the stone. This palace was embedded in her soul. She'd walked these corridors countless times, ran her fingers along every surface, roamed each hidden corner and darkened crevice. If she listened closely, she swore she could still hear the whispers of her past life rustling through the empty space. She envisioned the former kings and queens of Iona moving past, their heads dipped in close conversation, each face morphing into another as thousands of years flowed through her.

Kai tried to fend off the waves of nostalgia sweeping over her—both the sweet and the bitter. It was a reminder of what she'd lost. She needed to remember what she'd *gained*. Why did she keep having to remind herself that *this* was what she'd always wanted? What she had right now, with Aidan?

Being back on this island was doing things to her mind, dredging up memories and moments that belonged deep below the surface.

Sebastian dismissed his guards and Lord Everett, then turned to the rest of them. "Would you like to stay for a night cap?" he asked as they came upon their wing of the palace, gesturing to the couches surrounding a short table in the common room.

Rynn and Jade shared a glance—something Kai didn't think she would ever get used to—and started to decline, but Kai stepped forward.

"Oh no, you don't. This is the first time we've been together in months. You're going to sit here and drink with us like we're *friends*," she said, grabbing the bottle from Sebastian's hands and pointing it at Rynn and Jade.

A shadow grew on the table in front of Kai, and Sebastian's eyes flicked over her shoulder.

"Am I invited, too?" a familiar voice asked behind Kai. Turning, she met bright purple eyes.

"Hello, Kai."

CHAPTER SEVENTEEN

Kai

"I got more glasses," Bri called from down the hall. "I think I scared the poor servant, but—" She stopped in her tracks when she saw Isla, her fingers slipping and dropping the glass flutes.

Instantly, a strong wind filtered through the air, rushing past Kai and making her blonde waves swirl around her face. Before the glasses could shatter, their descent halted midair, as if balanced on an invisible cloud.

Annalise gasped at the sight and, to Kai's right, Rynn gripped his cane with both hands, his jaw tight and the veins in his neck bulging. His gaze was fixed on Isla—no, not Isla, but her *wind*. He looked like he'd been punched in the gut.

Bri glanced at the glasses resting peacefully on the ground, then back up at Isla before launching over the flutes and sprinting to her best friend. She flung her arms around Isla's neck, burying her face in her hair.

"I may be mad at you, but gods, am I glad you're alive."

Isla appeared a bit stunned, but recovered quickly and clutched Bri tight. "I'm so sorry, Bri, I know I should've found a way to—"

"Shut it, you freaky, purple-eyed elemental. We can fight later." Bri tore away from Isla, tears filling her eyes. "Right now, I want to make sure this is real." She cupped Isla's cheek in her hand. "Are you actually here? This isn't some...some sort of spirit magic?"

Isla's hand covered hers as she smiled. "It's real. I'm not going anywhere, if I can help it."

A shaky breath left Bri's lips before she lunged at Isla again, enveloping her in another hug. "I missed you so much. You have no idea."

"Trust me, I do. I really do. I missed you too, Bri. Every day. I'm so sorry I didn't—"

"Hush!" Bri pulled back and slapped a hand over Isla's mouth. "Don't ruin the moment."

Isla chuckled before her face suddenly fell. "Wait, why *are* you here?" She turned to Sebastian, fire blazing in her eyes. "Why did you bring her? This is dangerous! What were you thinking?"

Sebastian spun his flute between his fingers. "I don't presume to have control over your feisty friend here. She wouldn't take no for an answer," he said simply before taking a sip, the brief clenching of his fingers the only sign he wasn't as calm and collected as he appeared.

The wind picked up around them. "You could've said *no*, Sebastian. It's *your* ship. She could get hurt!"

"Next time, I'll be sure to toss her in the water." Sebastian's words were casual, but his tone held a challenge. Kai was immediately thrown back to the many times she witnessed Rynn lose himself to his lack of control, grasping at straws to keep others within his idea of safety.

She recalled a very similar conversation taking place between herself, Isla, and Rynn mere months before. Interesting. Perhaps the girl wasn't so different from them, after all.

Isla held Sebastian's stare for a moment, tension churning in the air. Then, the wind stopped and Isla sucked in a breath, regret forming on her features. In a softer voice, she said, "That's not what I—I'm sorry. I was out of line. I just don't know what I'd do if something happened to you." The last part was aimed at Bri who, to Kai's surprise, scoffed and stepped away.

"Well, something *did* happen to you, Isla. And I've mourned you for *four months*. Four months where you've been alive the whole time!"

"I think we've reached the 'fighting' stage of the evening," Aidan's low, deep voice rumbled in Kai's ear.

"Oh, you bet we have," Bri shot back. "You know what? While we're at it, I'm just going to put this out there—why did none of you do anything to save her on that beach? What were all of you doing the whole time?"

Jade sighed heavily. "We've been over this, Brielle. You know what happened. There was nothing we could do with Celesine controlling Sebastian, and—"

"No, *Jade*," Bri rounded on Jade, punctuating her name sharply, "I *don't* know what happened. Not really. The five of you"—she gestured to the former elementals and Sebastian—"and Luca came back from the beach to get me, and all I saw was Sebastian and Rynn both covered in blood, Arden in Luca's arms, and the rest of you walking around like ghosts. I couldn't even get you to talk to me!" Her breathing hitched as she held back sobs of anger.

"Luca had to tell me that—that Isla was gone. Stabbed through the chest. He didn't deserve *any* of this. You left him to mourn his children and relive their deaths over and over with no explanation, no reason for why they'd been sacrificed—*nothing*."

Isla stood behind Bri, arms wrapped around her middle, eyes closed tight as she listened. Bri's ire was aimed at the four elementals, but Isla seemed to be bearing the brunt of the guilt.

"While you all shut yourselves off, Luca and I had to sit on that ship, wondering how we'd explain this to the town and how we'd move forward with our lives—and I had to watch him lie next to his son's body, praying we could bury him in time." Bri swiped angrily at the tears on her cheeks. "Do you understand that we needed the four of you? And maybe, just *maybe*, you needed *us*?"

The wind picked up around them again, and Isla turned away with shaking shoulders, her hands clenched at her sides.

"I think that's enough for now," Sebastian said as he leapt to his feet and strode to Isla.

Bri took a deep breath, her voice softening. "I'm sorry if that's hard to hear, but it's the truth. I can't imagine what all of you went through—what it was like to lose your powers, or to have to go back to ruling a kingdom, or what happened when you disappeared, Isla," she said, looking at each of them as she spoke. "But you weren't the only victims of Celesine's games, and I just—I think Luca and I deserved to know there was even a *chance* Isla was alive. Some shred of hope to hold on to, because our lives changed forever that day, too."

"You're right, Bri," Isla said quietly, pulling from Sebastian's grasp. She faced her friend, whose eyes glistened as Isla continued. "And I'm sorry I didn't find a way to get to you. I still don't know how to explain what happened after—after I disappeared. It's like the spirit magic wasn't working for me, and I couldn't force it to take me to you. And the truth is, I didn't know if I could handle seeing Papa again." She shook her head in frustration. "That's a poor excuse, and I'm angry with myself for hiding. I'm sorry I didn't think about what this was doing to you. You deserved answers."

"I get it," Bri said with a nod, then scrunched her nose. "Well, alright, not *really*, but I'm trying to. It's just been a hard few months." She sniffed and reached out a hand to Isla. "I'm mad at the world and…at the gods, honestly, and you know how terrible I am at all this." Choking on a laugh, she waved her other hand in the air. "You know. *Emotions.*"

"You really are." Isla half chuckled, half sobbed as she wiped a tear from Bri's cheek. "Does that mean you forgive me? You're not angry with me?"

Bri hesitated. "No, I'm not. I want to understand. And we need to tell your papa, Isla. You have no idea what this time has been like for him."

Isla nodded and opened her mouth to respond when Jade cut in, her tone clipped and heated. "And will you forgive us as easily, Brielle? I've been trying to talk to you for months, trying to show you that we haven't abandoned you.

I know we didn't respond well after the beach, but we didn't forget about you and Luca. Why else do you think Rynn and I moved to that hole of a village? It wasn't for the beautiful weather."

Aidan cleared his throat. "Maybe not the best way to get on her good side."

Bri scoffed. "Yes, because spying on me from the bar every couple of weeks and leaving after ten minutes has done *wonders* to help me feel less abandoned."

Jade's face reddened. "I didn't know what else to do, Brielle! You said you wanted us to leave you alone, but we couldn't. Not when Luca could still be in danger, and not after everything you had been through. Watching you from the corner of a bar seemed like my only option, so I took it."

"Wait, what do you mean, my father could still be in danger?" Isla jumped in.

Jade blinked and turned to Isla. "Your blood triggers the abilities of the Dagger of Volnus. As in, your *bloodline*. Your father is the only other living member of the Vasileia line—that we know of."

Closing her eyes, Isla pinched the bridge of her nose. "And if anyone is searching for the dagger, they'd need him." Her eyes shot open, fear crawling across her features. "Gods, he's alone back in Evonlea. If something happens to him—"

"I left several guards stationed on his street." Sebastian grazed a finger up Isla's arm, making Kai glance over at Aidan. When had those two gotten so close? "They may not be able to stop every threat, but they're good at their job, and he's not unprotected. I promise," Sebastian added.

"And I told Hamil to check on him every day," Bri piped up.

"Alright, I'm sorry to interrupt, but why is Isla's father in danger? And what is this dagger you're going on about?"

Kai's neck snapped to the left in the direction of the voice, only to find Annalise standing by the window, an empty glass in her hand.

"Gods, Annalise, I forgot you were here," Kai said, huffing out a laugh.

"Should we be talking about all of this with her present?" Jade asked.

"You have *got* to be kidding me." Annalise pushed off the wall and stalked to the center, the slit in her green dress showing her dark golden thighs. "She's kidding, right?"

"Afraid not," Aidan said. "Jade doesn't trust very easily."

Jade shot him a sharp glare. "I'm making sure we're being careful. Every time we bring humans into this, it doesn't end well."

"We can trust her," Rynn said in his low voice, and all eyes turned to him, each bearing various degrees of shock. Aidan nudged Kai with his elbow.

"Yes, we can," Sebastian echoed slowly, giving Rynn a strange look before turning his attention to Annalise. "Anna, there are...some things I've failed to tell you." For the first time, he looked rather uncomfortable.

"You think?" Annalise crossed her arms. "Seb, I've let you have your space and respected that you needed to work through whatever's been plaguing you. But have you ever stopped to think about how I felt these last two years, watching my best friend become someone I didn't even recognize?" Sebastian's face fell, and Kai could practically feel the guilt seeping from him. Annalise's tone wasn't accusatory or spiteful, simply...hurt. Kai could tell how much the royal advisor cared for her king, and the many layers of shame Sebastian still carried with him.

"You didn't want to talk about it before, and I get that," Annalise continued. "But we're here now, and she just—she just stopped those glasses *in midair.*" She brandished an arm toward Isla. "I think it's far past time for you to tell me what's going on, *especially* if people could be in danger. What happened to you, Sebastian? And what happened on this island four months ago?"

"I would also like to hear this. The *full* version," Bri said, plopping down on an open chair and grabbing the bottle of wine.

Rynn, Jade, Aidan, and Kai all shared a look. Kai hadn't talked about that day with anyone besides Aidan, the four of them collectively choosing to turn a blind eye to the pain those memories caused.

Kai held a glass out to Bri. "Pour me one of those, if we're doing this." Bri obliged, and Isla shot Kai a concerned look before taking a seat on the arm of Bri's chair.

"Is no one else going to start?" Aidan said, looking around the room at the silent faces, then shrugging. "Settle in, friends."

This should be good, Kai thought. She took a sip of her drink and promptly wrinkled her nose. The palace had spared no expenses on the lavish feast, but their sparkling wine was cheap. It tasted like water.

"To start, I think we need to go back a thousand years ago, when—"

Jade cut Aidan off with a groan, and threw his hands in the air. "What? What could I have possibly done wrong already?" he asked.

"I just didn't realize we would be going quite that far back," she replied.

Aidan pointed a finger at her. "Then you should've volunteered to tell the story. Alright, then. So, one thousand years ago, the four of us"—he motioned to himself, Kai, Jade, and Rynn—"lived here on Iona. We had the power of the elements of nature and had been on this island for millennia, working alongside the kings and queens to help build their kingdom. Everything ran smoothly, until we eventually got caught up in the idea of exerting our control over the people and, long story short, things didn't end well between us and the monarchy.

"The kingdom went through a civil war—some people fought *for* us and wanted to put us on the throne, and others wanted the rightful Ionan dynasty to stay in power. It was...brutal." Aidan paused and rubbed at his jaw, and Kai sensed his muscles clenching next to her. "Many people died. And the four of us made many, many mistakes. This world didn't deserve the disaster such a war brought.

"And so, with the help of the spirit element, the Aether, we ended the war, closed off the island to outsiders, and went into a deep sleep. Where we couldn't cause any more damage or be tempted by our power."

The room was silent, and Kai gripped Aidan's hand as he continued. "Fast forward a thousand years, give or take a couple, and we were summoned awake under the premise of stopping a dark force that threatened us and our powers. Turned out, that was all a ruse—but I'm getting ahead of myself." Aidan cracked his neck. "That's where Isla enters the picture. She met Rynn when trying to save her family from an attack—or something like that; those details are a bit fuzzy to me. Anyway, the point is, the four of us eventually met Isla." His voice lowered. "We should've sent her back to her village. We were idiots."

"Why didn't you, then?" Annalise asked.

"Because she was having nightmares," Rynn began, quiet yet powerful. "Encounters with the 'dark god,' who had developed an obsession with her. He was a seemingly unstoppable enemy, for he could control our minds and force us to do his bidding." His head cocked, dark locks falling down the side of his face. "Your beloved king."

Annalise snuck a glance at Sebastian, but kept her face impassive. Sebastian stared into his glass, his elbows resting on spread knees.

"It wasn't really him, of course," Kai cut in, internally promising to smack Rynn later. He always found a way to make everything sound so dramatic. "But we didn't know that yet. He kept appearing to her, and we thought Isla would be safer if she traveled with us instead of staying in her village.

"We soon found a prophecy pointing us to a weapon that could be used to stop him. Over the course of a couple weeks, we learned about this weapon's powers. It was created by the Primeval gods a very long time ago, and is the only blade that could kill us—immortal beings." Annalise's eyes widened at that, but Kai kept going. "It also has the ability to take away our powers and give them to someone else. We figured Sebastian—or rather, the 'dark god'—was after it so he could take our powers for himself.

"We found the dagger a little way out from here, in a shipwreck under the sea. Sebastian caught up to us when we reached the island. That's when everything changed." Kai swallowed hard as images from that day flashed through her mind.

"What happened then?" Annalise prompted when Kai fell silent.

"Sebastian forced the elementals to fight each other," Isla said softly. "He got into their minds and made them use their power over nature to try and kill each other. I felt so helpless watching them, and knew the only way to stop it was to use the dagger to take away their powers so they couldn't use them against one another. It's what the prophecy had been leading us to the whole time—at least, that's what I *thought*. Who knows what it actually meant. So, one by one, I cut each of them with the dagger and took away their magic and immortality."

Annalise cut in. "Why didn't you simply use the dagger on Sebastian?"

Isla chewed on her lip. "The short answer is that I didn't know if it would work on him."

"And the long answer?"

Isla hesitated, glancing at Sebastian before turning her gaze away, a slight blush blossoming on her cheeks. "We had no idea how he'd come into his powers. At that point, we knew he was actually the King of Karstos, but didn't know what had happened to give him this magic. There were too many unknowns. Was he immortal? Was the magic his own, or someone else's? What if he wasn't in control of himself? Would the dagger take away his powers or just hurt him? I couldn't—I didn't want to do that. Hurt him. Not when I was convinced it wasn't really *him*. He was being used, like us."

"How did you know it wasn't him?" Annalise asked, her brow crinkling.

"I was with him for those two years, and I—I didn't know how to help him. Didn't know what had happened." Her voice was disappointed, like she thought she had failed her king.

"Nobody would've expected you to," Isla assured her. "I mean, how could you have known about this world of magic and immortals? There's nothing you could've done, no reason for you to have suspected anything like this." Her attention shifted to Sebastian. "I just...I knew something wasn't right. He changed a little more every time we saw each other. I think he dropped hints when he could, and it was...different, at the end. I knew he was fighting something outside of his control."

Annalise looked at the king, whose attention was locked on Isla.

"I took away each of the elementals' powers and held them in the dagger," Isla continued. "But that meant all anyone had to do was take the dagger, and they'd possess that power. So I made the decision to take the magic myself."

"What happened after you took their powers?" Annalise asked. Isla's jaw tightened, her purple eyes shining.

To Kai's surprise, Rynn spoke up. "The Aether—the same spirit elemental who assisted us in closing off Iona and entering our deep slumber a millennium ago—appeared and revealed that she had been the one behind Sebastian's actions. She desired to rid the world of us and assume our roles as the elementals to ensure mistakes such as the ones we had made in the past never transpired again."

"She was behind *everything*," Jade spat, indignation and betrayal prominent on her features. "Every step. Every move. And we had no idea."

"Well, *you* had no idea," Rynn muttered.

"We're not doing this again," she shot back.

"Anyway," Aidan cut in, "She and Isla fought—Celesine with her spirit magic, and Isla with all four elements. And you were an impressive sight, Isla, honestly—it's like you were made for it." His deep voice was gruff and emotional, and Kai understood exactly how he felt. Watching Isla wield their elements had been an experience she would never forget. Even when Isla didn't know what she was doing, the effortless way they flowed from her had been beautiful...and heartbreaking, that these pieces of their souls had so readily latched onto another.

"But it wasn't enough." Isla's tone turned to steel. "She still won, and I still failed. There wasn't anything I could do to stop her when she—" Her voice broke off. She took a deep breath and rubbed at the back of her neck, an errant spark flying from her fingertips.

"Is that when Arden...when she killed him?" Bri asked quietly. The thick silence that filled the air was answer enough. "I'm so sorry, Isla," Bri said as she leaned into her friend's side.

"Honestly, after that, I'm not entirely sure what happened," Aidan confessed, looking at Sebastian. "You may be better at filling in these blanks."

The king nodded, his gaze never leaving Isla. "Celesine disappeared right after that. I suppose Isla had weakened her enough to force her back to the spirit plane. I told Isla to use the dagger on me, thinking it might exhaust the Aether even further, considering it was her power inside of me. I hoped it would take my magic away as it had the elementals, but I didn't know for certain.

"Needless to say, it worked. Her influence left me instantly, and I was back to—well, perhaps not *normal*, but human. Powerless. The small sliver of magic Celesine had given to me now resided inside the dagger. That's when she reappeared, and—" Sebastian paused and ran his fingers through his blonde hair, causing a lock to fall onto his forehead. He cleared his throat. "She stabbed Isla with my sword." His voice was pained, and Kai didn't think she'd ever seen him lose his composure like this before.

Annalise's eyes had been slowly widening as she listened. "Then how are you here? How did you survive?" she asked Isla.

"Because she's brilliant," Aidan interjected. "Rynn was right. You took Sebastian's blood, didn't you? From the dagger? You knew it would give you the power of the Aether and transport you to the spirit realm to heal."

Isla bit down on her fingernail. "I think you're giving me too much credit. I was barely conscious at that point. But yes, I think a small part of me hoped it would do *something*. I didn't anticipate this, though."

"So what *happened* to you? Where have you been these last four months?" Bri asked, and all heads turned to Isla. That was the big question, the one each and every one of them had wondered since the moment they learned Isla was alive. Kai could practically feel the anticipation swirling through the air.

"I've been on the spirit plane." Isla shuffled her feet. "It—it's difficult to explain. It showed me things. I learned a little about how to use the spirit magic, but it's different from the physical elements. It's harder to control. I appeared to Sebastian twice and barely knew what I was doing—"

"Wait, you showed up *twice*?" Annalise asked in bewilderment. "I remember seeing you once, during the earthquake. How did I not know about the other time?"

"Anna, you're not with me every moment of the day," Sebastian said. "Besides, the first time was in the middle of the night." He crossed one leg over the other and sipped his wine casually, eyeing Isla with a hint of his usual cockiness. "In my bedchambers."

Isla rolled her eyes, but a blush crept up her neck. "That wasn't my intention, *Your Majesty*, and you know that."

"You won't find me complaining, love."

"As fun as this is, can we get back to the important parts?" Jade said, raising an eyebrow. "How have you been able to stay on the physical plane for so long, Isla? Celesine was usually only able to stay for a couple hours at a time. You don't even look like you're tiring."

"I sort of...met the Primeval gods," Isla said hesitantly. "They told me the balance of nature is off since I have all five elements, and that's why the world has been experiencing such crazy natural disasters. They said I need to restore the elements to their rightful place by finding the dagger and transferring all of this power back where it's supposed to be."

A tide of uncertainty rose inside Kai as Isla paused. She wasn't sure what those words meant, but it sounded an awful lot like...

"Does that mean *us*?" Jade asked. Her brow was furrowed, but hope lined her features.

Kai's stomach twisted and churned, a wave of anxiety crashing into her at the prospect. She'd pushed away any thought over the last four months about getting her water back, forcing herself to live in the present and be grateful for this new life she'd been given. This was everything she'd ever wanted. Were the gods saying that, to stop these disasters from happening, she would have to give it all up?

"I honestly don't know," Isla said. "They're annoyingly cryptic. They told me about this week-long event and that the dagger was still here on the island. The only helpful thing they did was give me the ability to stay in a physical body for long periods of time." Isla smoothed out her red dress. "So that I can be here for the entire week, they took away my power over the Aether. I still have all four of the physical elements and their spirit-related abilities, but that's it."

"Then why didn't your eyes go back to normal?" Bri asked.

Isla shrugged. "I guess because I'm still technically the Aether. This is only temporary. They gave me until the end of the festival. If we don't find the dagger and figure out what they mean by restoring the elements by the Spring Equinox, I'll have to go back to the spirit plane. For good."

Their group sat in silence, the weight of her statement and how little time they had falling heavily onto their shoulders.

As usual, Aidan broke the stillness. Clapping his hands, he said, "When do we start?"

Kai snorted and glanced at an ornate clock on the wall. It was well after midnight. "Absolutely not tonight. I need some time to process this, and I don't think anyone is going to be able to offer a good solution right now."

"Wait, you're going to bed? After this news was just dropped on us?" Jade asked in disbelief.

"Yes, Jade, that's exactly what I'm doing. I'm exhausted. We spent the last few days traveling and have barely had time to catch our breath. I think some sleep would do all of us a lot of good," Kai responded as she stood and stretched.

The rest of them seemed more hesitant to rise, but with a few shrugs and nods, they came to the same conclusion. The air filled with the rustling of fabric, clinking of glasses, and murmured farewells as their small group began to make their way to their respective chambers.

Hands grasped Kai's arm, and she turned to meet Isla's violet gaze before the girl looked away.

Kai wondered if Isla felt the shift that had taken place between all of them, knowing she held parts of who they used to be within the palm of her hand. What was she feeling now that she possessed their magic? Could she feel bits of *them*, the former elementals? Kai had no idea what she'd seen on the spirit plane, but her attitude toward the four of them felt...different.

"It's good to see you," Kai said, offering her a small smile.

Isla nodded, looking out the rain-flecked panes of the window. "Look, I know this is weird, me being back after everything that happened. It'll probably take some getting used to, for all of us." Isla turned to face Kai and Aidan. "But I'm glad to see you're alright." She hesitated and softened her voice. "And—I'm happy for you. All three of you."

It took Kai a moment to register her words, and she glanced around to see who stood beside her. Nobody else was there. When she turned back, she saw Isla retreating down the hall to her bedroom.

Kai's heart stilled.

Slowly, she raised her eyes to Aidan, who looked down at her with parted lips. A fog fell over her mind as her pulse began to race, pounding so hard she could hear it in her ears.

Aidan blinked. "Did she just..."

Putting her hand to her lips, Kai merely stared at him. At the same time, they both lowered their gaze to the inch of exposed skin at Kai's stomach.

All three of you.

CHAPTER EIGHTEEN

Isla

Isla sat in a cushioned lounge chair by the window of her room, twisting her clammy hands in the folds of her velvet dress as she reflected on the first evening on Iona. Physically, she was exhausted, but couldn't seem to get her mind to rest.

What had she been *thinking*, barging into the feast like that? It seemed like a bold move at the time—a way to make a statement and give herself a proper place in the festival. But the more she thought about it, the more reckless it felt. At least she had a nice bedroom, she supposed, even if she had placed a target on her back.

The only vacant room in the Karstos wing had been the one adjoining Sebastian's chambers. A large, canopied bed rested in the center, with a bathing room attached to the side. The furniture was simple but elegant: an oak dresser, a pair of matching bedside tables, a lush ivory rug covering the floor, and the chair she was currently slumped in. She twirled the gold ring she'd kept with her all night, staring at the door connecting her room with its owner's.

The conversation in the common room had gone as well as she expected. Guilt and shame licked at her as she recalled Bri's side of the story, envisioning their miserable journey back to Evonlea and the weight they'd carried for so long. How near-sighted Isla had been, to not think of how everything had affected *them*, as well. She was so happy to see her best friend again, but she didn't feel that she deserved her forgiveness.

The rest of the group had taken the news of her quest in stride. The clock was ticking; she *should* be devising a plan to find the dagger. Instead, she was fixated on the door and the mysterious man beyond.

She scoffed to herself and rubbed at her tired eyes. The whole night felt like a fever dream. From her dramatic entrance at the feast, to breaking into Sebastian's room and stealing his ring...she didn't know what had come over her. She'd been lonely, bored, and in need of a distraction—never a good combination.

Lately, her emotions had been shifting too easily. It was as if her personality had taken on new dimensions with the elements she now had. Coyness, anger, mischief, shame. She switched from one to the next so quickly it left her reeling. Her elements seemed to coax new, deeper reactions from her, often reminding her of the very people she'd taken them from.

But now, she felt hollow, with only a stolen ring and a handsome king occupying space in her mind.

With the pressure of her mission weighing over her, not to mention the tangled web of grief and regret and relief from seeing everyone again, she shouldn't even be *thinking* about him. Not in this way. Not in a way that made her heart beat a little faster and her skin flush a little warmer.

Gods, there couldn't be a worse time for this. She still heard the crack of her brother's neck when she closed her eyes, still saw her father's screaming face, still felt the scorching heat slice through her as the blade plunged into her abdomen. The changes she'd gone through, the knowledge she'd gained, the responsibilities that had been placed on her...they overwhelmed her daily, turning her into a different person. Someone she wasn't sure she recognized. She couldn't add...*whatever* this was between her and the king to her already mangled, fragile heart.

She bit down on her fingernail, thinking of that moment on the beach where his blue eyes had cleared, and he'd looked at her like he was seeing the sun for the first time. Like a new man. There was so much they hadn't talked about, so many explanations they owed one another.

And, as much as she tried, she couldn't seem to stay away. She'd never been able to—not since the moment he gave her his blood and made her question everything.

Standing, she knocked on the door.

A moment later, the man stood before her, a dip of confusion appearing between those blue eyes before widening as he took her in. A smile formed on his lips.

"Well, isn't this a surprise."

That smirk.

"I came to return this," Isla said in response, holding out his gold ring. As she did, her eyes trailed the length of his body, her cheeks heating at the sight of his black dress pants and a white button-down folded over his arm. His chest was bare and shadowed in the soft candlelight flickering from the walls of his room. Her gaze snapped back to his face as his smirk widened even further.

"I didn't take you for a thief, Isla," he *tsk*ed as he took his ring back. "What were you doing in my bedchamber alone?" He shifted and leaned his free arm against the doorframe, muscles flexing in the shadows.

"I'm sorry, I didn't mean to—"

"You misunderstand me, love," he cut her off. "I have no problem with you being here. It just seems a bit boring on your own—I'd much rather be with you." He flashed her a wink.

Gods, she forgot what a flirt he could be.

"Although, perhaps a warning next time you use those nifty little tricks, unless you enjoy watching me squirm." He removed his arm from the door-frame and stared down at the ring as he rolled it between his fingers. His words were casual, but he wouldn't meet her eyes, and the way his muscles tightened slightly made her think something was off...

Her thoughts stuttered for a moment as the realization of what she'd done crashed into her. She'd spoken into his mind—the same way Celesine used to.

It had felt harmless; perhaps a little cheeky, but safe. She hadn't even *considered* how he would feel having someone use any sort of magic on him, no matter how small. She'd violated his thoughts, forced her own words into *his* head. The thought that her "nifty little trick" might've reminded him of what he'd been through with Celesine made the blood drain from her face.

She inhaled sharply, her words stammered and nervous. "Sebastian, I'm so sorry. I didn't even *think*. I was so careless, I—"

He looked up and furrowed his brow. "Why are you upset?" he asked, taking a step toward her. "You didn't do anything wrong."

"Because—because that's something *she* would've done, isn't it? I used my powers on you, and I can see how uncomfortable it made you—gods, I'm sorry." Isla's words caught in her throat, and he took another step forward. "I don't want to do that...I don't want to ever make you feel like she did, or take away your choice in the matter. I know I probably remind you of her, with these ridiculous eyes"—she brandished an annoyed hand at her face—"and this only makes it harder—"

His hand came up to cup her jaw, his blue eyes melting into hers as his thumb gently brushed along her cheek. "Isla, don't compare yourself to her for even a moment. You are absolutely nothing like her."

"But you don't even know me," she whispered, a tear escaping the corner of her eye.

She didn't realize she'd started crying. Her heart beat erratically in her chest, a myriad of emotions twining with her elements. They were always right at the surface these days, and this conversation was hitting too close to the parts of her she'd tried to bury, the worries and doubts that had been festering since she saw those visions of the past on the spirit plane.

What if she *was* like Celesine? What if she was like all of the elementals? Their scars, their baggage, their anger...it all funneled into her through their magic. She'd had that single, jarring moment back in the spirit realm where she'd been so hurt, so furious with watching the callous actions of the elementals from centuries ago, that she'd wondered if the Aether had been justified. Even now, her stomach churned at the thought, disgusted with herself for experiencing so much as an *inkling* of sympathy toward Celesine.

And yet, similarities continued to arise. What was wrong with her?

To Isla's surprise, Sebastian smiled faintly. "You think I don't know you?" His soft exhale fanned across her nose and cheeks. The world faded away, save for his skin on hers and the words circling around them. "I've watched you for two years, Isla, and however lost I may have been to her control, *you* became the one thing I knew better than myself."

She looked away, the intensity of his gaze more than she could handle. But he gently turned her face back to his, refusing to let her hide.

"You think I don't know how your eyes light up when you hold your bow and arrow?" His eyes searched hers, like he was seeing into a different lifetime. "Or how you sometimes fail to hold that beautiful tongue of yours, and bite your nails when you're nervous?" His free hand found hers as he spoke, a soft touch grazing her fingertips and sending goosebumps up her arm.

"I saw how you cried yourself to sleep when your mother died. I know how you raised your eyes to the stars when you lost your first love and prayed to have the pain lifted from you." He grasped her hand and slowly brought it to his chest, flattening her palm over his rapidly beating heart. "I know how deeply your compassion runs and how much you care for your people, how an entire *village* loves you enough to call you their own. I know you'd give up everything for those you love, and fight for those who cannot defend themselves." Bringing her hand to his lips, he pressed a featherlight kiss on her knuckles.

"I know the darkness you fear within yourself, the one that whispers to you when anxiety clouds your mind, telling you you're not strong enough to fight. But you *are*. You're the strongest person I've ever met." He traced the scar on her cheek with his thumb, wetness from her tears spreading across her skin. "And I know that you saw me, Isla, when I had no hope left in this world. When I had nothing. When I *was* nothing."

Her breath hitched, and she flinched at his words—not because they hurt her, but because she hated that he'd ever been made to feel like he was nothing. Maybe the sentiment hit too close to her, as well.

Noticing her reaction, he instantly let her go. "I apologize, I shouldn't have done that."

"What are you talking about?" she asked, her eyes flitting between his.

"Said those things. Touched you. I just—" He paused, his hand flexing at his side with a slight tremble, as if he was nervous for her response. Or holding himself back.

"I know how I used to act around you. Possessive and claiming. I suppose, like you, I don't want to remind you of that time. I would never wish to make you uncomfortable, but I haven't been able to stop thinking about you, about *this*, and—"

Before he could finish, a tidal wave of urgency rolled through Isla's chest. He thought she was still frightened of him? Uneasy around him? Gods, that hadn't been true for far too long.

She did the only thing she could think of. Lifting onto her toes, she crushed her lips against his.

A sharp intake of breath was the only sign that he was surprised before his fingers wound their way through her hair. His other hand found the small of her back, pulling her flush to his chest. She could feel his heart pumping wildly, and her air element heightened the sound of its beats, mixing with her own in a rhythmic thrum. As her arms wrapped around his neck, his tongue lightly flicked a question against her lips, and she parted for him.

For the first time in months, Isla allowed herself to get lost in the moment, forgetting the crushing weight of the past to focus solely on the present. On the man before her, whose words cut to her core and reminded her that she wasn't alone. She wasn't the only one who had been irrevocably changed, irreparably broken.

A small part of her knew this was happening too quickly. She'd barely spent any time with him, and the gods only knew their minds were too chaotic, too delicate to jump into anything like this. But as his fingers dug into the bare skin of her back and his lips moved against hers, she couldn't deny how *right* it felt, how easy, like she'd been waiting for this her whole life.

His teeth nipped her bottom lip, heating her entire body. A small sound escaped her, which only made him grasp her tighter, his feet urging her backward until her spine hit a wall in her bedroom. Her hands snaked their way down his back as a fever mounted inside of her, flowing from her core to her arms and fingers—

Suddenly, Sebastian hissed and jerked away. Isla gasped at the quick movement, putting a hand to her chest to catch her breath.

"I think you burned me, love," he said, cheeks flushed and lips parted.

She'd *burned* him?

"What? Let me see," she said, pushing off the wall with wide eyes. Oh, gods, Aidan would have so much fun with this...

When she reached out a hand to turn him around, he gently grabbed her wrist. "I'm sure it's fine," he said. "I'll tend to it later."

"Can you even reach it? Let me get some cool water and ointment for it," she insisted.

He began to walk backward through the door adjoining their room, picking up his discarded shirt along the way. "I can take care of it."

Isla's eyes narrowed as she followed him. He was acting strange, but she didn't know why. "Why won't you let me see it, Sebastian?"

He didn't respond, his jaw shifting and fingers clenching around the shirt.

"You may not be used to people telling you what to do, *Your Majesty*, but I'm not leaving. Now turn around," she commanded, twirling her fingers in the air.

His eyes flashed. "I'm alarmed by how much that made me want to kiss you again."

She raised an eyebrow and crossed her arms, refusing to let him charm his way out of this. Releasing a long sigh, his features softened slightly as he relented.

"Fine." He set the shirt on the back of a nearby chair and stepped into the glow of the moonlight coming through the window. When he finally turned his back to her, Isla let out a gasp.

She'd seen them before, when she'd visited him on his ship the night she and Kai found the Dagger of Volnus. But she had completely forgotten.

The skin on his back was marred by faded pink scars, crisscrossing in short lashes, some more jagged than others. At the top, in between his shoulder blades, was the worst—dozens of harsh lines intersecting, creating deep gouges that were more red than pink, despite how much time must have passed since they were inflicted. A few inches down was the imprint of her hand, the charred edges already beginning to fade.

Whispering his name, she reached out a shaking finger. He sucked in a breath and straightened as she lightly traced scar after scar, feeling the ridges against her skin, wishing her touch could take away all he had suffered.

"Who did this to you?" she asked quietly.

It took him a moment to respond, but he relaxed as her fingers kept gliding over his back. "Celesine."

Isla's hand faltered. "What did she do?"

He took a breath, his head turning to gaze at her over his shoulder. She wanted to freeze time in that moment: the silver moonlight drifting over his body, making him glow against the shadows of the room. A lock of blonde hair swept across his forehead, his lashes fluttering on the tops of his cheeks as he closed his eyes.

"It was her way of punishing me when I fought her control. Some were done with her shadows, some with a blade—whatever was most easily accessible." His throat bobbed as he looked out the window. "I remember each of them. Each...indiscretion. Most of the time, it worked. She got me back in line."

"Most of the time?"

"Do you see the spot between my shoulders?" Isla looked at the patchwork of scars, her vision reddening and body tingling with the fury coursing through her. "That happened when I refused to have your father and brother attacked on the road through Aataran. It was the first time I'd completely broken free of her compulsion—I'd had moments of clarity here and there throughout the months, moments I took for myself, but she'd always been in the background of my mind. Lurking.

"But when she asked me to do that, to hurt them...I couldn't. I kept imagining what you went through when you lost your mother, and how this might break you." He ran a hand over his jaw. "And yet, she was the one who broke *me*. Weakened me enough so I had no choice but to obey her."

Isla slammed her eyes shut and snatched her hand away from his back, curling her fingers into a ball at her side. Her elements were roused and hungry beneath her skin.

He spun to face her, his expression pained. "Isla, I'm so sorry for what I—"

She held a hand up to stop him, an unfamiliar wave of rage boiling inside of her. "Don't you dare apologize for her, Sebastian," she seethed, her arms heating. "I can't believe what she did to you. *Gods*, if she's still alive, I swear I'll find her and rip her hands from her body for touching you."

Was the floor moving, or was it just her? Her body trembled uncontrollably as she spoke. With concerned eyes, Sebastian moved as if to grab her, and she jumped back.

"Don't touch me right now, please. I don't want to burn you again," she said through gritted teeth. The elements were responding to her anger, coiling and snapping and gnashing their teeth as if they smelled blood in the water. But she didn't know how to stop them.

The dresser next to them rattled on the wooden boards, and a mirror above it banged into the wall. Smoke filled the room like a dense fog rising from the ground. Sebastian approached again, more calmly this time. His hair whirled around his head. Was that wind? Was *she* doing that?

The vision of Celesine whipping Sebastian kept playing through Isla's mind. All because of *her*. Because the Aether needed her. How many other lashes had he received that were indirectly her fault? She saw Sebastian on his knees, blood dripping down the fresh cuts, Celesine raising her shadows and slicing them into his flesh—

Soft, warm hands grasped her cheeks. Blue eyes broke through the haze.

"Isla, listen to me. You need to breathe. Take one deep breath...that's it, love, now let it out. Breathe with me." She followed the sound of his voice, the inhale and exhale of his lungs. Slowly, she obeyed, feeling the elements begin to calm as she came back to herself.

"Are you alright?" he asked cautiously, his hands still cupping her face.

Glancing around the room, Isla saw a portrait dangling by a corner from the wall, a glass decanter shattered on the ground beside the bed, and scorch marks where her bare feet stood. Her eyes widened as she took it all in.

"I—I'm sorry, I've never lost control like that before." She ran her fingers through her hair, her body still buzzing. "Gods, this is such a mess. What will the servants think?"

"That we were having a bit more fun than we actually were," Sebastian said with a devilish smile. Isla snorted, the tension and anger from before melting away.

"I'm sorry," she repeated as he led her to sit on the edge of his bed. "I just couldn't stop thinking about what she did to you, and how unfair it is, and how—" She pinched the bridge of her nose, willing the elements to stay calm.

"How you believe it's your fault?" he finished for her, leaning against the post of the bed. When she looked up at him in surprise, he smiled grimly. "I know how your mind works. Your guilt touches almost every piece of what's happened. I feel it too. But you are *not* responsible for a single moment of my pain. I told you that story not to make you feel guilty, but because I haven't spoken of it with anyone else, and as much as it hurts to relive, my scars are a part of me now. I wanted someone to see them. I wanted *you* to see them. The person who helped me get through the last two years."

Isla scoffed quietly and squirmed. "You think too highly of me, Sebastian. I didn't even know who you were for most of that time, and then once I did, I hated you."

He leaned toward her, a finger sliding under her chin and tilting her head up. "And now?" His whisper skated across her cheeks and down her spine, making her shiver.

Now...

The door to the bedchamber opened with a bang. Isla jumped backward, sparks flying from her hand as her heart hammered in her chest.

Sebastian eyed the errant flame and winked. "Save that fire for me, love. I plan to be thoroughly burned by you."

Annalise cursed as she barged through the door, no doubt seeing the aftermath of Isla's rampage.

"*What* is going on?" Catching sight of a shirtless Sebastian, she threw her hands in the air. "You know what? I don't want to know. But just to confirm, is anyone dead?"

"Honestly, Anna, why would that be your first thought?" Sebastian rolled his eyes and grabbed a crumpled black shirt from the floor. "Isla got a little carried away, that's all."

Isla's eyes bulged out of her head. Cheeks flaming in embarrassment, she kept her head low, refusing to meet Annalise's eyes. *Gods, just strike me down now.*

"Right," Annalise said, drawing out the word. She eyed the shattered glass and broken wall decor. "The ground started shaking, and when I heard something crash inside here, I got worried."

"I appreciate the concern, but we're alive and well, as you can see," Sebastian said casually.

"Okay, well...I guess I'll leave you to whatever this"—Annalise waved a finger in the air at them—"is." She gave them one last suspicious glance before turning on her heel and walking out the door.

Isla groaned and buried her face in her hands. "I can't believe that just happened." Her head snapped up. "And you!" She smacked his chest. "You made it sound like I did all of this while we—"

His eyes flashed humorously. "While we, what?" He *tsk*ed. "How presumptuous of you. We barely know each other," he mocked as he wrapped his hand around her arm, pulling her closer to him.

Isla let out a breath, her skin suddenly cold. He may have been teasing her, but it was the truth. She barely knew him at all. Outside of their shared trauma with the elementals and a few stolen kisses, he was a stranger.

This was a mistake. She'd gotten so caught up in his pretty words and grand gestures, in the feel of a warm body next to hers after months of isolation. He may feel connected to the *old* Isla, the Isla he'd watched for two years, but recent events had changed her. Had changed *him*.

How could he possibly know her now, when she didn't even know herself? She wasn't the same innocent, selfless, anxiety-prone yet lovable girl he seemed to be infatuated with. And when he realized he didn't want whoever she'd become, she would once again be left alone. She should stop it before it got to that point. Before either of them got hurt.

"Actually, it's getting late." She gave a tight-lipped smile and put her other hand on his arm, pushing to extricate herself from his grasp. "I should go."

His roguish grin disappeared. "What? Is it because of Annalise? Or something I said?"

"No, it's not her, it's just—I'm tired, Sebastian. We both need sleep before we do anything we'll regret."

He reached out to grasp her hand again. "There's nothing about you or this night that I'd ever regret, Isla. What is this truly about?"

Ignoring his questions, she pulled away and motioned to his back. "You should get someone to come take care of that burn." She edged closer to the door between their rooms, her insecurities trying to crush the fleeting moments of happiness out of her.

He stalked to the door and pushed it shut, using the frame to support himself as he leaned into her. "Forget about the burn, Isla. Stop walking away and *talk* to me."

She was being irrational. Why couldn't she do what he wanted? The words bubbled inside of her, but she didn't know what to say, how to make him understand what a mess she was, how he wouldn't be happy with her, how the inside of her own mind made her want to hide.

"I don't know how," she whispered.

His hand closed around hers again, and this time, she didn't try to move. "Then just stay with me," he said softly, rubbing circles on her knuckles.

"Don't run, even if you're scared. I want to know what's going on inside your head. Every thought." He leaned forward and placed a kiss on her hand. "Every fear." He kissed her cheek. "Every worry." His lips moved to her neck, and she closed her eyes, her shoulders loosening as his breath warmed her skin.

"I don't want you to have to hide from me," he said, pulling away and meeting her eyes. "You don't need to figure this all out on your own. You're not alone anymore. But you have to be willing to talk to me, love. There's nothing you can say that would make me walk away. Gods, if anything, *I'm* the one scaring *you* away." He tenderly brushed a curl behind her ear, and she swallowed the lump in her throat. "Please, Isla. Let me in. Let me help."

She closed her eyes and breathed in, his sweet scent filling the space between them. "You're right, I *am* scared. Doesn't this feel too...sudden? That after everything we've been through, we're just trying to find something easy to take away the pain?"

"Nothing about this situation has been easy, Isla, but even if it were—if sharing these moments helps us find happiness, what's wrong with that?"

"Because—because what if it's not real? Everything you've said, everything you think you feel for me...it's all based on someone I *used* to be. You say you know me because you've watched me these last two years, but you don't know how different I am now. You don't know what I went through on that beach, what it felt like to watch my family be torn apart, and to be so turned around that I didn't know who I could trust.

"And these last few months...they changed me, Sebastian. I saw things I can't even begin to explain, and there's so much about the world I don't understand. So much about *myself* I don't understand, like these powers and what they've made me become." She let out a breath and rubbed the back of her neck. He simply watched her, giving her space to collect her thoughts.

"I guess part of what I'm scared of is that...just because you saw something in my past, doesn't mean you'll see it now. So maybe I *am* hiding. Hiding from whatever this is"—she motioned between them, her brow furrowing—"be-cause it...it's not real, is it? How can it be? You're holding onto these feelings for a girl who's not even here anymore. I'm worried I'll never live up to this idea in your mind of who you think I am."

His face was attentive and earnest, and she was surprised that she felt a little better after getting her thoughts out, even if she didn't know how he'd respond.

"Come here," he said, taking her hand and leading her to the edge of his bed. She sank onto the soft mattress, his hand firm and steady as he faced her.

"We've *both* changed in many ways, Isla. I understand your fear, but I also think there are some parts about us that can't be taken away. Your fierce loyalty, your burning compassion...that's all the same. And it's just as beautiful as it was before." He brought her hand to his lips and kissed the back. "I'm truly sorry if I've made things feel sudden between us. I realize I've been trying to leap into the middle of something without giving it time to grow and without giving you space to process what's happened. I forget I've had much more time to think about what I want than you have."

Isla looked at their intertwined hands, the sight filling her with a sense of hope she hadn't had before. "How can you be so sure of what you want?" *How can you be so sure of* me?

"Because I've wanted it for a very long time." He smiled and squeezed her hand. "I don't wish to scare you or push you further away, but the truth is, I can think of nothing but how much I want you. You remind me of the kind of man I hope to be, Isla. You make me feel like I am more than the sum of my past."

He gripped her hand a little tighter. "I understand this may not be as real for you yet, and I agree that we should get to know each other as we are *now*. But please, love, don't brush aside those two years I spent in a living hell with you as my only reprieve. Don't try and tell me that everything before this wasn't real. Because it was painfully, brutally, blessedly real for me."

His blue eyes swam with such intensity, with such genuine care, that words failed her. Her chest ached with sudden relief and understanding, like they were finally seeing one another, scars and all. All she could do was nod as he cupped the back of her neck, a sigh leaving her lips.

"I want to know you in any life, in any way, Isla Vasileia. And if that means starting over, then that's what we'll do."

"I think I'd like that," she whispered. Her lips curved upward as he pulled away, surprise dancing in his eyes.

"You would?"

"Yes," she said with a laugh. "As long as you're sure you can handle my chaos."

"Is that supposed to scare me?" He leaned over to kiss her, separating after a moment to murmur against her lips. "I'm a little broken too, you know."

She smiled. Gods, weren't they all.

CHAPTER NINETEEN

Rynn

Rynn could not remember the last time he had slept a full night. Definitely not since his accident. Perhaps in his time at Aataran, when his pride and confidence in his powers outweighed any concerns for the future. Now, however, attempting to sleep was futile. Not with the growing anxiety of what was to come, and this incessant pain in his leg constantly reminding him of his newfound fallibility.

He had stayed awake far later than was wise the previous night, reading in the common room well into the early hours of the morning. He had not been alone the entire time, however. Annalise had taken up residence in a chair by the single window, her head buried in papers and ink for the majority of the night. They kept their distance, rarely acknowledging one another's existence, but there was comfort in their silence.

The only interruption had been a little after one in the morning, when they heard a crash from the king's chambers, and the very floor beneath them trembled slightly, rolling Rynn's cane out of reach. Annalise had swiftly vacated her seat, retrieved his cane without so much as a parting glance, and rushed to Sebastian's room.

When she returned, she looked more bemused than concerned.

"What was that?" he had asked. "An earthquake?"

"Something like that," she had muttered. "I didn't ask too many questions. Isla and Sebastian are fine, though."

The rest of the night, he had been consumed by his own intrusive thoughts; the idea of Isla being there with the king needling him like the pain in his leg. But he could not figure out *why* it irked him so deeply. He had had four months to reflect and address his feelings toward Isla and all that had occurred.

Memories of the limited time he had spent with her in his arms and the peace he had found in her presence replayed over and over in the early weeks after they returned to Evonlea. And yes, there was a part of him that longed for those moments. Part of him still felt the pang of bitterness at the secrets she had kept from him, at the hidden closeness she had developed with the enemy.

But the king had never been the enemy. Not truly. Yet another flaw in Rynn's fatal pride—he should have believed her.

While he admired Isla greatly, he did not think it was necessarily *her* that he missed; rather, he missed the idea of having someone who gave him a purpose. Someone who needed him, but also knew how to be their own person. Isla was strong and capable, a quality he had not respected enough through his own personal need to save her. To bring her assurance. To be her rock.

It had taken him far too long to realize that a rock would only hold her down—and that was exactly what he had done, over and over again, to the point where he had lost control and harmed her. That was something he still had not forgiven himself for.

As much as it pained Rynn to think of his own mistakes, in the end, he knew Sebastian would treat her better than he had.

And so, here he was, just after sunrise, still reclined on the couch in the common room. Sleep had found him for a handful of hours, sometime after Annalise left. The hustle and bustle of the palace raked at his sleep-deprived nerves: maids beginning their morning routines, guards passing by to switch shifts, birds awakening and pecking at the glass window. He already missed the quiet solitude of the night, when the world slowed and slumbered, time passing like molasses while he mulled through events of the previous day.

He could not help but feel a bit of satisfaction that he had been right about Isla—she was alive, with not merely four, but all *five* elements of nature in her possession. Her mission from the gods was sorely lacking in details, however. He abhorred the idea of missing information, and they were barely given enough facts to carry the task out. How were they supposed to find a dagger that could vanish into thin air? They had mere days before the Primeval gods forced Isla back to the spirit plane, and who knew what would happen if they failed to bring the elements back into balance.

"Good morning," Annalise said from behind him, jerking him from his thoughts. She made her way to her spot by the window, her black pants tucked into boots, a loose emerald green tunic billowing at the arms. A stack of papers rested in her hand as she sipped steaming liquid from a mug.

"Did you stay here all night?"

"Yes," he replied.

She simply nodded, sat, and got to work. Her auburn hair fell onto dark golden cheeks as she leaned over to scribble on her papers, the end of the pencil catching against her lips when she paused.

Normally, Rynn would be appreciative of blessed silence. The gods only knew if it were any of the others out there, they would be pestering him with questions of what he was doing there all night. And yet, he now found himself curious.

"What is that you're working on?" he asked, nodding his head toward her. "You seemed to be quite enamored by it last night, as well."

Annalise scoffed. "I'm not sure if 'enamored' is the word. I was working out the guard rotation. We brought three with us from Karstos, but one of them didn't bother to show his face after dinner. And while Iona also offered to provide some of their own security if we required additional men, I don't trust them any farther than I can throw them."

Rynn had to smother a snort at that.

"This morning," Annalise continued, waving a fresh piece of parchment in the air, "the itinerary for the week was slipped under each of our doors. I'm reviewing it for Seb—His Majesty."

"Hmm." Rynn used his cane to stand and made his way to the center table, where a maid had set a tray of tea and mugs. "And what do our esteemed hosts have planned for today?"

"For you? Not much. The rulers of each kingdom will be in meetings most of the morning and afternoon, discussing potential trade routes and resource division. It seems like the auxiliary guests have free rein of the island."

"How generous of them."

Rynn studied the tray of tea, familiar irritation bubbling inside of him. He attempted to lean over with his cane tucked into his side to pour a cup, but pain shot up his leg at the movement. Gritting his teeth, he sturdied himself on the cane, using one hand to pour the tea, setting it back down, and grabbing the hot mug. He caught Annalise watching him struggle, and heat crawled up his neck, but he found no pity in her eyes.

"My thoughts exactly," she said to his previous response, her tone bland.

"And you? What will you do today, Miss Dalgard?"

"I suppose I'll go wherever His Majesty needs me."

Rynn had to refrain from rolling his eyes. It seemed to be instinct at this point. Truly, he was trying to let go of his past feelings for the king, but it was difficult to separate him from the dark god.

Annalise must have seen the brief look on his face, however, for she pursed her lips, her eyes flashing.

"What, are you still holding grudges against Sebastian, as well? Must I educate you like I did that ignorant pig last night?"

His eyebrow quirked up. She was an enigma, this woman. A member of a royal court, someone who held principles and propriety in high regard, yet was a spitfire when provoked.

"I want nothing to do with that man," Rynn said quietly. "Ottorius was out of line, disrespecting you and your position. He let his emotions cloud his judgment." The irony of his words and how he had once treated Isla coiled painfully in his chest. "I understand your loyalty to Sebastian."

Growing chatter at Rynn's back made him turn his head to see Kai, Aidan, Jade, Brielle, and Isla making their way to him and Annalise. He had not realized how much he had been—what, enjoying? tolerating?—conversation with Annalise until the band of obnoxiously chipper morning people graced them with their presence.

"Rynn, did you even go to bed last night? You're wearing the same clothes!" Kai exclaimed when he turned to greet them.

"You look rough, brother. Are you feeling alright?" Aidan followed up.

"We were going to see if you wanted to eat breakfast and then wander around the market in town. That is"—Jade eyed him—"if you're not too busy."

A dry chuckle sounded inside Rynn's head. Too predictable, all of them.

Yet somehow, he did not mind it as much this time.

CHAPTER TWENTY

Isla

Their group—minus Sebastian, Annalise, and the Karstos guards—ate a quick breakfast in the common room, then made their way through the grand palace and into the streets of Iona.

The last time she was here, Isla had only gone so far as the treeline at the western beach. From afar, she'd seen the jungle teeming with wildlife and greenery, the tip of the snow capped Mount Elani, the clear skies and crystalline waters. Now that she was inside the magical barriers that had once blocked trespassers from entering the heart of the island, she was able to see the hidden kingdom in its fullness.

In a way, the villages in Iona felt similar to the towns in her own kingdom. The streets bustled with families selling and trading wares, smells of local cuisine saturated the air, and the occasional merchant waved cloth at them to advertise their sale of the day. Taverns along the main square sat with their doors wide open, letting sounds of satisfied customers waft into the street and draw new patrons.

And yet, Farrow—the capital of Iona—was also so very different from anything Isla had experienced. Unlike the buildings at home, which were mostly made of brick, these structures were white stone, bright and gleaming against the cobblestone ground. They were stacked on top of one another in what Jade called a "haphazard manner," but that Kai and Bri thought looked cozy and modern. Some were piled three or even four stories high, with people leaning out the top windows, hanging clothes on a laundry line or waving across the street to neighbors passing by.

On the sides of the white buildings, splatters of colorful paint covered the stone. There were beautiful hand drawn murals of all sorts of subjects—animals, faceless people, abstract shapes and patterns. Some were names or dates that meant nothing to Isla, while some were words or short phrases such as "long live the Chamber," poems, declarations of love, and other indecipherable messages someone felt compelled to bring to life in the streets. A few of these pieces of art were crossed out or marked over with bright red paint. When Isla tried to see what was beneath, it was hard to make out anything other than what looked like various triangular shapes.

Perhaps the most incredible sight in Farrow was all of the animals. And not just house pets or small rodents, like Isla was used to seeing in Evonlea.

These were large, wild animals. Jaguars and jungle cats strolled down the streets, colorful birds with enormous beaks swooped low and made Isla's hair flutter, and even an occasional lion cub would pass by and rub its head against a stranger's leg. The first time their group had come across one of them, Bri had screamed. Jade and the others had only chuckled. Isla had watched in wonder as Jade knelt and ran a hand along the cub's small, round ears, not even slightly nervous about the wildlife running amuck.

"It's good to see some things haven't changed," she had said. "Iona has always welcomed the creatures of the land into its home—it's just as much theirs as it is ours. We all live off of what the earth provides for us, don't we?"

Bri still seemed skeptical and flinched anytime a bird's wing brushed against her cheek or a big cat swiped its tail in her face. But Isla was fascinated.

And the creatures were fascinated by her too, to say the least. Birds kept trying to nest in her hair, jaguars and bobcats trailed at her feet, nipping the back of her legs playfully, and a couple of monkeys had even launched themselves at her body, wrapping their skinny tails around her limbs, chattering at her animatedly. She felt a kinship to the wildlife, a part of her soul that reached out to them and longed to roam free through the mountside and jungles, the breeze in her hair and solid ground beneath her pounding feet.

It was hard not to notice the look on Jade's face as nature continued to mark Isla as one of theirs. There was pain there, a bit of tension and yearning, but also more contentment than she expected to see. Jade still interacted with the creatures, her features lighting with every touch or caw or purr, and Isla hoped her friend was beginning to find some sort of peace, or at least coming to terms with her humanity.

Perhaps she wouldn't have to stay human for long, if Isla's theories about what the Primevals were leading her to do were correct.

They had been wandering for most of the morning, stopping here and there to try various delicacies served by merchants across Farrow's marketplace. Sebastian had evidently given Bri a large amount of coin for a wardrobe, so she and Isla spent an hour or so in a local seamstress shop picking out gowns and casual wear for Isla, since she'd had nothing to bring with her for the week. The red dress she'd worn the previous night had been one that she...*borrowed*. The Primevals had dropped her in the middle of Iona with no money or directions, only the date and time of the welcome feast. She'd passed the beautiful velvet gown in a shop's window and knew she needed to look the part.

Kai wasn't wrong when she used to say how convenient her power of compulsion was. Isla had felt so guilty afterward, she left the dress and enough money to cover the cost at the doorstep of the shop that very morning.

As the sun climbed higher in the sky, Jade, who was ahead of Isla and Bri, stopped suddenly in front of an apothecary. "Would you like to see my favorite spot on the island?" she asked them, a sparkle in her eyes.

It was difficult not to smile when Jade's entire face lit up. "Of course," Isla answered, her arm looping with Bri's. "Lead the way."

"You four go on without us," Aidan said, sharing a look with Kai. "We're going to keep strolling."

"There's a shop I want to visit," Kai added as she took his hand, her eyes flicking to the apothecary sign above them and back again. Understanding swept through Isla, and she nodded knowingly.

Cocking her head, Jade said, "Well, we can all go to the shop, and then show them the ledge."

Isla could see Kai and Aidan grappling for an excuse to go off on their own. They probably wanted to find a healer who could confirm what Isla had told them the previous night—that Kai was with child. It was the strangest thing, sensing the life inside of Kai. The dregs of her spirit magic must give her some sort of awareness of life and death, allowing her to see an essence of one's spirit. If she concentrated enough, she could see a sort of...vibrance emanating from the people around her. Not beams of light, necessarily, just a brightness. And Kai's brightness was not merely her own. Isla could *feel* the additional life within her.

Honestly, she thought they'd already known, until she saw Kai begin to drink the sparkling wine. Isla had discreetly turned the alcohol to water and given them a not-so-subtle hint about Kai's condition. If the two of them didn't want to tell anyone else yet, that was their decision.

"It's fine, Jade," Isla cut in. "We should get back to the palace before too long anyway. It'll be faster if we split up."

Jade held Kai's gaze for a second longer, and Isla thought she would argue again, but she finally shrugged. "We'll see you back at Palace Noctem, then," she said to Kai and Aidan, who gave Isla an appreciative smile when Jade turned away.

Bri followed closely behind Jade as she led them to the end of the street then took a left, leaving the busy village behind. A quietness settled over Isla as she found herself shoulder to shoulder with Rynn, the sound of people milling about soon becoming background noise to the music of the jungle. There was a wide, gravel road at their feet, leading deeper and deeper into the trees, surrounded by the rustling of leaves and joyous screeches of native creatures.

She hadn't been alone with Rynn since that moment on the ship four months ago, right before they reached Iona. She'd told him she forgave him for the way he'd treated her, for the possessive claim he'd felt that had led him to make decisions for her and ultimately let his anger take control. And she truly *had* forgiven him; she wanted him to find contentment, to find a way to show his deep compassion.

Those weeks with him seemed like a lifetime ago. So much had changed since then; those lingering touches, desperate kisses, and stolen moments all felt like they'd happened to an innocent girl in need of comfort. In need of safety. That's who she had been—and he'd been there for her. She would always be grateful to him, to the man who had shown her how to move on with her life, how to find that joy and excitement she'd gone so long without.

She'd feared seeing him again would be uncomfortable—or worse, make her long for those days, for what they'd shared. But there was none of that. Even walking side by side with him through the jungle, she merely felt a distant sort of familiarity. Friendship.

Those two people who'd found each other in the mountains were gone.

"I'm glad you are back," he said, his voice barely discernible over the snapping of twigs underfoot. "These last months...I'm sure they have not been easy."

She twisted her lips, remembering Bri's words from the night before. "For anyone, it seems. I'm sorry about your leg, by the way," she said, nodding to his cane as it dug into the soft earth.

Irritation passed over his features. "Yes, well, we all must live with the hands fate has dealt us."

They trudged along in silence for a couple of minutes, keeping an eye on Jade's swinging brunette braid and Bri's occasional spurt of laughter to guide their way. While Isla thought she'd received all the closure she needed from their past, she realized there was one thing she'd failed to say.

"Tell me, Isla—"

"Look, I'm sor—"

They both stopped mid sentence and glanced at one another, her small, embarrassed smile mirrored on his hard edges and stoic lines.

"Please," he said, holding his free hand out. "You should speak first."

She bit down on her lip, suddenly nervous. "I wanted to say that I—I'm sorry for what I did all those months ago. For keeping things from you. From *all* of you. I should've told you about Sebastian's blood and how I'd met with him, and—" She stopped, her cheeks heating.

"And how you kissed him?" Rynn finished for her, and her head snapped up to look at him. Instead of quiet anger, she found acceptance, perhaps a hint of sadness, as he stared into the trees. "I recall his words to you on the beach. And I saw the way you looked at one another, Isla. I am not a fool. You were perceptive, being able to see the truth behind Celesine's hold on him."

"Still, I shouldn't have hidden things from the rest of you. And the kiss...it wasn't supposed to happen," she said, the memory of Sebastian surprising her with that first kiss coming back to her—barely a brush against her lips, but she'd instantly craved more, hadn't been able to stop the heat that pulsed through her. "I shouldn't have done that, not when you and I were, well..." She trailed off, awkwardly glancing at him out of the corner of her eye.

"I appreciate your apology," he said. "But you do not need to be sorry. I understand the...fleetingness of the situation we found ourselves in." He cleared his throat. "My feelings for you were real, Isla, and I am sure you would say the same. But neither of us were naive enough to believe it could have been anything more than transient happiness. An escape. And you deserve far more than that."

"So do you," she said quietly.

"I think you are good for one another, you know," he mused. "As much as he vexes me."

She snorted and lightly bumped his shoulder with hers, a weight lifting from her chest at the ease with which she could talk to him now. "He can be quite *vexing*," she mocked. "Although, his advisor seems to keep him in line. I haven't talked to her much, but I think I like her." She snuck a peek at Rynn, but his face was as composed as ever. He merely hummed in response, and Isla smiled to herself.

Before either of them could say anything else, she felt a faint thrumming in her blood, telling her something new was close. Jade looked back and motioned for them to hurry.

Excitement rose and swirled within Isla, flowing under her skin and tugging at her core. Even while being on a strange land she knew almost nothing about, she knew where they were going. Where Jade was taking them.

The sea.

It called to her like a song dancing across the waves, bringing a smile to her lips. As much as Isla wanted her life to go back to normal, *this* was something she would miss—the undiluted peace and freedom she found in her elements, the way they made her aware of everything around her, helped her find joy in mundane parts of life she never would've noticed before.

She picked up her pace and, sure enough, a few minutes of walking brought the undeniable crashing of waves against rock, the scent of salt and a hint of sweetness hanging in the air.

"Is that...the ocean?" Bri asked, looking confusedly back into the trees behind them. "Weren't we just in the middle of a jungle? How small is this island?"

Jade chuckled. "A bit smaller than your land of ice. Back in our time, there were only a couple of major villages. Farrow has always been closest to the shore, with only the jungle separating it from the water on three sides. The mountains are to the east." She nodded behind them, where Isla could barely make out the tip of Mount Elani over the swath of trees. "It's a much longer trek back that way. One could most likely travel the entire distance from east to west in a day." Jade reached out to push a cluster of vines to the side. "Perhaps it's small, but do you have a view like *this* in any of your kingdoms?"

Isla greedily drank in the sight, her mouth parting slightly. Beyond the last of the trees stood a wide, open expanse of rocky outcrop, shades of beige, burgundy, orange, and gray granite overlapping one another with rounded edges. Dazzlingly clear water appeared several yards below the edge of the cliffs as she stepped further forward, the sun skipping across the waves in a blinding flash.

Straight ahead stood a divide in the rocks, each side expanding to the left and right as far as the eye could see, the space between them giving way to turquoise depths. Connecting the two rocky cliffs was an enormous bridge, hewn from the same beautiful granite as the rest of the land. A woman and a young boy walked hand-in-hand across the bridge, and a handful of other sightseers lounged about the cliffside, basking in the warm sunlight.

"This is amazing," she breathed. Her eyes traveled across the water until she spotted a smattering of tiny islands nearby, far too small to be inhabited but large enough for her to clearly make out the rocky ridges and bluffs, and close enough for her to see waves cresting against the bottom of the escarpments. Sounds of seagulls flying overhead wound around her, the wind lifting her hair and settling against her skin like a caress.

"It was always one of our favorite places to go together," Jade said, wisps of her brown hair floating on the breeze as she faced the sun. Even Rynn looked more comfortable than Isla had seen him in a long time. His eyes were closed as he breathed deeply and leaned on his cane.

"I can see why." Bri pulled on Isla's arm, trying to drag her in the direction of the bridge. "Come on!" she said excitedly, and Isla didn't have to be told twice. The two of them sprinted toward the landing like a couple of giddy school girls, pausing to take off their sandals so they could feel the coolness of the rock on their feet.

Isla had missed this. She'd missed Bri *so much* it hurt. Missed the ease of their time together, their unbridled joy, the way her best friend could get her to step out of her comfort zone and take a leap. It was like a fog had been hovering over Isla for over two years now, the burden of her grief and accompanying anxieties that followed making her see life in shades of gray. And she still didn't know if she would ever get back the vibrancy and light she once knew—not after Arden, not after everything she'd lost. But in these moments...color peeked through the clouds, a ray of warmth to banish the darkness.

They reached the start of the natural bridge, smiling at families as they passed. Bri rushed forward onto the rocky platform that was barely wide enough to fit two people side by side, and Isla's heart lurched in her chest.

"Bri, be careful!" she called out with an exasperated, amused sigh.

"What? It'll be fine. You can catch me if I fall with your *air* thing."

"Just because I *can* doesn't mean I want to *have* to," Isla retorted, following her onto the landing. The wind picked up dramatically when there wasn't land on either side of them, and Isla held her arms out to balance. With a familiar tug on her core, she envisioned wrapping the air around her outstretched hand, and it immediately calmed so it was safe to walk.

"Gods, you're so cool," Bri said, smiling. Isla playfully shoved her, then latched onto her arm and leaned her head on her friend's shoulder. They stood like that for a moment, gazing into the neverending blanket of deep blue, turquoise, and white, nothing but a few feet of stone keeping them from joining the tide. Gray clouds had begun to float across the sky, offering a slight reprieve from the hot sun.

"Never thought you'd be here, did you?" Isla asked. "Look at you, living out your grand adventure."

Bri snorted. "I wish it didn't take you disappearing and the entire balance of nature hanging by a thread to get me here, but other than that, sure, I'm living the dream," she said. "This feels nothing like in the books, you know."

"As in, better or worse?"

"Oh, way better. Look at this!" She swept her hand out in front of them. "But also way more terrifying." Her expression sobered. "When I'm reading and getting lost in those worlds, life is always there to snap me back to reality. I can enjoy all the stories I want and never worry about the consequences. It's an escape. A wonderful, chaotic escape." Bri let out a long breath. "There's no escaping this, though. People can get hurt. People *did* get hurt. How do I come back from it if something happens to you this time?" Her soft words twisted and twined in the breeze, gripping at Isla's heart.

She squeezed Bri's arm. "We can do this, Bri. We'll find the dagger, figure out how to get the elements back where they belong, and I'll be able to come home with you."

"That's what you said last time," Bri murmured. "And you never came back. We don't know what's going to happen, Isla. You can't make promises like that."

Isla swallowed, the exhilaration of the water and scenery now replaced with disquiet and unease. Bri was right. It was unfair to make promises she wasn't sure she could keep. But what else was she supposed to say? How could she make any of this alright?

"You're right. We don't know how this will end. But let's say things *do* go badly, and someone gets hurt, or I disappear back into the Aether—"

"Is this supposed to be helping?"

"You're the one who said not to make promises," Isla reminded her, pointing a finger. "If I don't come back home, here's what will happen: you're going to cry. A lot. Probably scream and break things, because you tend to be dramatic." Bri rolled her eyes. "It'll be hard, Bri. And I hope to the gods I don't put you through that again." As Isla spoke, she absentmindedly twirled a finger, and a flower shot from the cracks in the rocks. She knew better than anyone how difficult it was to come back from a loss like that.

"But one day...you'll wake up, and the sun will still be shining, and your morning coffee will taste sweeter, and you'll find yourself smiling simply because you can." Isla reached for Bri's hand. "You'll take over the bookshop from your mother and spend your days between the pages of your own adventure."

Bri gave her a sad smile that quickly faded, her forehead creasing as she stared back out to the waters.

"Oh—make sure you keep my papa in line, though," Isla added, her tongue running away with her as she envisioned those she'd left behind. "He's going to get old and cranky, but just smile and nod when he starts trying to sell you squirrel tails or something crazy, okay? Maybe sit with him every once in a while. I think he'd like that." Tears had started to fill Isla's eyes, a couple of them tracking down her cheek.

"And you're going to fall in *love*." Isla drew out the word teasingly, and Bri snorted. "Don't laugh at me—it'll be an epic love. The kind they'll write stories about. You'll travel the kingdoms in your free time, maybe have a couple of children—or not, up to you. But if you have a girl, you'll name her Isla, of course. And you'll tell her all about her Aunt Isla and the trouble we got in together." She paused. "On second thought—maybe save *some* of the stories for when she's older."

They both chuckled, which subsided into a particularly loud sniffle from Bri as she wiped her nose on the back of her hand.

Isla interlaced their fingers. "Most of all, you're going to be *happy*. If all of this goes badly and I never see you again...don't do what I did. Don't close yourself off and forget who you are. I don't want you missing out on the rest of your life for a single second, Bri." Isla rested her head on Bri's shoulder again. "Well, alright, maybe for a second. I mean, I *am* your best friend."

"Oh, naturally." Bri's chin came to sit on top of Isla's head with a sigh. "Isla would be a good name for a dog, too."

Choking on a laugh, Isla dried her face with her sleeve. "Fine, you can name your dog after me."

"We're going to be fine," Bri said after a moment, the area around them silent save for the sounds of the waves churning below, becoming more restless as the wind picked up speed.

"Yeah," Isla whispered. "I think we are." Hope bloomed in her chest, her lips curving upward automatically from the weight of it.

Until a scream shattered the air.

CHAPTER TWENTY-ONE

Isla

Whipping away from Bri, Isla searched for the source of the cry. Her gaze landed on the water many yards below them and to the right, where bubbles rose to the surface and a splash followed by white waves beat against the rocks. Further down the bridge stood a sobbing woman, the same one they'd seen earlier walking with her son.

Her son. Isla's eyes widened.

A small crowd had already gathered near the woman, and her frantic words rose above the wind.

"Help! Somebody, please help my baby!"

The once harmless clouds were swiftly turning into dark gray blotches of anger across the sky, the pleasant breeze now a small torrent ripping through Isla's hair. Waves rose higher and higher, crashing into the rocks with so much force that the salty spray beat against her skin.

As Isla ran to the woman across the bridge, her eyes stayed fixed on the surface, searching for a sign of the little boy. A sharp, gray, triangular shape appeared in the water, only a short distance down from where they stood. She reached with her senses through the tumultuous sea and found the creature: a great shark with a wild nature and a sole focus as it flew through the water.

Somewhere in the group surrounding the sobbing mother, a voice shouted *"Shark!"* sparking a renewed bout of fear among the strangers. The mother fell to her knees, about to toss herself into the choppy water.

"Wait!" Isla cried, finally reaching them. "Stop, let me go—I can get him!"

The woman turned to her, puffy eyes and pale cheeks red with claw marks, like she had run her nails down her face in anguish. "Y-you can save him? My Amos?"

Isla nodded vigorously, preparing to dive, when Bri appeared at her back with a whispered warning. "What are you doing? If these people see you..."

"I don't have a choice, Bri," she replied sharply, then plunged into the waves.

She was falling, air whistling through her hair. She expected the cold water to shock her senses, but instead, it enveloped her like a lover's embrace, cushioning her fall and instantly calming where it wrapped around her body. It was the first time she'd been in the water since her deep dive with Kai to locate the Dagger of Volnus in a shipwreck. The tide seemed to know where she needed to go without her having to move; its silky caress effortlessly pushed her through the choppy waves, which died down the moment she glided through them.

Kicking her way across the churning sea, she was relieved when a mop of brown curls popped above the surface only a few yards ahead of her. The young boy—Amos—was maybe six years old, tears streaming down his small, frightened face as he gasped for breath. A wave rippled over his head, causing Isla to lose sight of him for a moment.

When he resurfaced, his choked screams met her ears. He'd caught sight of the shark, barely two arms-width away from him now, and his fear seemed to paralyze him. To Isla's horror, the boy began to sink.

With a flick of her finger, the water steadied beneath his feet, forming a solid ledge for him to stand on. In another moment, she was at his side, her arms wrapping around his waist.

"It's okay, Amos, I've got you. You're safe now." She kicked against the swirls lapping at her ankles and ran a hand along the boy's soaking curls, searching for any injuries. Sure enough, her fingers came back red from a small gash above his ear. That must have been what attracted the shark.

"I'm going to get you back to your mama, alright?"

Amos whimpered and slouched against her side, his little fingers shaking as he pointed to the shark circling them.

Smiling, Isla reached out a hand to the creature. Its rubbery nose pushed lightly against her, and she felt their bond tingle across her arm and down her spine.

The boy shrieked.

"It's okay, sweet boy, he won't hurt you," she reassured him in a calm voice. "See? He's just a curious little thing." She grinned at the sea creature and sent him on his way, his tail spraying them with water as he flipped around and sank into the depths.

"Let's get you home," she said, to which the boy nodded, wiped his cheeks, and wrapped his arms around her neck.

Isla swam back to the cliffs and, with a little boost from her power, she commanded rocks at the base of the escarpment to shift until they formed loose steps—nothing too extravagant as to make the onlookers suspicious, but enough for her and Amos to get back up to land. She helped him climb the steep slope, keeping an eye on his wound.

Shouts and conversation buzzed above her head as they approached the top. When they reached the edge, the boy's mother leaned over and pulled him into her lap, her cries of relief mixing with Amos's sobs.

"He has a cut on his head right here," Isla said a little breathlessly as she reached to point out the spot. To her surprise, the woman yanked Amos away from Isla's outstretched hand.

"Get away from my son, you monster!" she snarled, scuttling backward.

Isla's mouth dropped. "*What?* I was just—" She cut herself off as an alarm blared through her mind. She looked up to see the crowd from before glaring back at her with such malice, she almost stumbled from the shock.

"She's a witch!" a voice called out.

"One of *them*! What do we do with her?"

"They were right!"

More angry, indiscernible cries rang together as the people converged on her. *How had this happened?* She saved the boy—shouldn't they be thanking her?

Isla tried to plead with them, tried to convince them it was a misunderstanding, when a wrinkled hand grabbed her by the tunic. That's when she realized.

She wasn't wet. Not a single drop of water clung to her.

Isla looked down and back up into the eyes of the people, rage and hatred and fear evident on every face. Over their shoulders, an alarmed Jade, Rynn, and Bri raced across the bridge.

The crowd closed in, hands pulling at her clothes, her arms, her hair. Her breath quickened and heart raced, a surge building inside of her. She didn't want to hurt these people, but she couldn't think clearly, and wasn't strong enough to control all of them at once. Her foot scraped against a sharp rock, and her heel hit open air, her arms shooting out to balance her before she careened off the side of the cliff.

"Don't kill her! We need to take her to them!" a gruff voice yelled.

Another hand snaked out to grip her wrist, then released it with a hiss. "She burned me!" the owner of the hand yelped, causing the crowd to rear back.

Bri and Jade reached the back of the crowd, trying to muscle their way through and shouting at people to get out of their path. One woman spotted them and called, "These two—they're with her! They're helping her!"

Isla watched with growing rage as someone yanked Bri back by her tunic, and her best friend's shocked cry ignited something within her.

"Don't *touch* her!" Isla screamed, and suddenly, time went still.

CHAPTER TWENTY-TWO

Isla

A shiver crept down Isla's spine. Men and women who had been brave enough to get within touching distance of her were frozen, hands outstretched, mingled expressions of disgust and dread prominent on their faces. Hair and clothing still blew in the breeze, wrapping around unresponsive bodies that stared at her with glazed-over eyes. The surrounding crowd was just as still, just as rigid, like someone had paused them mid-action.

Had *she* done that?

A memory resurfaced, those white sands playing in her mind again. The moment Arden had died and she watched as his body crumpled to the ground, when her grief and rage had taken over...the world had stilled. Just for a moment. Had that been her, too?

She scanned the unfamiliar faces to find her friends, their obvious worry for her frozen on their features. Heart thumping wildly, Isla took a step away from the edge of the cliff, holding her breath when her chest brushed against a hard finger. When nobody moved, she inched forward, internally cringing every time stiff skin grazed her.

How was she supposed to stop this? Make everything go back to normal?

After she extricated herself from the masses, she closed her eyes and let her elements rise, let them glide beneath her skin in a rush of excitement. She hadn't had much opportunity to use her powers, especially the mind abilities associated with each element, but she knew what they did due to her time spent with the elementals. It was effortless to speak into another's mind on the wind, to influence thoughts and emotions with water's power, and although she hadn't tried it yet, she assumed she could easily create physical sensations on someone's body—magic given by her fire.

But, earth...

There.

A thin shadow blanketed her mind, unfurling at the corners as it stretched from her and across the entire rocky bank. It was quiet, steady, not easily roused and excitable like the other elements. She'd barely even noticed it before, but now that she had, everything made sense.

Her earth's ability was not to freeze time, but to freeze *minds*. People. Cause them to lock up from the inside and be unable to move freely. The realization of what she could do and what she had *failed* to do hit her in the chest like a brick.

She could have saved Arden.

She could have frozen Celesine moments before she attacked.

She could have prevented *everything*.

Her failure crashed around her in anger and despair, and with it, the spell dropped. Bodies sparked back to life, shouts of confusion ringing in her ears as the people searched for her, shocked at how she had moved from one place to another in the blink of an eye.

Isla ignored them. Her gaze locked on Jade's, guilt churning in her gut and coaxing itself into blame, her fire twisting that feeling away from herself and onto the person who had kept this knowledge from her.

This was Jade's fault. *All* of the elementals' faults. They should have told her about this power, should have given her all the information for what she was getting herself into. And now, Arden was dead...

Isla shoved away intruding hands that sought to hold her back and stalked toward Jade, Rynn, and Bri, her vision clouding with shadows.

Before she could say anything, Jade held her hands out. "Isla, I'm sorry—"

"No." Isla's hand closed around Jade's throat, her brown eyes widening as Isla's grip tightened. Jade knew what she was angry about. That her shrouded sense of *morality* had hidden this secret, had made Isla unprepared for this life...had kept her from saving her brother. "But you will be."

The crowd at her back grew louder. Bri jumped to Isla's side, crying out her name, and then Rynn appeared in her line of vision.

"You need to control it, Isla. Control your emotions. This is not the place—we need to get away from here."

"Isla, please," Bri pleaded with her, tugging at the sleeve of her shirt. Isla glanced at her friend, whose eyes were locked on the oncoming angry mob behind them.

With shaking hands and gritted teeth, Isla unlatched her fingers from Jade's throat and lowered her arms, fighting the cyclone of emotions whirling inside of her. She closed her eyes. *Breathe in. Push it down. Breathe out.*

"Come on," Bri said shakily, taking her hand to follow Rynn. "It's dangerous for you here."

Many of the Ionans had stopped advancing when they found Isla surrounded by three more people, choosing instead to glare at them in warning. A few men, however, continued inching closer and closer, as if preparing to attack and capture their prey.

"Stay back!" Isla shouted at them, pushing Bri behind her with one hand and holding the other out in front of her.

The men stopped in their tracks. Hatred spewed from their eyes and lips.

"They were right," one of them shouted. "The monsters are truly here!"

Isla continued backing up toward the jungle. "Look, I don't know what—"

"Just get off our island!" a second man said. "We don't want your kind."

"No," another hissed, taking a step. "We need to bring her to them."

A hand brushed the small of her back. Rynn's low voice rumbled, "We must go, Isla."

She nodded and spared the Ionans one last look before the four of them hurried away from the cliffs, away from the group of natives envisioning her head on a stake. The three men stopped chasing after them, but tracked her movements with narrowed eyes.

Why was this happening?

"Where do we go?" Bri asked, glancing over her shoulder. She had taken the lead, while Jade helped Rynn navigate the jungle terrain as quickly as they could.

"Back to Palace Noctem, I suppose," Rynn replied breathlessly.

"I have a better idea."

That familiar voice, old yet powerful, startled Isla. The others came to a halt as a tall figure emerged from a tangle of trees.

"Come, cousin," Akir said with a wry smile, his green eyes meeting her purple ones. "Follow me."

CHAPTER TWENTY-THREE

Sebastian

If Sebastian thought his own council meetings were a bore, they were nothing compared to what he'd been subjected to all morning.

Annalise had come to collect him—far too early for his taste—for breakfast before the meeting with the rest of the world's rulers began. She, Lord Everett, and he had been the first to arrive at the large, round chamber only a few corridors from where they had eaten the previous night. A circular table took up much of the space, with an enormous forest green tapestry bearing the crest of Iona hanging directly behind it. Golden candelabras dotted the room, a single floor-to-ceiling window on the center of the furthest wall providing natural light to the entire chamber.

He'd taken a seat at the round table and was promptly followed by the Triad—Xavion, Ayana, and Ottorius, whom Sebastian flashed a cheeky grin at—and then King Adrik and Queen Melanora of Evonlea, with various advisors trailing behind. Ten minutes later, the Chamber appeared.

Mariana de Faye, who seemed to be the unspoken leader of the group, was surprisingly quiet during much of the morning discussions. Sebastian observed her sitting back and merely listening, a long nail tapping against her armrest, while Stefan Rigaldi took up the position as spokesman for the Chamber.

Sebastian had sat through over three hours of tedious conversations regarding Iona's entrance into the global community, and what the other three kingdoms were willing to compromise to include them in their affairs.

Evonlea, Ara Mir, and Karstos had established a mutually beneficial, moderately peaceful—the past two years notwithstanding—relationship over the centuries, and Sebastian knew it would be difficult to break the status quo.

Each kingdom had a handful of resources and goods that were not readily available in the others. Ara Mir with their coal, copper, and other precious metals and jewels; Evonlea had rare animal pelts and meats, and by far the most effective hunting tools; and Karstos provided the best wines and harvested goods—like grain and chocolate—that could travel without perishing.

It had taken *years* for their ancestors to form a system of imports and exports that all three agreed upon. And these Ionans thought they could change that in a single week? It would almost be humorous, if he didn't want to put his head through the table listening to them.

Even if they did come to a resolution regarding amounts and frequency of trading, they would still have to work through trade routes—adding multiple new routes to a land further east than their ships normally traveled would take time. And plenty of arguing.

Sebastian was fairly certain he would die here.

Annalise, however, seemed to be lapping the discussions up. Her eyes were bright, her hands folded across the table, her head nodding or shaking aggressively at passing comments. Sebastian swore he saw her ears literally *perk* once.

What would he do without this woman?

A hand suddenly slapping wood jarred him from his thoughts of lunch. Ottorius stood on the other side of the table, his fist still resting where he'd slammed it down.

"We *cannot* afford to give up another ten percent of our metals, Rigaldi," he fumed. "We've already conceded the eastern region of coal mines, barring you provide the labor. But our uranium and copper are already limited as is. We must think of our people above all else."

Ayana and Xavion nodded solemnly beside Ottorius. Sebastian disguised his bark of laughter as a cough, his hand coming up to cover his mouth.

"Is something funny, Avax?" Ottorius asked, eyes blazing.

Well, since he asked, yes.

Ottorius Rejev was one of the most selfish, egotistical men Sebastian had ever met. Annalise had been spot-on the night before when she accused him of taking credit for work others did. One of the times Sebastian had visited Ara Mir as king, he'd witnessed the man making a grand speech to the citizens of the capital city about an upcoming charity project—a project Sebastian had heard one of the Aramian priests pitching the day before—in his own name, acting as if it was his noble idea. In addition, Sebastian's previous ambassadors to Ara Mir often informed him they suspected Ottorius manipulated numbers on the financial records in order to keep some of the coin his citizens paid in taxes. More recently, rumors had reached Sebastian's ears that the Triad member was paying for people's silence regarding his more...unsavory actions. Blackmail, extortion, harassment—the gossip was endless.

So, yes, Sebastian found the man's exclamation of thinking of his people "above all else" rather amusing.

"Not at all," Sebastian said, waving his hand in the air. "Please, continue. I *am* rather curious to see recent reports from these mines you mentioned. What are they yielding these days? Perhaps it would be beneficial for us all to see how production is decreasing, yes?"

"Well, Your Majesty, *perhaps* if you had not been previously engaged, you would have seen our correspondence over this matter," Ottorius shot back, and Sebastian stiffened.

"Now, Sebastian's absence aside, he surprisingly has a fair point," King Adrik said. *What a wonderfully backhanded compliment.* "I've been curious about that myself, Otto, since we've had smaller and smaller shipments from you over the past couple years. I want to make sure you're holding up your end of the agreement."

Ottorius's jaw clenched as he ran a hand through his jet black hair.

"Of course," Ayana cut in, attempting to diffuse the tension. "I'll have someone draw up the reports for all of you."

Sebastian held back a snort. The day he saw those reports would be the day he quit drinking. He simply wanted to rile the man up; he had no doubt the Triad was lying about their numbers in order to send less in their exports, and were now trying to use it as an excuse to refuse Iona completely.

"I look forward to reading them," Sebastian responded.

Annalise smirked at him when the attention turned back to the other side of the table. She'd always held a special hatred for Otto. "*Good one,*" she mouthed.

What could he say? If they were going to do this right, he would make sure everyone's cards were on the table.

Thirty minutes later, they were released for lunch, with the expectation that they would meet back in a couple of hours to continue hashing out details.

Sebastian was already exhausted. All he wanted was to go back to his chambers and sleep for hours.

"Anna," he started as he pushed in her chair and she gathered her notes, "do I pay you enough to attend these meetings for me while I go take a nap?"

She snorted and shoved a pencil behind her ear. "You pay me enough for me to line your bed with gold, Seb, but—"

"That sounds uncomfortable."

"—you know you can't skip this," she finished with a roll of her eyes.

He sighed, holding the door open as they exited the meeting hall. "Yes, yes, I know."

"Besides, you were great in there. Sometimes these monarchs need to be put in their place." She rounded on him before they could get down the hall. "You always act like it's such an inconvenience, but you know what you're doing, Sebastian. Don't think I didn't notice how every time they tried to weasel *you* into upping our exports, you turned it back around on someone else." Annalise poked him in the chest with a sly smile.

"Well, there's a reason they gave me this job."

She rolled her eyes again. "Yes, it's called *birthright*."

"Now, now, I worked very hard to be born into this family."

"Your Majesty, may I speak with you for a moment?" a voice called from behind him. Both Sebastian and Annalise turned to find Mariana de Faye waiting patiently by the meeting hall entrance, a sweet smile pasted on her red lips.

That did not sound good.

"Of course." Sebastian shot Annalise a wink. "Save me some lunch, yes?"

Her eyes were filled with caution, but she merely nodded before following the other dignitaries to the dining room.

"How are you enjoying your stay so far?" Mariana asked as he approached. Gray and silver hair sprang around her head in excited coils, framing her brown skin. Light from a nearby window caught her golden nose ring and reflected a beam onto the stone floor as she cocked her head and smiled.

"Palace Noctem is beautiful," he responded politely. "We appreciate your hospitality."

The woman scoffed. "So formal! What happened to the feisty king from this morning?" she tutted. "It's truly a pity the others do not seem to recognize your value. But I assure you, the Chamber does, Your Majesty."

"Well, I believe that's the kindest thing anyone has ever said to me," Sebastian replied with a bland smile.

"Will you walk with me?" she asked, beckoning him further down the hall.

Sebastian didn't like where this was going, but there was no room for refusal in her tone.

"Your time in power has been quite interesting," Mariana began as they walked. "The golden boy of Karstos...it has a nice ring to it, I must admit. I'm sure following in your father's footsteps was a difficult path to travel."

Sebastian's jaw twitched, and he grappled to maintain his normal, casual composure. "It's good to see seclusion has not kept you away from the gossip, Your Grace."

She gave him a wink, the wrinkles around her eyes deepening. "People *do* love to talk. Would you like to know what else I have heard?"

Not in the slightest.

"Do tell."

Mariana hummed. "That the king has lost his bite."

That was...not what he was expecting. "I assure you, my teeth are as sharp as ever," he said after a beat.

A forced laugh permeated the quiet hallway. "Oh, you were a wonderful child prodigy, from what we hear. The dutiful little prince, who enjoyed getting up to mischief but otherwise played the role splendidly. But the 'dark king'...now, *he* was interesting."

Sebastian froze at the same time Mariana stopped walking and turned to face him, awaiting his reaction with a smirk. He quickly reined in his frustration.

"I'm not sure 'interesting' is the word many of my people would use."

"Perhaps." She shrugged. "But I value a man who goes after what he wants. Who uses any means necessary to meet his goals." She ran a sharp nail along his arm. He couldn't tell if the woman was trying to seduce him or intimidate him, but either way, his body urged him to end the conversation.

Before he could disentangle himself, her hand fell away, her eyes sparking as she said, "Even if those goals were not your own."

Sebastian blinked, the only outward sign of his mind racing. What did the Chamber know?

"I wonder what your kingdom would say if they knew the extent of your crimes against them," she said absentmindedly, smoothing a wrinkle on his shoulder. Her eyes darted back to his face. "I apologize, I have taken up far too much of your time, Your Majesty." She patted his cheek. "I have high hopes that our discussions later this week with your kingdom will be fruitful." Flashing him a smile, she continued down the hall, leaving him to his thoughts.

She couldn't possibly know. Celesine was gone, and she was the only one who knew what he'd done. What she'd *made* him do. If his people found out...

Sebastian scrubbed a hand down his face once Mariana was out of sight. Cracking his neck from side to side, he took a deep, shaking breath, forcing the cloud of fear rising inside of him back down.

Well, Iona had certainly come to play.

CHAPTER TWENTY-FOUR

Jade

J ade recognized this man. Silver-flecked auburn hair and a long matching beard, kind green eyes, and pale, wrinkled cheeks. He was there that day on the beach.

"*Akir?*" Brielle's startled cry came from beside her as the girl moved forward to embrace the elderly man. "Where did you come from?"

"It's good to see you, Miss Brielle, although I wish it were under better circumstances. Please, you must come with me. This land is not safe for you."

Their group exchanged hesitant glances. As sincere as he sounded, Jade knew how well trusting others had gone for her in the past.

"Where are you taking us?" she inquired.

"Someplace they cannot find you," Akir answered. When they stayed rooted in place, he raised an eyebrow and sighed. "If I meant you any harm, don't you think I would have simply let the people follow you to the palace? Or exposed Isla last night at the feast?"

Jade's brow furrowed. "You were there?"

"I saw him," Isla confirmed quietly. "I'll come with you." She crossed the distance to the man, followed shortly by Brielle.

"Alright, come on," Jade said to Rynn, who also seemed less keen to trust the man. "Before those people back there change their minds."

They followed Akir through the dense trees and shrubbery, having to move swinging vines and loose branches out of their path as they trudged along.

"Akir, what's going *on* here?" Brielle asked.

"Not now, Miss Brielle. I will answer any questions once we are no longer out in the open."

They walked in silence, tension, heavy breaths, and confusion swirling in the air. Jade snuck a glance at Isla, who was resolutely facing forward, her fists balled at her side.

Jade had made a mistake.

She knew it the moment Isla had moved all the way from the cliffs to the back of the crowd in a mere heartbeat, a bewildered, dangerous expression on her flushed cheeks. Jade had never told the girl the depths of her abilities with the earth, the polarizing power over the human psyche that came with it. Unlike her fellow elementals, who didn't seem to think twice about using their mind abilities—whether it was for selfish purposes or self-proclaimed "altruism"—Jade had always refused.

Well, almost always.

She had used it in the war a thousand years ago. It was during one of the first true battles, long before the pained, labored cries of soldiers had become as common to her ears as crickets chirping on her windowsill. Their anguish had pricked her heart. Rebels, who fought in the elementals' name, in *her* name, were losing ground rapidly. Armies of loyalists had savagely cut them down, one by one, section by section. To prevent further carnage, Jade had frozen their bodies—only those of the loyalists, allowing the rebels to get their bearings and escape.

The coppery tang of blood still filled her nostrils, shouts of confusion still echoed in her ears as she remembered the swords clattering to the ground, no longer supported by cognizant hands. She had yelled at the rebels to run, to save their wounded and *get out*.

But instead, without so much as a moment's hesitation, they had raised their blades and began slaughtering the frozen statues of the loyalists. Even now, she could clearly envision the first head that fell, rolling across the blood-soaked grass to her feet, silent concentration still on the face of the victim who had never seen his death coming.

She had instantly let go of her power and unbound the loyalist army, but it was too late. The men were startled, completely caught off guard, and were annihilated.

The rebels sang her praises for months. The great goddess of earth who bestowed victory on those she favored.

Jade, however, had locked herself away. Refused to answer pleas for help, for aid, for relief. Never again would she involve herself in the affairs of men.

She hadn't spoken of it with the others, but that day changed something inside of her. Ever since then, her mind ability had gone dormant. Perhaps the violent way she had shut herself down and pushed it to the far recesses of her soul had cut it off for good. Anytime she had tried to awaken it, it was like nudging a hollow cavity.

It was gone.

But none of this was an excuse for why she hadn't told Isla of what she could do. It was not out of some selfish desire to keep the truth hidden—she'd simply never believed Isla would need to know. The idea of things getting to this point, of Isla *actually* taking their powers, had seemed so far-fetched to Jade that teaching her how to use her abilities hadn't crossed her mind.

She had thought about it so many times since that day on the beach. How if only Isla had been better equipped, she could have prevented her brother from dying. More than that, if only Jade herself had overcome her own mental block, she could have prevented *any* of it from happening. Simply stopped the king in his tracks, used the dagger on him, and been done with it before he even batted an eye.

Isla's ire was entirely warranted. Jade had been angry at herself for months now. If only she could *explain*...but words and emotions weren't her strong suit.

Their group approached a large boulder surrounded by a thicket of bushes and low-hanging vines. Akir stopped, pushed through the shrubbery, and disappeared on the other side. Jade exchanged a puzzled look with Brielle.

Suddenly, his auburn head popped back up over the hedge. "Well? Are you coming?"

The four of them merely blinked at him. With a shrug, Brielle moved forward, clearing a path through the bushes, Rynn following on her heels. Before Isla walked through, Jade put a hand on her elbow.

"Isla, can we please—"

"Not right now, Jade," she said, her tone short but no longer filled with anger. "Let's just...figure out what's going on. Then we can talk, I promise." Her eyes lingered around Jade's neck, where she'd gripped her earlier.

Jade didn't hold the girl's anger against her. She knew how easy it was to succumb to those strong emotions, and Isla had four times as much power surging through her veins than Jade ever had. Honestly, she was surprised the girl hadn't set her on fire.

Leaves and branches scratched against her as she pursued the others, and she finally saw where Akir had disappeared to. Behind the boulder lay a large, wooden door, built directly into the dirt. It was propped open, Akir's head still above ground, gesturing for them to come forward. Jade could see the tip of a rickety ladder as the man descended further. He helped Brielle and Isla down the hole, then turned to offer his hand to Jade.

"Help Rynn first," she suggested. "I'll go after him, to be safe."

"I am not an invalid," Rynn muttered as he threw his cane down the ladder and slowly lowered himself onto the wooden steps.

"Stop it," Jade commanded in a harsh whisper, gripping his shoulder before he took his next step. She was sick of his ungrateful attitude and spiteful words.

"So what if you are, Rynn? So what if you, for once in your life, must finally get over yourself and accept help? There is *nothing* wrong with that. For the love of the gods, you make me want to shove you down this hole." She tightened her grasp, keeping her voice low so the others wouldn't hear. "You have got to realize that this is who you are now. *We* have accepted it. And it has done nothing to change our love for you, you stubborn man. Now it's your turn."

She let him go and stared at his blank face, expecting a snide remark or an outright refusal to listen. But then, with a piercing gaze, he murmured, "What did I do to earn this friendship, Jade?"

Her expression softened. "Nothing. That's the point. You're stuck with me, I'm afraid."

"What's taking so long?" Brielle called up from the darkness.

Jade sighed. "And we are both stuck with all of them, it seems."

A hint of a smile flitted across Rynn's lips. "I suppose that's not so bad."

Giving him a faint smile of her own, she waved him down the steps, a weight she hadn't known existed lifting from her chest.

When her turn came and she reached the bottom, she found they were in a tunnel, the floors packed densely with dirt and stone. The rich scent of damp earth engulfed her, automatically putting her senses at ease. They followed Akir down the narrow, sloping tunnel, turning every once in a while as they descended down, down, down. Soon, mutterings of conversations from ahead reached them.

As they rounded a corner, the tunnel opened to reveal an enormous cavern. Jade took in the sight with wide eyes. Tables and benches, books, scrolls, blankets, makeshift beds, and boxes of supplies covered the huge space. Groups of people scurried in and out through various tunnels, some deep in conversation, some smiling and laughing, others walking alone with their heads buried in books. A few families lay in pallets on the floor in the furthest corner of the cave, fast asleep. Hand drawn maps hung haphazardly on the stone walls. Jade thought she saw a map of each of the four island kingdoms, plus one of Palace Noctem, and another she did not recognize—maybe the tunnel system, with its winding paths.

Jade immediately knew what this meant, what this place signified. A thousand years couldn't change the face of war.

"Akir, what is this?" Isla asked. "Where are we?"

"This, dear cousin, is why we had to keep silent out in the open." He looked back at them with a twinkle in his eye.

"Welcome to the resistance."

PART THREE:

DROWN

CHAPTER TWENTY-FIVE

Isla

The resistance. Gods, what had they walked into?

"And what, exactly, are you resisting?" Rynn asked, leaning on his cane.

Akir motioned for them to follow him down another side tunnel. "Come, and we can speak somewhere more private."

"Aren't these your people? Shouldn't you trust them?" Jade asked suspiciously.

"Yes, and I do. With my life," he responded. "But I do not expect you to yet, and pardon my assumption, but I don't think my cousin would like for this entire camp to know of her...situation."

"Why do you keep calling me that?" Isla insisted. "I thought all of my ancestors died, except for my father's line."

Akir ushered them inside a room—as much of a "room" as there could be in an underground cave, then began his story.

"Long ago, at the end of the civil war, the reigning king and queen—Medes and Nah-yomi Vasileia—took their family, servants, and whoever else wanted to leave the island to start a new life. They boarded a ship and set sail west. Weeks later, bits of wreckage from their ship floated back to shore. The people on Iona believed everyone had been lost at sea.

"However, Medes had an older brother named Satori. Satori was first in line to be king, but he renounced his title when they were young, choosing instead to marry a commoner and live his life away from the pressure of the

Vasileian crown. Rather than follow his brother, Satori and his family made the decision to stay on the island after the war. Satori had many children, as did his children after him, so on and so forth. I am the last of his line, although we no longer bear the Vasileia name."

Isla drank in the information, suddenly starving for more knowledge of her ancestors. "So, that means you're..."

"Well, perhaps 'cousin' was too simple." Akir chuckled, his beard bobbing slightly. "But, give or take forty generations, the sentiment stands."

A wave of hesitant excitement rushed over Isla. She had *family* here. Incredibly distant, yes, but still. A whole lineage of people bonded to her through time, with hundreds of years of history to learn.

"How do you know all of this?" Isla asked.

"Our ancestors were very keen on record-keeping, something I believe you are well aware of," he said, tapping his nose. "The Vasileia book in your possession is not the only one of its kind."

Her heart skipped a beat. "There are *more*? Can I see them?"

Akir nodded. "I think that can be arranged. I am also interested in seeing the one you have, if you would allow me."

"Of course," Isla agreed, her chest swelling at the idea of being able to share these discoveries with him. "Is there anyone else related to us here?"

He smiled, a bit of sadness in his light green eyes. "Most of my immediate family has passed on, and I never married or bore children. However, a few of us do remain. I have a nephew and a distant cousin on my father's side. And my sister, Eliza." His smile deepened, dimples appearing on his cheeks. "She is eager to meet you."

Isla returned his grin. She knew dozens of generations separated her from these practical strangers, but she couldn't help the desire to know them, to connect with this side of her lost heritage.

"Akir, you haven't yet told us what this resistance is for," Jade spoke up.

"No, I suppose I haven't." The old man sighed. "It began many decades ago, when the rule of the Chamber became too controlling, too dangerous, and a faction of people decided they desired a different future for Iona. One where they were not ruled by fear."

"What was the Chamber doing that made the people so fearful?" Rynn asked.

"That, Master Rynn, is a question not so easily answered." Akir brought his hands to a steeple in front of his chin. "When the great elementals of old"—he nodded toward Rynn and Jade—"left our lands and the kingdom closed itself off from outsiders, our ancestors struggled with how to carry on. How to govern an entire kingdom barely out of the chaos of war, in shambles and without a leader. They begged Satori to take the throne, but he refused, saying the people needed to come together to weather the storm instead of looking to force a crown on someone else. I believe he knew, even then, what the next millennia would bring.

"Different decades brought different power-hungry men and women, searching for the notoriety of the throne. Fairly early on, they established the Chamber: a group of elected individuals whose purpose was to understand the needs of the people and rule with their best interest in mind."

"I can imagine how that went," Jade said dryly.

"Indeed. From what our records show, the first Chamber was just and honorable, and brought the kingdom back from the brink of collapse. Unfortunately, the last several hundred years have proven that even a strong foundation can crumble. Anecdotes in our ancestor's journals and reports spread throughout the past have all shown footprints of a kingdom living in fear."

"Fear of what?" Jade prompted. "The Chamber?"

"I think that is the underlying current of it all, yes. But the Chamber has always been wise, you see. Multiple steps ahead in everything they plan. While the Chamber wants the fear of the kingdom, they do not want the kingdom to fear *them*."

Bri cleared her throat and said, "I'm not sure I'm following."

"They need something to elicit the fear of an entire nation, besides themselves," Rynn said quietly. "Humans are easily swayed when their energy and attention are diverted to something they believe is their largest threat. Like blind rats being led willingly off a cliff in order to run from the jaws of a cat."

"Well," Bri said, pursing her lips, "I don't think I appreciate that analogy."

With a chuckle, Akir clapped his hands. "Blind rats. Well, I have been called much worse. That is precisely right, Master Rynn. For hundreds of years, the Chamber has been cultivating an environment of fear and hatred, garnering the people's support by turning them against something they have no control over. Making the kingdom believe the Chamber is keeping them safe. Creating total dependency on them to ensure no danger befalls their families."

Isla remembered the gleam of unrestrained rage in the people's eyes at the cliffs and their constant reference to some omnipotent *they*...

She met Akir's gaze. "Are you saying the Chamber has turned everyone against elementals? Against...people like me?"

"Against *all* magic. But yes, most prominently, those possessing the power of the elements," Akir said with a nod.

Jade scoffed. "That's absurd. There has never been another being with abilities like ours, and we haven't entered this kingdom in a thousand years. Magic hasn't even been *seen* since the war. Surely, the people realized after centuries passed and nobody wielded magic that there was nothing to be afraid of."

Akir turned his attention to her. "Do not forget, Mistress Jade, that history is told by the victor."

"There was no *victor*. Nobody won that war," Jade shot back.

"Ah, then it is told by those left standing. Which you, my dear, were not."

Bri jumped in. "So, what, the Chamber has just been spreading lies over the past several hundred years that everyone should be afraid of magic? Didn't the elementals help *create* life here?"

"Yes, they certainly did, Miss Brielle." Akir stroked at his auburn beard. "And yet, they also helped start a war that led factions of people to slaughter one another, and sat back while the kingdom cracked and shattered from the inside out."

Rynn's hand whitened around his cane, a vein in his forehead throbbing as he clenched his teeth. "If you brought us down here for this, I do not—"

"No, you misunderstand me," replied Akir, putting a hand up quickly. "I apologize. I simply mean to show you how easy it is to argue the opposite. How easy it is to goad a reaction of anger from someone without using all of the facts. That is *precisely* what the Chamber has been doing for hundreds of years. Tell me, how are the people supposed to believe any differently when the turning point of their civilization, the entire reason for their seclusion from the rest of the world, all they have *ever* known, was built on the broken foundation of a kingdom ravaged by war? A war caused by *magical*, immortal beings?"

Jade and Rynn shifted uncomfortably. "You know that was not our intention. We did not follow you here for you to lay our sins before us, Akir." Rynn's tone was clear: get to the point, or they were leaving.

"I understand your frustration, and I'm sorry to be the cause of it. But I need you to see"—Akir's voice was now slightly strained, his body leaning forward with the urgency of his words—"why these people behaved the way they did today. Why this fear is so deeply ingrained in the blood of this kingdom, in our very bones, in our every breath. The Chamber feeds on this fear. That is how they keep the people in line and, by default, keep themselves in power."

"That crowd today, at the cliffs," Isla began. "It was like they immediately knew what I was. What I could do. They didn't even seem surprised, only angry. But there aren't other people out there like me, are there? Do other magical beings exist here?"

Akir shook his head. "No, they do not. Magic has not existed in these lands for a millennia, ever since the four elementals slumbered. But the people of Iona do not necessarily know that."

"Why would everyone still think magic is around, then?" Bri asked, holding her hands out. "There's no proof."

She hadn't even finished her question before Akir started nodding. "Yes, there has been no actual proof, as you say. That is why what the Chamber has done over the decades is so artfully crafted, so dangerously, deceptively perfect." He folded his wrinkled hands in front of him. "When times get difficult, when failures and tragedies strike, when a kingdom needs something to blame—who do they accuse first?"

"The leadership," Jade answered automatically.

Akir tapped his nose. "What if the leadership had the perfect scapegoat, a sacrificial lamb to offer on the altar of its peoples' mutiny?"

"Such as us." Rynn's tone was as dry as Isla's mouth.

"Such as *magic*, yes. Long ago, the Chamber saw the opportunity to strike fear into the hearts of its citizens by making them believe these people with power, with elemental magic, still existed and were in hiding. That they sought to slowly overthrow Iona, to bring it under their control once again—as they had centuries ago. When a blight destroys entire sections of crops, who does the Chamber blame? When a cyclone rips through the seaside villages, who do the people turn their anger to? When fires consume our farmland, how does the Chamber deflect responsibility?

"Over the centuries, it has become even more dangerous than simply cursing nonexistent elemental beings for their troubles. I have seen neighbors blaming neighbors for stolen property, kind, innocent civilians accused of heinous crimes against nature, my own kin thrown behind bars simply for being in the wrong place at the wrong time." Akir's hand curled at his side.

"There is no need for *proof* when one has *fear*. You cannot blame the people, as much as their actions may anger you. They are merely the product of a fractured kingdom, sheep who have been led astray for far too long. The history and truth about magic in the journals of my ancestors has made me wary of the leadership and kept me from falling prey to their manipulation, but the rest of our people...they simply don't know any better."

Up until this point, Isla had seen Akir as a somewhat endearing, wise yet eccentric old man. Someone with firm principles, but who stood in the background. Yet in this moment, he was a completely different person—blazing eyes, powerful voice, ironclad will. He spoke like a man who would give his life for these people. *His* people.

"You started the resistance, didn't you?" Isla finally asked.

Akir leveled his gaze with hers, his green eyes bright and steady. "It has been my life's work to banish fear with truth and lead this kingdom back to what it once was."

"Gods, how old are you, anyway?" Bri blurted, and Isla had to pinch her lips together to keep from laughing at the outburst.

Akir's mouth twitched. "Old enough that if I stopped moving, Miss Brielle, they would surely start digging my grave. Now," he said, clapping his hands together and jolting Isla from the thick tension of the room. "Any more questions?"

Before Isla could respond with the myriad of thoughts running through her mind, Rynn stepped forward and put a hand on her elbow.

"We should be getting back to the palace, Isla," he said. "We have been gone too long as it is."

Akir gave them a surprised look, a deep crease appearing on his already wrinkled brow. "Isla, you're not safe up there. The people have seen you and what you can do, and I must say, your eyes don't exactly keep you inconspicuous." He raised an eyebrow. "They will be spreading the news and searching for you far and wide."

Isla blanched. She hadn't thought about that. "What do you expect me to do, hide down here?"

"I thought you would understand that was why I brought you here, given the circumstances."

Isla scoffed, but her face fell when Akir continued to stare at her expectantly. "You can't be serious. I'm not staying down here for the rest of the week. I've got to—" She cut herself off.

Taking a step toward her, Akir said, "Cousin, whatever you came here for, maybe I can help. I'm under no delusion that you were sent to aid my resistance, but perhaps it was not mere chance that we ran into one another. Perhaps *we* can aid *you.*"

"How do you know I was *sent* for anything?"

"Why else would you come back to this island, the place that ripped everything from you?" He gave Isla a knowing look. "While I do not claim to understand everything that occurred here four months ago, I am not blind. *Something* happened that day, something that sparked a chain of events across the world. I do not believe you are here by happenstance. The question is, will you trust me with your quest?" Akir cocked his head, his eyes piercing into Isla's, hands once again steepled in front of his beard.

At the same time, Rynn and Jade both interjected.

"Isla, wait—"

"I don't think—"

Jade shot Rynn a glance and lowered her voice. "Isla, maybe we should talk for a moment."

Isla understood they had their suspicions—and she didn't blame them. They'd been turned on by their own people and betrayed by someone they thought they could trust. But this was *her* decision. And Akir had proven himself over and over, from helping keep Bri safe four months ago, to saving Isla from the wrath of the mob, and disclosing secrets he'd spent his whole life trying to keep.

Facing Jade, she said, "I appreciate your concern, but don't you think we need all the help we can get? We don't even know where to start. He's seen enough as it is—telling him the whole truth won't change much. And besides, if Akir or his people decide to betray us"—she turned to the man and gave him a slight smile—"I think we have information of our own the Chamber would be interested in. Not that I would ever want to use it, of course," she added.

Jade raised an eyebrow.

Chuckling, Akir said, "You know how to play the game already, it seems. Now, what is it that you are searching for?"

Isla straightened her shoulders. "Have you ever heard of the Dagger of Volnus?"

For a moment, the older man's eyes squinted in thought before widening. Surprise passed across his face. "Ah, yes. Yes, it's beginning to make sense now."

Isla and Bri exchanged a look. "So, you know what it is? What it can do?" Isla asked.

He paced the floor in front of them, his robe swishing at his heels. "Well, I know bits and pieces. Whispers, really. Certainly not as much as you. As I said earlier, my ancestor Satori kept a book similar to the one you have, where he recorded information about the treasures and myths of the Vasileia line. What is written is mostly based on his memory from before he renounced his title and left the family, something he scribed to be able to pass along to his descendants. There are multiple mentions of this dagger, although he was not certain how it worked."

"What *did* he say about it, then?" Isla asked eagerly.

"That it was a weapon he had only heard stories of, but never encountered on his own. Legends of its power over members of the family, how it called to them throughout the ages. Satori believed it had the ability to unite multiple sources of magic and would be incredibly dangerous if wielded together."

"That basically sums it up," Bri said with a nod.

"It's also the only weapon that can kill an immortal," Isla added.

Rynn grunted disapprovingly at her offering up so much knowledge, but Isla continued, briefly explaining the way the dagger worked and how she came into contact with it months ago.

"You found it in the shipwreck," Akir murmured, and Isla nodded. "And you wielded this dagger? That's how you gained the power of the elementals, and they were left as humans?"

Again, Isla nodded. "It disappeared after that, and we never found out where it went. But now, we need it back. The Primeval gods said finding the dagger and putting the elements back where they belong is the only way to stop all the natural disasters from worsening."

"So, you need to locate this dagger," Akir said, taking a deep breath as he stroked his beard. "Well, I suppose it's a good thing I found you today."

All eyes shot to him. Jade spoke first. "Do you know where it is?"

"Not for certain," he admitted, inclining his head to Jade. "But if I am correct, you have been very close, indeed. I believe," he said slowly, "it is in the palace."

CHAPTER TWENTY-SIX

Aidan

"D o these things come with instructions?" Aidan asked as he sat on the edge of their bed in Palace Noctem, holding a small packet of herbs in front of his face.

Kai's head popped out from the bathing chamber's door, a towel tied around her chest. "Aidan, they're tea leaves. Do you need instructions on how to make *tea*?"

He bristled and sniffed the tiny bag. "I *know* it's tea, I just didn't know if we had to do anything special with them. I've never done this before, Kai."

"What, made tea?"

His head rolled to the side as he gave her a look, her bright, mischievous smirk already melting away his irritation. "You know what I meant, sweetheart. All of these herbs and oils and concoctions for you and the baby"—he held his hand out to the basket of supplies they'd bought at the apothecary—"I don't want to do something wrong."

After separating from Jade and the others, Aidan and Kai had spent the afternoon at the local apothecary, The Greenhouse. The owner had talked with Kai about her recent symptoms and the fact that she hadn't had her monthly bleeding cycle in almost three months, all but confirming the pregnancy.

When Isla had mentioned a "third" along with him and Kai the previous night, he hadn't believed her. He'd almost thrown out the words as nothing more than a slip of the tongue. But...Isla was the *Aether*. She must have seen something from the spirit plane, or have an ability to sense these things now.

To see spirits and souls and life, even when unrecognizable to the human eye. And now, after learning of Kai's symptoms and speaking with the apothecary owner, they were both convinced.

And Aidan was losing his mind.

He couldn't believe she was *pregnant.* It's not as if that wasn't something they had talked about wanting. He knew their plan was to start a family eventually, to find a place they loved and lay down roots. But so quickly? They honestly weren't sure if they would be able to *get* pregnant, what with the whole...used-to-be-immortal bit.

They hadn't even been trying to have a baby anytime soon. Sure, he supposed they hadn't done a *great* job of preventing it. Kai took a weekly tonic Zephania made for her, but there had been several times she'd forgotten. They hadn't been too worried.

He shouldn't be surprised other parts of him were so...virile.

Aidan scrubbed at his beard, his thoughts racing as he looked at the basket of supplies. It was terrible timing. They were only four months into their new life, still trying to figure out where and *who* they wanted to be. And now Isla told them she'd been tasked with "righting the balance of nature" and needed their help. They had absolutely no idea what that would mean for any of them.

Despite all of this, Aidan was...excited. Absolutely giddy. When he didn't feel as though he would be sick, that was. His beautiful, wonderful wife was getting everything she'd ever dreamed of. Tears threatened to fill his eyes when he thought of Kai as a mother; she had so much love in her heart, so much joy to give. Getting to watch her bear his child and become a mother would surpass any idea of happiness he'd ever known previously in his life. And he would get to be a father.

A father.

Aidan's face fell. He'd never had a father. Gods, what if he was terrible at it? He knew how bad things had gotten a thousand years ago. What if he couldn't hold his temper? What if he—

"Aidan, are you spiraling on me?" Kai's voice broke through his inner turmoil.

He sighed. "Well, one of us has to."

Calmly, Kai set down her hairbrush and walked from the bathing chamber to the bed, getting on her knees before Aidan and reaching for the basket. She pulled out a black pouch and handed it to him, saying, "This one is a ginger root and peppermint mixture, for my nausea." Next, she fingered a glass vial. "These are raspberry leaves. I'll start taking this later, to help things go smoothly when the baby comes." Giving him another small vial, she explained, "This is lavender oil, to help me sleep."

As she spoke, his mind began to quiet, letting her sweet voice soothe him and bring him back from the edge.

"I'm glad one of us was paying attention at the shop," he said, leaning forward to kiss her forehead. "How are you feeling, sweetheart?"

She shrugged. "Honestly, I'm doing okay."

"You're *okay*?" He scoffed, and her big blue eyes stared up at him, a slight hint of wariness crossing over her calm features. "That's all I get? You're going to be a *mother*, Kai. I need a little more than 'okay,'" he said, unable to contain a smile.

When he grinned, the corner of Kai's mouth twitched. "I'm going to be a mother," she repeated in a whisper, eyes glistening as a brilliant beam broke across her face.

Gods, she was so beautiful. His sea temptress.

"We should be getting ready for dinner," she said after placing a quick kiss on his lips and dabbing her eyes with the back of her hand.

As she walked back to the sink and continued braiding her hair, Aidan began rifling through his new wardrobe. "Have you thought about telling the others yet?"

"Let's give it some time. I don't want to add this on top of everything that's going on, you know?"

Aidan's stomach churned uneasily. The previous night had been a whirlwind of information, and not only because of Kai's pregnancy. The two of them hadn't gotten the chance to talk about Isla being back and what their role in her new quest would be, given the circumstances. This wasn't the time for that conversation, though. Aidan had a plan for later that evening after dinner—a way to help his wife relax and for them to work through the chaos their lives had become.

"I hope Isla's doing okay," Kai added, padding into the bedroom and picking up the green outfit she'd layed out. "Last night was difficult. I can't imagine how she's feeling about leaving her family, along with juggling these new powers. I don't really remember what it was like in the beginning. I suppose we always knew how to use our elements, didn't we? It was almost like it was ingrained in us," she said thoughtfully.

Aidan chuckled as he pulled on a pair of brown trousers. "I don't know about that. I vaguely remember you using your influence over almost every human you spoke to without even realizing it, at first. You asked a fellow to 'lend you his hand' once and he almost sawed off his arm. Literally."

"Oh, gods." Kai ran a hand over her mouth, then turned her back to him so he could lace up her dress. "I forgot about that. And I wondered why there were so many horrible rumors about me." When Aidan laughed, she reached behind her to pinch his side. "You weren't any better! You set things on fire all the time. I went through so many sets of robes back then because they'd have scorch marks everywhere."

"Sweetheart, that wasn't an accident. I've been trying to take your clothes off for centuries," Aidan purred, running his nose up the side of her neck. He finished fastening the dress and snaked his hands around her waist to pull her flush to his chest. "Now, what do you say we get this dinner over with so I can get you back here and prove it?"

When they emerged from their room, they found Rynn and Jade lounging in the common area in their dinner attire, ready to head to the feast. The other members of their party hadn't shown up yet, but it was getting late, so the four of them made their way to the dining hall.

Rynn and Jade had griped about the constant need for frivolous clothing at these events, but Aidan had to admit, they all cleaned up nicely. He took in the dazzling gowns, the sharp suit jackets, the perfectly placed hair...it was a far cry from their weeks spent in the mountains.

And gods, did his wife look *good*.

Tonight, she'd picked an emerald number with jeweled sleeves hanging off her shoulders, her blonde hair pulled into an elegant braid that swung down her back. He'd thought it was a floor length dress, but when she moved, he realized they were pants that flowed like silk and lengthened her already long legs.

Aidan was tempted to lock them in their chambers for the rest of the night, but as they were leaving, she confessed she'd been rather nauseous from not eating most of the day, which in turn had him smashing down doors to get her to the feast.

Anything for his wife.

The banquet hall was as beautiful and extravagant the second night around, with its greenery, gold accents, and candles strung from the columns, illuminating the entire room in a flickering, golden haze. This time, the four Chamber members were already seated in their spot by the huge tree that took up the entire back part of the hall. Personally, Aidan didn't see the appeal; how did they even keep it alive? Did they have to worry about bugs and other pests in the branches?

Kai called it innovative. Aidan called it a fire hazard.

Guests from the other kingdoms trickled in as the minutes passed. He and Kai had been quickly introduced to most of the Evonlean royal family the day before. King Adrik and Queen Melanora looked tired after their day of negotiations. Their children, Klaus, Jessenia, and little Trystan, bounced around the room, refreshed as ever. He supposed the pampered life of a royal child would do that.

Behind Aidan, the server bent to pour the evening's wine selection into his and Kai's glasses, and they both put a hand over her flute. Rynn and Jade shot them a strange glance.

Aidan blinked. At the same time, he and Kai spoke.

"Kai's trying to stop drinking—"

"I already had a glass back in the room—"

He looked at his wife. Well, they had not thought this through.

"Just not tonight, thank you," Kai said sweetly to the server, who gave her a tight smile and kept moving down the line.

Across the table, Jade reached for a dinner roll. "You're acting odd," she said matter-of-factly, but before they could respond, Sebastian, Annalise, Lord Everett, and two of their guards walked up to take their seats. Sebastian and Annalise looked strained and exhausted, like many of the other rulers who had been in meetings all day.

"Where's Isla?" was the first thing out of Sebastian's mouth as he sat and went for his glass of wine.

"Oh, it's been a wonderful day, thank you for asking," Aidan said. When the king gave him a look, Aidan cleared his throat. "Probably getting ready. I'm sure she and Bri will be here soon."

"We had an...unexpected afternoon," Jade offered. Aidan's brow furrowed; they hadn't spoken to the others about their day after they'd split up.

That got Sebastian's attention. "Is everything alright?"

"I believe that is a question better answered with less inquisitive minds around," said Rynn from across the table, his voice low.

Annalise let out a sigh. "I thought Kingsley would already be here," she said in frustration, gesturing to the empty guard's seat next to Bri. "I haven't seen him all day. Frederick," she said, turning to one of the other guards, "has he spoken to you at all? He better have fallen ill, to have missed multiple shifts last night and today."

The guard shook his head. "No, ma'am. I saw one of the servants outside his door last night, so perhaps..." He trailed off, raising his eyebrows.

With a scoff and a roll of her eyes, Annalise sat down. "Honestly, I don't know sometimes whether we're paying them to guard our king, or to find people to stick their—"

"Alright, Anna, I believe the pre-dinner drinking needs to be kept to a minimum from now on, yes?" Sebastian cut in smoothly.

Now that he said it, Aidan *did* notice Annalise looked a bit flushed. In the short amount of time he'd know the royal advisor, he had never seen her remotely tipsy or unguarded. Her eyes were slightly pink and distant, and when Rynn tried to say something to her, she barely acknowledged him. Their meetings that day must've been a delight.

The same heavyset man from the previous night thunked his metal scepter onto the hardwood floor, calling everyone's attention to the large tree and the standing Chamber members. Tonight, they all wore their matching crowns and deep purple clothing, the mountain emblem of Iona embedded on their chests. As before, Mariana de Faye spoke for the rest, giving some short speech full of encouraging, superfluous platitudes. Beside Kai, Sebastian appeared rather stiff as she spoke, his fingers almost white around his flute.

What had *happened* that day? Everyone was so...tense.

The food was served, and Aidan instantly zeroed in on the roasted chicken, buttery rice, and brown sugar glazed carrots set before him. He and Kai took a bite at the same time, both emitting obnoxious groans as they chewed.

Sebastian lifted an eyebrow. "Hungry?"

"We haven't eaten since breakfast," Aidan said around a full mouth of rice and chicken.

"Why not?" the king asked.

Aidan swallowed. "We stayed busy, walking around the city and all."

"Indeed," a male voice said from behind them, and Aidan jerked in his seat. Nor Noxen and Ezeretta Bannock, the two quietest members of the Chamber, had appeared at their side of the table.

Nor continued, his deep, scratchy voice matching his rough-around-the-edges appearance. "We heard it was an eventful day on the island. And where, may I ask, is your friend? Isla, I believe?"

Jade and Rynn went still, holding Nor and Ezeretta's gazes in some sort of silent stand-off. Aidan's heart pounded. What was going on? What had he missed?

"Yes, we *do* hope everything is alright," Ezeretta added sweetly, but her quiet, kind tone did nothing to ease Aidan's bewildered mind.

"I appreciate the concern, but I promise, I'm fine."

Aidan's eyebrows shot up as he craned his neck to see around Nor and Ezeretta, finding Isla and Bri standing side by side, a confident smile painted on the former's burgundy lips.

"Oh, and I brought my own seat this time," Isla added, nodding to a servant behind her, who placed the decorative upholstered chair from their common room next to Bri's.

With a snort, Kai whispered to Aidan, "She gets that attitude from us."

Ezeretta narrowed her eyes for a split second before her expression shifted to that of a gracious host. Aidan didn't miss the glance she shot at Mariana up at the head of the table, who was watching the encounter over her glass of wine.

"We are most glad to see you again, Isla Vasileia. Please, enjoy the meal. I am sure we will have time to catch up later," Ezeretta said with a smile.

These vipers knew how to hide their fangs.

As the two Chamber members sauntered away to share pleasantries with the Aramian end of the table, Sebastian got to his feet and took Isla's arm, leading her to her newfound seat.

"You've been here for twenty-four hours, love. What could you have possibly gotten yourself into?" he murmured.

"I'll tell you about it later, I promise," Isla responded.

Across the table, Annalise chuckled loudly. "Oh, I bet she will."

"Anna, honestly," Sebastian said with a sigh. "Someone may need to take that glass away from you."

Glancing at Annalise, who rolled her eyes, Rynn said smoothly, "I think Miss Dalgard is capable of making her own decisions."

Aidan's mouth dropped open, a bit of carrot dangling from his lips before he clamped them shut. He wasn't sure he'd ever heard Rynn utter those words. Perhaps his friend had gained some perspective these last few months.

Annalise smirked and raised her glass in a toast. "Here's to another night of secrecy, espionage, and everyone wanting to kill someone else on this island."

Aidan tapped his glass with his wife's. "Well, I'll drink to that."

CHAPTER TWENTY-SEVEN

Kai

D inner passed without any more thinly veiled threats or outbursts, although it was far from boring.

The Evonlean royal children were shaping up to be an arrogant bunch, with their constant comparisons of the Ionan food to their own. Their remarks of, "Perhaps we can send them some wild game from home, it is *much* more fresh" and, "What an *interesting* choice of wine to pair with this cut" had Kai rolling her eyes more times than she could count. Ottorius, who, to Aidan's displeasure, was seated next to him for the entire week, attempted to strike up a discussion with him and Kai at one point, but was quickly shot down. Kai had no interest in his one-sided, aggressive agenda—especially after his display with Annalise the night before.

Right before dessert was brought out, a loud clatter and round of gasps arose from further down on the Ara Mir end of the table, drawing Kai's attention. She leaned to see over the people and found a figure in gold robes collapsed head-first onto his plate of food.

"It's one of the Aramian priests," Aidan whispered to her. A servant rushed forward from the shadows to help lift the unconscious man from his seat. His face was pale and dripping with brown gravy, and he blinked groggily as he came to.

"I think he just passed out," Aidan reassured her.

Kai's head was pounding, her stomach squeezing and contracting despite the food she'd eaten. What she wouldn't give for some of that ginger and peppermint tea right about now. She set her fork down and rubbed at her temple, just as Aidan leaned over to whisper, "Are you feeling okay, sweetheart?"

She nodded. "I'll be fine, just a little stomach ache," she responded quietly. "I guess I should get used to this."

"Do you want to get out of here?"

Kai tilted her head. "What did you have in mind?"

With a smirk, Aidan put his napkin down, stood, and reached for her hand. To the table, he said, "We're going to go explore. Don't wait up for us."

The two of them walked to the exit and up the staircase, Aidan towing Kai along while she chuckled. "Seriously, Aidan, where are we going?"

"Did you bring a bathing suit?" was his only answer as they walked toward the Karstos wing.

"A bathing—no, why would I have brought a *bathing suit*?" she said through a laugh.

"No matter, we might just get a little wet." His hand slid further down and gripped her backside, kissing the top of her head while they kept walking. She squealed his name in response.

Tugging at her waist, he slipped them into a shadowed alcove a few hallways from their chambers. "I'm sorry you're not feeling good, sweetheart," he whispered into her ear, his fingers grazing along her shoulder. Her breath hitched, the previous queasiness in her stomach suddenly replaced with something else.

"But," he said, lightly kissing at the groove between her neck and shoulder, "I have a plan that will hopefully help you relax. Come on."

He led her from the alcove and down the corridor. They navigated the path on distant memory and adrenaline alone, giggling like a couple of newlyweds about to get caught sneaking around. Rounding a corner, Kai squeezed Aidan's hand when she saw the kitchens come into view. She remembered how an underground network of tunnels and chambers rested beneath the palace. One thousand years ago, they had served as the servants' quarters. It

had also been home to a massive hot spring during their time, a hidden cavern
the two of them often retreated to when they needed to get away from the
world. Was that where he was taking her?

Beside the kitchens stood a statue of a lion guarding an enormous, decorated
tapestry. Aidan strode to it, checked to make sure no servants were watching,
and lifted the fabric out of the way, exposing a small wooden door.

"My lady," he said with a bow, and Kai led the way. Aidan grabbed a nearby
torch from its holder on the stone wall, and they carefully descended the steps
into the tunnels. She'd walked this path many times in her past, and even
in the dimness, with only the faint light from Aidan's torch behind her, her
feet still knew the way. Her fingers brushed against the damp stone as they
turned corner after corner, the musty scent of water and wood mixing with
the lingering freshly baked bread from the kitchen above.

Suddenly, Aidan reached out and grabbed her hand, the fire lighting his
face and bringing out the golden flecks dancing in his dark eyes. "Do you hear
that?" he asked, smiling. She quieted her thoughts and strained her ears until
she heard the gentle bubbling of water echo through the tunnels.

Returning his smile and quickly slipping out of her sandals, Kai winked and
said, "I'll race you."

And then she was off, bare feet pounding on the cool, hard stone, hair
whipping out of her braid and brushing her neck. The fabric of her emerald
jumpsuit was like water gliding along her skin. *Pants are so much better than
dresses*, she thought.

She'd felt sick throughout dinner, but the adrenaline and excitement of
their adventure made her forget her discomfort. As the sound of bubbling
water grew louder, steam billowed around the corner, and she shot towards
its warmth.

There it was. The beautiful, magical oasis that existed beneath the cold
exterior of palace life. A narrow archway expanded into an enormous rocky

ceiling, the hard stone beneath her feet shifting to smaller rocks as they neared the water. In the darkness, the pool before her looked black as midnight, the fireflies buzzing above creating specks of starlight on the surface. It was exactly as she remembered.

This place had been her solace for some time, especially during the cruel days of the war. Kai closed her eyes and tried to imagine how she once felt down here, the water calling to her, breathing life into her, her spirit ebbing and flowing in time to the frothing of the hot spring.

It was like grasping at straws.

But...she would be fine. She had something else to move her spirit now.

Without warning, warm hands pressed into her and lifted her over a hard shoulder. "I let you win that one," Aidan said as he rushed across the rocks and into the pool.

Kai gasped when the hot water hit the back of her legs. "We still have our clothes on, Aidan!" she said through a laugh. "We can't walk back through the palace like this!"

"Guess we'll have to stay down here long enough for them to dry, won't we?" He set her down, the water hitting right beneath her breasts. A comfortable heat emanated from the surface in clouds of steam, coiling and encasing them in its warmth. Aidan's forehead already glistened with sweat as he smiled down at her and pushed her damp hair out of her face.

"Do you remember all the nights we spent down here?" he murmured as he settled his hands around her waist. She could barely see, even with the torch he had stuck between two rocks at the entrance casting a faint glow that reached the edges of the pool.

"Hmm," she tapped her lip. "I seem to remember you *trying* to get me down here quite a few times."

"It did take a lot of convincing," he admitted, pulling her close and lowering his mouth to run light kisses down her neck. Kai bent her head to the side to give him more space.

"Well, I had better offers," she breathed.

"I don't believe you." He nipped at her shoulder and splayed his hand across her back possessively. Aidan did *not* share.

She bit back a smile, feeling rather dangerous. "There was that one human, Lord—"

A growl cut her off, his lips skimming the outer edge of her ear. "If I hear another man's name on your lips while my hands are on your body, it won't be pretty, sweetheart."

Kai shivered and pulled away an inch so she could see the outline of his face in the shadows and steam. Her playfulness melted away, replaced by a swelling in her chest that flooded her body, consuming her. His strength, his passion, his tender care...it burned through her, lighting her up from within.

"It's only ever been you. Always," she whispered, tracing his lips with her thumb, the black scruff at his chin tickling her hand.

He kissed her thumb. "To the edge of the world."

Kai shifted her hand to the back of his head and dragged his mouth to hers. His lips were soft and sweet against hers, taking their time, relishing in the thought of forever.

A forever they no longer had. A forever that Isla's mission from the gods might force them into once more.

The thought made her heart sink and her limbs stiffen, and she pulled away from Aidan.

"What's wrong?" he asked, confusion in his eyes.

"I'm sorry, I just...I keep thinking about what Isla told us. How there's a chance we might have to take our powers back in order to fix everything." She laid her head against his chest, voicing the fear that had been consuming her for the last twenty-four hours. "What if we have to give this up?"

"I'm not going to let that happen, Kai. We'll help Isla get the dagger, but they can't make us take our magic back. We'll find another way. Maybe Rynn and Jade will be enough, or maybe that's not even what the gods meant. No matter what happens, we're in this together, alright?" He kissed the top of her head, fierce protectiveness strengthening his words. "We've fought for many things in our lifetime, always so caught up in what we thought we deserved or what victory looked like.

"It took far too long for me to realize that *this* is it. This is what we should've been fighting for all along, and I promise you, sweetheart, I will not let it slip away from us. Not this time."

Kai could only nod as his arms closed around her. They could do this. They could help their friends, and still keep this beautiful future, the only thing she'd ever desired.

Not even the gods could take it away from them.

CHAPTER TWENTY-EIGHT

Isla

Isla soaked in the hot bath, letting the events from the day flow through her mind like the rivulets of warm water running along her skin. There were so many revelations and so much information all packed into one afternoon, and she desperately needed time to decompress. The elements seemed to respond to the tension in her body; they coiled tightly inside of her, nervous energy making them quiver and jump at the slightest reaction.

She tried to quiet her thoughts, but something kept pushing itself to the surface. Right before she and Bri walked up to dinner, Nor and Ezeretta had claimed to have heard about their "eventful day." How much did they know? Had they also seen Akir and his secret hideaway? Isla didn't know what she would do if his entire life's work, all the hope of those rebels, was ruined because he'd helped *her*. The Chamber members weren't idiots; they knew she was a Vasileia, knew it was probably no coincidence she was there. And she wouldn't be surprised if they knew she possessed magic. She hadn't exactly been the most inconspicuous. But she couldn't let them find out about the resistance.

The longer she lay in the now lukewarm tub, more questions sprang to her mind. Such as, why had the Chamber invited the former elementals to begin with? They held no significance to any of the kingdom's monarchies; to the world, they were simply normal, unknown humans with regular lives. And yet, the Chamber *had* to know who they were. Akir had. They'd practically been gods to these people. But why bring them here and then treat them like nobodies? Did they want to spy on them? To *hurt* them?

Isla rubbed at her temples. She was so sick of trying to get one step ahead of unknown foes. It was like four months ago all over again. Her anxiety always got worse when she spent this much time in her thoughts, worry after worry circling her mind until they spiraled out of control and she imagined every person was a threat, every loved one in danger. It was exhausting.

Suddenly, a knock sounded on her door.

"Just a minute!" she called, standing and stepping out of the tub. Grabbing a towel from the nearby basket, she quickly dried and slipped into a gray robe.

"Come in," she said, patting her hair with the towel. To her surprise, it wasn't the bedroom door that opened, but the adjoining one with Sebastian's room.

"I hope you don't mind, I wanted to—" He paused when he saw her. "I can come back later, if you are..." His gaze lingered where her robe started to part at her chest, then turned away.

"Are you going to finish either of those sentences, Your Majesty?" she teased, setting her towel aside and tightening the robe.

He huffed a laugh as he sauntered to her corner chair and sank into it, propping one leg atop the other. "It's been a long day, love."

"Don't I know it." Isla grabbed a loose pair of pants and a tunic and made her way back into the bathing chamber, slipping out of her robe behind the door. She heard glass clinking as she finished changing and asked, "How were your meetings today?"

"Negotiations are going as well as you'd expect. Iona wants more than they're willing to give, and everyone here has skeletons in their closets they're trying to sweep under the rug."

She walked back into the bedroom and sprawled across the mountain of pillows on her bed. "And what about you?"

He flashed her a devious smile. "Oh, you know me. I'm pulling them out, bone by bone. If these monarchs want to keep pretending we live in a perfectly balanced world, then I'm more than happy to show them how wrong they are."

Isla snorted. "I'm sure they loved you."

"Something like that," he murmured, running a finger along his lips. "I think Mariana and the Chamber know more about us than they're letting on."

Straightening, Isla crossed her arms. "What makes you say that?"

Sebastian tossed back the rest of his drink in one swallow, a haunted look appearing in his eyes, replacing the mask of confident indifference he so often tried to hide behind. "Just something she said to me earlier. But I'm probably reading too much into it. Enough about me—what happened to *you* today? Everyone has been so...annoyingly clandestine."

"I don't think you'll believe me when I tell you," Isla said, throwing her head back to look at the ceiling.

"After everything we've been through?"

"Fine." She met his eyes and bit her lip. "I don't think you'll *like* it, though."

"Ah, now we're getting somewhere."

Isla propped herself up. "Alright, well, we wandered through the towns and Jade wanted to show us a beautiful cliffside spot overlooking the ocean. It really was amazing—I wish we could've stayed longer. But then...a little boy fell from the cliffs into the water. Everyone was terrified, his mother was a wreck, and nobody knew what to do."

"So, naturally, you had to save him."

Isla shot Sebastian a flustered look. "Well...yes, of course. What was I going to do, let him drown? I dove in after him and brought him back up the cliffs. But I wasn't careful, and—" She took a breath, watching as Sebastian's features tightened. "The people saw me use my powers. They know what I am—or at

least, they know I'm not like *them*. They called me a monster and tried to..."
Shaking her head, she changed the train of thought. "I just wanted to help."

"What did they try to do?" Sebastian asked, a hard edge to his voice.

The memory of strange hands pulling at her, of her skin burning theirs, erupted in her mind. "Some of them wanted to kill me. To toss me back over the cliff. Others wanted to turn me in...probably to the Chamber. I think they know about me, Sebastian. Even if they didn't suspect it before, I'm sure some loyal citizen who saw me today went running to tell them everything. Akir wants me to hide, but I don't know if—"

Sebastian put a hand up, his forehead creased in confusion. "I'm sorry, *Akir*? What was he doing there?"

"We sort of ran into him today while trying to get away from the crowds. That's where it gets interesting."

He let out a humorless laugh. "Yes, because this was all so very dull."

Isla proceeded to tell him about the underground bunker and the resistance. Working her way from the beginning, she explained how Akir was a very distant relative, and how some of their ancestors stayed behind on Iona while others ventured out. She told Sebastian how the people of Iona were a bit lost after the war and the fall of the Vasileia line, and how the Chamber was eventually formed with good intentions that had soured over the passage of time.

He wasn't surprised by the fact that the people were itching to rise up against the Chamber. Isla relayed, as best she could, how, for centuries, the Chamber members had been brainwashing the kingdom into believing those who bore magic were evil and the source of all their problems. How they had so thoroughly convinced generation after generation that any negative act against them must be supernatural, and that it was acceptable to throw their own neighbors in the line of fire if they suspected them of this "witchcraft."

It chilled Isla to her bones. How many had died because of this fear? Because a group of powerful men and women had decided this was how they wanted to control their nation and keep themselves blameless? They had sacrificed the safety of their citizens for their own security and made the people so distrusting of one another that they would offer each other up to appease some sort of sick sense of loyalty.

It had to stop. But Isla had no idea how.

Sebastian stopped his pacing and sat on the foot of Isla's bed, turning to face her. "Simply another boring day on the island, I see. Threats against me, people attempting to kill you"—he tipped his glass toward her—"general insurrection and mutiny. We make quite the pair."

Narrowing her eyes, Isla said, "Threats? You failed to mention that part."

"Did I? Must have slipped my mind."

"Hmm." Isla got onto her knees and shifted across the soft comforter, plucked the glass from his hand, and held it above her head. "Now it's your turn. What really happened today?"

He glanced between the glass and her eyes, finally focusing on her and leaning backward to rest on his elbows. Isla tried not to take in how casual he looked on her bed, how the position made his white shirt strain against his chest, the veins in his forearms prominent beneath his rolled-up sleeves.

"Iona is asking for far more resources than I'd expected," he began, making her eyes snap back to his face. "It's a bold move, and a wise one, I suppose—ask for more than you need in hopes that, after negotiations, you are left with something, at least. But I'm not so easily swayed. I think the Chamber realized they weren't going to get much out of Karstos with the way things are going. And so, Mariana cornered me as we were breaking for lunch." He suddenly looked hesitant. Running his fingers through his hair, he continued. "What she said makes me believe she knows about how I wasn't fully in control over these last two years. Maybe even about Celesine, as wild as that sounds."

Hearing her name always sent a spike of anger through Isla. "What did she threaten you with?"

He looked up to the ceiling and closed his eyes. "Isla, I—I did something during my time under Celesine's influence. Something no one else knows about. And I can't take it back."

Pausing, his jaw tightened as his fingers began tapping on her comforter. She'd never seen him look so...fragile. Undone. Was he scared of what she might think of him? *He* wasn't to blame for his crimes of the past two years. She knew how much he cared for his kingdom and his people...but she also knew he hadn't forgiven himself, and probably never would.

His guilt and self-doubt crushed her. He wasn't ever hesitant to assure her of *her* worth and *her* healing, but he so rarely spoke of how he was dealing with his own past. Beneath the confident front he worked so hard to keep, Isla could see his wounds—the insecurities that ran deep, the constant need for validation, the desire to defeat the darkness still clinging to him like a shadow. Because she had the same scars.

They were simply two broken people, trying to sew together the pieces on a patchwork of their trauma.

Isla reached out her free hand and gently ran her fingers across his knuckles. He clenched at first, and then relaxed, finally opening his eyes.

"You don't have to hide from me," she said softly, recalling their conversation from the previous night where she had tried to do just that. "I'm not going to run away this time, I promise."

He turned to her, his eyes holding hers, the shimmer of humor she usually saw replaced by something else. Something raw, painful, and unsure. It was as if he was stripped bare before her, no longer a proud king but a shattered man, the past two years leaking from him like a cracked fountain.

"I don't want you to think less of me," he whispered.

Isla set his half-empty glass on her bedside table and took his hand again. "You once told me that none of what happened is my fault. Do you still believe that?" He lowered his eyes. "Then why can't you extend the same grace to yourself? You weren't in control of your actions, Sebastian. Yes, terrible things happened—but it wasn't *you*. The kingdoms may blame you, and I hate that you have to bear their distrust and clean up this mess. But you and I and the people who matter know the truth." When he still wouldn't look at her, she brought a hand to his chin and lifted until his gaze met hers. "Whatever it is that *she* made you do, it won't make me think any less of you. You're letting her win if you keep hiding."

He searched her eyes for a moment, and she saw when his resolve gave way. Nodding tightly, he took a breath, his hand still in hers.

"Toward the end of everything that happened last year, when Celesine could tell you were close to finding the dagger, I think she started to get worried. She became more erratic, more volatile. One day, she burst into my office with a contingency plan. I don't know if she anticipated her own failure or mine, but she obviously had a reason. She forced me to draft a declaration of succession and submit it to my council for approval—who, of course, all voted it into law, considering I manipulated each of them to accept."

"A successor? As in, if you die?"

He nodded. "To this day, I don't fully understand why she wanted to add this clause. It didn't make any sense to me, but I also wasn't in a position to do much thinking for myself. The only thing I can think of is that she was preparing for this to happen. Preparing for the fact that she may fail, and finding another way to get what she wanted."

Isla's heartbeat quickened. Celesine had always been many steps ahead. She thought they'd stopped her, but what if she was *still* ahead of them? Still out there, putting pieces into play?

His voice shook as he walked to her dresser and gripped the edges, his knuckles turning white. "The clause states that should I die or become unfit to rule, my entire kingdom falls into the hands of Ionan reign. Iona would have full control over the land and people. And because it was voted in by my council, I cannot redact it. Not without their full support, which I don't have."

A rushing sound began in Isla's ears. She blinked as she took in his words, his pained expression, his shallow breaths.

"*What?*" She pushed herself off the bed and started pacing. "Why would she do that? That doesn't make any sense. What does *she* get out of it?" Her thoughts turned bleaker by the second, but she shoved them away, continuing to vomit up useless questions. "Does Iona even know about this clause? Is she *working* with them? Gods, what if they're going to try and kill you to get your kingdom?"

"Isla," he said quietly, walking toward her and holding his hands up in warning.

Her elements rose beneath her skin, sensing her mounting distress. She didn't want him to say it, didn't want to acknowledge what his eyes were already telling her. It was *over*. They had won—whatever that meant for their broken, bloodied spirits. She was supposed to be done fighting.

Sebastian said her name again and reached for her elbow, his touch both grounding her and making her feel like the earth was about to swallow them whole.

"Yes, I think the Chamber is working with Celesine," he answered, his words wrapping around Isla like a noose. "But it's more than that. I—I'm afraid she might be *here*. On Iona."

CHAPTER TWENTY-NINE

Isla

I'm afraid she might be here.

It shouldn't have come as a shock. Rationally, it made perfect sense. Celesine had merely disappeared, exactly as Isla had—no body, no proof. It was painfully obvious. But Isla had forced herself into the delusion that they were safe, that Celesine couldn't harm them anymore. Even if she *was* alive, she had no power—did she? How could she, when Isla was now the Aether? If there was truly nothing to fear, why were her bones frozen, her breaths shallow, her muscles locked?

She had the power now. Nobody else. That was supposed to make her nightmares disappear, make the beasts with claws that once shredded her mind run away with their tails between their legs. She *hated* the weakness that came with fear. Hated the way her mind always shut down and burrowed into the darkest places. Hated the way it made her hide from life and hold herself back. When her mother and Waylan died, she hadn't been able to function. The idea of danger befalling her loved ones had crippled her to the point that she hadn't wanted her family to leave her sight. This same kind of fear took her mind captive and made her want to explode in a blast of pent-up emotion and anxiety.

And her elements could sense it, too. They reacted to her quicker than even her mind could catch up. At the mention of Celesine, they writhed within her, unsettled and temperamental. Flashes of cruel, violet eyes flew through Isla's mind; Arden's cold, lifeless fingers beneath her skin, the hard steel sliding through her chest. That all too familiar tension rose inside of her, the elements raging and pushing at her skin like they were begging to break free.

She had to get a hold of herself. If she didn't learn to control her fear, her anger, it would burn her alive.

I will not let this consume me, she thought. Her mother's soft voice filtered through her, words of comfort and pride taking shape against the shadows. *"The fiercest huntress in the land. Never let them stop you."*

Fear was a part of her. That wasn't something she could change. But so was ferocity. And it was a beautiful thing, how there could be power in both, if she only knew how to wield them.

Sebastian's hand came to her cheek, his warm breath blanketing her skin. "Breathe with me, love," he said, inhaling deeply. "In and out. Focus on my voice."

She did as he said, their chests rising and falling in tandem as she let his words soothe the edges of her fraying mind.

"Better?" he asked after a moment, and she nodded. He kissed her forehead before leaning away, and the tenderness of the action, the familiarity, made her breath catch.

"Why do you think Celesine might be here?" Isla asked quietly.

"When you used the dagger on the other elementals to take their power, they didn't die, so it's only natural that she didn't either. We just don't know where she went. But the Primevals told you the dagger is here, yes? Where else would she be, if not in the same place as the object she tore the world apart to find?"

Isla rubbed at her temple, taking in his relaxed demeanor, the way he appeared so put together. "How are you this calm about everything?"

His eyes fell away from hers and landed on the window of her bedroom, drinking in the moonlight. Slowly, he said, "I think I've always known she wasn't truly gone. There's been a weight, like a shadow, pressing in on me since that day. It feels as if I'll never be free of her." His gaze turned back to Isla. "I believed it was residual trauma, at first. Memories that plagued my dreams and were so vivid they left me unable to move or think. But maybe it was my subconscious telling me all along that I wasn't rid of her yet. That this nightmare wasn't finished.

"As I said, I don't think she was completely surprised by the turn of events on the beach. I think she planned for any scenario, and the fact that it's led us back *here*, to the lost kingdom I sold my soul and my people to, is not a coincidence."

"And you think she's working with the Chamber," Isla mused, trying to put the pieces together. "She could be the reason they suddenly want to be part of our world again, and are threatening you if you don't comply."

"I don't think it's merely *recent* events, Isla," he said. "You told me what Akir said of the history of this island. Of its hatred toward the elementals and those with magic. How for hundreds of years, they've been slowly poisoned by the leaders."

As he spoke, Isla sat back on her bed, running her finger along her lower lip in a daze. "You think none of it was the Chamber's idea. Celesine could have been pulling the strings this whole time—literally *hundreds* of years."

"It's what she does best," Sebastian said grimly.

Isla's head hurt. Not only had Celesine been biding her time for a millennium waiting to be able to use the Dagger of Volnus to capture the power of all the elements, but she'd been brainwashing an entire kingdom of people to fear the elementals. To what end, though?

Sinking back into her soft pillows with a groan, Isla said, "I just don't get what's in it for her. Why does she care if all these people hate magic?"

Sebastian sat and leaned back next to her, eyes on the ceiling. "If she truly has been working with the Chamber, maybe that's all part of some larger plan. Helping them build their kingdom while she held the power the whole time.

That's all it comes down to...that's all it ever comes down to with people like her. More power."

Isla turned to him and tucked her hands under her ear, pulling her knees so her body was curved toward the center of the bed. "What are we going to do?" she whispered.

He mirrored her, reaching out and gently brushing a strand of hair behind her ear. "We're going to find the dagger and put the elements back where they belong. And then Akir and his merry band of rebels will overthrow the Chamber and all will be right with the world."

Isla snorted. "You make it sound so easy."

"All in a day's work."

"And Celesine?" Isla swallowed. "What about her?"

A shadow passed over his features. "We'll find her and hand her over to the Primevals, I suppose."

The Primevals did nothing to stop the Aether the first time, and Isla doubted they would do much to punish her now. This was the creature who had ruined Sebastian's life, who had made him a prisoner in his own mind, who had upturned everything Isla had ever known and killed her brother. Her twin.

The elements churned and twisted inside of her, feeding off Isla's anger, but not overtaking her this time. They simply lifted their heads and smiled, caressing her thoughts of vengeance like vines wrapping around a tree.

"Or maybe," Isla said, dragging Sebastian's gaze to hers, "we show her what she's turned us into."

His eyes sparkled. "And what might that be?"

"Something to fear. She deserves to burn, and we deserve to light the match."

A slow smile unfurled on his lips. "Those teeth are as sharp as ever, beautiful."

She smiled back. He had no idea. But first, they had to find the dagger.

"I need to meet Akir tomorrow with the Vasileia book and see if the ones he has have any helpful information. And maybe he can tell us more about where the dagger might be. He thinks it's somewhere in the palace. I haven't sensed anything yet, but maybe...maybe there's some sort of block on it. I'm hoping now that I know it's here, my handy Vasileia blood will kick in and lead me to it."

"You make it sound so easy," he replied, mimicking her previous words.

She laughed. "I've done it once. I can do it again."

"I don't think there's much you can't do, love," he said, lifting his hand to run fingers down the side of her arm. Goosebumps erupted on her skin in their wake. She shivered involuntarily and let out a breath. She'd been scared the night before...scared of how strong his feelings were, and the effect he had on her. But the more time she spent with him, the more comfortable she grew. And she was surprised to find how well she knew him from only the quick encounters they'd had before—when he'd started to fight against Celesine's control, Isla had seen his true self. Their time together now was only helping her see him even better.

They laid in comfortable silence for several minutes, their breaths tangling in the flickering candlelight, his fingers on her arm lulling her closer to sleep.

"Sebastian?" she said with a yawn, her eyelids becoming heavy.

"Yes?"

"Will you stay with me tonight?"

Her eyes had already closed, but his lips gently brushed her forehead. "You never have to ask," he said, as she drifted off to sleep.

CHAPTER THIRTY

Isla

*L*ong nails dragged down the side of her face, cutting into her skin. She jerked awake, kicking back the twisted sheets and freeing her legs. She could have sworn someone had been standing over her bed, but there was no one there.

Looking to the right, she saw him—sound asleep, the burdens he bore in the day now gone under the glow of the moon and stars. She smiled, her fingers itching to run through his tousled blonde hair, but a curious sound coming from outside the open window stopped her. Turning, she saw the white curtains billowing in the night, a sudden windchill sending a shiver down her spine and rustling through her hair.

When had she opened the window?

Tick. Tick. Tick.

The mysterious noise drew her from the warmth of the bed. Slowly, she padded across the wood floor, her fingers finding the cold latch and pushing it closed. Then, silence.

Until...

Tick. Tick. Tick.

Forehead creasing, she let out a sigh. The sound now came from behind the door leading to his room. She tiptoed to the adjoining door, wrapping her hand around the handle and easing it open quietly.

She froze. This was not Sebastian's room.

Her bare feet sank into soft, white sand. Wind whistled faintly through nearby trees, a sweet grass and citrus scent wafting on the night air.

Tick. Tick. Tick.

The clouds overhead passed, allowing the moonlight to break through and illuminate the beach. Several yards away, by the familiar rocky outcrop, was a large, cloaked figure slumped to the ground.

Swallowing down the foreboding lump in her throat, she stepped toward the figure, granules of sand shifting beneath her feet. As she neared, the ticking sound grew louder. Clearer.

Tick. Tock. Tick. Tock.

She reached out a shaking hand to the hooded body, turning it onto its side. A silent scream formed on her lips. Staring back at her was a faceless head, save for two eyes of bright purple, with trails of blood leaking down ghostly cheeks.

Stumbling backward, she fell onto the cold sand. An eerie, high-pitched voice echoed inside her mind, the chimes of a clock ringing in the night.

"The end will come for all, my darling."

Isla woke to birds chirping outside the window and sunlight washing over her as she opened her eyes. There was a warmth at her back she wasn't used to—tender arms wrapped around her middle, hot breath against her neck, a strong body molded perfectly to hers.

Sebastian.

But even his heat couldn't shake the chill embedded deep in her bones.

Tick. Tock.

"Good morning," he said into her skin, the rumble of his voice momentarily distracting her from the memory of her nightmare.

"Good morning," she whispered back.

"Good morning," a third voice said, and Isla bolted upright, vines springing to life in her hands. She spotted Bri sitting casually on the dresser across the room, a wide smirk across her face.

"*Bri!* You almost gave me a heart attack!"

"Good thing you're probably immortal." Her best friend hopped off the dresser. "Sorry to interrupt, but I thought Isla would be—well, *alone.*" She winked at Sebastian, who leaned against the pillows like he wasn't remotely bothered by this encounter. "Annalise is about to have an aneurysm, by the way. She says you're late for your morning meetings."

Sebastian sighed. "I suppose they are rather important, unfortunately. Do you still plan to meet with Akir today?" he asked Isla, lifting the covers and rising from the bed.

She blinked, taking in the sight of his bare chest and arms, his toned stomach on display as he stretched and ran his fingers through his hair. Glancing at the dresser, she saw Bri staring slack jawed, and Isla cleared her throat loudly.

"Yes, hopefully," Isla said when Bri clamped her mouth shut with a snap. "Both about the dagger, and...well, I guess I just want to learn more about my ancestors, honestly. See what happened to the ones that stayed here after the war. I might even get to meet some of Akir's—*my* relatives." She was excited, but it was all so new. Jittery nerves crept in the more she thought about it.

Sebastian looked at her, seeming to see through her edgy behavior. "Don't be worried. They're going to adore you. And if they don't, you can always burn them. Or toss them in the ocean."

Isla choked on a laugh. "Because that's a great way to get an island full of people to stop hating me."

"Nobody could possibly hate you, Isla. They're only afraid of what they don't understand." He leaned down to kiss her cheek. "Will I see you later this evening?" he asked against the shell of her ear, his rough voice eliciting a shiver from her. Unsure what might come out of her mouth if she opened it, she simply nodded, and he flashed that cocky grin of his as he made his way to the door joining their rooms.

Panic flashed through her, the vision of what she'd seen beyond that door in her nightmare coming to the forefront of her mind. But when he opened it, all she saw was his normal bedroom. She shook off the eerie sensation.

"Good to see you as always, Bri," he said on his way out. Once the door clicked shut behind him, Bri rounded on her, jumping on the bed next to Isla.

"Okay, *what* just happened? Because that was hot."

Isla covered her face with her hands, letting out a loud groan. "Nothing happened."

"That didn't look like nothing."

"We just talked."

"That didn't look like talking, either."

"I swear! We talked about everything that happened yesterday, and then fell asleep." Isla pursed her lips before a smile could break across her face. "But the night *before...*"

Bri let out a piercing squeal. "I *knew* it!" Her short, black curls bounced against her forehead as she bobbed up and down on the bed.

Her friend's excitement was contagious. Isla giggled and swatted at Bri's hand. "We're not thirteen, Bri—it was only a kiss! Don't lose your mind."

"Yeah, a super hot kiss with a super hot *king* who used to be your enemy and now literally looks at you like you're a goddess he wants to worship on his knees. I couldn't write this stuff even if I tried."

Isla let out a breath with a loud *whoosh*. "He *is* pretty hot, isn't he?" she finally said, a smile creeping onto her face as Bri burst out laughing.

"Tell me *everything.*"

So Isla did. She told Bri about the two times she appeared to Sebastian while she was the Aether, and what happened on their first night in the palace, how they agreed to "start over" and try to get to know each other better. Isla's body began to relax as she spoke. She realized the two of them hadn't had much time alone together since they arrived on the island, and it felt like old times, just her and Bri, cuddled up around a fire with a cup of hot chocolate or apple cider. She missed it all—her old life, her best friend, her father, the friends she hadn't seen in months.

But more than that, she desperately missed her brother.

It would sometimes hit her in a wave of grief, rolling through and snuffing any spark of joy. When Arden had walked in on her and Bri talking about her first love, Waylan, all those years ago, he hadn't stopped teasing her for a month. His fifteen-year-old self chased her around the house making kissing noises until she smacked him across the face. She could almost picture him in the palace bedchamber now, his freckled face poking out the door behind Bri, wagging his eyebrows as Isla recounted her time with Sebastian.

Whenever she snuck a glance, he was gone, faded back into her memory like fog receding from the shoreline.

"What does his note say?" Bri suddenly asked when Isla paused, shimmying her shoulders.

Isla's brow furrowed. "What note?"

Pointing over to the little table by the door, Bri got up and took a folded piece of paper from beside the liquor bottles. "This note. I assume Sebastian left it for you?"

Isla hadn't seen that paper before. Standing and taking it from Bri's outstretched fingers, she unfolded it, and her eyes widened.

She handed it over to Bri. "This isn't from Sebastian."

Lion gargoyle, north gardens, 9 o'clock. Bring the book. The fewer faces, the better.

- A

"Very dramatic. I like his style." Bri gave it back to Isla. "I'm guessing that's from Akir?"

"I mean, I *think* so, but how did he get it in here? What if it's a trap?" Isla's mind whirled with possible scenarios. When did someone even have time to leave a note without her noticing? Those angry townspeople or the Chamber themselves could be trying to lure her out. She found it hard to trust anyone in this palace. In this *kingdom*.

Bri scoffed. "Then you can choke them with your vines or something. We'll be fine. Come on, it's almost nine. We don't have long to get ready!"

"Gods, why is everyone so violent this morning?" Isla said with an exasperated laugh as she followed Bri's instructions and got dressed. Truthfully, she was grateful to have a purpose; the thrill of secrecy and action had shoved thoughts of her nightmare and her brother from her mind.

After grabbing the Vasileia book from Bri's room, they told the others where they were headed and that Akir said to not bring many people. There was mild protesting from Jade, but Aidan and Kai seemed relieved to stay behind, and Rynn was nowhere to be found.

As they exited the common room, Bri mumbled to Isla, "Let's not get thrown off a cliff or chased by a mob today, okay?"

Isla laughed. "No promises, Bri."

Akir was waiting for them on a stone bench by the lion gargoyle, reading a news pamphlet with his legs crossed, a burgundy robe falling to his ankles. His light auburn beard tickled the paper as he glanced up.

"I see you received my message," he said politely as he folded his pamphlet and tucked it beneath his arm.

Glancing around to make sure no one could hear them, Isla asked, "How did you get it in my room?"

"We have members everywhere, cousin," he responded quietly, a twinkle in his green eyes. "A handful of the staff at Palace Noctem have found their way to our numbers. It is most convenient when needing to communicate discreetly." Standing, he said, "Come, we have much to discuss."

Akir nodded to his right and a moment later, a bird call echoed through the trees of the garden. He reached up and pulled at one of the stone lion's bared teeth. Isla heard a groan as the entire statue shifted to the side before her very eyes, revealing a small hole with a ladder, exactly like the one they'd escaped into in the forest.

"Quickly, quickly," he said, ushering her and Bri down. When all three of them were below the surface, he let out another bird call, then pushed against a beam on the wall. Slowly, the stone moved back into place, blotting out the sunlight and leaving them in the shadows of the tunnel.

Bri and Isla exchanged a glance in the flickering firelight from the torches lining the walls. "This feels ten times spookier now," Bri whispered.

Akir chuckled as he led them down the narrow dirt path. "We've had to place some tricks up our sleeves in order to stay hidden this long. Did you bring our ancestor's book?" he asked Isla, who held the delicate leather tome up in response. "Excellent. I've been scouring through mine as well, and I believe I have found some interesting entries by the late Satori."

The three of them made their way through the tunnel until they came to the familiar large, open cavern, with a network of paths leading to and from it. She'd learned yesterday that this was the base, the area where all paths connected and where most of the resistance leaders met and kept their projects and information. Like the day before, a handful of people milled about, either talking to one another in hushed tones or reviewing pieces of parchment.

Pallets were still layered across the ground with rolled up blankets and dented pillows—signs of more people having slept down there.

"What's all of this for?" she asked, gesturing to the sleeping arrangements.

"It's not uncommon for people here to be displaced from their homes. Over the past few years, we opened this underground route as an escape for those in need of refuge. The Byrnes, for instance," he said, nodding to what Isla assumed was a husband and wife and their small child resting in the corner, "were recently chased from their land by neighbors who accused them of using magic to set fire to their stables. And Donovan here has a bounty on his head for organizing an anti-Chamber rally in north Farrow." Akir put his hand on the shoulders of a young man as he passed by, who waved and smiled proudly before returning to his task.

"He's a rather...spirited boy," Akir said, quietly but fondly, while they proceeded to one of the adjacent chambers. "Does not quite understand the notion of keeping a low profile."

"So are these people forced to hide here indefinitely?" Bri asked.

"Many of them choose to return to their lives after they prove their innocence in whatever outlandish tale had been spun about them. But yes, some make the decision to stay in the relative safety of these walls. A few even join the cause, pledging their lives to bring down the Chamber. That's not a requirement, of course—we will provide a haven to any who need it, whether or not they wish to join our ranks."

"How can you be sure they won't run off and tell the Chamber about you the first chance they get?" Isla questioned.

"If these people have found their way to us, it is likely they have more of a reason to despise the Chamber than they do to aid it," Akir responded as he pulled a book off an old wooden shelf. "We have considered the risks, and are ultimately willing to take them if someone comes to us in need."

"Do you get a lot of people down here looking for help?"

He nodded gravely. "More and more every month. And fewer are able to return to the surface safely. I fear we will reach our limits soon, both in space and resources. These tunnels are filling up quickly, and it takes a large amount of work, food, and water to sustain this much life down here. But," he said, his countenance suddenly lifting, "that's not a problem for you nor for today. Here is Satori's record book, as promised."

Isla gingerly took the bound book from him after placing her own on the nearby table. This one was much smaller and made of cracked red leather instead of the smooth, brown covering on hers. A couple of bird feathers were scattered throughout the book and peeked out from the top. The pages fluttered violently as she opened it, like they might fall out with even the slightest breath. She began skimming through the entries, Bri reading over her shoulder excitedly. Her best friend looked like a child in a candy shop.

Akir's ancestor—which was hers too, she realized—was much more...blunt than the various writers of her Vasileia book. Very to the point, which Isla appreciated. Instead of reading through pages and pages of flowery royal decrees or deeply personal diary entries, she was presented with quick facts and the occasional candid opinion.

For example, one page had a handwritten copy of an announcement made by King Medes, Satori's brother, which detailed the reasons for an increase in taxes among the kingdom. The official statement said it was because the price of goods imported from the other three nations had increased, but in the margins, Satori had written: *"False. It was to fund the loyalist army at the start of the civil war."*

Another entry held a lengthy list of people who had been charged with treason and executed for working with the rebels. And still another was full of random names, each with attributes and deeds next to them, some scribbled out and rewritten. None of it made much sense, and Isla didn't think it was relevant to her cause. After a few more minutes in silence while they each scanned the contents of the books, Isla came across one of the bird feathers stuck between two pages.

"What's this for?"

"I marked a few sections I believed made mention of your dagger," Akir responded, enraptured in the Vasileia book Isla had given him.

Anticipation rising, she read each word carefully, hoping to find some sign or clue of where it had been kept before it was lost in the shipwreck, thinking perhaps it had magically found its way back to its original home in the palace. But the first feathered page yielded no results. It was barely a paragraph describing what Satori had heard rumors the dagger looked like—nothing they didn't already know.

The second page with a feather had slightly more information, but still nothing new. A diary entry on how one of Satori's ancestors struggled to sleep at night because they felt like they were being called to the dagger, somewhere in the palace. She couldn't help but think again how strange it was that she hadn't felt the dagger calling to *her* yet. If it truly was in the palace, wouldn't she know? Unless it was blocked somehow.

The third marked page wasn't even about the dagger. It told of one of the king's guards that had been found dead near some hot spring beneath the tunnels.

When she got to the fourth, a surge of excitement went through her. This entry included a detailed, hand drawn map of the palace. But as she read, her shoulders slumped. Satori had cataloged each hidden entrance in the palace and what secrets lay beyond the doors, but he hadn't found the dagger.

"Hey, don't be too disappointed," Bri said, bumping her shoulder. "This is still good information to have. Let me see if I can copy that map."

Isla handed her the journal when an unfamiliar voice sounded behind her.

"I was wondering how long my brother was going to keep you hidden from me."

Isla whirled to find an elderly woman with light green eyes behind narrow spectacles, silver hair pulled into a bun, and a welcoming smile on her thin lips. Instantly, she knew this must be Akir's sister, Eliza.

Much to Isla's surprise, the woman strode across the room and wrapped her frail arms around Isla's body, holding her in a shockingly strong grip. "I've been looking forward to meeting you, Isla."

Without warning, tears clogged Isla's eyes and words turned to ash in her mouth. She couldn't remember the last time she'd been hugged like this—so genuinely, so maternally. Eliza smelled like soap mixed with a bit of sweetness and sawdust, like the Belthare shop back in Lockhurt, and she couldn't help but think of her mother. Isla blinked rapidly, forcing back tears.

"It's good to meet you, too," Isla choked out as Eliza released her.

Still in his chair, Akir chuckled. "I apologize for my sister. She can come on a bit strong."

"No, no, I didn't mind. It's fine," Isla said, rubbing her palms nervously against the sides of her legs.

"Akir has told me so much about you. And this is your friend, Brielle?" Eliza turned to Bri with a smile, enveloping her in a hug, too. "We didn't get the chance to meet when you were here last. I'm so glad you stayed safe, dear."

I like her, Bri mouthed to Isla before Eliza let her go and backed away. She had to admit, she liked the older woman very much as well.

"So, what has my little brother been boring you with today?" Eliza asked, clapping her hands together.

"He's not boring us at all," Isla said. "Actually, I think this is so fascinating, everything you're doing for the people here and the information you've collected. We're just looking for something specific, and I don't think we've found it yet."

Eliza hummed, but before she could respond, a short, stocky man in overalls and a cap scrambled into the room, his breaths uneven and frantic.

"Mr. Akir!" he called, and Akir strode forward, a look of concern on his face.

"What is it, Clyde?"

"News from—from the palace," Clyde panted. "There's been an—attack."

Panic seized Isla, her elements responding in kind, fluttering and pushing at her skin. "Who was it? Who's hurt?" she asked quickly.

Clyde looked at her and back at Akir, and Isla's stomach plummeted with his next words. "I don't know. All I know is they found him in the Karstos wing."

CHAPTER THIRTY-ONE

Isla

T here was so much blood.

Annalise had found him in his chambers. During their break for lunch, the advisor had still been frustrated over the missing guard from Karstos and had finally gone to seek him out. Word traveled quickly among the servants, and Akir's messenger delivered the news fast enough for Isla to get back to their wing within an hour of Annalise finding the injured guard, Kingsley.

Isla knelt before him, watching his chest struggle to rise as she clutched his hand. A healer had been summoned shortly after he was found, and when Isla and Bri arrived, they had already removed the knife he'd been stabbed with and were trying to staunch the wound. But the moment Isla saw the blood pooling beneath Kingsley, tasted the copper in the air, heard his unsteady heartbeat growing fainter by the second...she knew there was nothing the healer could do.

Isla didn't even *know* this man, had never spoken a single word to him, but watching his life seep from him, his skin grow paler with each passing second, squeezed something inside of her. It was like she could feel his spirit within her grasp, each of his slow, labored breaths tearing at her.

Death was coming for him.

After sending his remaining guards to search the wing for signs of an intruder, Sebastian knelt across from her and Kingsley.

"Isla," he said softly, "is there anything you can do to help him?"

She shook her head, her fingers growing numb from holding onto Kingsley's so tight. He moaned around shortened breaths, his body jerking as he fought the pain. "It's too late."

Jade came into her line of sight, kneeling in the bloody pool beside Sebastian. Kingsley's eyes were clamped shut, and his mouth was contorted in a grimace, lips parting every few seconds to let out a grunt.

"You may not be able to save him, but you *can* take away his pain," Jade said.

Isla glanced up at her. "What do you mean?"

Jade looked to make sure the healer was out of earshot and responded. "Aidan's mind ability—you can get inside his head and make his pain go away. Or at least, make him believe it's gone. Replace it with something else."

Understanding clicked into place. Isla had never used this particular power before, but the moment she focused on what she desired, it sprang to life in her mind. Heat pulsed through her body and down her arms, into her fingertips until it connected with Kingsley's hand. She funneled sensations of peace and comfort into the connection, her own happiest memories coming to mind. Soft grass brushing her arms in an open field, warm flames filling a hearth, the press of a smile against her skin and hands enclosed around hers.

Kingsley's features began to loosen, his face no longer screwed tight in pain. His eyes fluttered open and met Isla's. He took a breath and coughed, a thin trail of blood leaking from the corner of his mouth, but his gaze remained calm. Serene.

"Thank you," he whispered with a cracked voice, and as the light left his hazel eyes, something clenched inside of Isla, like a fist had grasped a bit of her spirit and yanked it away. Tears ran down her cheeks and onto their clasped hands, flowing over the drying blood.

"He's gone," she whispered, extricating her fingers from his and sitting back on her heels. Exhaustion swept over her.

"You did well, Isla," Jade murmured. "He had comfort in his last moments. That's all anyone can ask for."

"He probably would've asked to not be dead," Isla said as she got to her feet, wiping the blood on her black dress. She wanted to get away from the stench of death, then bathe and fall into a deep sleep.

But she could not rest yet. Not when they had a murderer on the loose.

"What is the meaning of this?" Mariana de Faye's shrill voice rang out as she barged through the doorway, startling those standing at the entrance. The Chamber member's eyes darted across the scene.

"A question we would like to know the answer to, as well," Sebastian said, rising from his spot on the ground. His tone was icy, anger lacing his words. "We found my guard stabbed and left for dead in his own bedchamber. Tell me, Mariana, how does this display fit into your idea of camaraderie and peace?"

Her eyes glinted like steel. "If you are implying that Iona had anything to do with this, Your Maj—"

"Oh, do not misunderstand. I am not *implying* anything." Sebastian crossed to Mariana, all semblance of the man Isla had come to know gone. "A member of *my* royal guard, one of *my* people, has been brutally attacked and killed in your palace. We are here under the guise of political harmony and freedom, yes?" He cocked his head like a snake ready to strike. "I expect answers."

Mariana raised her chin. "Funny that you show such righteous indignation on behalf of your people now," she started, so quiet Isla could barely hear, "yet you let them die in your streets mere months ago."

The brief clenching of his hand was the only sign Sebastian had registered her words, but Isla's blood heated. Her elements raised their heads and sniffed, sensing blood in the water.

Sebastian took another step toward Mariana, speaking so low that Isla had to call on the wind to hear him. "Find out who did this, de Faye, or I will give your people the dark king you so wish to see."

Isla watched as Sebastian brushed by the Chamber member and stalked toward the door. Mariana quickly shook off his threat, cold determination lining her eyes. The healer and a handful of helpers rushed inside and began to move the body, and the rest of Isla's friends filed out one by one.

"Let our guests know that in light of recent events, the feast tonight is canceled, and dinner shall be delivered to each wing," Mariana barked at one of the servants, who nodded and scurried off.

As Isla made to exit the room, Mariana snuck an arm out and clawed at her wrist. Before she could jerk away, the woman whispered, "Your king should be careful with his threats." Brown eyes bore into hers. "We both know he will not be able to uphold them for long."

Even after scrubbing the blood from her skin, Kingsley's death lingered over Isla like a dark cloud. It's not as if she hadn't been around death before, but it was different now. Ever since she carried the spirit element, she had this sixth sense of...life. And death, she supposed. Watching him fade into nothing, into a cold, lifeless shell, had deeply unsettled her.

Although she didn't want to, she briefly wondered if that was how Celesine felt, except magnified by thousands of years. She couldn't imagine the toll it would take on one's mind.

Gods, she *hated* it when she empathized with that monster.

Isla had so many questions. She was still trying to process what had happened on the cliffs the previous day and the knowledge of Akir and his resistance, and now this? Someone had murdered Sebastian's guard, right in the middle of the festival. Was it a direct threat to Sebastian? To all of the kingdoms? If so, who was behind it?

Her first inclination was that it was the Chamber's doing. No matter what pretty words they said, Isla didn't trust them, especially after learning of their history and how Sebastian had been manipulated into giving his kingdom over to Iona. They had the perfect motivation to want him gone.

It was all becoming too much—who to trust, which conflict to focus on, who was going to be hurt next. Isla rested her forehead against the cool tile of the bathroom counter, the tightness in her chest growing and growing until it felt like she couldn't breathe. Her vision blackened at the edges. She slammed her eyes shut and tried to recall Sebastian's soothing voice from the night before. *Breathe with me, love.*

She didn't want to think about this tonight. She didn't want to let her anxiety consume her again. Mostly, she didn't want to be alone.

Straightening, she quickly brushed through her hair and threw on a pair of leggings and a sweater. She made her way to the door between her and Sebastian, and didn't hesitate before knocking.

He opened it a few moments later, a towel in hand and beads of water dripping from his blonde hair, his bare chest still damp from bathing. "Is something wrong?" he asked by way of greeting, his eyes taking in her tight features and roving over the room behind her for signs of harm.

"No, I'm fine," she said. "Just...wanted to see you. To check on you."

"Ah, well, as you can see," he said, brandishing an arm down his body, "I'm perfectly fine." He gave her a bland smile, one that didn't reach his blue eyes.

"You know what I mean." Isla leaned against the doorframe. "How's Annalise doing?"

"She's...well, she's Anna. The strongest, most stubborn woman I know. She says she's alright, but I know she feels guilty." He ushered her inside and motioned to his liquor cart, silently asking if she wanted a drink. She shook her head. "After spending yesterday and today complaining about him not showing up for his shifts, then assuming the worst of his character, only to find him bleeding out on his floor...she's not one to be kind to herself when she feels she is to blame."

Isla could relate. "Do we know where he was all this time, though? Maybe he'd been held against his will and that's why he disappeared for so long."

With a shrug, Sebastian said, "I suppose we'll never know. Although I do suspect he'd been with someone the night before, as Frederick claimed. We'll need to have the staff questioned. Perhaps someone saw something suspicious."

Isla nodded, and they sat in heavy silence while he grabbed a shirt from his bed, pulled it over his head, and poured himself a drink.

"Did you know him well?" she asked after a moment.

"Not as well as Anna and Frederick did. He was a fairly new addition to my royal guard, inducted only a year ago." He didn't need to explain to Isla what that meant. Anyone who came into his life within the last two years was practically a stranger to him.

"Why would someone want to kill him?"

"To send a message." Sebastian waved his short glass of amber liquid in the air. "These people are all the same. If you won't give them what they want, they do whatever they can to force it from you. It's a constant battle of who holds the power. You know what they stand to gain if I'm no longer fit to rule or out of the picture completely."

"Then why don't they simply come after *you*?"

"And have a dead royal on their hands, in their own palace, in the infancy of their rise to power?" He snorted. "They'd have a mutiny. Potentially a war. That's not something a kingdom like Iona can sustain right now. No, they won't try to assassinate me. Not yet, anyway."

Isla sucked in a breath. This was exactly the kind of conversation she wanted to avoid; she didn't want to think about someone hurting those close to her, or about finding Sebastian's body next. The thought made her shudder.

"I wish we could get away from all of this. Even for a night." She sighed and sat on the edge of his bed, resting her head against the bedpost. An idea struck her, something to distract her from the chaos. "There's one thing I find very unfair about all of this," she said.

"Just one? I think we need to work on your idea of fairness."

Isla chuckled and was surprised to find it was genuine. "You know *so much* about me and my life," she said the words mockingly, calling on their conversation from two nights before, "and I know next to nothing about yours. We said we wanted to start over, but you're already way ahead of me. I need to catch up."

When he didn't respond immediately, Isla glanced at him. His gaze was fixed on her, full of more emotion than she would've expected from her simple request. "Sebastian?"

He blinked and cleared his throat. "Not many people care to know about my life beyond my title and what I can give them."

Her heart constricted. "Then you need to find better people," she said, moving from the bed and reaching for his hand.

"What do you want to know, love?" he asked quietly.

Threading their fingers together, Isla smiled. "Everything."

To her surprise, Sebastian released her hand, set down his drink, and grabbed a thick blanket from the foot of his bed. When he looked back at her, she was relieved to find the familiar light back in his eyes.

He winked and said, "Come with me."

CHAPTER THIRTY-TWO

Sebastian

"How do you know about this place?" Isla asked, gazing up at the stars and twirling with that wide-eyed, awestruck wonder he loved so much.

"I spotted it on a map of the palace during our meetings today, then inquired with one of the guards as to how to get up here. They're a duplicitous lot, but I have to admit," Sebastian said, glancing at the greenery strung along the wooden canopy, "these Ionans have style."

The rooftop garden of Palace Noctem was everything he'd hoped it would be. A rickety staircase high in the northwestern corner of the palace led to a beautiful, cozy terrace filled with greenery climbing a wooden canopy, rows of blooming flowers, and multi-colored rugs lining the paved pathway. The canopy opened in the center to reveal the starry expanse of the heavens above them. Sebastian closed his eyes and reveled in the fresh night air, taking his first full breath since he arrived on the island.

"This is amazing." He opened his eyes to find her beaming at him under the starlight, and his chest felt so tight he thought it might burst. She looked lighter than she had in months, since long before elementals and mystical daggers and dark gods. He wished he could pluck the stars from the sky and settle them in the palm of her hand, if only to see that smile every day of his life.

He unfolded the blanket and spread it on the ground. "There's just something about the night. It makes our problems seem so much smaller." He sat down and motioned for her to follow, but she merely gave him a funny look.

"Are you saying that because you know that's what I'd want to hear? Because you know I'm the same way?"

Sebastian chuckled and pulled her to his side on the blanket. "If I thought a line like that would work on you, I would try many more of them." He leaned over and kissed her shoulder before sitting back on his elbows. "No, I think it's a passion my mother passed on to me. This was always 'our time'—she and my father would be in some meeting or another all day and then hosting in the evenings, so she would often come grab me far past my bedtime and bring me to the gardens along the estate. We would sit and talk for as long as I could keep my eyes open." A bubble of laughter escaped him as he remembered those nights. "She learned fairly quickly that I was an open book when tired enough. She exploited my exhaustion and fondness for sugar. I can't tell you how many times I confessed to the appalling things I'd done that week after she gave me a block of chocolate. I was a menace, honestly."

Isla laughed as she laid down, her arms behind her head, listening intently.

"I told her everything under those stars. My first love, my silly pranks with the boys, my first heartbreak. My loneliness. My fears of one day ruling a kingdom." He paused, an unexpected rush of emotion sweeping over him. "She was my everything."

"Was?" Isla asked softly, and he felt a light touch along his knuckles.

"She's still alive, if that's what you're wondering. In my palace, in fact. But she hasn't been herself for some time now." Sebastian swallowed thickly. "Several years before my father passed, her health and memory began to decline. She would forget things here and there—names of advisors, dates, and the like. Soon, she forgot my birthday and what year it was, and didn't recognize her closest friends of twenty years. My father's council advised him to keep her out of the public eye for fear of rumors starting. After a couple years, she'd lost many functioning abilities, and the healers wished to keep her confined to her quarters of the palace for her safety.

"Of course, that's when my father took a turn for the worse." Isla tightened her grip on his hand. "He had a series of heart attacks, each one more severe than the last, until—" He stopped and waved his hand in the air. "I don't know why I'm telling you this, of course you know—everybody in the realm knows how the great King Ryder Avax died. I suppose not many know what he left behind."

"So your mother is still living with you?" Isla asked.

He nodded. "I visit her as often as I can. She's in the best care I could find, with everything she needs to live the rest of her life comfortably. It's just..." He trailed off, scrubbing at his face in exasperation. He never spoke of her. Carrying the weight of his emotions was one thing, but sharing them with another? Every part of him screamed to retreat back to his safe shell of humor and wit, to hide behind words others wanted to hear. He glanced at Isla, seeking her strength, her comfort. She tilted her head to the side, waiting for him with a patience and tenderness that reminded him of his mother.

"It's breaking me. And I don't know what more I can do," he finally said. "She doesn't even *remember* me. It's as if I'm a ghost to her. A stranger. I can't bear walking into that room each time, knowing it won't make a difference. Knowing my own mother has no idea who I am, no idea what our life together was like. All I can do is watch her waste away." He leaned forward and ran his fingers through his hair in frustration, talking more to himself now than to Isla. "I hate myself for putting distance between us, but I don't know how much longer I can endure it. She's right there, *right* in front of me, and I—I miss her so much."

Isla moved until she was on her knees beside him, one hand on his shoulder. "I won't act like I know what that feels like or try to tell you things will get easier. I always hated it when people offered the same mindless phrases, over and over again." She rubbed her hand along the back of his arm. "I think it's cruel, how you've had to face the hardest years of your life alone. Or, mostly alone. I know your mother is still here, and of course, you have Annalise, but it's not the same...and I'm so sorry you've had to slowly lose the woman you knew. Gods, I can't imagine."

He closed his eyes. "I feel selfish, complaining about how difficult it is when my mother still lives, and you lost yours so recently."

Isla let out a huff, and her long hair brushed against his skin. When he opened his eyes, she was shaking her head. "Sebastian, that's the most ridiculous thing I've ever heard. You're allowed to have your own pain without comparing it to others. You've been through so much, things I can't begin to comprehend, with hardly anyone beside you." Her voice quieted. "Honestly, I wish I'd known you sooner. I wish I could've been there for you, the way I had friends and family there for me."

She *had* been there, even if she hadn't known it. He couldn't count the number of times he had wished for the same thing, for her to see him, to talk to him, to share in the burdens they'd carried. To know him *before* all of this. Before he was a mere shadow of a man.

But he didn't say any of that. Instead, he smiled halfheartedly. "I'm afraid you wouldn't have liked me at all if you had met me back then, love. I was much more immature. Not nearly as charming."

Isla raised an eyebrow. "And what makes you think I like you now?"

"The fact that you quite literally threw yourself on top of me the other night was a fairly good indicator," he said with a wink.

She rolled her eyes as pink began to creep up her neck. "Oh, gods, I did, didn't I?" she said with an embarrassed snort as she laid back down on the blanket and covered her face with a hand. "As if you need another boost to your ego."

"Oh, I'm definitely not complaining," he assured her, following her movements and propping his head up on his hand so he could see her beautiful blush. "And I'd be lying if I said that moment wasn't playing in my head over and over during the unbearably dull meetings today."

"You're so dramatic," she scoffed. "If threats to your kingdom and a bunch of hot headed monarchs arguing all day is *dull*, then I'd hate to see what your 'interesting' meetings are like."

"Well," he said, drawing out the word as he let his free hand trail up her arm. "I can tell you they don't involve much talking."

She smirked. "Had many meetings like that in your time, have you?"

"Ah, so we're having this conversation now, I take it?"

"It's not much of a conversation on my end. I suppose you already know about all of my...romantic entanglements, seeing as you spied on me for two years," she said teasingly.

"*Romantic entanglements?*" He bit back a laugh. "My, you're such a poet. But yes, I'd rather not think about how I was forced to watch you and the air elemental in your cozy little cave." Even the memory of those moments made his body spike with hot jealousy.

"And what about you?" Isla asked, shyness creeping into her voice. "I'm sure the handsome prince had all sorts of eligible ladies falling at his feet."

Her last remark was added hastily and with a forced grin, as if she was trying to hide her insecurity behind a mask. The humor from their banter suddenly left him, and he turned his head to face the stars.

"There have been many women in my life, yes. Whether placed strategically by my father in hopes of an advantageous marriage, or simply a means of escape for my younger self. They all only wanted two things from me: pleasure and power. That was all I was good for." He cleared his throat. "And who was I to complain, truly? I was a prince in line for the throne with the pick of any woman I wanted." He brandished a hand in the air.

"But I've only ever wanted to be seen for more than what I can offer someone. To be seen beyond the title, the crown, the role I have to play." He could feel Isla's gaze fixed on the side of his head, could hear her slow breaths as she waited. His heart beat in his ears. "I've never felt that with anyone but you, Isla. For two years, you've been the only woman to enter my thoughts. And I may be broken, but I promise you, there are far fewer shards than there would have been if you hadn't fought for me all those months ago."

He was still looking to the sky when her fingers grazed his chin and then his cheek, gently turning him so his eyes met hers. He lifted himself onto his elbows.

"And you call me a poet," she said, leaning toward him, emotion swimming in her eyes.

"Well, I couldn't have you showing me up," he whispered as his lips met hers.

This kiss was gentle. Tender. Unlike the others they'd shared, which had been filled with the urgency of danger or tension or denial. He wanted to savor her. The feel of her mouth against his, her fingers in his hair, the slight intake of her breath when he angled his head and brought his hand to cup her chin.

He didn't care where they were or what foes lurked around the corner. When he was with her, he was free.

Moving his hand to her waist, he carefully pushed her back to the ground and leaned over her. Red waves shone bright against the pale gray blanket, her violet eyes looking up at him like he was all she could see. He brought his lips to her neck and placed soft kisses against her smooth skin.

"I've been waiting for you my whole life, Isla," he murmured.

"I'm here," she whispered back, her breath hitching as his fingers explored the side of her leg. "I'm not going anywhere."

And, in those stolen moments under the stars, he could imagine it was true.

Chapter Thirty-Three

Aidan

"Where *are* they?" Annalise asked for the fifth time as she paced up and down the common room. The six of them—Aidan, Kai, Rynn, Jade, Bri, and Annalise—had been up for an hour waiting for Isla and the king to appear. The agenda for the day required Sebastian, Annalise, and his councilman to be at a breakfast meeting at eight o'clock sharp. At fifteen minutes past eight, Annalise started hammering on Sebastian's door and ordered Bri to check Isla's room, only to discover the two of them were missing.

Not a real shocker, in Aidan's opinion.

"I think it's pretty obvious what's going on here," he said, taking a sip of coffee and propping one leg on his knee.

To his right, Jade scoffed. "Here you go again with your insinuations. A man was *killed* last night, Aidan. What if somebody hurt Isla and Sebastian?"

"Gods, I feel sorry for the idiot who goes after Isla," Kai said.

Annalise threw her hands up in the air. "Alright, what about Sebastian, then? He could be dead!"

"Now, that seems more likely," Aidan interjected.

She quit pacing and flung herself onto the couch with a huff. "How can you be so casual about this when the murderer hasn't been caught?"

Aidan sighed. Of course, he was concerned about the attack and who might be behind it. But he was never a man to run and hide at the first sign of trouble. He knew he had a habit of covering upsetting situations with ill-timed humor, and not everyone appreciated his brand of distraction. If it helped alleviate the tension in the room, however, ill-timed humor it was.

"Forgive me if the fact that two young, attractive, cosmically traumatized people who have been ogling each other for the past three days disappearing in the middle of the night doesn't give me cause for concern."

"Well," Annalise started, shifting a pencil behind her ear, "I don't have the luxury of staying calm. Until our guards find the king or these Ionans catch the culprit, I can't rule out any possibility. I don't know what I'll do if something happens to him."

"That warms my heart, Anna. I didn't know you cared so much."

Sebastian appeared around the corner, rolling up the sleeves of his shirt. The same shirt he had on last night.

Oh, and look—there's Isla, Aidan thought as she trailed behind the king, her face bright red with embarrassment at finding them all waiting. *Right on time.*

"I hate it when you're right," Jade muttered next to him.

Annalise jumped to her feet. Aidan expected her to go off on a tirade, but instead, she shot Sebastian an icy look and strode toward his bedroom door.

"Your Majesty, Isla," she said curtly. "Both of you, in here. Now."

Sebastian looked like he was about to make some sarcastic remark, but when Isla gently touched his elbow, he closed his mouth. The two of them followed Annalise inside Sebastian's chambers.

"To be a fly on that wall," Aidan said with a longing sigh as the door shut with a *click.*

"It was highly irresponsible of them to disappear with no warning the same evening a man was attacked," Rynn said from his spot by the window, not bothering to look up from his book. "Miss Dalgard is well within her right to reprimand the both of them."

Aidan hummed in response, sharing a knowing look with his wife.

"So, what's the plan for today?" Bri, who leaned against the wall, said with a clap. "Chase down a killer?"

Aidan chuckled. "Glad to see your spirits aren't dampened, Bri."

"We need to start looking for the dagger," Jade said. "We've wasted two days now when we could have been searching. Akir told us he believes it's here. We know this palace better than anyone, and with the map Brielle copied when she and Isla met with him yesterday, we have plenty of places to start."

Jade had filled Aidan and Kai in on the incident with Isla at the cliffs, and how the crazy Ionan bastards tried to turn her over to the Chamber. The tale of Akir and his resistance came as a surprise, along with the deep history of corruption among this kingdom. Their cause resonated with Aidan. Another rebellion rising to overthrow those in power...it was like history was repeating itself.

"Is it smart to just go out in the open and act like nothing's happened?" Kai said from beside him, chewing on her lip. "We need to be careful. These walls aren't safe anymore."

"Kai, this entire *island* is not safe anymore. Do you want to help find the dagger and potentially get our abilities back, or do you want to hide in your chambers?" Rynn asked, his eyes still fixed on the book he was reading.

Kai and Aidan shared a glance. They still hadn't told anyone the truth, that they didn't *want* their magic back. Aidan kept hoping they'd find a different interpretation of "putting the elements back in their rightful place." And after what had happened to Kingsley, he didn't even want his wife so much as walking these halls alone. But they'd promised to at least help their friends find the dagger, then figure things out from there.

"He could've said it more nicely," Jade said, raising an eyebrow at Rynn, "but you both have good points. We should stay in pairs or small groups at all times, and maybe start carrying something to protect ourselves? Just to be safe?"

"Hmm, I do love seeing you with a weapon, sweetheart," Aidan quipped to Kai.

Ignoring him, Jade said, "I'll see if we can borrow some from the Karstos guards."

"Will you be ready to go soon?" Aidan asked, motioning to Rynn.

Rynn glanced at him over his book with a slight frown. "Actually, if you all do not need me, I was considering attending the meetings."

Scratching at his nose, Aidan asked, "You mean, the ones with the monarchs?"

"Yes, Aidan. What else would I be referring to?"

"You *do* realize you're not a king, right?"

"I'm not going to justify that with a response." Rynn sighed. "I thought it would be prudent to have eyes and ears on the Chamber to see what they might be planning. Miss Dalgard said they are allowing members of the court to sit in on discussions throughout the week."

Kai smirked. "Oh, well, if *Miss Dalgard* said so..." She trailed off, winking at Aidan.

"And when did you become a member of Sebastian's court?" Jade asked.

Rynn ignored her, shut his book with a *thud*, and reached for his cane. "I will take your amusing replies as a no, you do not need me," he said dryly. "Do none of you find it odd that we were invited here in the first place? We are not royalty, and we are not leaders. To these people, we are nothing. And yet, they bothered to find us in our little corners of the world. I want to know why."

He had a point. Aidan and Kai had thought the same thing multiple times, but their questions had quickly been overshadowed by the neverending list of problems that had arisen since.

"You're right. I think it's a good idea, Rynn," Jade said.

Aidan's jaw dropped open. "Did you just agree with him? *And* compliment him?"

"It is hard to argue with logic, *brother,*" Rynn mocked as he passed by the couch to head to his room, tapping Aidan's shoulder.

"What is *happening*?" Aidan asked incredulously.

"I think they're becoming friends," Kai said with a feigned gasp.

"You two are ridiculous." Jade shook her head. "Let's get ready. We have a palace to search."

CHAPTER THIRTY-FOUR

Isla

"What is *wrong* with you?" Annalise hissed as she smacked Sebastian in the arm with a stack of papers. "Running off in the middle of the night to gods know where in a foreign kingdom after a man was killed mere *feet* from your bedchambers?"

Sebastian sighed. "Anna, I'm sorry. I took Isla to the rooftop gardens and we simply fell asleep. We weren't planning to stay out all night."

"Oh, don't even get me started on that. You better hope no gossipping maid catches wind of your little rendezvous. Damage control would be a *nightmare.*"

"Annalise," Sebastian said, putting his hands on her shoulders. "Nothing happened. We're safe. I don't think anybody saw us, and I won't let it happen again." His voice softened. "I'm sorry I caused you any alarm. I don't mean to make your job more difficult."

Annalise's shoulders fell a fraction, the panic slowly leaving her face. Isla didn't know the woman very well, but she seemed to be more on edge as their stay progressed. With everything that had happened in the last forty-eight hours, Isla couldn't blame her.

"There you go, being all gentlemanly." Annalise glanced at Isla, then back at Sebastian. "I'm glad you're both alright. I don't want to be this overbearing, but you scared me. After Kingsley, I thought..." She bit down on her lip, and guilt surged within Isla.

They'd been careless to let themselves fall asleep on the roof. She should've known everyone would worry, especially after the murder, and Sebastian had a reputation to uphold—she hadn't even thought about what the consequences of people seeing a king gallivanting off with some girl would do to his image.

And yet...it had been one of the best nights of her life. Laying under the stars, talking for hours about everything and nothing, losing herself in his kiss, his arms...it was new and exciting, but it also felt like home. She wasn't sure it had been real until she woke up that morning with her head resting on his shoulder and his hand still wrapped around hers.

For a moment, before he awoke, she got to study his face—soft blonde hair brushing his forehead, long eyelashes fluttering against the top of his cheeks, contentment splayed across his features. The face of someone unburdened, who didn't have to wear a mask or play a role for the world to see. And she'd been gripped by the sudden idea that she wouldn't mind waking up to that face again.

Which was a dangerous thought. Dangerous and exhilarating.

When he'd opened his eyes, she saw a split second of unabashed, complete adoration before he tucked it away, and that single look sent a spike of realization through her. She finally understood this was *real* for him—and it might be real for her, too. Yet she couldn't help but think it was only going to be harder if and when they woke from this dream.

If they couldn't find the dagger and figure out how to bring the elements into balance, she'd be forced back to the spirit plane, separated from him by powers much stronger than herself. And even if they *did* manage to be successful...what about after? She had her father to go home to, not to mention the fact that Sebastian had an entire kingdom to rule. It didn't matter what he claimed his feelings for her were—his people came first, and she could never ask him to give that up.

Gods, she couldn't even believe she was *thinking* about this. About a life after...with him.

Annalise continued talking, snapping Isla back to reality. Sebastian had told her during their various conversations that his royal advisor was also his closest friend, and Isla could clearly see the shift now. The softening around her eyes, the casual slump of her shoulders, the heavy sigh leaving her lips like a weight lifting from her chest.

"I'm sorry I snapped, Seb. You deserve..." Her gaze slid to Isla and her lips twitched up a fraction. "Anyway, please just be careful. I don't like this palace or these people. Something is off."

"I promise," he responded, leaning in and giving her a quick peck on the cheek.

"Well, then," Annalise said as she straightened, "Now that's settled, we're late for meetings."

Sebastian grimaced. "They didn't cancel those after last night?" When Annalise shook her head, he sighed. "I'll meet you outside in a moment, Anna."

She gave a curt nod and walked out of the room, giving Isla a brief smile as she passed. Sebastian came to Isla's side and took her hand. The movement was so natural it made her chest tighten. She looked down at their hands, all of the things she didn't know how to say bubbling to the surface, her mind racing.

"Isla, look at me," he said, and she raised her gaze, his other hand cupping her cheek. "What's going on in that head of yours?"

How could he always tell? She bit her lip, fighting the urge to brush off her nerves and concerns, to act like nothing was wrong. But she had to stop hiding from him.

"I know I shouldn't be feeling this way, what with everything that's happened, but after last night...things just feel so right, and..."

"You say that like it's a bad thing, love," he said with a smile.

"I'm afraid it's not going to last," she whispered. "There are so many things outside of our control."

He was quiet for a moment, letting his thumb trace her jaw in slow, sweeping motions. "That may be true," he finally said, "but no matter what happens, I'm with you through it all. That's something I *can* control." He kissed her forehead, letting his lips linger over her skin as he murmured, "And I'm not going to let you slip away this time."

She closed her eyes and nodded, forcing a smile as he pulled away.

"See you tonight," he said, leading her to the door separating their rooms.

"Yes, see you tonight," she repeated as the door shut between them. She stared at the blank wood, his parting words ringing in her ears.

She didn't *want* to slip away again. If it were up to her, she'd never leave his side. But the thought didn't soothe her as he intended; instead, she was left wondering when this dream would end and something else would tear them apart.

CHAPTER THIRTY-FIVE

Isla

They'd been searching Palace Noctem for hours for any sign of the dagger, and Isla was getting tired of dead end after dead end.

Meandering through corridors under the guise of "touring the beautiful palace" only allowed them so much freedom. She, Bri, Kai, Aidan, and Jade had come across multiple restricted hallways and rooms, either guarded by Ionan soldiers or deadbolted so no one could enter. There had been a hushed, heated argument between Aidan and Jade over whether Isla should manipulate the guards to allow them access to such areas, ending with Aidan begrudgingly admitting that since Isla's mind manipulation was only temporary, the guards would soon remember what had happened and would be able to inform the Chamber they were snooping around.

So Isla found other ways.

The first guard they came upon, she set his pants on fire. Aidan was very fond of this solution, but, unsurprisingly, Jade was not.

As the man had scurried away with a yelp, their group had ventured down the restricted hall to find a library under construction. They wandered the shelves and inspected every nook and cranny, but saw nothing that might point them to the dagger.

The next locked door was easily picked by Isla's vines, and opened to a training room for the palace guards.

The third section was more promising: a small hallway with two doors, each of which was guarded by an armed Ionan soldier. To distract both of them at once, Isla found a glass chandelier in a nearby corridor and brought it crashing down with a flick of her wrist and a slash of her wind. When the guards sprinted to see the commotion, the five of them snuck into the rooms, which carried a myriad of priceless artifacts. One housed all manner of expensive weapons and tools—an entire armory of daggers, swords, spears, crossbows, and axes. Another held cases and cases of crowned jewels and precious stones; they had to pry Kai away once they were sure the dagger wasn't among the ranks.

Isla was exhausted. Room after room, wing after wing, and nothing to show for their efforts. Not even a *stirring* of the dagger's presence, as she'd so strongly felt the first time they'd found it on the ship to Iona. She knew it was her aggravation talking, but it seemed like their hope and time were both running out.

They were about to try hunting the gardens and courtyards, instead—thinking there might be more hidden entrances, like the one Akir had taken them through—when their group came upon a door in the far eastern wing with two guards standing before it.

"This wing is for the private use of the Chamber and is off-limits to guests," one of them said in a gruff voice, not even bothering to look at them. "Please make your way back to the main hall."

Isla didn't know what made her do it, aside from the fact that she was tired, frustrated, and knew their days were limited. Without thinking, she smiled sweetly at the guards, those little ribbons of coercion already reaching from her mind to theirs, dancing like silk into their subconscious.

"We're touring this beautiful palace. Surely it's alright for us to take a quick peek?"

Both guards faced her, their features slackened as they grinned back, her powers of compulsion taking effect. "Well, if it's just for a moment," the one on the right said, then opened the door to let them pass.

"Isla!" Jade hissed as they hurried into the chamber. "I thought we said you weren't going to use your abilities on anyone."

Isla shot her a look, her anger from two days ago rearing back. "*You* said it, Jade. I'm doing what needs to be done so we can find this gods-forsaken dagger and get off this island."

Before them stood an enormous chamber, easily three times the height of their personal rooms. Gilded buttresses domed above their heads, golden columns inlaid with intricate floral designs lining the sides. Built into the center of the back wall was a fireplace at least six people wide and twice as tall. On either side were two large bookshelves with rolling ladders. Several tables and chairs were placed in front of the fireplace and bookshelves, as if the Chamber often lounged there. Off to the left and right were four small, separate hallways leading to what Isla assumed were the private quarters of each member.

"Now, I could live like this," Aidan said with a deep chuckle from behind her.

Kai turned to Isla. "Do you think there could be anything helpful here?"

Isla shrugged. "It's the most interesting thing we've seen all day. Let's split up and look around." Glancing over her shoulder at the entrance they came through, she flicked her fingers and watched as a vine snaked its way through the handles, locking the door. "I'll keep an ear out in case anyone comes down the hall."

For the next ten minutes, their small group foraged the area, some choosing to venture down the individual hallways. Isla took to the bookshelves and soon, Jade approached her, exploring the other half of the shelves and fireplace.

"I never got to apologize," Jade said quietly, and Isla tensed. "For what happened the other day. And on the beach." Out of the corner of her eye, Isla saw her concentrating on the row of books, a crease in her forehead.

"We should have told you about my ability. *I* should have told you. It was foolish to keep it from you when there was the possibility you would someday need it."

Irritation laced through Isla, hot and sharp. "Then why didn't you? I could've stopped everything that day. Gods, for that matter, *you* could've done it. That whole mess could've been over with before I even—before my brother—" Isla choked on her words and lowered her voice. "I just don't understand."

"I couldn't have done anything, Isla. I haven't been able to access that part of my magic since the war started."

Startled, Isla faced her fully, and Jade sighed. "During the war, I used my power to do something I'm still ashamed of. Many people died because of me. It caused me to repress the spirit magic so strongly that it simply...disappeared. I couldn't use it again, even if I wanted to. I've thought *so many* times over the last few months how if I had only been able to find that part of myself, I could have prevented what came next. But I wasn't strong enough. And for that, I'm truly sorry, Isla," Jade said, her brown eyes flicking up to meet Isla's.

A bit of the resentment Isla had been carrying toward the female began to melt away. She knew how deeply Jade held to her convictions, she'd just never known why. And she understood the guilt Jade bore, how the weight of past mistakes could eat at one's mind, whether or not the blame fell on them.

"Thank you for telling me," Isla said. "I wish I'd known what I could do sooner, and how to use all of these powers. But I also get that this whole situation is a lot more complicated than we ever thought it would be."

Jade reached out and tentatively put a hand on Isla's arm. "It's not your fault, you know. Nothing that has happened has been your fault. You saved us that day, and sacrificed more than I think we've given you credit for."

"You sacrificed a lot, too. I hope I can fix that. I want you to be happy, Jade. All of you."

Squeezing her arm, Jade said, "Then let's find that dagger."

With a smile, Isla turned her attention back to the books, her fingers wandering over the freshly dusted titles. *A Brief History of Ionan Monarchy; The Trade Agreement Omnibus; Architectural Developments in a Post-War Nation; Friend or Foe? A Study in Gods and Magic.*

She reached for the last one when something further down the shelf caught her eye. Two smaller, black leather books with no title on the spines were pushed in slightly further than the rest. Curious, Isla pulled on the first one.

A low, whirring sound came from behind the bookshelf. Her eyes widened as, ever so slowly, the entire bookcase began to shift to the left.

"Umm...I think I found something!" she called out, not taking her eyes off the growing entrance. It stopped suddenly, leaving a gap wide enough for a single person to get through. Footsteps came from behind her as the others caught up.

Bri gasped. "This is amazing. I want one."

Isla snapped her fingers and a flame appeared at the tips. "Shall we?" she said before stepping into the hidden room. Jade and Bri followed quickly, but Kai and Aidan exchanged a look, one Isla didn't have to be omniscient to read.

She shouldn't be dragging those two into this. Not when they had just learned Kai was pregnant and had so many things they needed to figure out. This could be dangerous, and how could Isla ask them to sacrifice everything on a whim? How could she potentially ask them to give up their future at the end of this when they found the dagger?

But...how could she *not*? They had to follow the Primeval gods' orders. They had to stop nature from rebelling against the world. How could she protect them when she needed them? *All* of them?

Isla motioned to Kai and Aidan. "You don't have to come this time if you don't want to," she said softly.

"Why would they not?" Jade asked, her brow furrowing.

"No reason," Kai responded quickly, then took Aidan's hand. "We're right behind you."

Isla led them into the secret space, her fire casting a golden glow that dispersed the shadows of the rocky path. Single file, they quietly made their way through the narrow, sloping tunnel. Further and further they walked, the musty scent of dirt and stone walls mixing with the smoke of Isla's fire. The occasional rat or spider scuttled by, but other than that, there was no sign of life. Eventually, they came to a fork, both paths equally dark and foreboding.

"Which way should we go?" Bri whispered.

Closing her eyes, Isla's wind stirred within her, unfurling as it reached beyond her skin and branched off into the two tunnels, purring in her ear. Searching. Listening.

Then she heard it. From the right path came sounds of feet on hard floor, of metal clattering, of mundane mutterings and bells and sharp knives on wood.

From the left came...boiling water. A tide churning and frothing against stone. Something about it called to her.

"This way leads to the kitchens," she said, pointing to the right. "I can't tell what's on the left, but we're close to some body of water."

"The hot springs?" Aidan asked.

"Maybe that's what it is. You know about them?"

He smirked. "Yeah, we know about them. They've been beneath the palace for centuries."

"Wait, wasn't there an entry in Satori's journal about the hot springs?" Bri said to Isla. "Something about a guard hundreds of years ago dying down here?"

Aidan hummed. "Comforting."

Isla ignored them, her elements locked onto something down the shadowed path to the left. Her feet carried her toward it, a familiar sensation burrowing under her skin and crawling through her arms, her chest, her legs.

A humming. Just like the one she heard on the *Mekaisa* before she found the dagger.

Finally.

"It's this way," she said, mostly to herself, unsure if the others were even following her anymore. She quickened her steps, her fingers trailing along the wall and leaving a thin line of fire in its wake. Flames illuminated the path and pulsed within her as she neared the hot springs. The humming was faint but still there, calling to her.

Her salvation. Or, perhaps, her damnation. Either way, she would follow it to the end.

Suddenly, the trail stopped. Her fire flashed, exposing the ceiling and stone walls on all sides. There was nowhere else to go, no other curve to follow, no fork in the road.

"That's it?" Bri asked once the others caught up to her. "Where's the hot spring?"

Isla lifted her hand to the wall, feeling the thrum of water deep beneath her palms. "It's on the other side."

Where was the humming? Where was the dagger? She'd been *so sure*. The same calling, the same buzzing in her veins. And then it had just...disappeared.

"*Hello, daughter of the island. We were wondering when you would finally come,*" a familiar voice filtered through her mind.

A voice of multitudes.

Isla froze, unable to speak, unable to move. Her heart pounded so hard it echoed through her entire body. Flattening her hand against the wall, she leaned on it for support, the adrenaline racing through her making it hard to stand. She turned her face away from the others so they wouldn't hear.

"Where are you?" she hissed to the gods.

"Isla? What's wrong?" Bri asked.

"Ah, your mortal friends. We know you would sacrifice much to keep them from harm."

"And are you threatening to harm them?" Isla whispered, the elements still raging inside of her at the shock of the Primevals' presence.

A faint rumble sounded, and Isla swore the ends of her hair lifted. *"Not us, daughter. Return when you are ready, and return alone. Only then shall we reveal your next steps,"* they said, the last words twisting and fading into nothing.

A hand rested on her shoulder, and she whirled, fire collected in her palm.

"Woah, there," Aidan whistled, backing away with his hands in the air. "It's just me, little island. What happened?"

Isla put a hand to her head. She could hardly think, hardly breathe, her pulse racing. Her friends couldn't know. If the Primevals asked her to come alone, if they even so much as *hinted* the others wouldn't be safe, she had to keep them away. They couldn't be tempted to come down here again, not until she was sure any threat was gone.

Taking a deep breath, she offered them a forced smile. "Nothing. I was trying to see if I could sense the dagger, but I can't find it. I guess it's another dead end."

Jade narrowed her eyes. "Are you sure you—"

"I said it's not here, Jade," Isla snapped, instantly regretting her tone. She just needed to get them *out*. "Come on, let's get back. We've been gone too long."

Leading them away, she took one last glance at the darkened tunnel. Tomorrow, she would come back. Tomorrow, she would find the dagger and end this once and for all.

CHAPTER THIRTY-SIX

Rynn

The day had, in Rynn's opinion, been a monumental waste of time.

He sat through meeting after meeting with Annalise and the king, pretending to give his attention to the numerous conversations on treaties and resource allotment and squabbles over numbers, but it was all more or less the same. One kingdom desiring more than another was willing to give, thirty minutes of discussion, then settling on a compromise and moving to the next topic. He had to admit, he had expected there to be more...manipulation. Thinly veiled threats. High-strung, pretentious monarchs. Yet everyone was surprisingly reserved.

He supposed it made sense, in light of the Chamber's vague but grave announcement that morning about the death of the Karstosian guard. Everyone was rather subdued after the news. They did not give many details, in order to stave off inevitable panic, Rynn assumed, but it still cast a shadow over the entire day. Additional guards had been posted around the palace, and the monarchs were offered extra protection if they desired. The Chamber promised they had their best resources on the hunt for the murderer.

The day did not proffer any insight into who might be behind the attack or what the Chamber was hiding. Yet Rynn knew the four Ionans were hiding *something*. The initial wariness he had felt upon first seeing the invitation all those weeks ago had not died. He sought to understand *why* the Chamber had invited him and his companions—a question the others either glossed over in the wake of Isla's arrival and the larger quest, or one they simply did not find important. Rynn, however, could not let it rest.

There was no logical reason for the Chamber to bring the former elementals back to this island. He did not understand how they knew of their existence and where they had settled, since this kingdom had supposedly been cut off from the rest of the world for a millennia. And that was the assumption he had followed, until he began to realize this den of vipers knew far more than they should.

Which left two options. Either Iona had people on the outside this entire time, or they had someone *here*, at their disposal. Someone with a vested interest in access to the kingdoms and the old elementals. Someone who was accustomed to manipulating the lives of others and bending them to her will from the shadows.

Someone like Celesine.

And if she was here, he was going to find her.

He had hoped staying in close proximity to the Chamber would open his mind to their secrets, but so far, they had conducted the day's meetings with utmost caution and cordiality. It was incredibly dull. Rynn often found his thoughts drifting and his gaze wandering to mahogany hair and tawny cheeks, a pencil scribbling tirelessly across parchment, and sharp eyes that never missed a beat.

The previous day when Annalise had found Kingsley and burst from the guard's room with blood coating her hands, Rynn had shot to her side with the speed of his former self, ignoring the icy heat shattering in his calf. The thought of her injured in such a way made the edges of his vision darken with concern.

But she had been fine. It was not *her* blood. And he had realized what an absolute fool he was.

He had retreated to his chambers after they found the body. When a knock had sounded on his door, he knew it had been her. He had heard her familiar steps on the wooden floor, and the idea of her footfalls being so discernable to him made him realize even further that he was letting her get too close. He had not answered her call.

That morning, he found a hastily written note shoved underneath the door, inviting him to the meetings with her and the Karstos entourage. It was irritating, the way his eyes lingered on the curves of her letters, the way he fought a smile at the delicate loop on the "e" in her name.

And so, he went. To monitor the Chamber, and nothing else.

He did not need another person in his life to care for. Not when it inevitably ended in regret.

The sound of scraping wood startled him, and he blinked as the others rose from their chairs. Across the table, Annalise searched the room until her eyes landed on him and stopped. He tracked her as she gathered her notes and made her way around the room to him and Sebastian. She passed the side of the table where Ottorius and the other two Triad members were sitting, and flinched for a brief moment when her shoulder accidentally bumped against Ottorius's.

The man reached out to steady her, his fingers wrapping around her elbow and holding. Rynn could not see his face, but the man leaned to whisper something in Annalise's ear, and her eyes flashed as she quickly pulled out of his grip.

Next to him, Sebastian cursed. Rynn began moving through the crowd instinctively, parting people with his cane. By the time he reached Annalise, Ottorius had slipped away, but not before Rynn caught his hand sliding from her elbow to her shoulder, his eyes speaking more than the mere anger he had shown toward her in previous days.

"What was that?" Rynn hissed at her, his gaze locked on the Triad member's receding figure.

"Nothing," she responded coolly. "Come on, we need to get ready for dinner."

Sebastian appeared beside Rynn. "What did he say to you, Anna?" he asked, his tone low and dangerous.

"I just ran into him. It was an accident. You two are going to cause a scene." She stuck a pencil behind her ear before turning to the guards who would escort them back to their wing. But Rynn did not fail to notice the shake of her hand, and his fist clenched involuntarily at his side in response.

"So then it was the two of us against four of them, and I told Seb here we should go home because he had some fancy ceremony for his father the next week, and he didn't want to mess up his pretty face." Klaus, the eldest Prince of Evonlea, paused his story to hold back his laughter. "So he *asks* the gentleman who's about to punch him if it would be 'too terribly inconvenient to avoid anything above the neck,' and the fellow agrees!" He smacked the table in amusement as he spoke.

"Did they end up fighting, then?" Brielle asked from across the table.

"Of course, they did!" Klaus guffawed. "Came home with a couple of broken fingers and bruised ribs, but not a single hair on his perfect princely head was touched."

The Evonlea and Karstos sides of the enormous dining table burst into laughter, and Sebastian leaned back in his seat, swirling his glass with a smug look on his face.

"What can I say," he said with a shrug. "I must protect Karstos's most valuable asset."

Next to him, Brielle snorted and reached for her glass of wine. "Pretty sure that's not your *face*, Your Majesty," she said, giving him a pointed look as she took a sip.

The table howled. Klaus raised his glass to Brielle in a salute and chuckled. "Aren't you a little firecracker," he said, giving her an appreciative glance.

"Oh, honey," she purred. "I would rip you to shreds."

Beside Rynn, Jade choked on her water, and Kai and Aidan practically fell out of their chairs with laughter.

Had these Ionans spiked their drinks? Rynn had never seen his companions act so absurdly. And not even twenty-four hours after a man had died, with his murderer still on the loose. Perhaps dire times made some people avoid their fear rather than give into it.

Jessenia, Klaus's sister, raised her voice, and Rynn had to peer down the length of the table to see her. "Was that during the winter solstice celebration, when I was home from the academy?" she asked, tossing her light blonde hair over her shoulder with a pretentious wave. "I *do* remember that visit. And I'm very glad you didn't let them rough you up too much, Sebastian. It would have made the rest of the week much less fun," she said with a slight smirk.

Rynn rolled his eyes and, to his surprise, Annalise shifted closer to him.

"That princess has been trying to get back into Sebastian's bed for years. What I wouldn't give to shove my heels into those pretty little eyes."

"I think I would rather like to see that," Rynn murmured back.

"Give me access to any more of this wine, and you just might," Annalise said with a sigh, setting her glass down. "I'm sorry, that was unprofessional. I don't know what's gotten into me these last couple of days. Watching everyone act like nothing has happened, like everything is fine...it just sets me on edge." She grabbed her napkin and began twisting the fabric between her fingers in what Rynn had come to notice was her nervous habit.

Without thinking, he reached over and set his hand on top of hers. "Do not apologize, Annalise," he said, his voice low. "I would rather know what you are truly thinking, not what you believe others wish to see."

She looked over at him and blinked, her tongue running across her lower lip. "That's the first time you've said my name."

His brow furrowed. "I have said your name plenty of times."

"It's always been 'Miss Dalgard,'" she said with a ghost of a smile. "Never simply 'Annalise.'"

"Well, *Annalise*, I do not think there is anything simple about you."

He did not know what made him say it, nor what made his body lean into her. Perhaps the wine *was* imbued with something more. He could see the hazel flecks in her green eyes, could smell the sweet wine coming from her lips as she breathed in the small space between them. Did her eyes flicker to his mouth, or was the wine clouding his judgment?

Suddenly, Kai's voice broke through the haze. "How were the meetings today, you two?"

"Wholly unsatisfying," Rynn responded, unable to tear his gaze away from Annalise's.

"Oh, I'm sure they weren't that bad." Aidan smirked as he took another bite of his seared chicken. Kai held her water glass to her mouth to stifle her giggles.

Truly insufferable.

Lowering his voice, Rynn said, "There was nothing out of the ordinary. It was rather boring. I take it your quest failed to produce anything useful as well, considering we are still missing the dagger?"

Jade looked around to make sure nobody was paying attention before quietly saying, "It wasn't entirely unproductive. We're getting closer. Let's talk about it later, though."

His pulse spiked. Might they find the dagger soon and be rid of this island? When Sebastian had first come to him and Jade in Lockhurt and planted the idea that they could get their powers back, Rynn had been cautious but determined. Who would want to live encumbered by an injury such as his when he could regain his immortal life and never need another to aid him again?

And yet, as the weeks had gone on and they had arrived on this little island, something had changed. The notion of taking back his wind was still appealing, yes—it would always be part of him. But for some inexplicable reason, the fact that they may be close to completing their quest seemed to spark a sense of foreboding in him.

On his right, Annalise asked Ayana about the priest from Ara Mir who had fallen ill on the second evening.

"Oh, you didn't hear?" Ayana said, her tone turning grave. "He's still with the healers. He's been unconscious ever since. He had some sort of fit after they took him, and they haven't been able to get a response out of him. We are all so very worried."

Rynn snuck a glance across the table at Ottorius, who had not ceased gorging himself on the food and wine with a jovial grin since they arrived. Very worried, indeed.

"I'm sorry to hear that. Have the healers said what they think caused the reaction?" Annalise asked.

"Not that they have told me. They said he passed out at dinner, and began to seize uncontrollably when under their care in the healer's wing. We rotate who goes to check on him, but so far, his state remains unchanged."

"Perhaps I'll go pay him a visit later," Annalise said kindly.

"You're too sweet," Ayana said, patting her cheek. Ottorius watched the exchange with a curious gleam that had Rynn wanting to leap across the table.

The man always examined Annalise like she was something he wanted to either choke or devour, and Rynn's blood boiled every time Ottorius looked her way.

Raising his glass to hide his lips, Rynn muttered under his breath, "I do not like the way he looks at you. He has seen you as a challenge ever since you crossed him that first evening."

With a glance across the table at the man in question, Annalise paled ever so slightly. "It's nothing, Rynn. These people are all the same. Well, except for Seb, of course." She waved her fork in the air. "If you're not one of them, you're someone to step on or someone to conquer."

Rynn's nostrils flared. "You are neither a conquest nor a doormat, Annalise, and anyone who sees you as such is a fool."

"Two compliments in one evening. This wine must be making me hear things," she said, her lips curving into a smile.

In that moment, he felt he would do almost anything for that smile. And that scared him more than any hidden foe ever could.

Tapping his fingers against his leg—a relentlessly annoying tick he had picked up since becoming human—Rynn quickly finished his meal and stood from the table, needing to put space between himself and these dangerous urges.

"I'm heading to our wing, if anyone would like to accompany me."

Kai and Aidan followed suit, which took Rynn by surprise, for Kai's meal had barely been touched. The three of them made their way to the Karstos chambers.

"Would either of you care to expand on Jade's cryptic answer about your findings today?" Rynn asked as they walked.

Kai responded first. "Well, we spent hours searching without any luck, until we found the Chambers' private suites and had a look around. Turns out, there's a secret entrance there that leads to the underground tunnels. But it was another dead end—we didn't find the dagger, obviously," she said with a yawn and a wave of her hand.

Narrowing his eyes, Rynn glanced at her. Wheels began turning in his head. "Kai, are you ill?" he asked.

With a jolt, Kai gaped at him then snapped her mouth shut. "Of course not. Why?"

Now that he had time to examine the evidence, his thoughts spun faster. He ticked off points on his finger as they strode down the hallway.

"You hardly touched your meal tonight, you have had nothing to drink but water since we arrived, you are always first to retire for the evening—which is very unlike you. I saw you go off to speak privately with the healer last night after she was summoned for Kingsley. And Aidan is a very territorial man, we all know"—Aidan grunted at this—"but his behavior has been borderline possessive, even for him."

When he looked up, Aidan and Kai were both staring at him.

"One, I think that's the most I've ever heard you say in one go. And two, you're paying *way* too much attention to us, brother," Aidan said.

"I simply think if you are feeling unwell or are not up to the task at hand, you should seek help from one of the healers. We would not want you collapsing on us while searching for the dagger or trying to perform the power transfer later—"

"Gods, Rynn, I'm not *sick*," Kai said with a loud sigh. "I'm *expecting*."

Rynn stopped in his tracks, his mind going blank. "Expecting what?"

Clapping him on the back, Aidan barked a laugh. "A *baby*, Rynn. Kai is pregnant. But we haven't told anyone yet, alright? Please keep this between us for now."

Rynn blinked at him. "You—what? How did this happen?"

"Well, you see, when a man and a woman—"

Slapping a hand over Aidan's mouth, Rynn looked expectantly at Kai, who shook her head in amusement. "I don't know what to tell you, Rynn," she said. "We just found out. Isla clued us in, actually."

She and Aidan beamed at each other as the three of them resumed walking. Rynn struggled to put his thoughts together. A *child*? It was something he had never thought of in his entire existence, although he knew of Kai's desire after the events of the last year. How would this affect their willingness to help? Surely, if they ascended back into their powers, it would create complications, such as terminating the pregnancy or causing problems with Kai's health. After seeing his two companions so well-adjusted and happy with their new life, he suddenly felt like an imbecile for ever thinking they would be willing to give this up.

What did that mean for the elements?

His mind continued to race out of control but, for once, he held his tongue on his negativity and concerns. Something Jade said to him earlier pierced his thoughts: they were stuck with one another and, despite their flaws, loved each other. He desired to be better to them, as they were to him.

"I am...happy for you," he said slowly, and found he truly meant it. "And you have my word that I will not mention your condition to anyone else. I know this is what you have yearned for. The two of you deserve the life you always wanted."

Kai took his hand and turned her blue, misty eyes to him. "Thank you." As they neared the Karstos wing, she leaned her head on his shoulder. "You do too, Rynn. You do, too."

Over the next hour, the remaining members of their group trickled into the common room one by one.

Except for Annalise.

Rynn's concern grew with each passing minute, as did his irritation and the slicing pain in his leg. Where was she? Why had no one waited for her? *He* should have waited for her. With the prospect of danger lurking behind every corner, they had all agreed to avoid wandering the halls alone.

"Where is Miss Dalgard?" he hissed to Sebastian while the others were in deep conversation.

"She left dinner with the Aramians. Said she wanted to visit their sick priest, and one of their guards promised to bring her back here after," the king responded.

A spike of frustration went through Rynn. "And you let her go? We do not know if we can trust these people, Sebastian."

Sebastian turned to face Rynn fully. "I understand your concerns, and trust me, I know better than most how little we can trust the people in this place. But one thing you have to understand is that I did not *let* her do anything. If I tried to control that woman, I would inevitably wind up with poison in my whiskey." He gave Rynn a pointed look. "You care so much for the people in your life, Rynn, however hard you try to mask it. But you need to make sure your compassion doesn't drown them. Doesn't drown *her.* You must trust her to make her own decisions."

A war raged inside Rynn's mind. He knew the king was right—knew his possessive hold on others had led to their downfall, time and time again. But how could he ignore it, fight it, when it gripped his mind with such fear?

All of his existence, he had seen fear as a weakness. If he had the power, if he had the knowledge, if he had the *ability*, he would never need to know dread such as this.

Fear made one human, he understood that. But that did not mean it made him a fool.

Rynn grabbed his cane and stood. "I do trust her, Sebastian. It is *them* I do not trust. I will not see her as another broken body on this cursed island."

Before anybody could question him, he made his way through the halls and toward the healer's wing of the palace, ignoring the pain shooting through his leg with each labored step.

It was times like this when he wished the wind was still his to command. That he could still stop any foe with a snap of his fingers, could tear the very air from their body with barely a thought. It gave him peace of mind, knowing he was able to protect. Instead, he had to calm his thoughts in other ways—steadying his breaths, reminding himself that she had guards with her, that his body was overreacting and he would inevitably find her sitting safe and sound in the healer's wing. She would give him that quizzical frown of hers that said, "Really? You came all this way to bother me?" and he would find an excuse for his irrational behavior.

She was fine.

And if she was not, he would rip this palace apart.

Rynn reached the door of the healer's suite and pushed it open, his cane echoing on the hardwood floor. He took in the rows of cots, the shelves full of supplies, and the sharp scent of cleaning solution and peppermint. Some beds were occupied, and a few men and women bustled about in their white healer's cloaks, but other than that, the chamber was quiet as the palace prepared to sleep.

"May I help you, sir?" a pale woman with brown hair pulled back in a bun asked.

"Has anyone come to visit the Aramian priest this evening?"

She nodded. "Yes, a small group comes every night after dinner. You just missed them, actually."

If they had only recently left, he should have passed them in the halls. A tightness worked its way up his chest. "Do you know which direction they went?"

She shook her head. "I'm sorry, sir. I'm afraid I wasn't paying much attention. I believe some went toward the east wing"—she pointed out the door to the left—"but a couple of them went the other way."

It must be the guard escorting Annalise back to the Karstos chambers. Rynn tried to calm his erratic heart as he thanked the woman and began to retrace his path, unable to stop himself from pausing at every new hallway to listen for footsteps or catch a glimpse of mahogany hair. He shook his head and rubbed a hand over his face. He felt ludicrous. What had this woman done to him?

As he trudged down the corridors, the stillness of the palace washed over him, except for the crude tapping of his cane on wood. It seemed even the branches outside the windows ceased their scratching, and the insects chirping their nightly symphony fell silent. The hair on the back of his neck rose while a prickle crept down his spine.

The slight tremble at his feet was the only warning.

With his next breath, he flung himself to the ground, pain and adrenaline ricocheting through his leg. The window at his side shattered a heartbeat later, raining shards of glass that embedded themselves in his skin. The paintings on the wall rattled in the wind and the floor beneath him trembled violently. Rynn winced at the sharpness slicing through his back.

But above all, he heard her cries.

And then, he was crawling.

CHAPTER THIRTY-SEVEN

Rynn

When the ground halted its quaking, he gripped the side of the wall and hauled himself to his feet, ignoring the fragments of glass showering from his back and the stiffness in his leg. As an afterthought, he gingerly picked up the largest, sharpest piece he could find and placed it inside his pocket.

He did not know what was happening—a storm, perhaps, or an attack. All that mattered was reaching her.

He followed the sound of her shout. When he turned the next corner, he spied a dimly lit alcove spilling the shadows of two figures across the ground. Another window nearby had exploded, leaving broken glass in its wake, a tapestry billowing in the howling wind.

"Don't *touch* me!" he heard from the dark space.

His feet carried him across the hall, an aching, boiling rage deep inside of him bursting free like the very wind that ripped through the palace. Annalise was shoved into the wall, cast in shadows, with a tall figure pressed against her. Familiar black hair. Glittering jewels adorning pale ears.

Wrath consumed him.

"Not so mouthy now that you don't have your precious *king* to protect you, hmm?" Ottorius hissed as his hand snaked up her leg, pulling at the fabric on her black dress. "Nobody will be looking for us in this storm, I imagine." His other hand gripped Annalise's jaw. "I have *hours* to teach this pretty mouth some manners."

Rynn was almost to her, but time seemed to slow as his leg dragged behind him.

Ottorius released her face and, in a movement that made dark satisfaction well in Rynn's chest, Annalise spat at the man, her eyes churning with hatred. Growling a curse, Ottorius brought his fingers around her throat. She gasped and kicked against him as he swung his other hand back—

Rynn caught his wrist.

Ottorius let out a cry of frustration and whirled around, raising his fist when he laid eyes on Rynn. With his other hand, Rynn lifted his cane to block Ottorius's blow, then swiftly jabbed the tip into his chest. Ottorius stumbled backward, further into the shadows. Grabbing onto the cane with both hands, Rynn strode after the man, barely noticing the pain blazing up his leg as he backed Ottorius into the stone wall. He shoved his cane horizontally across Ottorius's neck, caging him in and cutting off his air.

A calmness blanketed Rynn's mind as he watched the man gasp for breath.

"I am going to make you regret touching a single hair on her head."

Holding the cane to the man's neck with one hand, Rynn reached into his pocket for the shard of glass. Ottorius's eyes widened as his face continued to turn purple. Behind him, Rynn faintly heard Annalise calling his name, but all he could see was Ottorius's spindly fingers wrapping around her throat, the angry tears staining her cheeks, his hand buried under her dress...

Rynn brought the sharpest edge of the glass to the man's lips. "What was that you said to her?" he asked, his voice low. "That you had hours to teach her pretty mouth some manners?" He scraped the glass around Ottorius's cheek and down to his chin, blood blossoming under his touch. Somewhere in the distance, thunder crashed, and the walls around them vibrated.

"I, too, have *hours*, Ottorius." He dropped the cane and grasped the man's chin before he could draw breath, forcing his lips apart and shoving the bloodied shard into his open mouth. A muffled scream escaped his lips before

Rynn slammed his jaw shut, watching the pain erupt in Ottorius's eyes as he slid to the ground. Red spilled from his lips when he unhinged his jaw and tried with flailing fingers to extract the glass.

Rynn felt a tugging on his tunic.

"Rynn, *please*—the storm is getting worse. We have to go!"

He looked at Annalise, then back to the pitiful excuse of a man wallowing on the hard floor. A vision of what would have happened to her had he not shown up flashed across his mind. This man deserved far worse than a bloodied mouth.

As if she could read his thoughts, Annalise put her hand on his cheek and turned him to face her. "Stop, Rynn. He's not worth it. We need to get away."

His nostrils flared and chest heaved at the self control it took to hold her gaze instead of plunging his cane down Ottorius's throat.

"He was going to hurt you," Rynn growled.

She lowered her hand to grab his. "Yes, he was. But now, we need to go."

He clenched his jaw as she bent to retrieve his cane, her hand never leaving his. Behind them, Ottorius let out a groan and mumbled something incoherently, but Annalise's grip prevented Rynn from turning back.

"We should send someone for him," she said, glancing over her shoulder as they made their way past broken windows and fallen paintings. A hardness glazed in her eyes. "Later."

His rage had not died, but his other senses slowly began to return. He took in the shattered glass covering the corridors, the splintered tree limbs falling through windows, the debris and cracked furniture lining the halls. Thunder boomed, followed by flashes of lightning that lit the shadows and ignited Annalise's face next to him in a fiery glow. Sheets of rain pounded against the walls.

He did not think he had ever seen a storm such as this.

Another crash of thunder and bolt of lightning lit the world and, further down, they heard echoes of an enormous collision. Screams rented the night air.

A guard sprinted down the hall. "What are you two doing out here?" he yelled. "You need to get to a safe room!"

Without waiting for a response, he grabbed Rynn's arm and shoved him in the direction of a nearby deserted pathway. "The closest one is two doors down. Leads to an old cellar. Hurry!"

Annalise shot Rynn a look of alarm. "We need to get back to the others."

"All of the other guests have been warned and led to safe rooms throughout the palace," the guard said desperately, glancing over his shoulder as another crash sounded. "You need to go. Now!"

Rynn nodded and squeezed Annalise's hand, guiding her toward the room. When she tried to pull away and protested about going to the Karstos wing, he snarled, "I am not letting you out of my sight, Annalise." They reached the door, and he threw it open with a *bang*. "You heard the guard. They are safe. And now, I am ensuring *you* stay safe."

He slammed the door behind them and she ripped her hand from his. "*I* have been the one to save myself for fourteen years, Rynn. I don't need you doing it for me now."

His breath caught. He no longer believed they were talking about the storm.

She turned her back on him and hastily felt along the floor for a latch leading to the cellar. The room had no windows, but he could still hear the storm beating against the outside walls, each peal of thunder shaking the ground at their feet. The door creaked open, and Rynn grabbed a torch from the wall to reveal a small wooden staircase lowering into the depths of the palace. Slowly, they eased their way down, until the musty scent of old earth and chittering of mice replaced the sounds of the storm.

When they reached the bottom, the fire from the torch revealed a small cellar with dirt floors and faded wooden barrels scattered against the walls. A broken shelf sat in one corner. A dusty, empty sconce hung from the wall, and Rynn carefully rested the torch inside of it. He turned to find Annalise slumped onto a barrel, her shaking fingers brushing through her hair.

"I apologize, Annalise," he said softly, keeping his distance.

She scoffed and rubbed at the kohl smudging under her eye. "Why? What, exactly, do you have to be sorry for?" When he did not answer, she looked away. "That's all anyone seems to be able to say."

"I apologize for not heeding your wishes the first time you asked me to stop. And I apologize for thinking it was my responsibility to save you. But I will not apologize for finding you and stopping him—"

"I didn't *need* you, Rynn!" she shouted through a choked sob. In a soft, shattered voice, she added, "I didn't *want* to need you."

"We all need someone, Annalise," he said, and suddenly his stomach dropped out beneath him.

He had spent months fighting against that very notion. Yet standing here, before the strongest woman he had ever met, he realized what his companions had been attempting to make him see. What Jade had been silently teaching him with every reprimand, every outstretched hand, every scowl.

There was strength in leaning on others. There was courage in falling to one's knees. There was power in humility.

"I do not presume to know what you are going through," he said slowly. "But you are always safe with me."

She swallowed and looked down to her hands resting on her knees. "I've never talked with anyone about this before."

There was pain and uncertainty in her voice, and it made his chest feel as if it were going to cave in. "We don't have to talk about anything you do not wish to."

"No, it—it's alright. I want to." She cleared her throat, leaving long pauses between her words when she continued speaking, as if dredging up each thought required effort.

"It...it's happened before. Fourteen years ago, on my eighteenth birthday. King Ryder had given my father permission to throw a ball in my honor at the castle, and I was ecstatic. The food, the wine, the decorations, the dancing. It was all for me.

"The boy I'd been trying to get to notice me for ages had finally told me he wanted to be my escort." She swallowed and took a deep breath. "Seb helped me find the perfect dress and teased me all week. I told him I was hoping Edgar—that was his name—would kiss me at midnight on the balcony, when the fireworks were in the sky and the promise of a new year of life was ahead of me. My own little fairytale." The bitterness in her words made Rynn flinch.

"I was naive. Fairytales are for princesses and storybooks. Edgar had his fill of wine and snuck me into an empty maid's cupboard. It was all wrong. I didn't want to go; I tried to stop him, but..." Her voice caught at the end and she paused, twisting her fingers in the edges of her dress.

The image of some faceless man using and discarding her in such a vulnerable state had rage whipping violently beneath Rynn's skin. He shifted on his feet and attempted to shove the feelings aside. She did not need his anger. She did not need his vows of retribution on her behalf. He noticed the slight tremble to her hands, the way she adjusted her head so her dark hair hid the side of her face from view. As if she could not bear to be seen when speaking of such a dark moment. But he *wanted* to see her. He wanted to see every piece of her, to know that she was here with him and *safe*.

"When he had his fill of *me*, he left. I spent the rest of the night alone in that cupboard, listening to the sounds of fireworks and celebration. All for me. But I couldn't feel their happiness. I—I couldn't feel anything. Just this...this hollowness." Her words were barely a whisper. "Like he had taken something from inside of me. Then...then Sebastian found me. I told him Edgar had simply walked out on me, nothing more." She gazed at Rynn through her curtain of hair, her eyes distant. "Seb was young, like me, and thought everything could be solved with a smile and a friend."

"And he still does not know?" Rynn asked quietly.

Shaking her head, she said, "I never told him. I suppose part of me thought I'd brought it upon myself. That it was *my* fault, in a way. I'd fancied Edgar for months. I thought..." She trailed off and rubbed at her forehead, a hint of a sob breaking through her even tone. "I don't know. Seb had always looked up to me, and I didn't want him to know how broken I was. How broken I still am. I was afraid he would look at me differently. I just wanted to be his Anna. He—he's my best friend."

Rynn could not fathom the thoughts that tormented her all these years, and the *strength* it took for her to be where she was today. This woman before him...she believed she was broken? Someone who had picked herself up time and time again, who constantly put the needs of others before her own, who ran an entire *kingdom* with none of the praise due her.

He wanted her to see all that he saw.

"You *are* different now, Annalise. Different than you were fourteen years ago. But 'different' does not mean 'broken.' You are stronger. More resilient." He took a tentative step toward her. "Most importantly, absolutely none of what has happened to you is your fault. You did not bring anything upon yourself, as you say. That man, and any other who makes such vile choices, is *entirely* to blame."

She let out a small scoff. "I know. I've told myself all that for *years*. But then things like this week happen, and tonight, and I just...I feel so helpless. I thought I was weak, being so scared to get near him. O-Ottorius." She stumbled on the name. "Told myself I was overreacting by feeling so uncomfortable around him. I thought I could handle it." She slumped against the wall and looked to the ceiling, shame and exhaustion etched onto her beautiful features. "I should've been able to handle it."

Rynn's chest tightened. "Annalise, there should have been nothing to 'handle' to begin with. *None* of this should have happened to you."

"But it did!" she suddenly shouted, green eyes blazing as she whipped her head to face him. "And I did *nothing*! Fourteen years of learning to protect myself, fourteen years of hiding my demons and trying to be better, *stronger*, and—gods, I was right back there in that maid's cupboard. Helpless."

His heart broke for her. He wished she could see herself as he did, wished she had not felt the need to keep her silence and carry this weight alone. Slowly, he stepped closer to her and, gripping his cane, lowered himself to his knees before her barrel, being sure not to touch her. His leg screamed at him, but he gritted his teeth and pushed the pain aside.

"I don't know what to say, other than I have not even known you for a week, and already I find you to be the most capable, most extraordinary woman. You are so brave, Annalise."

Wiping at her cheeks, she exhaled and closed her eyes, the fight from a moment ago leaving them. "I don't feel like it."

"But you *are*," he said, and the urgency in his tone made her eyes snap open. "I cannot imagine being in this position, reliving the nightmare that has plagued you for years. Even when you should not have to be, you are brave. For facing this life, day after day. For acknowledging your fears and not letting them consume you. For telling me of your past and permitting me to share in your burden, despite how difficult that must be."

He held his hand up to her as he knelt at her feet. "May I?" he asked gently, aching to feel her skin against his, desperate to prove the depth of his words. But only if she allowed him. Only if she was willing to let him in further.

She hesitated, and he held his breath, the silence of the dark cellar painstakingly loud inside his head. Then she nodded, placing her hand in his. Her soft touch soothed something within him.

He brought her palm to his heart. "Thank you for trusting me, Annalise. I don't ever want you to feel as if you are alone."

With a shaky breath and a tentative smile that sent his world spinning, she nodded. "I...I don't think I am. Not anymore."

Perhaps neither of them were.

CHAPTER THIRTY-EIGHT

Isla

Isla wasn't fast enough to stop the storm from decimating Farrow.

She hadn't even been able to sense it coming. It reminded her of when the earthquake and tornado had struck the day she visited Sebastian in Karstos—she couldn't feel the elements the way she should've been able to.

Her friends, minus Annalise and Rynn, were gathered in the common room when they heard the first boom of thunder. The palace walls shuddered, and in the distance, the tinkling of broken glass sounded from the halls.

"What in the—" Aidan started, then clutched the back of the couch to keep from falling as the ground shook, a low, echoing rumble making Isla's body hum.

"Everyone, get away from the windows," Jade commanded, pulling Bri to the opposite side of the hall. The others moved to follow, but Isla hesitated. She might not have been able to sense it, but she could still stop the storm before any damage was done.

She bolted to the window and flung it open, torrents of water and wind blowing the curtains back and drenching the wood floor. Taking in the tempest, her eyes widened. It was as if the heavens had collapsed and fallen to the earth. Lightning lit the horizon in a beautiful, terrifying dance, each strike chasing the one before across the dark sky.

"Isla, love, what are you—"

"Just get to a safe room!" she shouted over her shoulder, ignoring their cries as she pushed through the window and into the thick of the downpour, her skin immediately soaked. The wind and rain warred with one another, a battle that whipped through the trees and bashed against the palace, the scattered remains of broken branches, windows, and palace siding littering the landscape.

How had she not seen this coming? How had it gotten this bad so quickly?

She tried to leash the elements, to bring the wind and water into submission, but it was like something was fighting her. Every time she summoned them, they strained and snapped against her mind with a groan. Her connection was weak and distant, her magic diluted. Freezing rain pelted her. The wind made her skin raw and chilled her to the bone when it shouldn't have even *touched* her.

As she struggled to gain command, a bolt of lightning streaked across the sky and struck the tree right next to her. She flew backward, her body vibrating from the force.

She hit the ground with a gasp. Sharp pieces of bark and tree limbs splintered from the tree in the blast, slicing into her arms and neck. Her head spun.

How was she going to stop this? How was she supposed to help these people when the elements wouldn't listen to her? Hopelessness surged through her, flooding her with visions of the entire palace in ruins, villages destroyed, and families wasting away in the streets.

The sharp sting of pain and mounting distress had her elements slowly rising to the surface, working themselves into a frenzy as they sensed her panic. Wind swirled up her neck and through her hair, lifting the strands like it was begging her to *get up*.

"Oh, *now* you're here," she muttered, wincing as she stood. Jagged cuts marred her skin, but even as blood welled and spilled over, the edges began to sew themselves together, her healing abilities kicking in.

"Help me stop this," she begged her elements. "*Please.*"

Finally, they answered.

They broke through her skin with newfound fervor, reaching into the sky and ripping the storm straight from the heavens. The familiar tug on her core was white hot and excruciating, like the strands weaving the elements to her soul were fraying, separating from her as they brought the wind and rain under control. Gripping her head in her hands, she fell to her knees with a cry.

Then, it stopped.

The rain slowed to a mere trickle. Trees at the edge of the forest that had almost been uprooted now rustled calmly in a light breeze. Looking to the sky, she saw gray clouds rolling back to reveal midnight blue.

It was like nothing had even happened.

Her breaths were ragged as she pulled herself to her feet, staggering against the utter exhaustion sweeping through her. Several times she almost fell as she made her way back to the open window of their common room, now wrenched from its hinges and leaving a gaping hole. Forcing her body through, she stumbled down the hall and into her room, crumpling to the floor in a heap. Wet clothes stuck to her shivering body as water sluiced from her and pooled on the ground, but she didn't care. It hurt too much to move. To think.

Were the elements *slipping away*? Was this punishment for taking them to begin with, for disrupting the balance of nature? No ordinary storm should have been able to cause this. And she shouldn't have struggled so hard to stop it. The ache she felt when summoning her elements...it was like a piece of her had been irreparably severed.

She was terrified to tell the others, to dwell on what that might mean. When would the next event strike? And what if she couldn't do anything when it did?

These worries became hazy and muddled in her mind, however, as fatigue gripped her. She'd never expended that much power before; it was as if every cell in her body was screaming, alight with pain and pleading for relief. Her eyes fell shut as her back slumped against the wall. She just needed sleep...

Distantly, she heard the tapping of footsteps on the wood floor and the whispering of voices like fluttering wings grow closer. There was a soft creak of her door, and the glow of firelight turned the inside of her eyelids a muted red. Someone whispered her name as warm hands enveloped her body. She groaned when the hands tried to lift her, the dull throb in her nerves sparking to life at the movement.

"Isla, I need to get you somewhere warm." Soft lips brushed her forehead, and she relaxed into strong arms, her head rolling to the side and resting against a hard chest. She curled involuntarily toward his warmth. Only then did she realize how violently her body was shaking, how icy her skin was next to his heat.

He whispered soothing words into her hair as he walked, jostling her with each stride, but soon he set her onto the tiled floor. Her eyes were still too heavy to open. The sound of running water filled the room, and those gentle hands were on her again, cupping her face and skimming her cheeks.

"Isla, can you hear me? I need you to open your eyes, my love."

Slowly, painfully, she forced her eyes to open, meeting those of bright blue and filled with concern.

"Sebastian," she whimpered.

Relief flew across his face, his shoulders relaxing, his brow smoothing. "We need to warm you up. Can you get into the bath?"

She nodded and he helped her rise, supporting her weight as she looked down to see her dress, once light blue, now drenched and covered in mud and grass. Her arms and shoulders were littered with crusted blood, drying with the dirt caked on her body.

"Where are you hurt?" he asked softly, his thumb running along her collarbone and pulling back, red with her blood.

Everywhere. "It was just a cut, but it—it already healed," she said, her voice raw. With shaking hands, she slipped her thumb beneath the sleeve of her dress and pulled it down her shoulder. Sebastian's eyes lingered briefly before he turned away to pull a glass bottle from the counter. Unfastening the stopper, he poured oil in the water, the scent of lavender blooming in the air. Soon, the tub was filled with a cloud of bubbles beneath the rising steam. When his back was to her, Isla stepped out of her dress and eased her aching body into its sweet, warm caress.

A sigh escaped her lips, her head leaning against the hard edge. She lay there, taking deep breaths, letting the water loosen the grime. Her muscles began to release their tight hold under the layer of thick bubbles that hid her body from view.

As she reached for the bar of soap sitting on the edge, Sebastian appeared at her side, taking it from her fingers.

"Let me help you," he said, kissing her hand then moving behind her. A moment later, his hands were in her hair, working the soap through her tangles with gentle fingers. It was so intimate, so vulnerable, to be so wholly in the care of someone else. She couldn't imagine letting anyone else in like this.

"What happened?" he asked as he washed.

She took a deep breath. "The storm was...too strong. I didn't think I was going to be able to stop it. I've never felt that before, like the elements were...pulling away from me." His fingers moved to her scalp, massaging in slow circles, and she closed her eyes with an involuntary moan. He paused at the sound.

"Did I hurt you?"

"No, it doesn't hurt. Don't stop," she said. The pain had finally ebbed from her body, the elements quiet once again. She was spent, but no longer felt the weakness that had captured her entire being.

He slowly brought her head into the water, washing away the soap and dirt. "You scared me, Isla. When I saw you on the ground, I thought..." He trailed off, his hand tightening.

Isla grabbed his arm and carefully pulled him to the side of the tub, keeping her chest below the surface of the bubbles. His eyes were distant and haunted, like he was picturing her back on the floor, lifeless and covered in blood.

"I'm okay," she said quietly, running a wet hand through his soft hair. He leaned into her touch. "It's over now."

"I wish I could tell you to never do something like that again, but it wouldn't work, would it?"

She smiled. "I'm afraid not."

"That's what I thought." He sighed and pulled her to him, pressing his forehead to hers. "I wish this burden didn't fall on you. I just got you back. The idea of something happening to you, of you being taken from me...it's like being trapped in the darkness again."

She brushed her nose against his, their lips so close his shuddering breaths swept over her cheeks, and she could sense his erratic pulse as her hands wound around his neck. She didn't know what to say or how to stop either one of their fears, because the truth was...she didn't know what was going to happen. And that scared her more than any storm, any god, any foe.

"I wish I could make promises to you, Sebastian," she said, his lips a whisper on hers as she spoke his name. "But I don't know if I can keep them."

"I don't need your promises, love. We'll face whatever may come. I just need to know you're here, now. Safe and whole and with me."

"I'm here," she said, kissing the stubble at his jaw. "I'm safe." She moved to his cheek. "I'm yours." She placed a kiss on his lips, his breath catching as he brought her closer, water sloshing against the side of the tub.

"Let's get you to bed," he murmured against her mouth. When she raised an eyebrow, he chuckled. "To *sleep*, my love. You're exhausted."

She smiled and nodded, giving him one last kiss before he got up to retrieve a towel. Holding it out to cover her, she stepped into the plush fabric, weariness once again settling into her bones.

Sebastian slipped out while she changed into a nightgown, returning once she'd brushed her hair and tucked herself into bed, her eyes barely able to stay open.

"Rynn and Annalise just got back. I told everyone you're alright," he said, removing his shoes and sliding under the covers behind her, his chest pressed to her back. "They were worried about you."

"Well, they can stop worrying," she said with a yawn, her voice muffled and her mind foggy. "You're with me now."

He said something in response, but sleep had already claimed her, the safety of his arms pulling her into a deep, dreamless slumber.

CHAPTER THIRTY-NINE

Isla

When Isla woke the next morning, the other side of the bed was cold. She slapped a hand over her eyes to avoid the onslaught of the sun from the bedroom window. Flashes of the previous night came back to her, along with soreness from the exertion it took to use her powers. It wasn't a soreness in her muscles, like when she trained too hard or rode a horse for too long. It was a deep throbbing in her skin, her nerves, her bones. Like something had been torn from inside her.

Groaning, she flipped onto her side, only to see a note and a glass of water sitting on her bedside table. She shimmied up the mattress until she was leaning against the headrest, draining the water in seconds while reading the note.

Gone to the daily meetings. Wish I was with you instead. I've left you my signet ring in case you need anything—but please, save any filthy requests for when I'm not in the presence of others.

Hope you're feeling better today,

-S

P.S: Has anyone ever told you that you snore like a bear?

Choking on the water, she held back a snort. Sure enough, resting on the table was a dainty chain with his gold ring, the same one she'd used to speak to his mind the first night. The weight of it clunked against her chest as she fastened the clasp around her neck.

She wondered what everyone else would be doing that day. She expected they'd want to keep searching for the dagger, but she couldn't tell them yet that she already knew where it was. Her next course of action was clear, but how was she supposed to get back to the tunnels without the others trying to follow? She couldn't risk anything happening to them, not when the Primevals had warned her to come alone.

A tapping sounded on the bedroom door. Quickly trying to untangle her mess of hair, she made her way across the room, opening it to find Bri with a cup of steaming liquid and a muffin in hand.

"How are you feeling?" Bri asked, her normal, upbeat tone now worried.

Isla gave her a tired smile. "I've been better, but it's okay. Thanks for bringing this." She took the cup and food and urged Bri inside. "Did Sebastian tell you what happened?"

"Just that calming the storm took a lot out of you, but you were recovering. What *happened*?"

Isla recounted the night before as swiftly as she could, her mind already across the palace and deep in the tunnels, anxious to get down there again. As she spoke, an idea formed in her mind—one that would hopefully ensure some privacy over the next few hours.

She finished her story and, before Bri could react, said, "I promise, I'm already feeling so much better than I did last night. And actually, it's perfect that you're here. I need you to help me with something."

Bri narrowed her eyes. "Why do I get the feeling I'm not going to like this?"

Taking a sip of coffee then waving the mug in the air, Isla said, "It's not a big deal, and it won't be for long. I just don't want anyone trying to follow me."

"Follow you *where*?"

"I'm going back to the tunnels. I think the dagger is down there, and I need more time to find it. And no offense, but I'll be faster without all of you." The words twisted her stomach as she said them, even though it wasn't entirely a lie.

A little crease appeared on Bri's forehead. "But we were just there yesterday and didn't find anything."

"There was that other section we didn't check, remember?" Isla said, scrambling for an excuse.

"Are you sure you'll be safe?"

Isla nodded. "You've already seen what's down there. You know I'll be fine." Gods, she hated how easy it was to lie to her best friend. But she'd learned months ago the lengths she'd go to in order to keep potentially dangerous information from those she loved.

With a sigh, Bri said, "Alright, I'll cover for you. What do you want me to tell them?"

"Just...say I'm still tired and want to rest." It wasn't too far from the truth, considering what had happened the previous night.

"Okay, fine. But I still don't like this, you know," Bri said, leaning over to take a bite of Isla's muffin.

"You didn't have any problem offering to cover for me when I snuck off last winter," Isla said teasingly, remembering how Bri had supported her when she'd secretly met with Sebastian and didn't want the others to know.

"That was different," Bri said around a full mouth. "First, it was romantic. Second, it wasn't even your real body. I don't want you to get hurt." Her eyes showed how wary she was, and Isla's heart clenched.

"I know, Bri," she said softly, setting her cup and muffin down and wrapping an arm around her best friend. "It'll be okay, I promise."

"You said that last time."

"Yes, well...I learned my lesson." Isla swallowed and turned around, stripping out of her nightgown and into a pair of thick pants and a light sweater. She tucked Sebastian's ring beneath the fabric. "Thanks for doing this for me. I'll see you when I get back," she said, pulling on her boots.

As she made her way to the window, Bri asked, "Wait, why are you going that way?"

"I can't go barging through the common room. Everyone will see me."

"So you're going out the *window*?"

Shrugging, Isla unlatched the window and swung it open, letting the morning breeze and scent of a passing storm waft through the air.

"Come on, Bri, where's your sense of adventure?" Isla answered with a wink, then ducked beneath the frame and stepped into the sunlight.

She stuck close to the outer walls and shadows of the palace as she made her way to the eastern wing, careful to avoid anyone seeing her.

The aftermath of the storm was chilling. The western side, where the Karstos wing was located, remained mostly untouched. The north and east, however, had sustained great damage. An entire turret had collapsed, part of its wide base cracked in half and crumbled on the courtyard beneath. Dust and debris hung in the air like smoke, making it difficult to breathe or see properly. Entire walls had caved in, enormous trees uprooted and thrown aside, and servants ran around trying to salvage pieces of furniture or supplies.

Using her wind to listen to the sounds around her and locate the Chamber members, she found two of them in the north wing with mingled voices of what she thought were the other monarchs. The remaining two were making their way closer to her, Mariana's smooth voice and Ezeretta's dulcet tones growing more distinct.

If they were heading to their quarters, Isla had to hurry.

She sprinted around fallen tree limbs, hiding behind bits of stone and fragmented walls when she heard anyone approaching. Soon, through the cracks in the palace, she spied the same hall they had wandered down yesterday, the one leading to the Chamber's suite.

Within moments, she'd traversed the broken walls and slipped inside, the guards from yesterday gone—they had far more problems to deal with now than monitoring restricted rooms, she assumed. She strode straight to the bookshelf, pulled the book that opened the hidden door, and entered the dark, dank tunnel. She sent a vine slithering from the ground and to the bookshelf, twitching her finger and feeling it edge the second black book forward, rewarded by the sound of grinding and whirring as the bookshelf moved back into place. Her vines slinked to the ground. The last sliver of light grew smaller until it was gone, and she was left with only the sound of her breathing.

Once again, her flames flickered to life in her hand as she made her way down the familiar tunnels.

Her nerves threatened to spin out of control, but her sense of resolve overshadowed them. Not only did she know the dagger was down here, but also her chance to find out from the Primevals what she needed to do to end this. Anticipation made her chest tighten.

She came upon the fork and went left. As she drew nearer to the hot springs, her steps faltered. The entrancing pulse of the dagger beat in her veins, pulling her closer to the wall that led nowhere. Frustration bloomed inside her and she balled her hands into fists. How could she feel it so strongly when there was nothing there but stone and dirt?

On the other side of the wall, she could sense the hot springs bubbling and roiling excitedly, seeming to call to her. *Come*, the water beckoned.

"I'm trying," she said with a grunt, slamming her hand on the wall.

Not hard enough.

And then, it hit her. Her cheeks flamed; she was an *idiot.*

"Are you an elemental or not?" she grumbled to herself, pushing up her sleeves and placing her palms on the stone. Careful to avoid bringing down the entire wall, Isla felt for the vibrations of the earth and stone beneath her skin. With a tug on her core, the wall responded to her magic.

She watched as a crease appeared in the stone between her hands. Slowly, it pulled back like threads unknitting, a deep rumble emanating from the source. Something strange pushed against her earth from the other side. Bits of rock and small stones fell at her feet, but otherwise, the structure stood tall, the only change being the growing sliver in the wall—the only thing separating her from the hot springs—opening to let her pass.

Then, the first trickle of water appeared in the gap.

CHAPTER FORTY

Isla

With an echoing *crack*, the wall split open before her. Boiling hot water crashed through in a torrent, knocking her off her feet and momentarily shocking her senses. Grunting, she focused on holding the wall in place and gathering the flow of water spreading down the hall. Slowly, it began to recede, moving backward until the path was once again dry and the water was held back by an invisible force.

Isla took a moment to catch her breath, her muscles aching from the force it took to curb both elements, still tired from the events of last night. She left a human-sized slit in the wall, the rolling, tumbling water visible on the other side, like it was beating against a window.

Now that her heartbeat had evened out, the call of the dagger took her thoughts captive again. Except this time, it was stronger.

"Okay, dagger, what am I supposed to do?" she groaned aloud. Was this *another* dead end?

Earth.

Water.

She breathed deeply as the words flowed through her mind. The wall was earth, the hot springs were water. Did she need to find a source of fire and air, then? Was this some sort of millennia-old, cosmic trial to reach the dagger? Isla rolled her eyes at the thought. Where was she supposed to—

The hot springs. *Something* had to be naturally heating the water.

"You couldn't have made this easy, could you?" she muttered under her breath. Stepping past the hole she'd created and into the dark depths of the hot springs, she pushed against the pressure of the water trying to break through. She kept one hand on the rock while shoving out her other arm to force the boiling flood back. Her earth rumbled inside her and up into her hand, threading the gap in the stone back together.

Finally, she released her hold on the earth, slumping against the wall while the water covered her, finding a small pocket of peace in the dampened sound beneath the waves. She would never get used to this, to being able to *breathe* underwater, to see as clearly as if she were on the surface.

Fire.

It had to be heated from some source beneath the floor. Kneeling, she felt the smooth, slimy stone at her feet, and the flames under her skin leapt in response. The surface was scalding.

The idea of lowering herself into a pit of fire was slightly more disconcerting than water, even though she knew it wouldn't hurt her. Fire may be the most temperamental, but it still answered to her—she hoped.

Lowering herself, she called on earth to open the floor as she had the wall, being sure to keep the water *out* of the way this time. As the crack widened, a hissing grew increasingly louder. Heat licked up her body, almost uncomfortably so, like it was trying to seep through her skin to play with the fire in her veins.

"Knock it off," she grumbled, and the flames crackled in response. Once the new hole was wide enough for her to slip through, she took a deep breath. "Here goes nothing."

Then, she plunged, the earth automatically sewing itself up as she crossed. She fell.

And she fell.

Through skin-melting heat that threatened to burn her lungs with each painful breath, she fell.

How was she supposed to stop her descent?

Air.

Of course. Another challenge.

Swallowing what felt like daggers, she pulled at her air, pleading with it to respond quickly before she had to peel herself from the ground. Wind tickled at her cheeks excitedly, providing a slight reprieve from the heat, and wound its way down her body, cushioning her and slowing her fall.

Seconds later, the floor loomed beneath her, and it was like nothing she'd ever seen before. An undulating wave of deep orange, bright yellow, and dark crimson flowed on the surface. It cracked and flickered like fire but without the flames, almost like a burning sea. Her wind set her down, and she gingerly lifted her feet above the molten fire, surprised to find a solid surface. As she'd hoped, the flames didn't burn her. It was uncomfortable, yes, but it welcomed her anyway, and she found her body growing used to the extreme temperature.

Perhaps this was why the dagger transported itself down here, past so many impossible trials for humans. Because only an elemental was meant to find it again. Or, even further, a Vasileia.

Looking at her surroundings, she found the cave was actually quite small. Of all the places for the dagger to lead her—

There.

A bright orb floated across the cavern, its gravity pulling her in, its colors mesmerizing. It was shifting, throbbing, like it was alive with all four elements. Fire as orange as the dawn nipped at a spiderweb of vines, waves of dazzling blue pulsed and splashed against a clear wall of wind, each chasing one another in a sphere of life.

And there, between heartbeats, was the Dagger of Volnus, suspended in the center of the orb. Isla gasped and sprinted toward it, her hand outstretched to break through its cage.

Instead, she met a solid barrier. A scorching pain shot through her arm, and she cried out, clutching her hand to her chest.

"Careful, daughter," the Primevals spoke, their consuming presence rattling Isla's teeth.

"Isn't this what you wanted?" she growled, unsurprised to find them there. "For me to get the dagger?"

"Yes, but not before you understand the weight of what you are about to do. We have not revealed everything to you, Isla Vasileia."

As Aidan would say, that was the understatement of the century. "I know how the dagger works," she said. "I just need to know how it will help me. What did you mean when you said I needed to restore the elements to their rightful place?"

There was a shift in the atmosphere, a sudden tension filling the air. As if the Primevals were uncomfortable.

"You are the only one who can carry out this deed, daughter of the island. We had to ensure you would find your way here. And for that, we apologize."

"Apologize? What are you talking about?" A creeping sensation slid down Isla's spine, the hair on her neck raising.

"This was never meant to happen. A single soul was never meant to carry the weight of all elements. It is unconscionable. At the beginning of time, we created a way to restore balance, should calamity befall the elements. Were this to happen, each elemental would be able to give up their power of their own accord, sacrificing that shard of their soul. They would become mortals while their elemental magic continued on in the earth where it belonged, unhindered by the bindings of men. It would be free.

"Never did we expect a single being to embody all five elements at once."

Isla's heart pounded in her chest. Beads of sweat that had nothing to do with the molten core rolled down her back. "Okay, so why can't I do that? Sacrifice the elements and become human again?"

"Because, daughter," the voices said, pity lacing their magnanimous tones, *"with the amount of magic you possess in your soul, sacrificing it all will mean sacrificing yourself. There would be nothing left."*

Her blood ran cold. A buzzing began in her ears, but for once, her elements lay dormant. As if they knew. As if there was nothing they could do.

"You mean...it will kill me."

The air was silent.

"Well, why—why don't I just use the dagger to give the elements back to the elementals, and then they can all sacrifice that single part of them? That way nobody has to die, and nature will still be restored." She lurched toward the sphere that held the dagger. "Let me have it, and I can fix this."

She would do anything to protect those she loved, yes. But there had to be a way around this. A way to save herself *and* everyone else.

"Isla."

"Please!" she shouted over them. This couldn't be the only answer.

"Daughter, we—"

"Don't call me that!" she screamed, pounding her fist on the orb. Once again, pain lanced up her arm, but she didn't care. She continued to beat at the cage, her elements recoiling inside of her as she cried out.

"Stop!" the voices commanded, and an invisible force pulled her back, knocking her to her knees. *"The dagger will not work for you again."*

She blinked, the ringing in her ears increasing. "Wh-what do you mean?" she whispered.

"Did you think we would create an infallible weapon, one that could be used over and over, upsetting the balance of nature even further?" Their words

sunk into her skin. *"The Dagger of Volnus could only be activated once for each element in order to transfer immortal lifeblood and magic to another."*

Once. It could only be used...once.

And she'd already used it.

Her mind raced through every entry she'd read about the dagger, every piece of information they'd gleaned, *anything* that might offer another solution. There had to be a loophole, a way out. There always was. She couldn't have taken on this power, done everything to save the others on that beach four months ago, only for it to end like *this.*

"There is no other way, Isla Vasileia. We wish there were."

"Don't lie to me," she spat up at the ceiling, still collapsed on her knees. "You don't care about me. You don't care about *any* of us. If you did, you wouldn't let this happen! If you wished there was another way, then *create one!*"

Silence permeated the air, then what sounded like a sigh whistled through the wind, rustling her hair. *"Balance must be restored. We cannot create more elements when the ones we provided to this world so long ago still live within you. If you wish to put an end to the disasters that plague your earth, this is how it must be."*

This is how it must be.

Everything had led to this. Every plan, every dead end, every search. Because of a single, split-second decision she'd made months ago, she would have to die.

She thought of her father. How she hadn't seen him since that day, and had let him believe her to be dead all this time. Perhaps it was better this way. She supposed it wouldn't change much; he would still mourn his son and daughter, still feel the pangs of their loss.

He didn't have to know she'd survived. She didn't need to reopen the scabs of those wounds, only to cut a fresh scar.

She thought of Bri. The sister she'd never had. If a bond could exist between souls, there was surely one connecting theirs. How could she leave her *again*?

But...if she didn't, how much longer would any of them survive in a world trying to rip itself apart?

She thought of the former elementals. Gods, what a mess they were—but they were *her* mess, *her* family now. She didn't know how Kai and Aidan felt about getting their powers back, but she thought Jade and Rynn still hoped for it. And now, they never would. They would never have that piece of their spirit filled.

But they would get to *live*.

She thought of Sebastian. For a single moment, she had let herself dream of a life with him, someone who adored her, someone who *saw* her. A man who gave her courage to fight the monsters that lived within her, confidence to block out the voices of anxiety, and conviction to believe in herself.

A bitter pang shot through her heart. Some dreams were meant to stay in the dark.

"What is your decision, Isla Vasileia? Will you take the dagger and do what must be done?"

Isla closed her eyes. "How much time do I have?"

"At the stroke of midnight on the Spring Equinox, the powers of the Aether will be relinquished to you. Then, you may complete the transfer and release the elements to the earth."

The eve of the Spring Equinox was tomorrow. Less than forty-eight hours.

"Can I say goodbye?" she asked weakly.

The air around her tightened, and she could practically feel the pity rolling from the omniscient beings. *"Do what you must. Return here tomorrow evening, at the hot springs in the center of the palace, for this is where all four elements converge in the place of their birth."*

She stood on shaking legs and warily eyed the orb holding the dagger. "How do I get it out when I come back?"

"Your blood, of course."

Of course. One more thing her cursed blood was the answer to.

"Ready your mind, daughter of the island," the voices whispered through her. *"For tomorrow, you shall meet your end."*

CHAPTER FORTY-ONE

Jade

Something was wrong. Jade felt it in the air—like when she could sense a storm coming by the stillness of the trees, the fresh scent of rain before it blanketed her earth.

It wasn't that the palace and the people had gone still. No, everything seemed to be moving much faster after the destruction of the previous night. Servants, maids, and guards were frenzied, trying to salvage supplies from the wreckage and keep up with the areas of the palace that were still in commission. The Chamber was firm in their decision to hold the Spring Equinox ball the very next night, which Jade thought was an absolute waste of time and resources. Why did they feel the need for all of this pomp and circumstance when their city was in partial ruins? When their people were in the streets attempting to save their homes? When the injured had not yet been tallied, and their healers were up to their necks in the wounded?

Yes, a *party* sounded like a wonderful solution.

Jade and the others had spent most of the day in the village of Farrow, lending their hands in any way they could. Lifting broken limbs from yards and streets, collecting food, water, and clothing for the temporary shelters that had been set up, and tending to minor injuries. Jade had to admit, it felt good to be in the thick of the relief efforts. To be helping people and providing encouragement after such a calamity. She couldn't remember the last time she had felt such a kinship to others besides the elementals. Remembering what it was like to work toward a common goal, to be suffering in likeness, to be a *community*...it made her miss the old days, before power got in the way of purpose.

They had now cleaned up and were heading to the banquet hall, which was far enough away from the damaged side of the palace that it was still in perfect condition. As she descended the entrance stairs leading to the hall, Jade saw servants milling about, setting the table and handing out flutes of sparkling wine as the guests entered. Aidan and Kai veered off to the left as Jade, Rynn, and Bri took their glasses. Jade's sharp eyes monitored who was in attendance so far.

The Evonleans were already seated on their end: King Adrik with his over-powdered face and voluptuous robes, his wife helping their youngest son with a napkin, and Klaus, who stood as soon as he saw Brielle enter the room. Their sister, Jessenia, still hadn't appeared. Klaus's eyes followed Brielle with a sinful smirk as he took in her gown, a deep blue dress that dipped low in the back and clung to her every curve, with slits on both sides that began at the waist and trailed down her legs. It was held together by gold fastenings, accenting the gilded floral designs flowing across the fabric.

"He's looking at you like you're a meal," Jade said to Brielle behind her glass.

"Who?"

"Prince Klaus."

Brielle glanced at the man, then looked back at Jade with a smirk. "He's looking at *both* of us, Jade."

Sure enough, a moment later, he flashed a wink in Jade's direction before turning to his mother. Jade bristled. "That's preposterous."

"What's preposterous? That he could be attracted to you?" Brielle eyed her. "With curves like that, you shouldn't be surprised."

Jade waved off her comment. "No, not that. I meant that he would want to get involved with anyone from a different kingdom, especially at an event like this, where everyone is at each other's throats while pretending they don't want to sabotage one another."

"Oh, Jade," Brielle said, cocking her head while her lips turned up the slightest amount. "So innocent."

"Innocent?" Jade's mouth dropped open. She didn't think anyone had called her innocent in her millennia on this earth. Her reddened ledger proved quite the contrary.

Brielle chuckled. "Have you ever been in love?"

Rolling her eyes, Jade said, "Because I'm sure *love* is what's on that boy's mind right now."

"No, you're probably right," Bri said with a shrug. "But isn't that the point? Love is never on your mind until you're falling into it. I mean, come on, do you think Sebastian ever expected to fall in love with the woman he was forced to sabotage, as you say, for months?" She snorted, and Jade snuck a peek at the king, who was conversing with the Triad as his eyes kept straying to the entrance stairway.

Brielle continued. "I think, like many of us, the prince likes to find things to take his mind off real life. It may just be fun, but along the way, who knows? You might find something better."

"And have you? Found something better, that is?" Jade asked curiously.

The girl's laugh was like a bell. "Me? I'm still having too much fun for that," she said with a wink as she sauntered in the direction of the Evonleans. "It wouldn't kill you, you know," she shot back over her shoulder.

"What wouldn't?"

"Living a little," Brielle said, lifting her glass in the air before walking off.

Jade was sure she hadn't meant the suggestion as an insult, but the words stung slightly. Was that how Jade came across? How incredibly ironic, considering her passion, her *element*, was providing life to that which was around her. Was she so intent on what others were doing, on being the cautious one, the steadfast one, the conscientious one, that she had forgotten to live?

The rapping of a scepter on wood broke her from her thoughts as a servant announced the arrival of the Chamber. The guests took their usual seats as Mariana, Nor, Ezeretta, and Stefan entered and made their way to the far end of the table. Out of the corner of her eye, Jade saw Isla slip through the columns where the servants lurked and quietly rush to her spot by Brielle. Isla had been missing for most of the day; Brielle had said she was resting, still weakened from the storm the night before. The girl's face was an unreadable mask, her features even paler than normal.

Before Jade could whisper across the table to inquire further, Mariana's deep, smooth voice sounded from the Chamber's end.

"Our people have suffered a great tragedy," she began, steepling her hands at her chest in a gesture of solemnity. "While the fearsome storm has ravaged our home, we are proud to find our kingdom banding together and standing strong, with the help of many of you. It is a true sign of harmony and goodwill among our nations. This has been an insightful week of cooperation, and I speak for the entire Chamber when I say I am hopeful for a mutually beneficial relationship with each and every one of you." She gave the room a glowing smile and raised her glass. "A toast! To—"

But to what, they would never know, for at that moment three guards came bursting in from the side columns, the doors slamming with a *bang* that echoed throughout the hall.

"We apologize, Your Graces," one of them said, "but this could not wait." He quickly made his way to the Evonleans, stopped before King Adrik and Queen Melanora, and bent to whisper in their ears.

What little color there was leached from both of their faces, and Melanora let out a heartbreaking wail. Adrik jumped from his seat with a roar.

"What's going on?" Jade whispered as the other two guards murmured to one another, pointing in their direction.

Across the table, Isla's eyes widened. "The guard said that Princess Jessenia is dead. They found her in her room just now. She's been strangled."

None of them had time to respond as the guards strode toward Isla and Brielle. They pulled Isa's chair back and one of them grasped her arm, bringing the girl to her feet. She stumbled against their hold as both Brielle and Sebastian leapt from their seats.

The other guards held up their hands in warning.

"Isla Vasileia," the one holding her began, "by order of the Chamber of Iona, you are hereby charged with the attempted murder of High Priest Zolec Divola, and the murders of Kingsley James and Princess Jessenia Kegameth."

Jade blinked, her mouth dropping open.

Chaos broke loose.

Chapter Forty-Two

Jade

"What is the meaning of this?"

"She's *what?*"

"There's got to be some mistake—"

"You will take your hands off of her, or I will remove them for you."

Of all the exclamations, Sebastian's low, icy threat was the clearest. He pulled a cutting knife from the table and shoved it against the guard's throat, a silent threat to release the girl.

Giving Sebastian a sneer, the guard dropped Isla's arm. "You may threaten me all you like, Your Majesty, but it doesn't change the fact that we will be taking her to a holding cell to await further investigation. Willingly or not."

"And on what grounds do you make this accusation?" Sebastian asked heatedly.

"The High Priest Zolec Divola suffered a severe reaction three evenings ago, which the healers have deduced was caused by ingesting a liquid form of hemlock in his wine. Traces of hemlock were found in Miss Vasileia's private chambers when searched earlier today."

Brielle's eyes shot fire at the guard. "You searched her *room?*"

"Furthermore, the weapon used to wound and kill Kingsley James of Karstos has been identified as belonging to Isla Vasileia." He reached into his pocket and removed a dagger wrapped in cloth, and when he pulled the fabric back, both Brielle and Rynn breathed in sharply.

"I don't understand how this is possible," Rynn said next to Jade. "I had that dagger in my possession. I retrieved it from the ship four months ago and brought it here. I meant to give it to you, Isla, but had not yet found the opportunity."

Isla stood as still as a statue, seemingly nonresponsive to the pandemonium ensuing around her. When she looked down at the old dagger, however, she winced. Jade supposed it looked vaguely familiar; she recalled Isla wielding it during their weeks together in the mountains. She thought she remembered it being a gift from Isla's brother.

"Can anyone corroborate your claim, sir?" the guard asked Rynn, who stiffened.

"Is my word not proof enough?"

The guard shook his head. "As the handle of the dagger has Miss Vasileia's name engraved on it, our assumption must be that the dagger belongs to her and has since been used in the act of murder."

Brielle spoke up. "But I was with her the entire afternoon when Kingsley was killed. We weren't even in the palace! She couldn't have done it."

The guard looked at her with a furrowed brow, and Jade tried not to let her own fear show at Brielle's confession. If they asked about where they were...

Thankfully, Sebastian quickly deflected. "What of Jessenia, then?" he pressed.

"We do not have concrete evidence, but both Miss Vasileia and Princess Jessenia have been unaccounted for over the last several hours, and we believe there is motive for such an act of violence."

Sebastian threw his hands in the air. "What *motive?*"

The guard raised an eyebrow at him. "Did you, or did you not, have a romantic relationship with the Princess of Evonlea during the last five years?"

"I don't see how that's rele—"

"And do you not currently have a romantic relationship with Miss Vasileia?"

Sebastian glanced at Isla, his fists tightening. "You believe she harmed the princess out of *jealousy*?"

"Murder has been prompted by far less, Your Majesty," was the guard's only response.

"This is ridiculous!" Sebastian shouted, motioning toward the Chamber. "Do you have anything to say about this?"

Mariana crossed her arms, her expression unreadable. "We are just as shocked by the news of these allegations as any of you. However, if the head of our guard has reason to hold Miss Vasileia responsible, we have no choice but to trust him."

When she gave a curt nod to the guards, all three of them swarmed, one holding back Sebastian as the other two motioned for Isla to follow them.

Jade's heart hammered. Why wasn't Isla *fighting*?

"Where are you taking her?" Sebastian struggled against the guard, who slammed him onto the table. When one of the men forcefully gripped Isla's arm, Sebastian exploded.

With a roar, he lurched away from the table, his fist colliding with the guard's jaw and knocking him back a few steps. But before Sebastian could reach Isla, the guard pulled his sword and pressed it dangerously close to Sebastian's side. The entire Karstos section of the table jumped up, Sebastian's two remaining guards at the ready with their swords drawn. Gasps echoed down the hall, shock and fury mixing with the grieving cries of Queen Melanora, who was slumped in her husband's arms.

"This is all very dramatic," Isla said, finally breaking her silence. Her voice was calm, lethal. "I haven't killed or poisoned anyone, but if you hurt my king, I will bury that sword in your gut without so much as touching it."

"I think we've heard enough. Guards," Mariana said briskly, "you may also want to take her friend here in for questioning, given that she claims to have been in Miss Vasileia's company before the attack on Kingsley."

The guard nodded and reached for Brielle's arm. Before he made contact, a vine encircled his hand and snaked up to his shoulder, snapping it behind his back with a sickening *crunch*. The man cried out and fell to his knees. The room was in an uproar—more guards rushed in from the side while Rynn, Aidan, and Sebastian took various stances of defense, ready to attack.

"No!" Jade said to them in a low voice, holding an arm out to Rynn and catching Kai's attention. If they fought back, if they gave the Chamber *any* indication they were loyal to Isla and a threat to Iona, they would all be detained or banished.

Letting the chaos around them mask her words, she whispered, "We can't get involved. Isla needs us to stay neutral. She needs us *here*."

"But we can't let them take her," Aidan hissed across the table.

As he spoke, two guards who had converged on Isla suddenly collapsed to the ground, holding their heads in their hands and screaming in agony.

"I don't think that will be a problem," Kai said.

Three more burst from the side. With a wave of Isla's hand, they rose into the air, their legs kicking and dangling several feet off the ground. Frightened shouts sounded from the guests. The Ionan servants cowered on the ground, some holding up pieces of jewelry that looked like ancient protection amulets.

"Restrain her!" Stefan Rigaldi roared, stalking toward Isla.

Snapping her fingers, a low wall of fire rose from the ground in front of Isla, a line separating her and the Chamber. The guards who had rushed toward her stopped in place, flames highlighting the fear on their faces. Most of the Aramian and Evonlean guests who hadn't already vacated the table now staggered away from Isla with mixed expressions of shock, curiosity, and terror.

"Do you see what those with magic are capable of?" Mariana cried. "Terrorizing our people, murdering your loved ones! She has come here to rip away our crusade for peace!"

Isla scoffed. "Your crusade is not one of peace, de Faye, and it's time your people learned of your lies."

"Who do you think you are, speaking to us like that?" Stefan yelled.

Isla's features hardened, and Jade hardly recognized the girl. Something had happened over the last couple of days. Something that wiped the compassion from her eyes and replaced it with steadfast resolution. Her pale cheeks and violet eyes were aglow with the dancing flames before her.

"Me?" she asked, anger flashing over her. Heat swept through the hall. "I'm a *Vasileia*. I'm a child of the bones resting in this very palace, of the empire you buried beneath your reign of fear. You put those crowns atop your heads and called yourselves their salvation? Their *leaders*?" She shook her head, red curls waving like a sea of fire. "Soon, your people are going to see how broken and corrupt you really are."

With a wave of her hand, she sent out a force of air so strong it brought every person in the hall to the ground. Slamming into Jade like a brick wall, it knocked the breath from her lungs and sent a dull pain through her body as she landed on her back with a grunt.

Heart beating wildly in her chest, Jade scrambled to her knees.

All that was left in the spot Isla had occupied was smoke rising in the air like snakes of shadow and four shattered crowns, rolling in the empty silence.

CHAPTER FORTY-THREE

Isla

T he tunnels felt even more menacing under the blanket of night.

Akir had found Isla shortly after she'd fled the dining hall and quickly led her to the hidden entrance in the north gardens, where the lion gargoyle once again shifted to reveal the now familiar steps leading to the underground bunker. They'd barely managed to avoid a slew of Ionan guards hunting the palace grounds for her.

Isla's elements were a twisting, colliding cyclone, feeding off her adrenaline and anger and fear. Perhaps they also knew what was to come the next day. They clung to her stronger than usual, embedding themselves further into her spirit, as if that could keep them there permanently. It was like they didn't want to let her go.

"Is there any truth to their claims?" Akir asked as they made their way down the steps and into the headquarters of the resistance.

Isla balked. "No! How could you even ask me that?"

He stopped in his tracks and spun to face her, his robes swinging at his ankles. "Isla, I am preparing to harbor you in the relative safety of my life's work, surrounded by helpless people who cannot afford the risk your presence brings. But I am willing to do it, for I believe justice should prevail against fear, and you are my blood. Forgive me if I must be absolutely certain you will not betray me or my people."

Taking a deep breath, Isla shook her head. "I haven't hurt or killed anyone. I don't know how they found hemlock in my room—I guess someone put it there to frame me. I was down here with *you* when Kingsley was attacked. And I couldn't care less about the princess and Sebastian's past. I would never hurt her." She reached out and took Akir's wrinkled hand in her own. "I don't want to bring danger to your people, Akir. While I appreciate everything you've done, I can't accept your help. I don't want you risking what you've built here just for me. I can take care of myself."

"I know you can, cousin. But you should not always have to. You can stay here for as long as you need." He squeezed her hand. "Have you located the dagger?"

She hesitated. Her stomach fell at the reminder of all she had uncovered that day. "I know where it is, yes. This will all be over tomorrow."

Akir gave her a sad smile. "Perhaps *your* battle will be. The rest of us are not so lucky."

Isla lay awake on her pallet, snores and deep breathing filling the air. Her mind was unable to stop replaying those moments in the cave with the Primevals and the chaos of dinner.

How had things gone so badly? It was as if the last twenty-four hours had happened in a blur. The only piece of relief she'd gained from it all was that her friends weren't down here with her, hiding for their lives. They may not completely escape the Chamber's questioning, considering they were so close to her, but Isla could only hope the Chamber and their guards continued to see Isla as the sole guilty party and didn't take it out on her companions.

She knew the Chamber—or someone working for them—had planted the evidence against her. Nobody else had any reason to want her locked away. Not only was she the living embodiment of the magic they hated, but she was also a Vasileia. It was her own fault for flaunting that fact on her first night.

She'd created a target on her back, one the Chamber was threatened by in more ways than one.

It didn't really matter that she'd been accused of the crimes. She didn't fear what the Chamber could do to her. What she *did* fear was what they could do to those she loved. If she was right and the Chamber was trying to frame her, that could only mean they'd also committed the murders. This whole time, Isla had been so set on finding the dagger and completing her quest that she'd lost sight of the problems that would still exist once—*if*—she succeeded. Namely, this island being controlled by such fear-mongering, vindictive leaders. How could she leave the kingdom in this state?

But if she didn't, they would have much worse things to worry about.

Isla fingered the heavy ring still hanging around her neck, thanking the gods Sebastian had thought to leave it for her. She desperately missed him. It was surprising how she could grow so used to someone's presence in such a short amount of time. The door between their rooms had become a welcome invitation over the week. Knowing he was on the opposite side, eager to comfort her after a long day, to hold her and adore her and distract her...it was so natural, so expected. Gods, what she wouldn't give to be with him now.

Bringing his ring to her lips, she summoned her wind. She wasn't sure if Sebastian was awake or if her words would even reach him in his sleep. She just knew she needed to talk to him, if only to calm her mind.

After making sure none of the other sleeping rebels were close enough to hear, she whispered, "Sebastian...if you're awake, I want you to know I'm safe. I escaped with Akir to the tunnels and am staying here tonight. Please don't come looking for me. There's already so much tension between everyone, I don't want you jeopardizing your relationships with the other kingdoms. And—and tell everyone else I'm alright, too. I need you to keep them safe."

She paused, unsure how much to say and scared of the overwhelming emotions clogging her thoughts. Her entire being ached for peace. For him. For everything to be over.

She exhaled shakily. "I found the dagger. I know what to do, and hopefully by tomorrow night, it'll be over. Just...don't do anything rash, okay? I'm going to fix everything." She rolled onto her side and tucked her elbows in. "I'm sorry this turned into such a mess. I hope they don't take it out on you. Annalise is probably up to her ears in damage control as it is. But...I have to admit, knocking Mariana flat on her back was incredibly satisfying."

She felt ridiculous, blabbering to a piece of *jewelry* in the middle of the night, but slowly, the knots in her stomach loosened and the suffocating weight on her chest lifted.

"It actually reminded me of this one day a few months after my papa taught Arden and me how to use a bow and arrow. It was the first time he let us practice shooting real game in the forest. We were only eleven and barely knew what we were doing. I aimed for a squirrel high in the branches of a tree and didn't see Arden standing right below it. I *accidentally* let go of the string too early and it shot straight at him." She snorted at the memory of her twin's face. His eyes had been as wide as saucers. "I've never seen him move so fast. Fell straight to the snow on his back, just like Mariana and the rest of them."

Before she knew it, one whispered story turned into several, and her throat ached from speaking in hushed tones for so long. When she closed her eyes, it was easy to believe Sebastian was beside her, wrapping his hands in her hair, kissing her forehead, running his fingers along her arm.

"I miss you, Sebastian. This all happened so fast," she said, eyes closing, breaths slowing. "Who would've thought we'd be here? The mighty king and a huntress from a little town in the woods." Sighing, the ring slipped from her fingers as sleep circled above her.

"I just wish we had more time."

Chapter Forty-Four

Isla

Isla woke to the sounds of footsteps on stone, rustling papers, and murmuring voices. Slowly, she opened her eyes and stretched, the past twenty-four hours rushing back to her in painful spurts. Her hand pressed into something metal, and she looked down to find Sebastian's gold ring.

"I apologize if we woke you," someone said. Isla glanced up to see Eliza and Akir standing at a nearby table.

"It's fine," she said with a yawn. "Is there somewhere I can go to..."

"Freshen up?" Eliza finished for her. "Yes, dear. There's a room down this hall and to the left. It's one of the only areas where we have pipes to carry running water."

Isla nodded her thanks and followed Eliza's directions, taking a few minutes to splash her face with cold water and relieve herself. When she got back to the main chamber, she found Akir and a small group of people loading knapsacks with supplies.

"Are you going somewhere?" she asked him.

He nodded. "We spent most of the day yesterday in the village helping with storm relief. There's still much work to be done."

"But...what if you're spotted? Aren't most people down here because they're wanted for some sort of false crime?"

"Some, yes. These here with me"—Akir motioned to the handful of men and women—"are volunteers to the resistance. They are all free to live above ground." Turning to the group, he said, "Is everybody ready?"

"I want to come," Isla suddenly said.

Akir paused, then stepped closer and beckoned her into a corner. "Are you certain? I thought you would have other business to tend to today, since you have found the dagger."

She'd been trying to put off thinking about the "other business" for as long as possible. Whenever she dwelled too long on what the Primevals told her, on the fact that she only had one day left, on the idea of saying goodbye…it was too much. She was worried she'd give in and refuse to follow through.

And truthfully, using her last day to help heal this island in whatever way she could seemed like a good way to go.

Nodding, she said, "I can't do what needs to be done with the dagger until tonight. I have time, and I want to help."

He bowed his head. "Then it would be our honor, Isla Vasileia."

Eliza shoved a thick, dark cloak into Isla's hands. "You may want to put this on to hide yourself," she said. "I have a feeling people may be looking for you."

Eliza's concerns were for naught, considering when Isla, Akir, and his crew reappeared above ground, the town was bustling with far too much activity for anyone to pay attention to them.

The main village of the island was in even worse shape than the palace. What was left of the white-stacked buildings that had lined the streets when she roamed Farrow several days ago now lay crumpled on the cobblestone. Wild animals wandered through the rubble. Some homes had been completely wiped out, while others still appeared liveable, if not disheveled. Tree branches and debris from nearby fallen structures littered the area. People with dirt and dust covering every inch of their bodies scurried about as they cleared the most obtrusive objects from the streets.

At the end of the main square stood a series of taverns and inns that had been mostly unaffected, save for minor damage, and when Isla passed by, she saw they were filled to the brim with people. Blankets covered all available floor space, and bodies were crammed together with barely enough room for others to get by as they carried food and water through the crowds.

As Isla drank in the sight through the window, she was surprised to find the people were...smiling. Laughing, even. Conversing and joking with their neighbors while folding stacks of blankets and clothes or sorting through piles of food. These people, who had suffered so much and had such a cloud over their future, had come together in good spirits, refusing to let their circumstances take even more from them.

It was a very different picture from that day on the cliffs, where the mob had let their fear and anger take control.

"You see? They are not all what you think," Akir said softly. "The Chamber has not yet won, no matter how bleak it may seem at times. Where there is still joy, there is hope. And I see quite a bit of joy in there, don't you agree?" he asked, tapping his nose with that twinkle in his light green eyes.

Yes, she could see it. And it was a curious thing, how that very hope could bloom in her own chest while her end drew nearer with each passing breath.

Akir divided the volunteers and doled out instructions for the day. When he reached Isla, he paused.

"What can I do?" she asked.

He chuckled. "Oh, dear cousin, I believe the question is whether there is anything you *cannot* do."

"You know what I mean," she said with a smile and a shake of her head. "I don't want to do anything that will...attract too much attention. We don't need another riot on our hands."

"I think you will find people to be more amenable in the throes of disaster. But yes, discretion is wise. Come," he said, motioning for her to follow. "I have just the thing."

Curious, she trailed behind him as he strode out of the main square and into the surrounding forest—the same path she and the others had taken to reach the cliffs earlier in the week. Instead of staying straight, Akir veered off to the right, down another dirt road that looked as if it were often traveled, but had now been destroyed. Before them, as far as Isla could see, acres of splintered trees, sinkholes, twisted and gnarled roots stretched, as well as remnants of buildings from the nearby village that had blown this way.

"This path leads to the largest cropland our kingdom possesses," Akir explained. "A few men ventured out yesterday and reported the fields have been almost entirely ruined. We have lost the majority of the crops we were to harvest later this spring, and will need to start over on preparing the land for summer and fall rotations. And, as you can see"—he brandished an arm—"our access to the fields is severely limited now. I had hoped you might—"

Isla stopped him mid sentence. "I think I can help with that," she said, a hint of a smile forming on her lips.

Her earth was already awakening with a slow, powerful ease. It stretched its limbs and unfolded beneath her skin like a canvas. Nature turned its attention to her as she lifted her arms; every leaf swayed in her direction, animals curled around her calves and pressed into her before retreating, rock and stone rumbled beneath her feet. With that familiar tug at her core, vines snaked from the ground and wound their way around broken logs and scattered trees, pulling them from the path and stitching them back together. Sinkholes filled with dirt and rocks until they were once again solid land.

Within minutes, the damage from the storm had been repaired, the path cleared and smoothed, the deadened foliage enlivened and radiant.

Akir beamed and clapped his hands. "My, we could use you around here more often."

"What's next?" she asked, a little breathless from the power and rush of adrenaline. It was invigorating, how she could help the land, how her magic could *give* and bring life.

Over the next couple hours, Isla repaired the forest surrounding Farrow. When a man came to find Akir and told him they were in need of more firewood, Isla waited until he was gone and, with a snap of her fingers, sent stacks and stacks of logs to the edge of the village. They heard another complaint that the underground reservoir holding most of the accessible water was cut off by a collapsing tunnel, and Isla located the source and easily molded the earth back to its original state.

She lost herself in the work, in the life teeming all around her and the earth bending itself to her will as easily as breathing. It almost made her forget what was to come.

As Isla finished clearing the furthest section of the forest, Akir reappeared from behind a thicket of trees.

"How far out are the fields you talked about earlier?" she asked the elder. "The ones that got ruined."

"Just a mile that way." He pointed north.

She nodded her thanks and wiped dirt and sweat from her brow. "I'm going to see what the damage was."

The two of them made their way through the newly cleared forest until they came upon the wide fields Akir had spoken of. Bright trees and bushes gave way to a rickety wooden fence stretching all the way down the treeline in either direction. Most of the fence had been destroyed, some posts leaning onto the field while others were violently ripped out of the ground. Beyond the fence lay acres and acres of farmland. Parallel rows of crops in what Isla assumed used to be neat lines were now a scattered mess of roots and stalks, upturned soil and torn plants.

"The people salvaged what they could, but most of this spring's crops are dead," Akir said.

Isla walked further into the field, her fingers running along a patch of vegetation that had been uprooted from the soil. Immediately, their roots extended and dug through the earth, the plants righting themselves and blooming under her touch.

A small section of land was easy. But this? Acres of ruined crops? This was different from moving earth or water, from stopping storms or raising a blaze. This was creating *life* from nothing.

Pressing her palms into the earth so she could feel it surrounding her, Isla closed her eyes. She imagined that well of power breaking into hundreds of tendrils and pushing away from her, slithering through the ground and giving life wherever it touched. It was like she could see each individual strand foraging the earth. She felt each root take hold, each stalk straighten, each vine grow.

"Isla," Akir said softly beside her. "Open your eyes."

Carefully, she blinked against the bright sun. Around her lay a field of green rows and fertile soil, herbs, vegetables, and crops of all kinds blooming before her very eyes. Even now after she'd paused, they grew, their stalks rising from the ground inch by inch.

But that was not what Akir was referring to.

Off to the side, behind the fence line, stood a small group of men, women, and children. They watched her with wide, wary eyes, not quite believing what they were seeing.

Panic clutched at her. Nobody was supposed to be here. What if they reacted like the others did? What if they hated her? Feared her?

"Let them come to you," Akir whispered, as if speaking of timid animals. Slowly, Isla took her hands from the earth and rose from the ground.

The first one to approach her was a child. Maybe ten years old, the little girl's chestnut braids swung around her tan face as she bit her lip with a shy smile. A woman, who Isla assumed was her mother, followed a few steps behind, but didn't stop her daughter from walking straight up to Isla.

"Hello," Isla said kindly, crouching to the girl's eye level. "My name is Isla. What's yours?"

"Rayna," the girl said, looking at her and then glancing over at the fully grown crops, her hazel eyes drinking in the sight. "Are you a fairy?" she suddenly asked.

Chuckling, Isla shook her head. "Nice to meet you, Rayna. And no, I'm not a fairy." Looking over the girl's head and meeting the gaze of her mother, Isla added, "I'm just someone who wants to help."

"What you did—" The woman stepped forward hesitantly, then stopped herself, grasping at her dirty apron. Her bright eyes scanned Isla with bewilderment, a small crease forming between her brows. "I've never seen anything like it."

Isla stood and put her hands out in a show of peace. "Please, don't be afraid. I would never do anything to hurt any of you."

"Afraid?" a gruff voice said behind the woman. A middle-aged man with gray in his bushy black beard put his hand on the woman's shoulder. "You have this magic the Chamber warned us about, don't you?"

Wetting her lips, Isla nodded.

His gaze bore into her as he squinted, and Isla felt like her soul was being sifted and weighed by this single human. She didn't realize she was holding her breath in the silence until her chest began to burn.

"Well, then," the man finally said, "I suppose it's not so bad after all."

And just like that, the rest of the people cautiously made their way to her and the rows of crops around her, stopping to examine and marvel over each one. Isla exhaled and caught Akir's eye. He winked and smiled, as if he knew all along what would happen. *They are not all what you think,* he had said.

Isla spent the next hour talking with the Ionans. They were eager to show her their irrigation systems, to see her reactions to their innovative farming practices—they didn't seem to understand she knew absolutely nothing about farming. She was presented wheelbarrows with steel blades attached to the ends—so they could plow more efficiently—and a demonstration of their crop rotations throughout the harvest seasons, as well as a new breed of fruit they'd experimented with that looked like a cross between a strawberry and an orange. One man took her to the far east side of the fields and asked her if there was a way to block a family of moles that kept burrowing. At one point, Rayna brought her a little pink peony that Isla stuck in her hair with a smile.

Her heart was so full. These people trusted and appreciated her. It gave her hope that not everyone had been brainwashed by the Chamber's twisted words.

When she and Akir said goodbye to the families, Rayna ran to her and wrapped her arms around Isla's waist. Isla cupped her cheek as her freckled face looked up with a wide smile, full of such beautiful innocence.

"Will you come back and visit, Miss Isla?"

Isla's stomach fell, a coldness washing over her. Struggling to keep a grin pasted on her lips, she said, "I'd love to, sweet girl, but I don't know if I can. You better take care of everyone here, okay?"

Rayna nodded and let go, rushing back to her mother with her braids swishing at her back. Isla waved one last time and crossed over the fence line with Akir at her side.

"What's wrong, cousin?" he asked, concern written on his wrinkled features as he stopped her a few minutes down the path. "Why do you cry?"

Raising a hand, Isla felt wet tears running down her cheeks. She forced out a shaky laugh and wiped at her eyes.

"I guess I'm just not very good at goodbyes," she said.

She picked up speed and trudged ahead of him. Had she taken time to look back, she may have noticed her answer didn't appease the old man, for his grave face stayed fixed on her, the wrinkles in his forehead deepening in suspicion with each stride.

CHAPTER FORTY-FIVE

Sebastian

O ne would never know by the king's finest formal wear, his dashing smile, or his carefully groomed hair that half of his heart was currently seeking refuge in the hidden tunnels.

He hadn't seen Isla in almost twenty-four hours, when she was accused of murder and made her escape from the Chamber and its guards. If they hadn't known of her abilities by then, they certainly did now. The whole palace did.

The Chamber had placed a guard at every door in the Karstos wing, and small groups had been sent to search the palace grounds. Mariana and Ezeretta had personally escorted Sebastian and his entourage from the dining hall after Isla's display. He knew what Jade had warned them, how they needed to remain compliant and give no reason for others to believe them guilty, but he had found it difficult not to try and fight his way out from under Ionan surveillance to make sure Isla was safe.

What she had done that night...it was incredible. Breathtaking. And while he had no doubt she could take care of herself, he could not quiet the growing unease at knowing she would not be in his bed, wrapped in his arms.

The *only* bit of consolation he'd received the rest of the evening were the whispered words that echoed through his mind late into the night, her beautiful voice haunting him as he fell asleep. Even without being near her, he could hear the love and longing in her voice as she told stories of her childhood, comfort mixed with the sting of unhealed grief. His arms ached to hold her, to kiss away her tears and soothe the jagged edges of her sorrow.

As today marked the last full day of the Reign of Dawn festival, the four kingdoms were supposed to finalize the various trade agreements and treaties before ending with a grand celebration at the Spring Equinox ball. Given the previous night's events, however, all meetings had been canceled. Sebastian caught word that the King and Queen of Evonlea had sequestered themselves in their chambers with their two sons and commanded their servants to prepare their ship to set sail early the following morning. He hadn't heard an update on the Aramian high priest, Zolec, but assumed he was still in the care of the healers.

The day had been spent in painful silence. Guards were positioned down the length of the Karstos hallways, and it was an unspoken rule that while they were "highly honored guests," they were under careful observation and were unable to leave the wing until nightfall for the ball. As such, none of them were comfortable speaking openly with one another, afraid word would get back to prying ears and spin their conversations into a confession of treason against the Chamber. Sebastian was able to covertly slip the news to the others that Isla was safe, but hadn't given them any more details than that.

He had been anxiously pacing in his room for the last half hour, fully dressed and prepared for the ball far earlier than was necessary. The idea of a *party* in the midst of this chaos was absurd, but he knew they needed to keep up appearances to avoid the Chamber looking more closely than they already were.

He was waiting for the guards to summon him and escort them to the ballroom. It was a surprise, then, when the familiar knock of his advisor sounded on the door.

"Come in, Anna," he said absently.

The door creaked open and shut swiftly. "I hate how they're watching us like we're all going to break loose and murder someone," she said by way of greeting, striding to the armchair by the window and heatedly throwing herself onto the cushion.

"What did that chair ever do to you?"

She shot him an unamused glare. "Where is she, anyway?" *Straight to the point.* "How do you even know she's alright?"

He shook his head as he walked to the liquor cart and poured them each a healthy portion of whiskey. "She got word to me earlier," was all he said, inclining his head to the door to imply he didn't want to take any chances they were being listened to.

"So what are we supposed to do, exactly?" Annalise asked exasperatedly, accepting the drink. "Stay quiet? Go to the ball? *Not* act like our friend was accused of murder and used magical powers to escape in front of the entire festival?"

Sebastian ran a hand through his hair. "Look, Anna, I'm as on edge as you are about the whole ordeal. But she told me that she found the dagger and knows what to do with it to end everything *tonight*. We have to trust her. I would love nothing more than to cut each of these guards down and run off to find her, but that would do more harm than good. You know that."

Annalise sighed heavily, lifted her glass to her lips, and gulped it down in seconds before slamming it onto the table.

Sebastian raised an eyebrow. "Thirsty?"

She winced. "Sorry, I'm just...you're right. We have to trust her. I just want to get off this island."

Needing to distract himself from the worries plaguing his mind and pretend, for a moment, that it was simply him and his Anna, Sebastian teasingly said, "I'm surprised you're eager to leave, considering you and a certain moody male who shall remain nameless have hit it off so well."

Annalise jerked her head to him, her eyes narrowing while her bronze cheeks deepened in a blush.

She opened her mouth to retort, and he clicked his tongue at her. "Now, Anna, you don't think I haven't noticed how he's constantly around you? How you spend your mornings together, all quiet and cozy in the common room? Or how he chased off after you like a hellbent lover when you disappeared the night of the storm?"

When he mentioned that night, her flushed cheeks suddenly lightened and she dropped her gaze to her lap. Concern shot through him. Softening his voice, he said, "Did something happen that night, Anna? Did he hurt you?"

"No, he didn't," she said quickly. "He was...what I needed, in that moment." Pausing, she twisted her fingers against her dress, and Sebastian took in her ball attire for the first time. She was stunning in a floor-length, ash gray gown with a full skirt that billowed out at the waist, making it look like her legs were encased in whirling smoke. The top half was long-sleeved and made entirely of lace that showed hints of her golden skin beneath the delicate silver designs. Black kohl lined her eyes and flecks of silver dust shimmered on her cheeks, her long, mahogany curls brushing against them as she moved a strand behind her ears.

He knelt before her, took her hand, and kissed it. "When he sees you tonight, he's going to beg to come back to Karstos with us." Her shy eyes met his, and she gave him a close-lipped smile. Sebastian had a feeling there was something she was holding back, but the gods knew he wasn't one to judge secrecy.

"You know you can talk to me about anything, right, Anna?" he asked, her cold hand still in his.

She squeezed his fingers. "I know, Seb. Just give me a little time."

Nodding, he stood and straightened his dress coat. "Save me a dance, yes?"

Her green eyes sparkled with humor. "I suppose, if only to stop you from pining after Isla for five minutes."

"I do not *pine*."

"My gods, Seb," she said with a snort. "You're absolutely pitiful when she's not around. 'Isla this' and 'Isla that.'" She approached him and reached up to fix his collar, her tone dropping its playful edge and filling with compassion. "I've never seen you look at anyone the way you look at her."

He held his breath, his heart pumping faster while flurries erupted in his stomach. "I think I'm in love with her," he breathed.

Her lips lifted. "Are you just now realizing that, oh wise king?"

"Have I ever told you that you have a way of making me feel so good about myself?" he joked, then scrubbed a hand down his face and sat at the edge of his bed. "What am I going to do if we can't figure out this mess with the dagger and her powers?"

"Aren't you the one who said we have to trust her? She'll find a way," Annalise said simply. "You thought you had lost her after everything on the beach, and look what happened. It'll work out, Seb." She put a hand on his shoulder, a smirk playing on her lips. "What you *should* be worrying about is whether she feels the same about you."

He scoffed. "Please, Anna. I'm a king. Everyone is in love with me." When she laughed and rolled her eyes, he sobered, letting that mask fall once again. "I don't know how she feels. Sometimes I think...we could be more. That she feels it, too. But I suppose that's the problem with being in love with someone long before they know who you are, isn't it? Falling with the fear that they may never meet you at the end?"

She patted his cheek. "Or catching them when they fall, too."

A brisk knock came at the door, followed by a muffled voice telling them it was time to leave. Annalise straightened her dress. "How do I look?"

"Like you'll bring Rynn to his knees. How do *I* look?"

"Like a love struck puppy. Shall we?" she asked, looping her arm through his.

"If we must."

The music reached him long before they reached their destination: a low symphony with a haunting, alluring melody that echoed through the halls and beckoned them nearer. When the guards threw open the enormous double doors, Sebastian was momentarily stunned.

Beyond the doors stood a ballroom rivaling the ones in his own palace. Even with half of Palace Noctem in ruins and the other half up in arms, the Ionans had somehow made the space look like something out of a dark fairytale.

The room stood at least three stories high, glass windows inlaid with gold running down the length of the walls and revealing the forest and night sky beyond. Deep blue tapestries that glistened in the firelight hung from the ceiling and clung in the space between the windows until they amassed on the reflective gold floor. Candles flickered from multiple chandeliers overhead and sconces lining the walls, casting the room in a hazy glow. Floral arrangements lined the tall tables and overflowed onto the floor in a sea of greenery, amethyst irises, blood red roses, and a myriad of other jewel-toned flowers that made it feel like he was stepping into a gilded garden at midnight.

They were some of the last to arrive, it seemed. Sebastian wasn't sure where all of these people had come from. With the Evonleans in mourning, there were only three kingdoms in attendance, but it looked as if the Chamber had invited the entire island. Men and women he didn't recognize glided along the floor, laughing and drinking like they didn't have a care in the world. Servants dressed in black from head to toe stood alert at the tables, offering glasses of sparkling wine and trays of hors d'oeuvres to anyone passing by.

"Well, they certainly aren't holding back, are they?" Bri said beside him. Looking over, he took in her strapless crimson ball gown, the top half of which was studded with varying shades of red gemstones. Her red gloves extended past her elbows, a glass of wine already situated in one hand and a bite-sized piece of bread with salmon atop in the other. When she caught the candlelight just right, it looked like she had been set ablaze.

"Have you heard anything else from her?" she murmured, using her flute to hide her lips.

Sebastian knew she was referring to Isla. He imagined her best friend had been taking this the hardest, unsure where Isla was and with no way to communicate. "Not since I told you last," he replied. "She said she was safe and with Akir, belowground. She told us not to do anything *rash*." He forced a small chuckle from his lips, attempting to ease the concern on Bri's face.

She smiled. "Who, us? Do something rash? She doesn't know us at all." Taking a sip of her wine, she said, "Well, we may both be nervous wrecks, but at least some of us are enjoying ourselves."

Sebastian trained his eyes on what Bri was looking at and saw Rynn leaning on his cane behind a tall table, partially hidden in the shadows of a large floral arrangement. His stoic gaze was fixed on Annalise's back as she struck up a conversation with Ayana of the Triad.

"Gods, he could be a bit less creepy, couldn't he?" Kai said lowly from behind Sebastian and Bri as she and Aidan strode up to them, turning down a drink from a nearby servant.

"To be fair, I think Annalise may be into that," Aidan piped in, snaking his arm around Kai's waist. Her dress was smooth and the exact turquoise shade of her eyes as it flowed like waves down her body. Aidan looked equally as charming in his all-black ensemble, gold kohl outlining dark eyes that kept scanning the area every few seconds.

"Our esteemed hosts have yet to arrive," said Jade as she joined the group. While she walked, she pinned back a section of her shoulder-length brown hair, showing off light pink earrings that matched her blush gown. Gray vines stretched down the skirt of the dress, leading to silver heels that clicked against the hard floor.

Sebastian glanced around with a tight smile. "Waiting for their grand entrance, I assume."

The five of them felt out of place among the joyful partygoers, apprehension swirling in the air around them despite their attempt at levity.

"Has anyone seen her?" Kai asked quietly.

Sebastian gave an almost imperceptible shake of his head. "From what she told me last night, she has things under control. We just need to get through the night without raising suspicion."

"I hate to say it, friends, but we *do* look rather suspicious at the moment," Aidan said, raising an eyebrow and taking his wife's hand. "It's a ball. We might as well dance." He led her off into the crowd of beaming couples, and Sebastian soon lost sight of them.

"They have a point. May I have this dance?" Sebastian asked Bri, offering his hand.

"Never thought I'd get to dance with a *king*, Your Majesty," she said, chuckling as he swept her into his arms.

"Yes, you've truly peaked now, I imagine." When she smacked his ear, he laughed, his chest lightening ever so slightly. "I'm kidding, of course. I'll miss you when this is all over, Bri. I'm glad we had this week together."

"You act as if one of us is dying. It's not like I won't see you all the time when you come visit Isla in Lockhurt," she said, rolling her eyes playfully, but he didn't miss the distress in her eyes when she said Isla's name.

He bit down on his lip as he led her in a waltz around the dance floor. He hadn't thought much of what would come after the festival ended—he had been more focused on getting through the week. Truthfully, his idea of the future always included Isla. It wasn't something he had to think about.

But what would *she* want? That frightened him more than anything. He'd been too selfish, too caught up in his own happiness to consider what her life would look like when this week came to an end.

"Do you think..." he began, then cleared his throat nervously. He wasn't used to this—the idea of rejection, the constant insecurity over what Isla might be feeling. He supposed he'd never allowed himself to care this much. "Do you think she would want me to visit her? Or that she would ever consider...relocating?"

Bri blinked at him, her mouth opening slightly before she shut it. "To Karstos?"

"Preferably, as I am rather tied up there."

"I don't know, Sebastian. I'm all for this whirlwind romance bit you two have going on, but her whole *life* is in Evonlea. Her family's business, her father and friends. She's never been one to jump at the idea of change."

He nodded understandingly, but inside, his heart twisted. Bri was right, of course. It was foolish of him to even think such a thing.

"You just need to talk to her," Bri said. "Are you serious about this? About *her*?"

He met her brown eyes, emotion rushing to the surface and brimming over. He'd admitted it to himself before, but somehow, saying it out loud for a second time tonight released something inside of him.

"I love her, Bri. I think I've loved her since the first time I saw her, even while under Celesine's influence." He swallowed, unsure of how to put the breadth of his feelings into words. "It's like there are pieces of me missing, and while I know I'll never be the person I once was, when I'm with her...I feel whole again. She's not replacing the missing parts with what they used to be, it's more that...her pieces fit with mine to make something new. Something stronger. We both may be broken, but we're not incomplete." He shook his head and looked away. "I'm sorry, that doesn't make any sense."

Bri's sniffle made him turn back to her. "If she doesn't want to run away to Karstos with you, I will," she said, dabbing at her cheeks with her gloved hand.

"Are you propositioning me, Miss Harvish?" he said with a laugh and spun her with one hand as the music changed to a faster beat.

"I would, if my best friend wasn't probably in love with you, too." She winked, then her face fell slightly. "Are you *sure* she's safe? Do you know what her plan is?"

"As sure as I can be, and no," he murmured, making sure nobody was close enough to hear. "She didn't go into detail about her plan. Simply that she would take care of everything tonight."

"Gods, I hate this," Bri said through a sigh. "Let me know if she talks to you again, okay?" She squeezed his shoulder as the music stopped and they broke away. "Thanks for the dance, Your Majesty," she said, curtseying before going off toward Jade.

Meandering to a nearby table with drinks, Sebastian eyed the crowd for his friends and found Kai and Aidan still dancing, Jade and Bri talking by the doors, and Rynn and Annalise tucked away on a gold-plated bench. He hid a smile as he took a sip of sparkling wine.

The glass almost slipped from his fingers when a voice echoed in his mind.

"Sebastian, if you can hear me...come meet me at the north gardens."

His heart picked up speed as thoughts flew through his head. Was Isla alright? Had something happened?

Time seemed to slow as he waited for the servants to pass and for the guards to turn their attention the other way. Sticking close to the walls so he could blend into the background, he made his way to the double doors, smiling politely and raising his glass at those who glanced his way. Thankfully, as he reached the exit, a small group of guests had just arrived, and he was able to slip out unnoticed.

Letting out a long breath, he quickly strode in the direction of the north gardens, sending a prayer of thanks to the Primeval gods that nobody had crossed paths with him. He exited through a side door of the palace, the large silver gazebo marking the gardens within sight. In moments, he reached it, padding along the cobblestone steps that opened to an enchanting landscape. Towering vines snaked up wooden beams, lanterns hung from the edge of the gazebo, and an assortment of flower beds arrayed the ground in a blend of colors.

But the most stunning sight was that of the woman in the center, gazing at the stars.

Her back was to him, the red waves of her hair cascading down a green gown of gossamer and flowers. The light fabric cinched at her waist, where it flowed to the ground and trailed several feet behind her. Under the firelight, it looked like green waves upon the water, rippling in dozens of shades: emerald, sage, and forest, some moments blue like the sea, others dark like a jewel. Real vines twisted up the top half of the dress to her shoulders, where they bloomed into delicate flowers that twined down her arms. A crown of matching cream blossoms adorned her head.

His footsteps must have alerted her to his presence, for she turned slowly, her pink cheeks and freckled face shadowed. Still, when her gaze met his, it took his breath away. She was all he could see; she made beauty look effortless, made the starlight gather around her like it shone for her and her alone.

She was here. She was safe.

He was seized with the sudden urge to touch her, and crossed the path to her in swift movement. She met his stride and they collided in the center, his hands winding around her neck and into her hair as he brought his lips to hers.

How could he have gone his whole life without her? Without this, without someone who filled him with so much passion and hope and peace that he could burst. She didn't simply spark a flame inside of him; she set his entire soul ablaze, an inferno that was stoked with each stroke of her tongue, each sigh from her lips.

His hands slid down her back and rested on her hips. She breathed out his name, whispering, "I missed you," as he pulled her even closer, her soft body against hard edges.

He moved to kiss the slope of her neck. "I don't know if you realize how much of a mess you've made me," he said against her skin.

"Been worried about me, have you?"

"Not *about* you," he corrected between kisses along her neck, her collar, the dip below her ear. "I worry for anyone who tries to cross you." Pulling away, he searched her violet eyes and found them clouded with both desire and anguish. "But I don't know what's happening, Isla. We're almost out of the time the Primevals gave, and we still don't have any clue what Celesine has planned or if she's truly here." He took a breath. "Please, tell me—"

Pushing onto her toes, she silenced him with another kiss, crushing her lips to his as if she wanted to make him forget his every thought, every worry. Desperate. Urgent.

Like a goodbye.

She broke away and he rested his forehead against hers, their chests heaving.

"Can we pretend none of that matters? Just for a moment?" She weaved her arms around his neck and kissed his jaw. "Dance with me, Sebastian. Please."

And so, he did.

CHAPTER FORTY-SIX

Isla

S he didn't know how she was supposed to do this. Didn't know why she had snuck into her chambers to retrieve this ridiculous gown or why she felt the need to break her heart even further by calling him here. Maybe she wanted to imagine, if only for one night, they were simply two people sharing a dream under the stars. Two people who weren't destined to be shattered again and again, who could smile and dance and fall in love without fate ripping it from them once more.

For a moment, she believed it.

She'd spent weeks fighting the pull to him when he was the nameless dark god. When she thought he'd willfully kidnapped her family and was mercilessly hunting her and her friends...she'd been disgusted with herself for the reaction her body had to him. Quickened breath, racing heart, boiling blood. And when she began to notice something was off...

If she was honest with herself, that's when everything changed.

Even under Celesine's influence, he'd fought for her. He'd always had faith in her, always saw her strength and believed she could do anything she set her mind to. However wrong it may be, *he* had been the one she sought when on the spirit plane, the one she appeared to when she had no control over her power. Because he understood her. Sebastian didn't see her as the timid, anxious girl who hated taking chances, who secluded herself when things got hard. He saw parts of her she never knew existed. He pushed her outside of her comfort zone and didn't let her lock herself away or get buried beneath the demons that plagued her mind. He wanted *all* of her—not only the good parts.

And since he'd been freed from Celesine's grip...it *terrified* her how much she wanted him, too. It felt like almost everything good she'd ever had in her life had been taken from her.

But she'd been foolish and full of hope, and had let herself start over with him. Had let herself imagine what happiness would be like at his side, and had seen how wonderful he was. Compassionate, understanding, vulnerable, charming. He cared deeply for his people and about doing right by them after everything they'd been through. The way he loved Annalise, his mother, even the rest of their friends who had once stood against him...his heart was so big, so beautiful. And it fit perfectly to hers without trying.

It was laughable, truly, how quickly she was falling. He was more than she'd ever dared to dream of. She only wished it wasn't too late.

"Did I ever tell you," he murmured as they swayed to the sound of wind whistling through the flowers, "of the first time I saw you?"

She turned her head so it was flush to his chest, his heartbeat echoing through her. Breathing in his sweet scent of wine and cypress, she quietly answered, "No."

"I suppose it was a little over two years ago now. Celesine had sent me to Evonlea to find you. She didn't yet trust me well enough to tell me why, just that you were important to her plans and I was to keep an eye on you and your family.

"It was soon after you had lost your mother and the boy, Waylan." His voice softened. "I tracked down your home, but you weren't there the night I showed up. I ventured along the path behind your house and was drawn to the river. Celesine's magic was so incredibly strong in those early days, and I had completely forgotten who I was. But something about that river and the nearby clearing at nightfall made me pause. I felt a whisper of my old self try to break free.

"And suddenly, there you were. In that small clearing in the woods, where it was far too cold and lonely, sat a woman with the most striking red hair." One hand remained at her lower back while another strayed to her curls, wrapping a strand around his finger. "You were crying. I could hear your pain before I saw you. And I was intrigued. Many people, when grieving, tend to hide themselves from the world in every way, shedding tears with their head in their hands or prostrate to the ground. I think what fascinated me the most was how your face was toward the sky, like you were opening your pain to the stars, begging them to see you.

"It was beautifully heartbreaking. I still think about it, about how much I wished I could wipe those tears from your eyes," he said, leaning back and letting a finger brush like a ghost against her cheek. "A woman I'd never met, whom I was destined to harm time and time again." His hand moved to her chin and tilted her head to meet his gaze. "I wish that wasn't how our story started, Isla. I wish we didn't have so much darkness staining our past. But you are the greatest light I could've ever asked for."

He placed a tender kiss on her lips, and the tears welling in Isla's eyes spilled over as she squeezed them shut. She could taste them on his lips as they pulled apart.

"Why did you have to be so perfect?" she whispered, her eyes still closed, his breath fanning across her cheeks and nose as he brought a hand to the back of her neck.

"Is something wrong?" His tone was full of uncertainty, and when she finally looked at him, fear swam in his blue eyes.

Gods, she couldn't do this. Her heart was already breaking.

She blinked away the tears smearing her vision and covered his hand with hers. "This time with you...it's meant everything to me, Sebastian. Even with all the chaos around us, this week and our nights together have been some of the best of my life. But I—I can't—" She choked on her words, her chest swelling so sharply she couldn't breathe. The air around them thickened and swirled, leaves rustling at their feet.

He took a small step back. His jaw pulsed as he clenched his teeth. "I understand if...if you don't feel the same way. If I haven't given you enough time."

Her eyes widened. He thought her feelings weren't *strong* enough? Perhaps that was how it should be. Perhaps this was the easy way out—letting him believe she didn't want him, giving him a clean break to move on with his life when she left. In some ways, she supposed, that would be better.

In a different time, a different life, she may have gone that route. Covered her pain under the guise of the "greater good" to spare him additional heartache. But he deserved more than that. He deserved the truth. All of it.

Gripping his hand that was still at her neck, she stopped him from moving further away. "No, that—that's not what I meant. I don't need more time. Well, I do, but not in the way you think. Gods,"—she held a finger to her temple—"you're so much better at this than me."

He stared at her, waiting, while the wind shifted around them, the tips of his blonde hair swaying and falling to his forehead. Shoving down the panic rising inside her and quelling her elements, she kissed the palm of his hand.

"I was wrong. Days ago, when I said I didn't know how this could be real, I was...scared. Of so many things, honestly, but mostly that you would realize I wasn't the girl I used to be, the girl in that field two years ago. I thought you would leave me, or something would happen to you, or life would just...get in the way. If I could stop it before it got to that point, I could save us both the inevitable unhappiness.

"But, like always, you fought for it anyway. You wouldn't let me sabotage myself." She shook her head and let out a soft laugh. "We haven't even been here a week, and we've barely spent any time together. I know it's fast, I know it's...it's absurd, but—"

"It's not absurd," he said quickly, stepping closer and tucking a windswept curl behind her ear.

She suddenly felt shy under his intense gaze, her cheeks heating at his nearness. "I think it would be very easy to fall in love with you, Your Majesty."

A tentative, hopeful smile spilled across his lips. "There's still time for that."

The air left her lungs as her stomach dropped to her feet.

"No," she said, swallowing. "There isn't. I—I need to tell you something."

"What do you mean, 'no'?" he asked, his brow furrowing. "I thought you said you found the dagger and knew what to do."

She nodded and without thinking, took a step back. "I did, and I do. I found it beneath the palace, near those hot springs Aidan and Kai said they used to always visit. The Primevals showed up before I could take it and explained some things we didn't know. Like how...how exactly I'm supposed to put the elements back into nature to restore balance."

"This sounds like good news. I don't understand what's wrong," he said, moving forward to fill the space between them. She wanted nothing more than to lean into his touch, but she knew if she let him comfort her, she wouldn't be able to do this.

Turning so only her profile was to him, she anchored herself in the earth around her, feeling it steady her bones. "According to them, a single being was never supposed to be able to hold all five elements. It's unnatural. *I'm* unnatural. It goes against everything the Primevals intended. There's a sort of...safeguard in place if anything ever happened to the elementals, one where they could all willingly give up their elements to restore balance."

Out of the corner of her eye, she saw him blink at her, taking in her words.

"The thing is...for me to do that, to give them up, it's going to take a lot more power than if it were five individuals with each element."

"How much power?" When she didn't immediately respond, he grabbed her hand and pulled her to face him. "How much, Isla?"

"All of it," she whispered.

His eyes flashed. "So you will give up your magic, all of it, and simply be human again?"

The ache in her chest deepened, consuming her, threatening to pull her under. "Sebastian..."

"Don't say it," he said fiercely, tugging her to him and resting his forehead against hers. "Don't say it, love." His words were softer this time, pleading. He shook in her arms, his heartbeats rapid and breaths labored.

"They said there's nothing I can do. That doing this will—it will kill me." She closed her eyes and breathed him in, the pit in her stomach and the pang in her heart worsening each second. "I don't have a choice. I have to go."

"No, you don't." He pulled away swiftly, his features hard and unrelenting. "You don't have to do any of this. This should not be *your* responsibility!"

"I know, I know," she whispered, tears now streaming down her cheeks. "But if I don't, what happens with the elements? How many more disasters can your people take? The same storm that hit this village could be happening across the entire world, and I—I can't let it keep getting worse."

He shook his head. "This isn't on you, Isla. The safety of this world doesn't need to rest solely on your shoulders. Use the dagger and give the others back their powers—they can stop this just as easily."

"That's what I thought too, but the Primevals said the dagger would only work once," she choked out. "And we already used it. I can't give their magic back."

He angrily thrust his fingers through his hair. "Then...then you refuse. Let the storms come, if they must, and we can figure it out when they do."

Seeing him like this, pacing back and forth, thoughts churning in his mind as he tried to think of a solution, though she knew there was none...it chipped away at her jagged edges even further. The same ideas had circled her head for hours, but it was like grasping at the open air. There was no hope.

Breathing deeply, she said, "My time runs out tomorrow either way, remember? They gave me these seven days. I'll be sent back to the spirit plane forever, only able to see you or Bri or my father whenever I have enough strength." She bit down on her lip to suppress a fresh wave of tears. "That's not a life, Sebastian. I couldn't be with you. I couldn't be with *anyone*."

"But you'd be *alive!*" he shouted, clutching at her shoulders. "We'd have more time to negotiate with the gods, maybe they'd find another way. It would give us a chance."

Gods, she wanted to believe him. And maybe it could work; maybe, given the time, another solution would come along. But how long could she live in that empty pocket of space, above and beyond the world and all she loved, an onlooker as days and months and *years* passed? Was it selfish of her to rather end this now than simply...exist? To know she was doing the right thing instead of prolonging the aching loneliness, the soul-crushing isolation, in the hope that one day she could be with them again?

Even if she was willing to refuse the Primevals' solution and wait for another to present itself, that wouldn't solve the problem with the elements. It would only get worse the longer she held onto her power. What kind of world would she be subjecting her loved ones to? Villages and people destroyed, famines and droughts, danger hiding in the very nature they used to trust. She would never forget the visions she'd seen on the spirit plane, where families burned and islands crumbled. If she had a way to stop that pain, how could she not do it?

The look on her face must have given away her answer, for he was shaking his head again before she could even reply.

"You've already made your decision, haven't you? So what was this, a goodbye?" he spat, taking a few steps back and holding his arms out wide, a vein in his neck pulsing under his frustration. "Is that why you brought me here?"

She went numb, the despair in his eyes enough to freeze her heart. "Good, you're angry—you should be. I know it was selfish, and I'm—"

In a flash, he was before her again, clutching her hand. "I'm not *angry* with you. Gods, I'm *terrified.* I'm desperate." He put her hand to his heart, and she could feel it pumping erratically, mirroring her own distress. "I love you, Isla, and I—I don't know what to do. I can already feel you slipping away. This is killing me."

His words flowed through her and wrapped around her tightly. How could one feel so many agonizingly intense emotions at once? His love and her pain threatened to bring her to her knees, but she couldn't stop the way her breath caught at his confession, how her heart fluttered beneath the weight.

"Say that again," she whispered.

His forehead creased as he cupped a hand around her cheek. "I love you, Isla Vasileia. Every part of you, every broken piece. My heart was yours long ago."

I love you. Her chest was bursting, her elements practically ripping themselves from her and the catastrophic tempest swirling within. She knew she could love this man, knew she could spend an eternity at his side. If only that were enough.

If only they had more time.

If only fate had not given them this.

"This isn't fair," she said without meaning to, another sob wracking her body as he pulled her into him and wrapped his arms around her. Her head fit perfectly against his chest. She tried to soak the feel of him into her skin—his warmth, his scent, his strength. Holding onto this last moment of comfort and peace, allowing it to banish the shadows and wipe away the stains darkening their canvas.

"Stay with me," he begged. A plea. A promise. One she couldn't answer and couldn't keep.

"I can't," she said into his coat jacket, already soaked through with her tears.

"Then I'm going with you."

At that, she pulled back sharply. "You can't, Sebastian. I don't know what's going to happen. It's too dangerous for anyone else to come."

Resolution shone on his features, drying the wetness that had clouded his eyes. "I don't care. Let me talk to the gods. We can find a way out of this."

She shook her head, panic setting in. She imagined him going through those tunnels, facing the challenges of the elements as she had, and all of the things that could go wrong. What if the gods simply struck him dead? What if Celesine showed up? What if, when she gave up her power, something happened and he was harmed? She didn't know what to expect, and the idea of him being anywhere *near* the tunnels when there could be collateral damage made it difficult to breathe.

"You can't risk it. It's not safe down there, and there's nothing I can do to protect you if things go wrong." He was about to argue, so she forged ahead, her tone laced with urgency. "*Please,* Sebastian. Think about what it would mean if something happened to you! Your kingdom would fall into the hands of the Chamber. Your mother is back home, and Annalise is here...they need you. Your *people* need you."

"And what about what I need?" He stepped closer and trailed his fingers along her arm, staring at her with such pained focus, like he was trying to memorize every freckle on her cheeks. "Does that not matter?"

"Of course it does. But this—it's bigger than you and me." Another sob broke loose, and she wiped away more tears. "It's not like I wanted any of this to happen. I just want *you.* I want this"—she motioned between them—"but it's too late. You have to let me go."

"I don't think I can." His words were soft and strained, and his hand shook as he looked down and scrubbed at his face, like he was at war with himself. "How am I supposed to watch you walk away, Isla? How am I supposed to stop myself from chasing after you?"

"Don't watch, then," she whispered back, and when his eyes met hers, she knew she couldn't put it off any longer. "Just kiss me."

His jaw clenched, and she thought he may refuse, may keep fighting, knowing this was it. This was goodbye. But, as if he felt the same unavoidable pull that she did, he cursed and wrapped a hand around the back of her head, yanked her to him, and molded his lips to hers.

This kiss was her undoing. Raw, broken, unyielding. Salty tears mixed with the taste of him as he slid his tongue along her lips, and she let out a whimper. He turned her body and forced her backward until her spine crashed into the side of the gazebo, but she barely noticed. All she could feel was him: his fingers pulling her head closer, his other hand at her waist, gripping her tighter and tighter as he pressed himself into her.

With each breath they shared, each graze of his tongue, each sigh from her lips, she pushed her tangled web of thoughts from her mind into his, uncoiling that tendril of spirit magic and wrapping it around him. Not to manipulate, but to *show*.

She wished she had time to tell him everything. To make him understand what she saw when she looked at him. How loved he was, how capable and worthy and *good*. How much his people needed him, and how wonderful of a king he was to them. Through their thoughts, she showed him all the pieces she hadn't been able to give before. The way his smirk made heat pool in her core; the way she felt when he'd kissed her for the first time all those months ago, like she had been lit up from the inside; the way she'd wanted to burn the world down when she saw the scars on his back.

He gasped into her as she flooded his mind with thought after thought, vision after vision.

When he had her pinned beneath him in his bed, the night she appeared to him on the Wyndsor Sea. When his eyes finally became a clear, beautiful blue that day on the beach. That first time she'd come to him as the Aether, how his sorrow and desperation had crushed her.

Stay with me.

Their first night here in Iona, when he'd broken her open with his words and healed her with his promises. When they spent the night together under the stars and she realized that was what she wanted. *He* was what she wanted. A lifetime of morning kisses and playful smirks and honest truths without hiding behind a mask.

He stiffened under her touch and broke away, his eyes dark and breaths uneven. "What...was all of that real?"

"It was real. It was *us*," she breathed out. "And I'm sorry, Sebastian. I'm so, so sorry." She pushed up on her toes to press her lips to his one last time. Before drawing away, she murmured against his skin and down the bond through their mind, "Close your eyes."

His eyes stayed shut, his chest heaving as he released her and clenched his fists together. She slipped from his side as tears muddied her vision and a scream built in her chest. Each step away from him was like tearing her limbs from her body, cleaving her heart into little pieces. Clutching at her throat, she forced herself along the candlelit path back to the palace, not sure what she would do if he followed after her.

But he didn't. Her command over him held. His roar and the splintering of wood rent the night, and her heart shattered beneath the stars as she ran to meet her end.

PART FOUR:

IGNITE

CHAPTER FORTY-SEVEN

Isla

I sla raced along the pathway to the eastern wing of Palace Noctem, struggling to breathe as her chest tightened. At one point she stumbled, barely able to see through the darkness of the night and the tears in her eyes. Angrily ripping the crown of flowers from her head and yanking off her heels, she threw it all into the rubble of the palace with a scream and crumpled to her knees, the rocks and jagged stone pressing into her dress and skin.

She had never felt so alone. And it was her own fault; her own decisions that led her here. Her own unrelenting urge to take everything upon herself with no regard for what may happen to *her*. Jade had been right all those months ago; she'd seen it in Isla, even then. The need to be the savior. The hero.

Yet could she say that she would take back a single decision she'd made? Perhaps she should've given Celesine the dagger when she'd asked for it. It would have sentenced the world to her injustice, yes...but it would have saved her twin. Would have let her go back home to her simple life with those she loved.

Letting her head roll back on her neck, she looked up at the sky, the bright stars swirling in the inky expanse. Tears continued to spill freely to the ground. Her wind caressed her body, her cheeks, her hair, trying to comfort her aching spirit. Beneath her hands and feet sprouted a soft patch of grass whose blades twisted up her arms, brushing her skin. Even her water and fire soothed her, a warmth spreading through her limbs while she closed her eyes and let the calmness of the sea wash over her.

She loved these elements. They were a piece of her, a blessing she'd never imagined receiving. And they reminded her of other blessings that had come with the last few months. She felt Rynn, Jade, Kai, and Aidan in every breath she took; these beings who were forever connected to her in a way she couldn't express. Now, they had a chance at true happiness. No longer burdened by the weight of immortality and power, but free to live their normal lives as they pleased. If anyone deserved it, they did.

And Sebastian...if she hadn't made that fateful choice on the beach all those weeks ago, he might still be under Celesine's control. Or dead. A world without him in it, without his hope for a better future, his willingness to serve his people, his wit and charm and compassion...it was unbearable. So for that decision, too, she had no regrets.

Her best friend's face appeared in her mind, as familiar as her own. This would be unfairly hard for her, having to mourn Isla's death a second time, and Isla hated that more than anything. But she had never seen Bri light up the way she had during their escapades this week, or even months ago when the stubborn girl had forced her way into their plans. Bri wasn't born to stay in a small town for the rest of her life; she was made for the world, made for joy, made for adventure. And now...she could seize it. Make her life her own. Maybe some good would come from this mess. Isla had said as much in a letter she wrote and left in Bri's room when she'd gone to get dressed for the ball. Facing Sebastian had been nearly impossible, but facing her best friend...she wouldn't have been able to follow through with her plans if she said goodbye to Bri.

Her body began to ease, her mind more resolved, until one final image burst through her thoughts.

Papa.

Where was the silver lining in his story? What good would he glean from her decisions? Because of her, he'd lost his son and unnecessarily mourned his daughter for months. She was too much of a coward to even go see him during her time as the Aether, and now she was leaving him for good.

She thought of him every day. The man who had raised her, who taught her to wield a dagger and shoot an arrow, and showed her women could be as fierce warriors and hunters as any of the men. Her father may have kept the truths of her and Arden's ancestry from them, but she knew he loved them so completely, so unconditionally, that she'd forgiven him for it long ago.

He'd suffered so much loss, perhaps more than herself, and he didn't deserve this.

That was her one regret as she summoned her strength and lifted herself from the ground, wiping the last of the wetness from her face.

No more tears. She would face her final moments as the fierce huntress, with memories of her mother, father, and twin at her side.

Isla crept through the quiet palace—a much more chilling and empty vessel while all of its inhabitants were at the ball. Instead of going through the secret tunnel beneath the Chamber's private quarters, she headed for the kitchens, where Kai and Aidan said the entrance to the hot springs was.

A clock chimed eleven o'clock down the corridor. Only one more hour until her allotted time was up, and the Aether would flow through her once more. That's when the Primevals said she needed to release the elements.

Listening on the wind for the distant sound of bubbling water, she let the elements guide her to a large tapestry near the kitchens, quietly sneaking past servants who were bustling to prepare more food and drinks. When she shifted the tapestry, she found a wooden door and slipped through it with ease.

A thrumming began beneath her skin as she descended further into the underground tunnels. The familiar hum signifying the Dagger of Volnus was close pulsed in her ears. She didn't take in much of her surroundings as she strode purposefully down the narrow dirt path, a small fire lit in the palm of her hand. Soon, the gurgling and boiling of water greeted her, and steam reached out from around the corner to lick at her skin.

When the walls curved, she stepped into an enormous rocky cavern, aglow with iridescent fireflies fluttering over the dark, frothing waves. The sight made her mouth drop open. She hadn't seen it in all of its glory the first time she was down there, considering she'd entered through a gap in the middle of the pool. She hadn't realized then how massive the cave was.

With a flick of her wrist, balls of fire shot from her hand and sailed through the cavern, lighting the entire space. Jagged rocks hung from the domed ceiling. Stones covered the floor, becoming damper and warmer as they led to the hot waters. While she thought she would be at peace surrounded by all of her elements, an inexplicable shiver crept down her spine, the air thick with tension she couldn't place—a foreboding energy that set her on edge.

Shaking off the strange sensation, she forged ahead into the hot spring, the warm water lapping at her heels and enveloping her as she stepped further. Her skin and gown stayed dry, as always, but she could still feel its heat seeping into her muscles. Taking one last, strengthening breath, she plunged below the surface and swam to the bottom, where she repeated the same steps as last time and opened the earth to the fiery core beneath.

Immediately, she knew something was wrong.

When she fell into the depths, using her wind to guide her to a stop, the blazing heat of this second cavern was *scorching*. She almost couldn't stand it. The moment her bare feet touched the burning sea of embers, she let out a yelp and flew back into the air, looking down to see blackened, blistered skin at the soles of her feet.

How had the fire *burned* her?

Vines sprouted from her hands and wrapped around her feet, encasing them in a protective shield. As she landed on the fiery surface, the earth rumbled and she almost lost her balance. Whereas last time the floor had been a peaceful wave of crimson, orange, and yellow, this time...it was an uncontrollable furnace. Plumes of fire blasted erratically from random pockets of the surface, the ground beneath her feet rolling and quaking like an angry beast. She tried to reach out to it, to sense the source of its ire, but it gnashed its teeth at her.

Concern ignited within her. This felt like the storm she'd barely been able to calm the other night. Like then, it was outright rejecting her and her elements.

More flames burst to her right and a deep tremble rocked the cave. Why was this fire so out of control? And what would happen to the tunnels above it, to the entire *palace*, if it worsened?

She spotted the same enchanting, glowing sphere of power across the space, all four elements pulsing and floating around the Dagger of Volnus. With anxious steps, she crossed the cavern, remembering how the Primevals told her that her blood was the answer to retrieving it. Looking above her to the jagged rocks embedded in the ceiling, she summoned a sharp stone. Cracking from its position, it flew down to her outstretched grasp. In one quick movement, she sliced the skin of her hand, wincing slightly as blood bloomed across the wound. She raised her palm to the orb and ran it down the curve, eyes locked on the streak of red that melted into the glow of the elements.

Instantly, the cavern shook even more fiercely, each element in the sphere receding and fading into nothing, one by one. First the vines, then the waves, followed by wind and finally, flames. The dagger clattered to the stone, echoing off the walls.

As Isla bent to retrieve the weapon, she mentally prepared for the onslaught of power and possessiveness that would overwhelm her, like it always had when she touched the blade in the past. Except this time, when her palm closed around the handle, she felt...nothing. Simply the cold, hard steel beneath her skin. No lightning bolt of power, no staggering shock of energy, no obtrusive wave of violence.

The Primevals had told her it could only be used once, and they were right; it wouldn't work for her again.

To her left, flames shot from the ground with such force, they singed her skin. A crack began to form in the fiery earth, creating lines like a spiderweb through the molten floor. Isla's eyes widened. If the cavern exploded...

With a burst of energy, she flew back to her hole in the ceiling and hurtled into the hot springs, sealing the entrance to the hot core. Instantly, the water seared her lungs and soaked her clothes and skin. She struggled to get a handle on her pocket of air, the shock of her water trying to turn against her costing her precious seconds.

What was *happening*? Why was she wet, and why was it so hard to breathe? Were the elements leaving her?

She quickly swam to the surface, her eyesight trained on the rocky shoreline, her heart pounding as she raced against time to stop the fire from obliterating the palace.

She almost missed the four silhouettes lurking in the shadows.

As she hauled her sopping body over the rocks, three words pierced the damp air.

"Hello, Isla Vasileia."

Chapter Forty-Eight

Isla

The four Chamber members stepped out of the shadows, still in their sweeping ballgowns and tailored jackets, ever the image of superiority and power. Isla's heart raced, the dagger in her hand pulsing against her forearm as if it sensed danger ahead.

"What are you doing here?" she asked, forcing as much bravado into her words as she could.

"Really, Isla," Mariana said with a laugh. "It's our palace. Did you think we would not know everything that's been going on this past week? That you and your friends could roam the halls, uncover your little secrets"—she wiggled her fingers at Isla—"without us seeing every step? We've been waiting for you to arrive. Stefan here did not think you would show, but she was right, as usual."

"*She?*"

A slow grin unfurled on Mariana's lips. "The Aether, of course."

Although she'd been expecting it, the confirmation made Isla's stomach drop to her feet. She and Sebastian had speculated that Celesine and the Chamber had been working together this whole time, but she still didn't know *how*. Isla's eyes flitted around the cave, as if she might find the Aether hiding in the shadows, preparing to pounce.

"She's not here, if that's what you're thinking," Nor Noxen said, his steel eyes tracking her gaze.

"Then where is she?"

He chuckled. "Everywhere, I suppose. She *is* the Aether, after all."

She needed to figure out what was going on. Needed one of them to crack.

Narrowing her eyes, Isla scoffed. "So, she sent you to do her bidding. Typical. Always using those she thinks are lesser than her to do her dirty work. I bet you don't even know her plans, you just obey her like good little—"

"You don't know what you're talking about," Nor snarled, stepping toward her. "She will be here soon, once she has her full powers back, and then—"

"Silence, Nor," Mariana commanded, holding an arm out to cut him off. "It's rude to interrupt our guest." Her voice was even, but her eyes flashed in anger.

Good. Isla was getting to them.

Celesine didn't have access to her full powers. That made sense, considering there had been no sign of her in four months. But how much power *did* she retain from their fight on the beach? Isla assumed she had taken it all when she used the dagger against Sebastian, but it sounded like that wasn't the case. Perhaps that was only a fraction of Celesine's magic, and she still had the rest, though in a weakened state. How much time did Isla have until she appeared?

"Your *guest*," Isla said, rolling her eyes, trying to get them to continue talking. "Yes, because you've treated me so well. Do you always accuse your guests of murder and attack them openly during dinner, or am I just lucky?"

"We had to go a bit off script," Mariana said casually. "You arriving at the welcome feast on that first night was not part of our initial plan, I admit, but it worked in our favor. The Aether was the one who encouraged us to invite the four elementals of old, hoping their presence here would draw you out, especially after learning of your quest from the gods.

"Getting you here was the easy part. We assumed you would stay hidden and we would need to track you more closely, so imagine our surprise when you walked right through our front doors, practically serving your own head on a silver platter." She chuckled and shook her head, her deep gray curls bobbing around her ears. "That's when we cultivated a new plan. One that would allow us to kill two birds with one stone, if you will."

"Figuratively and literally," Stefan rumbled next to her, his eyes lit with mirth.

Isla's brow furrowed. "You *did* kill Kingsley and Jessenia, then." Her stomach churned with anger at their callous attitude toward the lives they'd taken, standing there and making jokes as if they hadn't broken families. "Just so you could frame it on me? What did I ever do to you?"

"Your mere *existence* is a nuisance, Isla," Ezeretta answered with a hiss. Her pale skin glowed in the firelight of the cave as she moved closer. "The name you bear and the legacy you carry could be detrimental for our reign, should the people learn a precious *Vasileia* has come back to them."

"I—I don't even *want* your throne!" Isla spluttered, eyes widening. This was unbelievable. The smallest *hint* at a threat, and this was what they'd done? "I didn't come back here to claim any sort of birthright you think I have!"

"It doesn't matter what your intentions were. It's about *perception*. If our people knew you existed and began to think of life under a different leadership, it could topple everything we have built. We couldn't allow that. And so," Mariana said, straightening the sleeve of her burgundy dress, "we did what we had to do. No monarch of the other three kingdoms would accept you as an heir to this throne if they believed you had harmed their loved ones, and no Ionan would respect you as their queen if they saw you as the vengeful, heinous murderer who swept in to claim her crown."

Two innocent people had lost their lives, and a third was lying unconscious in a bed, all because these selfish beings before her had such insecurity over losing their place of power. Revulsion swept through Isla, the elements practically growling under the surface of her skin.

"You're despicable," she spat. The water at her back rolled and sizzled. with her anger. "It won't be me, but someday, someone is going to take this kingdom out from under you."

Mariana gave her a cruel smile. "I don't think so. Not after what the Aether will do for us."

"I don't know what she's promised you, de Faye, but she won't keep it. You're fools for thinking she'd do anything but use you and discard you the second you stop being beneficial to her."

"You're wrong, little Vasileia," Stefan sneered. "She has been helping Iona for centuries. We know she'll do right by us this time, as well."

Isla blinked, shocked to hear Stefan admit the truth, even if she and Sebastian *had* been suspicious of it. "All the fear and hatred around magic these people have been brainwashed into believing for hundreds of years is because of *her*?"

"You act as if magic is not the very thing that first tore this kingdom apart, Isla," Mariana said. "The Aether first appeared to our predecessors long ago, in the wake of the civil war. She helped rebuild Iona, offering counsel to the leaders throughout the decades and creating the possibility of a future that would never know such violence and unrest again. Unlike when the former elementals walked the land, this kingdom hasn't faced threats of mutiny or war under the reign of the Chamber, thanks to her."

Isla's mouth gaped. "Because everyone's hope and free will were taken away! Of course the people won't revolt when they can barely leave their houses for fear of what might happen to them!"

Ezeretta bristled and moved her white hair over her shoulder. "We, Celesine, and those who came before us merely wanted what's best for everyone—a people who abide by the law and know their leaders will protect them. Give them something to fear, and they will stay in line."

"That's a very eloquent way of saying *tyranny*."

"Call it what you will, it makes no difference to us." Mariana waved her hand in the air. "Despite what you may think, we have always cared for our people. And now, once the Aether holds the power of the gods, we will never have to be concerned about the future of our kingdom again."

The power of the gods? Isla's hands flexed involuntarily at her side. "You can't trust Cel—the Aether. What exactly was this arrangement you came to, anyway?"

Gesturing to the other three, Mariana answered, "We lure you and the former elementals here, where the Dagger of Volnus is, and ensure you find it and perform the magic transference. In exchange, she will grant us power our ancestors only dreamed of."

Before Isla could respond, shouting and a loud crash came from the tunnels beyond the hot springs entrance, and all five of them turned at the sound. Three guards appeared with a slumped figure carried between two of them.

"We found him, Your Graces. He was already coming down the tunnels, like you said." The third guard gestured to the limp man, whose blood began to stain the stone.

Isla would know that figure in her dreams. Sweat-slicked hands trembled at her sides, her vision tinging with blackness at her sudden fury.

"Ah, yes," Stefan said, clapping his hands together. "The other piece of our *arrangement.*" He casually flicked his wrist to the third guard and said, "Kill him."

When Sebastian lifted his head, blonde hair falling over a darkened bruise on one of his blue eyes, Isla snapped.

Thrusting out an arm, she sent a wave of air to the guard who was raising his sword, pinning him by the throat to the tunnel wall behind him. With her other hand she summoned a vine and whipped it at the guard on Sebastian's left. It lashed around his ankles, his legs buckling as she tugged, the vine dragging him along the rocky floor. She stalked toward the remaining man, who had the decency to show fear, and latched her hand around his throat, pushing blazing heat through her skin until the scent of burning flesh filled her nose.

"Let go of him," she said, her voice a deadly calm. Immediately, he released Sebastian, who stumbled to the ground. Isla shoved the man away and watched him clutch his neck with wheezing sobs, rushing to the guard who lay on the stones, wrapped in thorny vines.

She took one look at Sebastian and fell to her knees. "What did they do to you?" she asked softly. Reaching out, she brushed a strand of hair from his eyes, the deep red bruise still warm under her touch. His other cheek had a long, bloody gash from ear to nose, and he gripped at his midsection as if he'd been injured. His white shirt and black dress pants were torn and covered in streaks of dirt.

Despite his obvious discomfort, he gave a half-hearted smirk. "I'm afraid they've ruined my pretty face, love."

She choked down a laugh and skimmed her finger along his bloody cheek. "I have a thing for scars."

The answering smile on his cracked lips made her heart ache. "You shouldn't have come, Sebastian. I should've forced you to stay away when I had the chance," she murmured.

"I told you, I can't lose you again."

She memorized his features—the curve of his lips, the sharp cheekbones now bruised and battered, the strong jawline, the clear, blue eyes.

"Stay here," she commanded, both of them standing while she kept him at her back.

"I'm not going anywhere." His low voice was in her ear, coating her in courage and sending a shiver down her spine.

When she faced the Chamber again, Mariana began speaking in a deep, commanding voice.

"*On behalf of His Majesty, Sebastian Avax, twenty-third ruler of the fifth dynasty, King of Karstos, we decree by executive order the following terms.*" Recognition flashed in Isla's mind; this must be the clause Sebastian had told her of several nights ago. "*Should the presiding king become unfit for rule, whether by death, abdication, or on any physical or temperamental grounds itemized subsequently, the king forfeits his position and property to none other than the Chamber of the Kingdom of Iona.*"

"Honestly, de Faye, who has the time to memorize that?" Sebastian asked.

The leader of the Chamber simply smirked. "*That* was the final part of our agreement with the Aether. When she had you set the amendment in place last year, we had no hopes it would come to fruition so quickly. You are the only thing standing in the way of us claiming your kingdom, Avax."

"You're going to need a lot more than three men to take him from me," Isla snarled, lifting her hands.

A humorless smile played on the edges of Ezeretta's mouth. "You may be powerful, Isla Vasileia, but do you *really* think you can stand alone against the might of the Ionan empire with the Aether on our side?"

"Well, then," a familiar voice boomed from the tunnels. Suddenly, Aidan's hulking figure appeared in the entrance. "It's a good thing she's not alone."

Chapter Forty-Nine

Kai

Her feet hurt from hours of dancing, and blisters formed on her heels where the straps of her shoes had rubbed against them all night. It had been easy to lose herself with Aidan, easy to get swept away by the enchanting music and the candlelight. To momentarily forget their burdens and the danger lurking around every corner. But as the glow from the Spring Equinox ball began to dim, the shadows crept back, and Kai was once again reminded of what lay before them and the limited time they had left.

Isla still hadn't reappeared, and although Sebastian said she'd contacted him to assure him of her safety and that she'd found the dagger, it was all so cryptic. Where *was* she? Did she still need them? What was the Chamber planning now that she had a target over her head?

Midnight quickly approached, and exhaustion had set in, heightening her constant questions and concerns. She and Aidan found their friends and made their way back to the Karstos wing. The whole group was shrouded in a heavy haze of worry and weariness. Annalise and Rynn stuck close together, heads tilted toward one another as their hushed, anxious whispers reached Kai's ears. The Karstos guards lingered behind them. Bri and Jade walked on Kai's right, and when Bri linked her arms with both Kai and Jade in a show of comfort, Kai gave her a small smile.

The only one missing was—

"Has anyone seen Sebastian?" Annalise asked, breaking away from Rynn to look back at them.

Now that she thought about it, Kai hadn't seen the king since shortly after they arrived at the ball. She assumed he'd been fraternizing with the other royals. Puzzlement crossed everyone's faces, and Annalise stopped abruptly.

"You two," she pointed to the Karstos guards, whose eyes went wide, "are fired. Effective upon our arrival back to Karstos." She threw her hands in the air. "How do you lose your *king*? He is your one and only job!"

The two glanced at each other and mumbled their apologies before promising to find him and sprinting off in the opposite direction. Annalise put a finger to her temple and massaged it angrily.

"Gods, I have to do everything myself," she muttered. "When was the last time any of you saw the Chamber?"

Sharp steps on stone and a slightly familiar voice distracted them before anyone could respond.

"Ah, there you are. I was worried I would not find you." An elderly man whom Kai recognized as Akir ambled up to them. "You must hurry!"

Bri jumped back in alarm. "Where do you keep *coming* from?" she said, clutching at her chest.

"I make it my responsibility to know what is occurring at any time in this palace, Miss Brielle, and at this moment, your king and Isla are facing imminent danger."

"King? As in, King Sebastian?" Annalise asked as she pushed to Kai's side. "Wait...who are you?"

"Annalise, this is our...friend, Akir." Rynn gestured to him. "He has been assisting us in locating the dagger."

Akir surveyed the group with concern. "I'm afraid our Isla has not been entirely forthcoming with any of us. My men have reported they recently witnessed her entering the tunnels by the kitchens, and your king followed not long after."

Sharing a glance with Aidan, Kai's brow furrowed. The tunnels that led to the hot springs? What could Isla possibly need down there? They'd already searched that area.

Annalise strode forward and gripped the elderly man's arm. "Which way?" she asked briskly.

He nodded his head toward the left. "Be swift," he said, locking his hand across Annalise's fingers. "I fear that if you don't stop them, multiple lives may be lost tonight."

"Gods, could he be any more dramatic?" Bri muttered under her breath as she leaned against Kai to slip off her shoes, then hiked up her dress.

Kai's heart thundered in her chest. What was Isla up to? Glancing into her husband's dark eyes, her same hesitancy stared back at her. Isla must have found a way to stop the storms and put the elements back in place. That was the goal all along, Kai knew, but fear paralyzed her at the thought that she was out of time. That she might have to give up everything they'd hoped for *tonight*.

For a split second, she wanted to run.

But if Isla was in danger...

"We don't have to do this, sweetheart," Aidan said softly, his thoughts mirroring her own. Her stomach churned, disgust at her own cowardice clawing at her.

Lifting a hand to his cheek, Kai responded, "She did it for us."

"Alright, *what* is going on with you two?" Jade asked exasperatedly.

Kai and Aidan turned to find Annalise and Rynn already heading in the direction of the kitchens, while Jade and Bri still waited for them. At Jade's demanding question, Rynn and Annalise slowed.

"You've been acting strange all week. And I've never seen you turn back from a challenge," Jade said, crossing her arms.

Kai bit her lip and reached for Aidan's hand, comforted by his fingers between hers. *Well, it's now or never.*

"Aidan and I...we're going to have a baby." At the awkward, stunned silence that followed, Kai cleared her throat. "As in, I'm pregnant." Jade and Bri continued to blink at her, and Kai shuffled her feet. "With child."

"Yes, I got that, thank you," Jade said, her mouth snapping shut. "Why didn't you—what—*how*?" Pointing a finger at Aidan, she added, "Do *not* answer that." She breathed out slowly. "This complicates things."

"How does that complicate things?" Bri asked, crossing to Kai and wrapping her in a tight embrace. "That's amazing, Kai! I'm so happy for you."

Kai smiled weakly and returned the hug, but her gaze didn't leave Jade's, who swallowed and said, "That's wonderful news. I know how much you've wanted this." Her eyes betrayed her words, though, as they were filled with skepticism. When Bri released her, Kai walked to Jade and took her hand.

"What does this mean?" Jade whispered.

Kai didn't take her cynicism or lack of enthusiasm to heart; she knew her best friend, knew she was fearful of the unknown and scared of the myriad of problems this revelation caused. Her deep brown eyes were guarded and full of trepidation, showing her uncanny ability to see past unspoken words and into the heart of the issue.

"I don't know." Kai said quietly. "But our friend needs our help. We'll figure it out; we always do."

To her surprise, Rynn snorted.

"What's so funny?" Kai asked as she, Jade, and Aidan caught up to the others.

"Your optimism amuses me. We rarely ever 'figure it out' the first time around."

Aidan clapped him on the back. "Well, there's a first time for everything."

"Why are you not surprised about this news, Rynn?" Jade asked suspiciously as they scurried down the corridor toward the kitchen.

"Because I already knew."

"*Excuse* me? How did he know before I did?" The pout Jade gave Kai made her burst into unexpected laughter, followed by a rush of compassion. Even when diving headfirst into uncharted waters, her companions never failed to warm her heart. Their bickering, their love, their bond...this family was one of the greatest gifts she could ever receive.

She quickly blinked back fresh tears. *Gods, these emotions are annoying.*

"He cornered us a couple nights ago and we told him. Don't worry, *Aunt* Jade, we'll make it up to you," Kai said, bumping Jade's shoulder with a smile that fell away when she remembered what they were running toward.

They reached the kitchens quickly with Kai and Aidan directing them down the winding corridors. Aidan moved the tapestry covering the entrance, and the six of them entered the tunnels.

Immediately, something felt *off*. Kai couldn't put her finger on it, but the air was filled with heated tension, like a string stretched too tight. The further they descended, the warmer it grew, and distant shouts reached her ears.

The reality of what they were walking into hit her again. They had *no idea* what to expect. She thought they were searching for the dagger to perform a simple power transference, something they'd already done once before. But now, after the way Akir sounded so frightened for Sebastian and Isla's lives, Kai wasn't so sure. What had happened in the last couple of days that made this so dire? That would lead to someone's *death*? Perhaps the Chamber was much more of a threat than they'd originally thought. Or the Primevals had changed their minds and were punishing Isla for what she'd done on the beach.

Aidan must have been having the same internal conversation, for he turned to Kai as they hurried and murmured, "No matter what happens, you stay behind me, alright? And if things get out of hand, you need to get out."

"What, and leave you? Not a chance, Aidan," she hissed.

"Promise me, sweetheart. I can't go down there knowing there's a possibility you'll get hurt."

"Then we might as well turn back now, because there's *always* a possibility I'll get hurt," she retorted, then sighed at the stubbornness written on his face. "I promise, Aidan. I'll stay out of trouble."

He nodded and grabbed her hand, placing a kiss on her knuckles as they approached the last corner before the hot springs. Anticipation coiled in Kai's stomach, the gut-churning suspense heightening her already queasy state. They could hear the boiling waters, so much louder and angrier than the last time she'd been down there.

Voices rang out above the crashing waves—one sounded like Isla, and the others were the Chamber members. Sharing a look with Aidan, they broke into a run, their friends close on their heels.

Her eyes widened at the scene before her. On the ground by the banks of the hot springs were three Ionan guards, all in various states of distress. To the left stood the four Chamber members, their hardened features set on Isla and Sebastian, who stood with their backs to the entrance. Sebastian's clothes were a dirty, bloody mess, and Isla's ball gown was sopping wet. Her red hair whirled around both of them as she kept her body in front of his.

"You're going to need a lot more than three men to take him from me," Kai caught Isla saying as she lifted her hands in warning.

Ezeretta flashed her a cruel smile. "You may be powerful, Isla Vasileia, but do you *really* think you can stand alone against the might of the Ionan empire with the Aether on our side?"

Aidan, no doubt emboldened by the adrenaline he lived for, took a step forward. "Well, then," he shouted. "It's a good thing she's not alone."

The four Chamber members plus Sebastian and Isla snapped to attention at his voice. Kai sucked in a breath when she saw the king's face: dried blood smeared down his cheek from a clotted gash, his bright eyes now red and swollen, an angry bruise beneath one of them. Annalise whispered a soft *"Seb"* behind her.

"What is going on here?" Rynn asked from the shadows, stepping into the cavern beside Kai.

"We don't have time to explain, Rynn. You need to take Sebastian with you and *get out*," Isla said hastily, practically shoving Sebastian into Aidan's arms, then reaching into a pocket of her green dress to pull out—

Kai's eyes widened. Was that the Dagger of Volnus? When had Isla found it?

A deep rumble shook the cave, waves of hot water roiling and spilling onto the stone. Kai grabbed Aidan's arm to steady herself.

"Was that you?" Aidan asked Isla.

She shook her head. "It's the underground furnace below that heats the hot springs. It's dangerous for you to be here. You all need to *go*," Isla insisted again, brandishing the dagger toward the exit.

"Hold on. When did you get the dagger back?" Bri asked, popping her head over Kai's shoulder.

"Sebastian, what in the gods' name happened to you?" Annalise added.

"Is nobody going to ask why we're all down here?" Jade hissed.

Mariana de Faye's deep chuckle broke up the countless questions. "My, you've brought an entire show with you! It's too bad we must cut the entertainment short." She snapped her fingers at the entrance, and Kai glanced around in confusion to see who she was motioning to.

Within seconds, boots on stone and metal armor clattering and creaking echoed down the path. Aidan quickly grabbed Kai and pulled her deeper into the cave, putting as much distance between them and the oncoming invisible army as he could. The soldiers must've been waiting for them to come down into the tunnels and followed them.

Shadows appeared first, then boots, followed by armored guards bearing the crest of Iona on their breastplates. Ranks of soldiers filed into the cavern, two by two, an endless march of silent figures with swords and daggers drawn as they stepped in line behind the four Chamber members. Kai and her friends continued to back up to the water, taking in the sight of dozens and dozens of guards lining the stone walls.

Ezeretta faced Isla and Sebastian, who were only a few feet ahead of Kai and the rest. The female cocked her head. "As we said"—she held an arm out—"the might of the Ionan empire."

What happened next seemed to occur in slow motion.

Several guards ran to the Chamber and threw up shields around their bodies. Another man stepped forward and tossed a small, round object toward the water. Kai watched it arc over the heads of the Chamber, heard Aidan's cry of "*get down!*" and felt his warm hands surround her and pull her to the ground.

And then, the cavern exploded.

CHAPTER FIFTY

Rynn

Ringing filled his ears and a gray fog muddled Rynn's vision. Slowly, his senses came back to him, the dull pain in his leg growing to a searing heat, his back and head thudding sharply with every heartbeat.

"Annalise?" he croaked, fighting through the dizziness as he sat up to take in his surroundings.

A soft hand touched his. "I'm fine," she said in between coughs, calling with a strained voice for Sebastian, who'd been thrown backward in the explosion. He stirred at her words, the wound in his cheek bleeding again but otherwise unscathed.

Rynn groped for his cane and eased himself off the ground. A few steps away, Aidan helped Kai to her feet, and Jade brushed dust from her hair right beside Brielle. Isla stood ahead of them all, her expression murderous. On the ground where the explosive landed were charred and splintered vines lying in a heap, as if Isla had covered it at the last moment to avoid them all being hit with the brunt of the blast.

Isla cursed. "What was *that* for? What have they ever done to you?"

"We were told to detain you," Mariana answered, "at whatever cost."

Rynn furrowed his brow. "Told by whom?" When Mariana did not answer, but merely smirked at him, Rynn's gut clenched. Meeting Isla's violet eyes, he instantly knew.

"Celesine," he hissed.

Sharp intakes of breath sounded around him, but he was not surprised. Celesine was back, as he suspected she would be. She was a nagging insect, always lurking in the hidden crevices of their lives, evading capture while she bided her time in the darkness. She was surely after Isla's power, the one desire sustaining her after all these centuries. He knew how crippling it was to hold so tightly to a skewed vision of reality, to a yearning that warped one's mind until they were unrecognizable. He was loath to admit it, but he and Celesine were similar in that respect—they both felt a pull to the temptation of power, felt a sweet release when giving in to their darker instincts.

But, unlike him, she had never learned when to stop. Had never had companions to care for her so deeply that it cut through the shadowed haze. And for that, he pitied her.

"Where is she?" he asked impatiently.

"She'll be here," Mariana said.

Rynn gripped his cane as a rumbling began at the back of the hot springs and worked its way forward, causing the rocks at his feet to quake and the boiling water to coil and snap.

Suddenly, Isla's head jerked up, the blood draining from her face. "Midnight," she whispered, and Rynn understood she must be hearing the chimes of the clock through the wind.

"That's what she's waiting for," she continued, grasping the Dagger of Volnus. "At midnight, when I get my full powers of the Aether, Celesine will too. I have to get rid of these elements before she comes ba—"

Isla choked on her words and clutched at her chest, the dagger falling to the stone with a *clang*. Several people shouted her name as she staggered backward, then suddenly flung her arms out, her mouth agape and pupils blown wide. A purple glow emanated from her chest, as if it were *under* her skin, stretching and brightening with every breath.

The spirit magic was returning to her.

In a flash, the light faded, and Isla groaned, collapsing to the ground.

The others were too preoccupied with Isla to notice the purple shadows gathering several yards away from them.

Hair rose on the back of Rynn's neck. His eyes shifted to the growing mass of shadows, reflexively moving to stand between it and Annalise. Slowly, the purple magic shifted, gaining in length as a figure began to take form. Aidan cursed behind him. The shadows billowed and curled around one another, beams of bright purple breaking through the darkness like lightning, crackling and snapping. Wind whirled around them as the shadows finally dissipated.

A female remained. Raven hair curled down her shoulders and loose, black gown, her olive skin darker under the dim firelight, red lips smiling cruelly beneath a set of vibrant, violet eyes. What shocked him most, however, was the raw and blistered skin along her cheek, the patchwork of deformed scars from forehead to chin. He had almost forgotten Isla's fiery assault on the female after she had killed Arden. Apparently, her spirit magic had failed to heal her completely.

"So kind of you to wait for me," Celesine said, and the sound of her voice sent chills through Rynn's body. He had dreamt of that voice for months. Recalled her betrayal and taunts over and over, imagining being able to wrap his hands around her throat and silence her lies.

She had taken everything from them.

"You've done well, my darlings," she crooned as she walked to the Chamber, dragging a sharp nail down the side of Nor Noxen's cheek. "You will be most rewarded."

"What have you done, Celesine?" Jade asked, her voice a combination of disbelief and lingering pain.

"*The* Celesine?" Brielle interrupted, recognition dawning across her face. "You're the one who killed Arden?"

Celesine turned to face the girl, her expression impassive. She brought her hands together as she sauntered to Brielle and Isla. Rynn's muscles tightened, anticipating Celesine's every move.

"My, my. Who do we have here?" she asked. Looking back at Rynn and the others, she *tsk*ed. "You surprise me, honestly. Bringing another human into this mess after what happened last time."

"She's not your concern," Jade said, moving to put herself between Celesine, Brielle, and Isla. Celesine simply chuckled and drew closer to Brielle, who had the sense to straighten in fear but kept the look of disgust on her features.

"You must love your friend very much, mortal girl. Tell me," Celesine tapped a finger against her chin, "Did she say goodbye before she led herself to her death tonight?"

Brielle's face crumbled as tension swept across the cave. "Wh-what are you talking about?"

With a look of feigned surprise, Celesine said, "Has Isla here not told you why she was down in these tunnels? What the Primeval gods revealed to her *days* ago?"

"You're lying," Brielle seethed.

The words sunk into Rynn. Akir had said Isla was withholding information from them. A part of him did not want to believe she would be so foolish, so reckless, as to keep this from them, yet he knew in his bones that Celesine spoke the truth. He did not know what the Primeval gods had said to her, but Isla was self-sacrificing to a fault, quick to make decisions for herself and those around her without consulting them or allowing them to change her mind. And now her beautiful, brave spirit was going to be her demise.

"Am I?" Celesine said, amused. "Perhaps you are not as close as you believed. What kind of person knows they are about to die and doesn't tell a soul?"

The air was taut with unspoken truths, the gravity of her accusation sinking into them all. To Rynn's right, he saw Aidan blocking Kai and keeping a vigilant eye on the rows of soldiers lying in wait. Jade was still stationed near Celesine, her jaw clenched and eyes narrowed. Annalise had found her way to Sebastian, a few steps from where Rynn stood.

"Isla wouldn't do that," Brielle insisted weakly, looking back at Isla, who was still motionless on the hard ground.

"Why don't you ask her yourself?" Celesine's smile grew as her arm shot out, purple shadows unfurling and aiming straight for Isla. With a cry of panic, Brielle lurched forward in its path, the spirit magic slamming into her chest before it reached her best friend.

"No!" Rynn shouted, right as Jade screamed the girl's name. Aidan and Jade barreled to her and Rynn cursed at his leg; he would never reach them in time.

Brielle threw her head back and let out a shriek as the shadows twisted around her body. Jade made it to her first and tried to grab for her, but the shadows hissed, making her withdraw her hand with a groan.

"Stop, Celesine! She has nothing to do with this!" Jade snarled.

Celesine simply raised an eyebrow. "She got in my way. Humans must learn their lesson somehow; actions have consequences."

"Yes, they do."

Rynn's eyes snapped to behind Brielle where the voice came from, and had to suppress a shudder. Isla stood—no, *hovered*—above the ground, her red hair billowing around her as if by magic. His eyes traveled up the green gown that clung to her body until they reached her eyes, a more violet shade of purple than he had ever seen. Her features were practically glowing, the scar on her left cheek bright pink and fearsome. The undiluted rage flashing across her face as she raised her arm made him take a step back.

Suddenly, the purple shadows left Brielle's body, and Celesine was raised in the air by an invisible force of wind. She spluttered and choked as if it were grasping her by the neck. Vines snaked around her body, binding her hands and working their way up her throat and around her head. Her face turned an alarming shade of red, but as she opened her mouth to scream, nothing but water poured free.

"You will never lay another finger on them," Isla said, her words slow and deep as she stepped back to the ground and crept toward her victim. Torrents of water flowed from Celesine's mouth. She thrashed against her bindings, trying to summon her spirit magic, but the distress she was under must have made it difficult to concentrate.

Unease built inside of Rynn at the sight. He was not one to shy away from retribution, and if anyone deserved this, it was Celesine. But this...this was not Isla. This cruel being before him enacting punishment as if it brought her pleasure was not the girl he had held all those months ago.

Nobody moved for a heartbeat as they watched Celesine begin to lose her struggle against the restraints, her gagging and choking becoming more and more strangled. Even the Chamber and their obedient guards did not seem to know what to do, choosing to stand in silent fear.

Sebastian broke away from Annalise and charged to Isla, her name on his lips as a soft plea. Before he could reach her, the sound of crumbling rocks and a distant roar overtook the air.

The stone beneath their feet shifted once again as the boiling water rose and fell in massive waves, spraying them with a fiery deluge that blistered Rynn's skin. He stumbled over his cane and watched as the others lost their balance as well, the earth continuing to shake as if the entire floor was preparing to erupt.

Finally, Isla broke from her trance. The vines around Celesine receded, and she crumpled to the stone. Isla steadied herself and shook her head to clear her thoughts, her eyes widening.

"I—I'm sorry, I don't know what I was doing—" She cut herself off, glancing at the raging water, then at the stone still sliding and trembling around the cave.

"There's not enough time," she whispered. "This cave is about to explode, and I'm not strong enough to stop it. And if Celesine finds a way to get my powers..." Her breathing became erratic and hurried, her blazing eyes finding each of her friends. The look she gave them was full of such regret, such heartache, that Rynn felt his own heart stutter.

"Everything Celesine said is true. Please—*please* understand, I never meant to hurt any of you by keeping this a secret. I just didn't know what else to do." Looking directly at Brielle, she bit down on her lip and wiped a tear from her cheek. "I love you so much, Bri. Since the day you walked into my life, I've never been alone. You've brought me out of my worst times—I don't think I'd be here if it weren't for you. Please...forgive me," she finished with a whisper.

Rynn's body jolted. He knew what was about to happen, but once again, he was not quick enough.

Isla held out her arm, the Dagger of Volnus flying from the ground and into her grip. In one fluid motion, she lifted the blade and dragged it along her forearm. The skin flayed open as the dagger began to glow. Isla dropped the weapon with a gasp, blood seeping from the wound to the stone.

Back where the Chamber stood, Mariana let out a sharp screech and shouted, "*Stop her!*"

Soldiers moved forward, then stopped in their tracks once they saw what was happening around Isla. Even Rynn was not quite sure what he was witnessing.

What appeared to be strands of light poured from Isla's arm, weaving with crimson blood as it sank, five multi-colored rivulets streaming across the ground. They flowed faster and stronger as Isla's blood continued to fall.

It was the elements, he was sure of it. The magic was leaving her body—and taking her life with it. Surely, that was what Celesine had meant when she said Isla had come to her death, the truth the Primeval gods had planted in her mind. To release the elements and balance nature, she must forfeit her life.

Which was exactly what she had done.

A guttural cry of frustration broke his focus, and he watched in horror as Celesine leapt from the ground, regaining strength after Isla's attack. Her eyes locked on the strands of power.

The elements. The blood. She was going to try and intercede.

In a burst of energy, he ran forward, ignoring the pain cutting into his leg as adrenaline surged through him. Brielle and Jade sprinted for Isla as well, and Rynn glanced back to find Sebastian on his heels.

He was almost there. If they could reach the dagger before Celesine, they could stop her from—

Celesine's hand connected with the dagger, and a brilliant sphere of power erupted at the contact. He thought of nothing except getting the weapon away from her as he gave one final push and launched himself into the bubble, his fingers latching onto the blade. A sharp, searing pain lanced over his skin, but he refused to let go. Jade and Brielle stumbled into the strange web of magic, their knees hitting the stone and soaking with Isla's blood.

The five strands of light broke away from each other and snaked separate paths through the blood and stone. Rynn furrowed his brow, his mind racing to put the pieces together. It looked like one of them was heading directly toward him.

The four other elements branched off and shot across the crimson flow.

One to Celesine.

One to Jade.

One to Brielle.

And one to—

At the last second, Annalise shouted Sebastian's name. Before the king could cross over into the sphere of magic, he was knocked off his feet. Rynn let out a strangled cry of warning, but it was too late.

Annalise fell into the circle, her brow slick with sweat and her breaths uneven.

And the fifth element sank into her skin.

CHAPTER FIFTY-ONE

Rynn

T he instant the thin strand of magic entered his veins was like coming home.

His wind rushed back to him as a lover's embrace, his skin tingling with awareness, his lungs filling with fresh air. It swooped and swirled within him, covering the dark spaces he had long forgotten about.

It was as he remembered. Colors were brighter, sounds were clearer, the thumping of his heart was stronger than ever. Even that incessant pain in his leg dulled compared to the onslaught of senses soaring through his blood. He immediately found Jade staring back at him, a look of immense awe radiating in her eyes. She felt it, too. Their missing pieces had found their way back, stitching the broken fragments of their souls together again. He could not stop a small smile from blooming across his lips as a vine shot from Jade's hand, stretching and curling up her arm as if it were welcoming her back to its fold.

He looked down at his leg, hoping to find it healing now that he had obtained his magic, but it still bore that hideous scar, his muscles sunken and weak at the shin. But it was a light affliction, nothing like the all-consuming pain he had suffered for months. Before he raised his head, though, something else caught his attention.

The ground had ceased its quaking. Perhaps the balance of nature had already begun to shift once Isla released the magic. The glowing sphere of light they had been entrapped in had also vanished, and Isla was still alive—weak, but alive.

Brielle suddenly cursed next to Jade, her voice panicked and shaking as her hands ran up and down her side in hysteria. When she lifted her chin, Rynn's mouth fell slightly ajar.

Looking back at him were deep brown eyes, blazing with foreign fire.

"What—what's wrong with me?" she asked, holding out her arm as errant sparks lit her fingertips.

His mind raced. When he and the others had interfered with the flow of magic, those kernels of power had traveled through Isla's blood to embed themselves in the closest living beings. Air and earth had once again found their original vessels. And it appeared that Brielle...she had become the fire elemental. That meant—

Rynn turned swiftly to Annalise, wind whipping from him and gliding through her mahogany hair like silk. *It liked her.* His wind was as possessive as he was, caressing her skin and purring its satisfaction. Those thoughts were quickly stunted when he saw the confusion flooding her endlessly green eyes. Confusion, but also...curiosity. Her inquisitive gaze snapped to the raging water beyond, as if she were drawn to it.

Annalise stumbled for several steps until she oriented herself, her movements accelerating when she reached the edge of the water and let out a soft gasp of wonder. Rynn followed, allured by her, his wind begging to leap into the depths.

"It...it's alive," she said, the water springing in excitement to thread between her fingers, glistening her bronze skin. Her eyes met his, and her trepidation was gone. Instead, she was brimming with life, more free than he had ever seen her.

She was glorious.

"Isla," Sebastian said with a groan from behind them. Rynn turned to find the king cradling Isla to his chest, her arm still dripping with blood and her face a ghostly pale. She managed to lift her head and look around, her eyes fluttering.

Her *green* eyes.

The Aether had left her. *All* the elements had left her. Isla was mortal once more. Even though she had given up her powers, it had not killed her as the Primevals said it would. Perhaps their accidental interference had saved her life. This was not a path any god could have foreseen.

"Enough of this!" Celesine snarled as she rose to her feet, violet eyes flashing in rage. Her black hair was tangled and windswept around her neck and shoulders, giving her the appearance of a crazed goddess of vengeance.

The Chamber and the Ionan guards leapt into action at her call. Soldiers strode across the stone, weapons drawn, grim determination in their eyes.

Rynn heard the whistling steel before he saw it.

In a breath, his arm jerked out to close around the handle of a dagger, inches from Annalise's throat. She gasped and instinctually lifted her hands, a cascade of water tumbling from her fingertips.

Growling, Rynn flipped the dagger and launched it back where it came from, the blade finding with ease the unfortunate soul who had signed his own death warrant. When it sank into the flesh at his neck, chaos broke loose.

CHAPTER FIFTY-TWO

Aidan

Aidan seized Kai's arm and dragged her behind him, ducking low as more weapons flew through the air. Closer to the water line, Sebastian carried Isla out of harm's way, blood still streaming from her arm and her face growing paler by the second.

Guards were *everywhere*. Aidan didn't know who to watch in all the madness.

Rynn and Annalise ran toward the Ionans, using their collective powers to keep them at bay. Rynn handled the oncoming soldiers effortlessly, as always. He was right back in his element. Men fell to the floor, clawing at their necks and gasping for breath when Rynn so much as looked at them. He'd formed a shield of air to wrap around Annalise, and whenever a stray dagger or sword got too close, it rebounded off the invisible barrier. Aidan could tell she was desperate to help, but was struggling to gain control of the water.

Celesine rounded on Jade and Bri and began attacking with newfound fury. Jade's earth magic barely managed to stop the onslaught. Celesine shot purple beams of shadows straight at each of them in quick succession, met each time with a wall of rock. Jade was able to slow her down by summoning huge stone spikes from the ground, forcing Celesine to maneuver out of the way, but with Jade having to protect both herself *and* Bri, Aidan didn't know how long she'd last.

Bri was trying, he had to give her that. Every few seconds, he'd spot a ball of fire or two spit from her hands and ignite along the ground at Celesine's feet, causing the latter to jump and lose her concentration. But it only seemed to further anger the spirit elemental.

Annalise and Bri were so far in over their heads. He had to do something.

Keeping his body in front of Kai's, they quickly made their way to Isla and Sebastian. Kai knelt to the ground and ripped off a bit of Isla's green dress, wrapping it tightly around the gash to create a tourniquet.

"Isla, I need you to talk to me," she commanded sternly. "I know you're tired, but you have to stay awake."

While Kai treated Isla as best she could, Sebastian watched the battle unfold and clenched his jaw. "They're never going to hold up."

"Never say never." Aidan clapped Sebastian on the shoulder. "I have to get out there. Annalise and Bri have no idea what they're doing."

"Find me a sword, Aidan, and I'll fight beside you."

Aidan looked at the king, fierce resolve in his bruised eyes. It suddenly hit him how far he'd come, from the dark god who inspired fear and hatred, to this man who would willingly fight at his side, ready to jump into danger to help the ones they loved.

He nodded and squeezed Sebastian's shoulder. "Then let's get you a weapon. I hope you're not just a pretty face, Your Majesty."

"I know my way around a blade," he said with a wink, which was more of a gruesome twitch that pulled at the wound on his cheek.

"Noted," Aidan replied. "Kai, we need to get you and Isla over to the wall, out of sight as much as possible. Can you carry her?" he asked Sebastian, who nodded, but Isla grunted as she wobbled to her feet.

"I can walk," she insisted.

Aidan refrained from rolling his eyes. *Stubborn girl.* "Fine," he said firmly, then reached out to steady her. "We have a lot to talk about when we get out of here, little island, and trust me—we *will* get out of here. But for what it's worth, I'm glad you're not dead." He gave her the smallest of grins before turning his mind to forming a plan.

The idea of his wife being down here, feet away from an attack, and him not having the power he used to in order to get everyone out safely...it was terrifying. The fear of being without control while his loved ones stood in the line of fire was killing him. His eyes darted to every possible threat, assessing them with racing thoughts, trying to figure out how to get them *out of here*.

The four of them rushed to the nearest rounded wall, still much too far away from the exit. "You two"—he motioned to Kai and Isla—"stay as low to the ground as you can. We'll be back soon."

"Wait—the dagger!" Isla cried, tripping to get to the drying pool of blood where she'd fallen earlier.

"You're *kidding* me," Aidan grumbled. "If I don't see that gods-forsaken dagger again for the rest of my life, it'll be too soon. Stay here," he said, jogging back to retrieve the weapon.

As he reached down to grab it, Kai shrieked his name.

Without thought, he took the dagger and spun in place, planting it through the neck of an oncoming Ionan guard.

"Sorry," he said, removing the blade from slick skin as the man fell to the ground. "I was aiming for your arm." Tossing the dagger to his other hand, he cracked his neck. "Guess this thing is useful, after all."

Aidan's attention was drawn to Rynn and Annalise, where they battled over a dozen foes across the cave. Annalise seemed to have adjusted to her newfound powers rather quickly, able to blast her opponents with jets of water to distract before pouncing on them with a sword.

They weren't aiming to kill, only to wound or incapacitate, which unfortunately gave the soldiers a bit of an edge—because they *were* aiming to kill. Celesine and the Chamber were going for blood. Now that the Aether knew there was a way to get their powers, she would stop at nothing.

Aidan saw two guards sneak up on Rynn's back, and his stomach dropped. "Behind you!" he bellowed, and Rynn turned at the last second.

"Lovely," Rynn snarled as he raised a hand and batted away an oncoming sword with his wind. Lunging at the owner with incredible speed, he grabbed the man's wrist and twisted it until bone cracked, then Rynn grabbed the sword from his slackened grip.

Aidan raised his eyebrows and gave him a thumbs up. *That's one way to do it.*

Making his way back to his wife, Sebastian, and Isla, he narrowly avoided several attacks and fended off two guards who stalked toward the three huddled at the wall.

"They can't keep this up forever," Aidan panted as he reached them. Kai hugged him tightly and wiped specks of blood from his jaw.

"We have to stop her." Isla pushed against the rock wall with her sights set on Celesine. She was still unsteady on her feet, but her face had already regained some color.

"Isla, love," Sebastian said with a growl. "I think I speak for everyone when I say *absolutely not*. You're not stepping a foot into that fight."

Aidan whistled. "I get what you see in him. Quite sexy, that king of yours," he said, nodding to Isla.

"This is my fight, too," she responded, green eyes blazing despite the weariness in them.

Gently grasping her shoulders, Aidan forced Isla to face him. "You gave everything for us that day on the beach. You sacrificed the life you knew to follow us, a bunch of strangers, into the unknown. You gave Kai and me the chance at this life, and I owe you *everything*." His voice came out gruff and thick. "You're wrong, little island. This was never meant to be your fight. So let us protect *you* for once, hmm? Let *us* finish this." He jerked her to him and kissed the top of her head, her green eyes swimming with emotion when he pulled away.

"And for the love of the gods, please try not to get yourself killed for five seconds, okay?" he added with a smirk, then turned to Sebastian.

"No kiss for me?" Sebastian deadpanned.

Aidan winked at him. "Keep me alive, and we'll see."

A scream echoed through the air, and Aidan pivoted to see Jade stagger backward with a whip of purple magic tightening around her throat. Bri formed flames in her hands, but they sputtered out within seconds, so she threw her arms up in frustration and charged at Celesine, tackling the female to the ground and breaking her hold on Jade. It gave Jade enough time to collect herself and form a rock barrier, ushering Bri back to safety while she held Celesine off with a web of vines.

"Go," Kai urged him. "We'll be fine."

"I'm sorry, sweetheart." Guilt warred within him. How could he leave his wife when he'd made her promise to escape at the first sign of danger? And here he was, planning to jump into the action.

"Don't be sorry for wanting to protect the people we love, Aidan." Standing on her toes, she placed a kiss on his lips. "If you're that sorry, make it up to me later."

He groaned. "Gods, I love you."

That playful smirk he loved so much twisted at the corner of her mouth. "I love you too. Now go help our friends."

"Take this," he said, shoving the Dagger of Volnus into her hands. "If a single hair on your perfect little head is hurt, I'm dragging every one of these bastards into the Wyndsor Sea."

"Violent Aidan," she purred. "My favorite."

Aidan kissed her cheek before grabbing Sebastian's arm, whose forehead was pressed to Isla's, whispered words that Aidan couldn't hear pouring from his lips.

"Ready, brother?"

Sebastian gave Isla a sweet kiss, and Aidan raised his eyebrows.

"Ready," the king responded, squaring his shoulders and following Aidan.

"You want to talk about that?" Aidan muttered and flicked his gaze back to Isla.

"Keep me alive, and we'll see," he said, clapping Aidan on the back.

Aidan barked out a laugh and shook his head as the two of them ran headfirst into the nearest pack of soldiers. Slamming his fist into the face of the first guard he could reach, Aidan grabbed the man's head and brought his knee up to meet his nose, hearing a sickening *crunch*. He plucked the sword from the man's hand and kicked him to the ground. Next to him, Sebastian had secured his own weapon, and they faced off against several soldiers who had heard the skirmish.

These Ionans were skilled fighters, Aidan had to admit, but he'd been around for millennia. He was pretty sure he'd taught their ancient ancestors how to wield a sword. Aidan cut through them easily, bending low to swipe at their ankles then swinging high to crack the hilt over their heads, aiming for any opening in their armor he could find.

"You weren't lying," he said in between heavy breaths, sparing a glance at Sebastian, who'd also carved his way through a handful of soldiers. "You do know your way around a blade."

"And I do still have a pretty face," Sebastian responded as he brought his sword up to block an attack, the clash of steel ringing in the cave. With a grunt, he planted his heel into the ground and thrust against the enemy sword, bringing his other foot up to kick him in the chest and then swiping his blade at the guard's head. The man wailed and dropped to his knees, blood pouring from his eye.

Rynn and Annalise appeared nearby. Rynn kept a continual barrier of solid wind over his body as he sliced his dual daggers through the air at lightning speed. He'd always been the best of them with weapons—well, next to Aidan. Annalise had grown even more into her powers over the last few minutes. She'd figured out how to form her water into a solid object, creating blades of ice that she used to combat oncoming guards. She parried and blocked, slashing at their swords and strengthening her ice daggers with each passing second so they didn't crack and break. Aidan had to admit, he was impressed.

"I think she's better than you, though," he said to Sebastian.

"Well, I *did* teach her everything she knows."

"First, that's a lie," Annalise shouted as she blasted scalding water at a man running straight at Aidan. He doubled over, scraping at the welts already forming on his skin. "And second, what are you doing here, Seb? We're trying to *protect* you, you idiot!"

"*I* am trying to prevent a power-hungry immortal from stealing our powers and conquering the kingdoms, but sure," Rynn huffed, bringing a dagger down on his opponent's neck, "we are doing this for the *king.*"

"I couldn't let you have all the glory for yourself, Anna," Sebastian said.

Annalise flicked her hands and the guard she was fighting choked as water spouted from his mouth and nostrils. She drove the hilt of her blade into the side of his face, and he tumbled to the ground. Sebastian's mouth fell open. Smirking, Annalise bumped his shoulder with her own.

"I'm imagining these are the lords on your council back home. This is basically like an advisory meeting."

Sebastian scratched at his chin. "We must be attending drastically different meetings."

She smiled viciously, swiping her blade against the arm of a guard and slamming her foot into his ankle before finishing him off with an elbow to the nose. "Try being the only woman at them."

Two guards lunged from behind Annalise, their blades outstretched and aimed at her neck. Rynn burst from the right and, with a powerful sweep of his arm, sent the men flying through the air and straight into the boiling hot springs.

"Watch your back, Annalise," he murmured, lifting his hand to tuck a strand of hair behind her ear. When he slipped away to face the next slew of soldiers, her cheeks reddened in a blush.

Not long after Rynn turned, however, another Ionan came from the side, out of Rynn's line of sight. The man paused, grabbed a dagger from his weapons belt, and prepared to launch it at Rynn's unprotected back. Aidan sucked in a breath and leapt from the ground, but his efforts were in vain.

A spinning blade of ice hurtled through the air, sharper than any blade, and impaled itself through the man's eye. He fell like a rock.

Rynn whirled to face Annalise, his eyes darting from the body and back to her, first in confusion, then surprise, then wild determination.

"You should watch *your* back, Rynn," she said in a challenge.

Without hesitation, he replied, "Marry me."

Aidan, Sebastian, and Annalise's jaws dropped.

"What?" she yelled.

"*What?*" Sebastian echoed, crouching to plunge his sword into another guard's ankles.

Aidan broke into laughter, his booming chuckles cutting through the cries and clashing of metal. "You've got some nerve, Rynn," he said as he landed a punch to the side of someone's face and kicked an unconscious body across the stone.

"You're joking," said Annalise, another ice blade forming in her hands. Her face fell when she looked back at Rynn. "I'm a little busy, if you hadn't noticed!"

Rynn held up his hand, and five guards were blasted off their feet, knocking into the hard wall. "I have lived thousands of years. I'm a patient man, Annalise."

Aidan and Sebastian continued attacking with frenzy at any sight of uncovered skin: necks, ankles, under the arm. Their blades and fists were a blur of silver and flesh, and soon, Ionan guards were scattered around them. The Chamber was furious; Aidan caught them across the cavern angrily roaring commands, faces red and spit flying from their mouths. Only a handful of opponents were left standing.

Aidan smiled. They were actually going to pull this off.

CHAPTER FIFTY-THREE

Jade

S he never thought she would be in this position. Her once great confidant, her loving mentor, her rock when life had crumbled. This powerful figurehead of her past now faced her with such hostility, such open hatred, ready to end her without a backward glance.

Jade thought she had known betrayal and hardship. She'd clashed against mortals and oppressions of this world, and warred with inner demons in a battle she feared would never end. But *this*...this was the fight of Jade's life.

Every block against Celesine's spirit magic, every vine that burst from Jade's hands, every beat of the precious earth beneath her feet was a reminder that for *thousands* of years, she'd been lied to. For thousands of years, she'd blindly placed her faith in a being who had pretended to care for them, slowly sinking deeper and deeper into bitterness and resentment until it swallowed her whole, only to break free and emerge as something completely unrecognizable.

Jade didn't know the female standing across from her anymore.

"Haven't you had enough of this yet, Celesine?" Jade shouted as she dodged yet another lash of purple smoke, which barely grazed Brielle's shoulder. A ball of fire appeared in the girl's hand in response, her eyes narrowing on Celesine.

"Darling, I'm just getting started," Celesine responded, circling Jade. "I have been trapped in the spirit plane for *months*, half of my power split with the mortal, but unlike her, I could not form a physical body. Until now." Her purple eyes gleamed hungrily. "I have not felt this strong in ages."

"That makes two of us," Jade said with a grunt, lowering herself and slamming her hands into the ground. With a boom, fissures appeared in the stone, snaking from her hands and branching off along the floor, causing the earth to rumble. Beyond Celesine, she saw the others had managed to halt the human soldiers, perhaps half a dozen left standing amidst Annalise, Sebastian, Rynn, and Aidan. Closing her eyes, she felt the earth tremble with anticipation beneath her, surging through her fingertips as vines joined the cracks and spread to the remaining Ionans, wrapping their tendrils around weapons and yanking them to the ground.

"Stop this, Celesine," she said, looking into the eyes of her old mentor. "Or I will bring this entire palace down, taking your precious puppets and dagger with it. You know I can," she challenged as she stood, the stone still quivering at their feet.

"There she is," Celesine said with a wicked smile. "You and your righteous indignation, always the one to decide what's right and what's wrong. You call these loyal people my puppets, but how do you know they are not following me because they truly believe in my cause?" She held her arm behind her to the Chamber and their guards. "They understand how much better I can make this world. How much I will be able to provide once I have the powers of the elements. No more hunger, no more fighting, no more lack."

"Yes, until the first person disagrees with you. Do you plan to simply kill anyone who stands against you?" Jade cried in frustration. "Withhold resources from people who don't want to live under your thumb? That's not *leadership*, Celesine. These powers, our elements...they won't help you dominate a world that was designed to have free will."

"And how much good did that free will do them a millennia ago?" Celesine said, cocking her head.

Jade took a deep breath. "We made mistakes, and the humans made mistakes—and that's going to keep happening. That's how kingdoms and people grow. You can't rule them with fear in hopes of creating some perfect, impossible world. Fear is not the answer to power."

"No, darling," she said with a sneer. "Fear *is* power. And you cannot get anywhere in this life without either. That's something the Primeval gods did not understand upon creating us, but I have learned the truth."

Behind Celesine, motion caught Jade's eye. Rynn and Aidan crept slowly toward her, the former silencing their footsteps using his wind.

Jade knew what was coming. Knew they would not get through to Celesine with logic or compassion, and it was always meant to end like this. A piece of her heart broke knowing she wasn't able to help Celesine from this darkness, the way Celesine helped her centuries ago. But the Aether had chosen this path. It was time they ended it.

"We loved you, Celesine," Jade said softly. "*I* loved you."

For a fraction of a second, Jade thought her old friend looked back at her through soft, purple eyes. But the expression was quickly erased, replaced by a solemn smile. "Love has no place among gods."

It was then that Rynn brought his hands together and Aidan raised a sword at Celesine's back.

In the blink of an eye, Celesine whirled.

Purple cords enveloped Rynn and Aidan's necks, lifting them from the ground while they strained and kicked against its hold. Shouts filled the air as their companions ran forward to help. Sebastian charged at Celesine with his sword held high, Annalise at his heels with a cyclone of water whipping a path across the stone. Brielle shot daggers of fire at Celesine's raven-haired head, but one by one, Jade's friends all froze in their tracks, trapped in silent screams as they were strangled by the spirit magic. Sebastian, Annalise, Brielle, and even Kai, who had jumped from the wall as soon as Aidan had been attacked.

It felt like the walls were closing in on Jade. Her eyes scanned their faces, their anguish slicing through her heart. She wasn't strong enough. She was going to fail them, these people who were relying on her, who *needed* her—they were all going to die. Their eyes were already dimming, their breaths already becoming labored and pained, all while Celesine smiled in cruel victory.

Jade was transported to those later days of the war, where the people cried for her, begging her to help them. *Save us.* She had failed them, sentenced them to a brutal annihilation, because she was weak. Defective.

That day on the beach, she could have *so easily* prevented catastrophe had she been able to access all of her powers. She could have halted time and stopped Sebastian from turning them against one another, could have saved Isla's brother, could have reversed everything that had happened since. Everyone's pain, everyone's heartache, everyone's despair was on her shoulders. Guilt and blame ruptured through her like a tidal wave, reaching to the deepest parts of her, pulling at her weaknesses and bringing them into the light.

"Jade," a voice whispered, and her breath caught.

Isla. Where had she come from?

"Jade, *do it.* You have to stop her," Isla pleaded, but Jade didn't want to turn around in case Celesine noticed. "I know you have the power, and I know what you've been through. But this isn't about you. This isn't about what you did back then—this is about our friends, our *family*, needing you." Her voice was low and hurried, coming from right behind Jade. "Whatever you think you've done in the past, they've forgiven you a thousand times over."

Jade's breaths quickened as ahead of her, Brielle thrashed harder against her restraints, the fire slowly dying from her features. At the same time, Kai went slack in the purple shadow's grip.

To her surprise, cool metal pressed into the palm of her hand, along with Isla's gentle touch. "I thought everything was my fault that day with Arden. I thought I should've been able to fix it all. None of that was *either* of our faults, and neither is this. You don't need our forgiveness, because you've done nothing wrong." Isla closed Jade's fingers around the hilt of the dagger. "I think...you have to forgive yourself."

Her heart thudded in her chest, her mind racing. Her tendrils of earth were solid and steady in her veins, as they had always been—her earth had never abandoned her. It had always been there for her, even when she didn't deserve it. It hummed at Isla's words as if it agreed, as if it, too, had forgiven her long ago. Forgiven her for the way she'd abused its power, wanting the glory for herself instead of using it to create and nurture and grow.

Perhaps...forgiveness was not something anyone *deserved*, least of all herself. One is not granted love or forgiveness or loyalty out of their own merit. It's freely given in love, despite flaws, despite past sins.

Tears fell down her cheeks, but they were not tears of pain or sadness. They were tears of...relief.

Her magic wrapped itself around her in a strong embrace, guiding her deeper into that well of power she hadn't touched in a millennium.

And there it was. A soft, delicate blanket in her mind, stretching to welcome her home.

"Thank you," she whispered—to Isla or to her earth, she wasn't sure. With a vigorous tug, she pulled at those strands, and marveled as everything around her froze. Her friends' legs ceased kicking, the Chamber paused in the middle of sprinting to Celesine's side, and the Aether's face was locked on her victims, her features unmoving as Jade approached her slowly.

Looking back to where she had been standing, she saw Isla crouched low to the stone, her red hair blowing from the steam and wind off the water, but her face completely still. The many guards scattered on the ground in various stages of recovery were now rigid, immobile.

She had done it.

It was shocking, the stillness surrounding her, with only the sounds of the hot spring bubbling at her back, the faint wind whistling through her hair. Peaceful, almost.

The Dagger of Volnus pounded in her grasp. The only way to kill an immortal, resting in the palm of her hands. Fate had a twisted sense of humor, she thought, for this to be how it ended. In the quiet of the night, when shadows came out to play and there was no one to watch her break.

With a deep breath, she thrust the blade into Celesine's heart, and let her hold on her magic drop.

"I'm sorry," Jade whispered as Celesine's face flinched, realization crashing into her eyes. Celesine fell to the ground, and Jade with her, more movement around her as her friends were released from their bonds. But Jade's focus stayed on those purple eyes, dimming by the second.

Celesine coughed, and blood trickled out of the corner of her mouth. Jade clutched at her body as she slumped into her lap.

"You finally fought," Celesine said, her voice scratchy and dull as another cough wracked her body. Tears splashed onto her olive cheeks, and Jade realized as her heart clenched that they were her own. Reaching up, Celesine placed a cold hand on Jade's cheek, her next blink slow as her eyes fluttered shut. Her hand fell away.

She was gone.

CHAPTER FIFTY-FOUR

Isla

Everything happened so fast, Isla almost couldn't believe it was over. One second, she'd been handing Jade the dagger, and the next, Jade was on the ground, Celesine's body draped over her lap, blood seeping from the fatal wound in her chest.

Jade had done it. Celesine was dead.

Not only that, but the Aether had also been released from her hold, the same thin strand of light that had flowed from Isla's arm now mixing with Celesine's blood on the dark stone floor. As it sank into the earth, the light suddenly disappeared, and a shudder went through the cavern.

Jade looked back at her, mouth agape. "The spirit, it...it's gone. I can't feel it anymore." She turned her head to Rynn, as if seeking confirmation, and he nodded grimly.

With a dagger now in their all-powerful commander's heart, the Chamber was surprisingly quiet, seeming to understand they were done. They had nobody backing them, nobody defending them, nobody delivering empty promises. The fight had entirely left their haughty faces, leaving behind haggard remnants of a broken leadership that realized their mistake.

Annalise sprung into action and took up the mantle of organizer, instructing Kai, Aidan, and Sebastian to gather the fallen soldiers and help the injured. Rynn kept watch over the Chamber while Jade silently wrapped their wrists with vines, keeping them isolated against the back wall until they could figure out how to best handle the situation.

Jade was...detached. She went through the motions quietly and with hardly any emotion, and Isla couldn't imagine what she was feeling. The burden of being the one to kill Celesine, someone who had been her friend, her *hero*, for so long...she didn't deserve that responsibility. And yet, she'd done it, and because of her, they were safe.

Bri approached Isla and they watched as Annalise ordered the boys and Kai around, while Rynn sullenly hovered over the four Chamber members. The heat coming from Bri made sweat break out on Isla's forehead.

"This was the craziest night of my life," Bri said with a deep sigh.

Isla huffed out a laugh, but the sound didn't have much heart. Despite their victory, she felt weak and exhausted, defeated in a different sense.

She was hollow. Vacant. The absence of her elements consumed her, a gnawing, aching pit in her soul. Those last moments she'd had with them, when the magic realized what she was about to do, had been excruciating. The elements hadn't wanted to leave her, and it was like ripping her body in half when she drove the dagger into her arm. And then they were simply...gone. She would never feel them again, and that thought made it difficult to breathe.

"How are you feeling?" Bri asked, touching Isla's injured arm, which was wrapped in green fabric from her gown, now streaked with red.

Isla glanced at it and looked away. "I'm fine. It doesn't hurt that bad anymore."

"I didn't just mean your arm."

She looked up into Bri's eyes, always so expressive, but even more so with the heightened emotions of the fire element blazing through them. The anger and hurt she held back brimmed on the surface. Gods, Isla had messed up. Again. She knew they needed to talk, but it would have to wait. There were still things they had to take care of.

Isla averted her gaze. "How about you, Bri? How do you feel about all of this?" she asked tentatively, pointing to Bri's hand as a ball of flames flickered to light.

Bri flipped her hand over, and the blazing sphere rolled with it, spinning animatedly up her arm. The frustration in her tone lightened as she stared at it. "I won't lie, it's...it's pretty amazing." They both watched as the fire moved back to her hand, licking at her fingers playfully. Bri's eyes were a mesmerizing blend of deep brown and vibrant orange.

"But I don't want this life, Isla," she said suddenly, snuffing the flames out with a clench of her fist. "I watched what having this kind of power did to you, and I know it tore Aidan apart way back then. It's so...*big*, if that makes sense. I can already feel it pushing parts of me away to make space for itself, like there's not enough room for both the fire and me. How did you do this with all *five* of them?"

This description surprised Isla. To her, it hadn't felt like the elements were pushing her away at all. If anything, they molded to her, making her into something new. Something stronger. But she could understand how that kind of magic might work differently for someone else—technically, Bri hadn't chosen this path. Maybe the distinction lay in the fact that Isla had willingly accepted them.

"I got used to it, I suppose," she answered. "They became part of me."

"What if I can't get rid of it?"

It hurt Isla to see the terror on Bri's face. Her brave best friend, her ferocious and feisty Bri, who so rarely showed fear. Isla bit the inside of her cheek. "I don't know if it'll work, Bri, but...there might be a way."

The only problem was, her idea included all four elementals.

When Celesine had been stabbed by the Dagger of Volnus, her element was released, as all five had left Isla when she cut herself. Isla assumed it was because the dagger didn't work in the same way it had those months ago on the beach—it would no longer *store* the magic in itself, but would set it free.

The flaw in her plan was the same as it was with any other plan they'd made: the unknown. The Aether was gone, set loose back into nature. What if it wasn't possible for some of the elements to be free, and some to still dwell inside the elementals? The Primevals had made it very clear that they had created the five elementals to host the magic, and if that balance was disrupted, it could be catastrophic. Well, it was definitely unbalanced now, with one of them already freed.

Looking at Rynn and Jade, who had come alive when they got their powers back, Isla didn't know if she could convince them to give it up. *Again.* She now knew firsthand how agonizing it felt.

"Come on," she said to Bri, looping her uninjured arm through Bri's and trudging toward the others, who had finished sending soldiers back through the tunnel. To Isla's surprise, Akir and a few of his followers had shown up while she and Bri were deep in conversation.

"Cousin," he said by way of greeting, his concerned green eyes zeroing in on her wrapped arm. "What happened to you?"

Aidan jumped in and patted Isla on the shoulder. "It's better than dead."

Isla shot him a look. "We have a lot to catch up on, Akir, but it might need to wait until later."

He nodded. "I take it you will be staying on the island a little while longer?"

Instinctively, she snuck a glance at Sebastian, whose eyes had already found hers. "I can spare a few days," she responded.

Eyebrows raised, Akir said, "I fear we have missed something vital, but am I correct in assuming you need assistance with our dear Chamber?" He inclined his head to the four members, who glared daggers at him from their slumped, tied position at the stone wall.

Isla held back a snort. "Do you think you and your group"—she gestured to the handful of men and women who stood behind him—"could deliver them somewhere...safe?" *Like a dungeon.* "Until we figure out what to do with them and who will take their place."

His eyes twinkled. "I think I know where to take them."

As he bowed his head and turned to give instructions, a sudden thought struck Isla, and she straightened. "Wait...Akir?"

"Yes?" he replied over his shoulder.

"How would *you* feel about taking their place?"

He froze, even the wispy hairs on the end of his long hair seeming to still. The eyes of all his rebels were on him. Slowly, he turned to face her, the wrinkles at his forehead more pronounced in his confusion.

"I don't believe I understand, cousin."

A smile crept onto Isla's lips. "By blood, you have as much a claim to this throne as I do. But this isn't about birthright or lineage—you're exactly what Iona needs, Akir. Even in this short week, I've seen how much you care about these people and their rights. You started an entire *resistance* because you saw what this kingdom was going through. You devoted your life to helping those who got on the wrong side of an oppressive leadership." Conviction bloomed in her voice as visions of the last few days flew back to her. "The way these people look at you...you're their hero, Akir. You love this kingdom, you respect their freedom, and you cherish them as individuals—not as bodies simply there to serve you."

"She's right," Kai said, appearing at Isla's side. "Trust me, I've seen many kings and queens come and go on this island. Some were excellent and just, some were harmful. But hardly any of them had the passion to do good that you have."

"You may be a bit idealistic for my taste," Jade chimed in from behind them, and Isla turned to find a small smile on her face. "But you would do what is right by this kingdom. And that's the most important part."

Sebastian's fingers brushed against the small of Isla's back as he said, "For what it's worth, you would be the least annoying monarch I'd have to deal with."

At that, Akir chuckled, his eyes glistening with emotion.

"Be good to them," Rynn said simply, his arms crossed as he leaned against the wall and nodded in approval at the elderly man.

"Well, you have my vote," Aidan boomed as he came behind Kai and snaked his arms around her stomach.

Akir took them all in, his expression full of gratitude and wonder. Pride swelled in Isla's chest. She found Sebastian's hand and laced her fingers through his.

"I—I don't know what to say." Akir steepled his hands together in front of his long beard. "There are many laws in place, many regulations we would need to amend and put in front of a council before making a change such as this. It may not be possible. I will have to inquire with the record keepers to see if there is a precedent for such a motion." Isla could see wheels spinning in his head, his inquisitive mind already many, many steps ahead.

Bri smirked. "'King Akir'...it has a nice ring to it, don't you think?"

The rest of them chuckled in agreement, and Akir looked at them again, tilting his head to the side.

"Thank you," he said quietly. "You have helped bring peace to this kingdom and given hope that we can be without fear once more, as it was in the old days."

"You've been doing that for years," Isla said. "We just...accelerated it a bit. *You're* the hope for Iona, Akir."

He pressed his lips together and nodded tightly before clearing his throat and clapping his hands together. "Come! Before you make an old man weep. There is much to be done." He winked at Isla and turned to his rebels, doling out instructions for getting the Chamber members out and helping the wounded soldiers.

"He would have gladly passed the Ionan crown to you, you know," Sebastian whispered in her ear.

"It's not mine to take," she responded with a shrug.

"What of a different crown, then?" he asked, and she whipped her head around, her eyes wide.

He raised a brow and smirked, backing away before she could question what he meant. Bri and Jade took his place, the latter still looking weary and distant. Isla reached out to take Jade's hand, surprised that she didn't pull away.

"So, what do we need to do?" Jade asked, and Isla blinked.

"About what?"

Jade sighed. "Getting rid of our elements." When Isla stared at her, Jade gave a half-smile. "I'm not a fool, Isla. I know that's where this is heading. We both do," she said, looking over Isla's shoulder.

Isla craned her neck to find Rynn approaching quietly, his piercing gray eyes steady. "This was never permanent," he said.

"And you're okay with that?" Isla asked hesitantly, looking between him and Jade.

"This was a gift." Jade released Isla's hand. "A chance to say goodbye, since we couldn't last time. I think a part of me has known that the time for the elements to be contained in a single being has passed. We aren't what this world needs anymore, and haven't been for quite a while."

Rynn nodded solemnly, moving to stand beside Jade and Bri. "A thousand years ago, I could not have imagined my life without the wind under my control. And that's the problem, is it not? They are not ours to command."

His gaze found Annalise as she drifted toward them. "Perhaps there is a different life for us here, after all this time."

Aidan and Kai slipped among them, his nose nuzzled in his wife's neck as they rocked back and forth. "A *better* life, brother," Aidan said.

Tears filled Isla's eyes. For herself and the bonds she shared with each and every one of the friends standing before her. And for the elementals. They'd finally found the peace they'd been striving for their entire lives.

"If you're sure," Isla said, "then I just need the dagger."

Rynn pulled it from his pocket, clean of blood. He must have retrieved it from the body before they covered her with Aidan's jacket.

"Who wants to go first?" Isla asked as she took it by the hilt.

Annalise stepped forward. "This was quite the adventure, but I think I'm made for life within four walls and a ceiling, not open waters. Although," she paused, meeting Kai's eyes, "I see why this would be hard to give up. It's very..."

"Freeing?" Kai offered. "The sea suits you, Annalise. Maybe you can embrace your wild side every once in a while." She winked, and Annalise smiled.

"Well, let's get this over with." She held out her arm to Isla, who grasped it firmly and pressed the blade against her forearm.

"This might sting a little," Isla warned, before pushing it into the skin until a bead of blood bloomed. Annalise gasped, but held still.

Isla created a small gash, enough to cause deep red blood to trickle from Annalise's arm and to the ground. Within seconds, veins of bright light oozed from the cut, dripping to the stone and slowly sinking until it disappeared from sight, the same way the Aether had left Celesine. A shockwave pulsed through the night and the water at their back gurgled energetically as its element was released.

When Isla let go, Sebastian came and wrapped a piece of fabric from his shirt around Annalise's forearm, staunching the flow of blood.

"How do you feel, Anna?" he asked.

"Back to normal, I suppose," she said with a shaky breath. "The water is gone."

Next, Isla turned to Bri.

"It was fun while it lasted," her best friend said, offering her arm. Isla repeated the process, watching as the element dimmed from Bri's eyes, knowing it had lit a spark that would be hard to contain. Bri had always had fire—now, she had to stoke it on her own.

The space between them heated when her strands of power fell and faded. Two down, two to go.

"Rynn," Isla said, turning and holding her hand out.

"If you do not mind," he reached to take the dagger from her, "I would rather do this myself."

She smiled knowingly and gave it to him. He cut a jagged line on his arm and, with closed eyes and a tense face, said goodbye to his element as his magic leaked away, wind whipping through their hair.

Isla took the dagger and glanced at Jade questioningly, knowing this would be hardest for her. The depth of love and connection to the earth...it was different from the others. More intimate. Isla felt its loss in her core, and knew giving it up for a second time would take incredible strength.

"Just do it," Jade said with gritted teeth.

Isla sliced at her arm, the entire group watching in reflective silence as her blood dripped, dripped, dripped to the stone, the earth rumbling in its wake.

And finally, the elements were free.

CHAPTER FIFTY-FIVE

Isla

T he following days passed in a blur. Isla and the rest stayed on the island a few days longer than expected, busy with various tasks.

Sebastian and Annalise offered to help Akir devise a plan of action to formally dismiss the four Chamber members, draft a declaration to the citizens of Iona, and begin treaties with the other three kingdoms that better aligned with the new goals Akir wished to set in place.

The others involved themselves in a little bit of everything. Kai, Aidan, and Jade spent most of the days in the nearby villages, still aiding with storm relief. Rynn split his time between politics and the people, seeming to enjoy the give-and-take of the advisory meetings and observing the inner workings of a court starting from scratch. After Isla received proper care for her arm, she and Bri worked in the temporary shelters of Farrow, lending a hand wherever they were needed.

Isla and Bri finally had the conversation that had been weighing on Isla since that night. Four mornings after Celesine's death, when they were supposed to be packing to leave the island, Isla pulled Bri into her room, prepared to grovel and fill her best friend in on everything she'd kept secret.

"What's going on?" Bri asked as she stepped inside, taking in the plates of cinnamon rolls, mugs of warm coffee, and bottles of wine placed neatly on the bed. "It's a bit too early for this, but I'm not complaining." She picked up a wine bottle and gave Isla a look.

Biting her lip, Isla said, "This is me...trying to say I'm sorry." She winced. *Sorry* didn't even begin to encompass the emotions running through her, but she didn't know where to start. Didn't know how her best friend could possibly forgive her after she'd lied to her and run away with the intention of never coming back. But she supposed sweets and wine would be a good place to start.

"I know you probably can't trust me easily after this," she continued, taking a deep breath and trying to remember the words she'd been reciting in her head for days. "I messed up. Again. When the Primevals told me sacrificing myself and my powers was the only option, I didn't know what to think. I felt like I was alone and couldn't put this on anyone else. While I thought it was the right decision, I know it wasn't fair to you—to anyone. I was trying to protect you, Bri, and—"

Bri scoffed with a bite of cinnamon roll in her mouth. "That's the oldest excuse in the book, and you know it. You were *afraid*, Isla. And that's okay. But you're not responsible for our protection. You're not in charge of what we should and shouldn't know, especially when it affects us all. If you had just come to us, we could've found a different way, or at least not been blind-sided!"

Isla flinched. "You're right. I know—I'm so sorry. I was scared. *Unbelievably* scared. And so stupid. These last few months have just..." Her shoulders raised involuntarily, as if she was trying to burrow into herself. "It's made everything so twisted inside of me. The things I've seen, the magic, it—I don't know what to *be* anymore. *Who* to be. It's like—" She cut herself off with a sigh and rubbed her hand against her neck. Putting her thoughts into words, trying to articulate these emotions, felt like an impossible task.

"Before this, when it was just us in our small village, dealing with our own burdens and daily life...that felt so *big*. It was all I knew. Me, Papa, and Arden;

you and Hamil and the others; our shop, our town. That was it. That's all I needed to care about.

"And then the elementals showed up. They opened my eyes to so much more than I had ever dreamed of—magic and far-away kingdoms and...honestly, *purpose*. I felt needed and important on such a greater scale. That's dangerous, I know, but it didn't change the thrill I got when realizing I could make a difference. I was *special*.

"When I got the elemental magic, it was...well, you know." Isla gestured to Bri. "It was like this rush of power and belonging and completeness I'd never felt before. And it was beautiful. But there's another side to all that power, something I didn't realize until I was stuck on the spirit plane, watching centuries and centuries of the world unfold around me. All of the chaos and difficulties and mistakes...it made my old life and troubles seem so small, you know? There are three other kingdoms out there besides my own, thousands of people, and countless problems. When the Primevals told me I had the chance to help them, to prevent anything worse from happening, how could I not take it?

"I'm not saying I went about it the right way," Isla said hurriedly as Bri opened her mouth to argue. "I'm just saying this was why I made the decision. But not talking to you, not trusting you with everything going on inside my head...that was wrong. After what we've been through, I should've come to you, Bri. You didn't deserve this."

Bri gave her a long look, her jaw clenching and unclenching as she searched Isla's eyes. "As far as apologies go, that could've been worse," Bri finally said grudgingly.

Isla lifted an eyebrow. "Are we...okay?"

Sighing, Bri slumped her shoulders. "Isla, you know I'll always love you. You're my sister. This will take some time to get over, but what did you think I was going to do, walk away?" She crossed to Isla and wrapped an arm around her waist, squeezing her tight. "If you haven't noticed, I'm pretty hard to get rid of. Especially when you ply me with cinnamon rolls and wine."

"That's good, because I don't want to get rid of you," Isla said, leaning her head on Bri's shoulder.

"Well, now that *that's* out of the way, tell me about Sebastian."

Isla reared back to see Bri's mischievous smile, and couldn't help but let out a laugh. They spent the next hours gorging themselves on sweets and packing their bags while Isla told her everything that had happened, from her mysterious meeting with the Primevals to dancing in the gardens with Sebastian.

When she reached the part about Sebastian telling her he loved her, Bri kicked her feet in the air, spilling red wine onto the sheets.

"Gods, he's perfect. *Why* are you heading back to Evonlea with me instead of jumping on the boat to Karstos? And jumping on *him*, for that matter."

Isla launched a pillow at her. "I have to go home, Bri. I need to see Papa. You know that."

It really shouldn't have been a difficult decision. Her father was her number one priority, and she wanted to see him so badly it hurt. Her life was in Lockhurt—her friends, her job, her legacy.

Yet...she was worried a part of her would never truly belong there again. Not after everything she'd been through, everything she'd seen. Not after finding Sebastian.

She'd tried not to think about that over the past days. Sebastian had respected her wishes to return home, even though she could tell it broke him. It was so easy to fall in love with him on this island, where a mere door separated them and they were thousands of miles away from the rest of the world and who they used to be. But real life beckoned them now. They had more people to think about. She didn't know what the future held, and her feelings for him hadn't changed. It was just...complicated.

A terse knock sounded on the door, and Bri and Isla looked at each other.

"Yes, Annalise?" they said in unison, then broke into giggles.

"Are you girls almost ready?"

"We'll be out in a minute!" Bri called.

They fastened the buckles on their travel cases and headed out the door. The rest of the group was already in the common room, and after some shuffling around, they made their way through the palace and to the main entrance, where carriages waited to take them to the docks.

Akir, Eliza, and his newly formed council stood by the grand entrance doors when they arrived. Eliza beamed at Isla and enveloped her in a warm embrace, her sweet, clean scent washing over Isla.

"Don't be a stranger," she whispered in her ear, and Isla nodded, her chin hitting the top of the elderly woman's shoulder.

"You are welcome here anytime, cousin," Akir said, holding his arms out to her. When she squeezed him tight, he murmured, "I wish it had not taken so many near-death experiences to bring us together, but, alas. Here we are." He pulled away, both of them misty eyed. "And I am proud to call you family."

Family. Kindred spirits she hadn't even known existed until that week, now bonded for the rest of their lives.

"Don't have too much fun here without me, okay?" she said jokingly, wiping a tear from her cheek.

"I suppose you will simply have to visit often, then."

Sebastian slid an arm around her waist. "A ship will be at her disposal whenever she wishes," he said, shaking Akir's hand with his free one. Her heart swelled at his words, knowing he was still taking care of her, even with their future such a mess.

Soon, the carriages were loaded and they were on their way to the shore. The path led through the jungles, the vibrant greenery and chattering wildlife waving a final farewell as they passed.

The beach came into view, that glistening white sand and dazzling turquoise water where everything had changed. Isla's eyes found the spot by the large group of boulders where Arden had died, and she let out a slow breath. His green eyes stared back at her when she closed hers, the freckles that dotted his cheeks and nose like stars mapped in the heavens. Sebastian, who had been lazily running his fingers up and down the leggings at her thigh while they rode, grabbed her hand and gently rubbed his thumb over her knuckles, seeming to know where her head was at.

"He's still with you," he said quietly, placing a kiss on her temple. She leaned into the touch, his breath warming her skin. "And your mother." He brushed another kiss at her cheek. "They will always be watching you."

"And your father, too," she added as his arm came to her other side and held her against him. She breathed deeply and let the sound of his heartbeat calm her. "He'd be so proud of the king you've become, Sebastian."

"He would have loved you." His fingers traced light circles on her arm.

Next to her, Bri had her head out the carriage window, happily drinking in the last moments of fresh air before the upcoming days on the water. On the bench across from them, Annalise was absorbed in a book Akir had given her.

"Speaking of fathers," Sebastian said, his tone taking on a playful edge that made Isla's heart pump a little faster. "When will I get to meet yours?"

She blinked rapidly, holding back a laugh as she imagined the look on her papa's face if the *King of Karstos* were to waltz into their little cabin.

"Why do you need to meet him?" she asked coyly.

"Well, I've heard it's the proper thing to do."

Isla twisted to look at him, a teasing smile on her lips. "I didn't take you for a proper man."

"For you, I can be." He gripped her chin between his thumb and forefinger, his deep blue eyes suddenly full of intensity. "You're it for me, Isla," he said, low so the others wouldn't hear him. "Whenever, however you want, I'll be ready."

She swallowed the lump in her throat, the tension between them thick as she flicked her eyes to his lips.

"Wait until you have your own room on the boat, please," Annalise said, making Isla jump in her seat. She looked across the narrow gap to find Annalise still engrossed in her book. Isla's cheeks flamed as Bri brought her head inside long enough to wink at her.

"Gladly," Sebastian murmured, and Isla was pretty sure her heart was going to burst.

The days of travel back to Evonlea were so unlike the last time she'd voyaged to Iona, where she'd been preoccupied with worries and panic and questions. This time, it didn't last nearly long enough.

Her group of friends spent their days playing games on the main deck, talking about their lives over the past few months, and sharing stories of the three different kingdoms. Isla had never been to Ara Mir, and she was fascinated by the tales Kai and Aidan told, especially of his daring adventures deep in the mines. The two of them planned to return to the desert kingdom, but weren't set on if that would be their permanent residence. Isla didn't understand how they could be so casual about their future, especially with a baby on the way. She would be a raging pit of anxiety right about now. She'd come to realize, however, that those two were at ease and content as long as they had each other. They could make a life anywhere, anytime. There was something beautiful about the freedom of their spirits.

The most shocking thing that occurred on the trip was during their third day at sea. Rynn had fallen into a habit of reading in an alcove on the main deck with a cup of tea at sunrise. That morning, as soon as Sebastian awoke, he found the broody male and offered him a job on his royal council.

And Rynn accepted.

The entire ship had been abuzz with the news for the rest of the day. Kai and Aidan, as expected, were positively giddy over the information, and teased him incessantly for hours; Aidan's new nickname for him became "Lord Rynn." When Annalise found out, she'd stormed across the deck, grabbed Sebastian by the shirt, and dragged him to the nearby captain's quarters. The entire boat heard their argument. Apparently, she hadn't known he was going to make such a decision, and wasn't fond of being caught off guard.

When they emerged thirty minutes later, Sebastian bore the largest smirk Isla had ever seen, and Annalise's cheeks were pink, her eyes churning with resolve.

Rynn had walked up to her, his face as impassive as ever, and calmly said, "I suppose you are technically my overseer now."

"Oh, shut up," she'd hissed, before grabbing the back of his neck and pulling his lips to hers, right in the middle of the deck.

Isla had hollered and clapped with the rest of them, a huge grin on each of their faces as Rynn threw his cane to the floor and lifted Annalise off her feet.

Even Jade looked pleased for their happiness, although she remained distant over the next few days. Isla didn't know what her plans going forward were. She'd set up her life in Evonlea for the sole purpose of taking care of Rynn, who would now be moving to Karstos with very new developments to focus on. Isla wished she knew how to help, wished she could find what would fill the vacant look in Jade's dark eyes. But that was for her to discover on her own—she needed to figure out what life looked like after an entire existence of finding purpose in others.

And Bri...well, Bri was the same Bri she had always been, with a little more adventure filling her dreams. She made plans to visit Kai and Aidan, talked with the ship's crew about what a job on the water was like, and hounded Sebastian until he promised her he'd have a guest room set up entirely in her honor for whenever she felt like exploring Karstos.

"And for other reasons," she'd said with a wink at Isla.

That was one conversation Isla managed to avoid the entire trip. She and Sebastian stayed up late each night, talking about everything under the sun, from their childhoods to their favorite foods to the losses of the past years that still haunted them. But any mention of the future, any question of where she wanted to end up, and she froze.

Not because she wasn't sure about her feelings, but because she was *too* sure, and she had other people in her life to consider. Namely, her papa. She felt incredibly selfish to think of leaving him so soon after coming back to him, mere months after he'd watched his son die. He'd spent this time mourning both of his children while living in an empty house, memories of his family ingrained in every corner.

She was all he had left. She couldn't abandon him.

When they reached Vyros, the southern port in Evonlea, Isla could hardly believe how quickly the time had passed. She, Bri, Rynn, and Jade were to meet with their old friend August, who would take them up to Lockhurt, where Rynn would gather his belongings before heading to his new home in Delarossi. Kai and Aidan had decided to vacation in the capital city of Karstos before heading to Ara Mir—because an entire week on a faraway island wasn't "vacation" enough for them, Isla supposed—and would accompany Sebastian and Annalise further south.

Sebastian had insisted on coming with Isla all the way to Lockhurt, but she knew he needed to get back to his responsibilities at home, and if she'd let him come with her...she wouldn't be able to say goodbye. She needed time to think about the paths that lay ahead of her without his annoyingly perfect and distracting presence drawing her closer and closer in.

Maybe it was a good thing their departure from Vyros was so rushed. Leaving the others had tears filling Isla's eyes before they even said anything.

Aidan pulled her in for a tight hug as August's men loaded their belongings into saddlebags. "Hey now, this isn't goodbye, little island," he said, her tears already dripping onto his shirt. She sniffed into his shoulder. "I expect you there when the baby's born. She's going to need to meet her Aunt Isla and hear about all the crazy adventures we went on."

"*She*?" Isla asked, pulling away and raising an eyebrow.

He grinned sheepishly. "Well, I don't know, of course, but gods forbid we have a little *me* running around the place."

At that, Jade snorted, and he turned to say goodbye to her and Rynn while Kai slipped her arms around Isla's neck.

"Thank you," she whispered softly. "I've probably said it before, but what you did for us, this life you gave us...it means everything to me."

"You deserve it, Kai. I'm so grateful to have met you—all of you. You've changed my life too, you know." Isla squeezed harder. "I just hope it doesn't take another dangerous threat to the world for us to see each other again."

Kai dropped her arms and wiped at her cheeks. "We're going to see you all the time, just you wait."

"Yes, because living three kingdoms apart makes traveling so easy," Isla said, laughing through the tears clouding her vision.

"Who knows?" Kai shrugged, that mischievous gleam in her bright blue eyes. "Fate does funny things sometimes."

While the others finished talking, Sebastian snagged Isla's arm and dragged her away, closer to the ships lining the rocky port. He brought his lips to hers and she immediately twined her arms around his neck, pulling up on her toes to deepen the kiss.

She didn't know how to read this kiss. It was urgent but tender, like a goodbye mixed with hope for tomorrow. It broke her heart but filled the cracks at the same time. Knowing this man loved her, that he would wait for her, was more than she could bear. More than she deserved.

From far off, she heard August call her name, and she tore away to press her forehead against Sebastian's.

"I didn't think leaving you would be this hard." Her breath hitched, already missing him so much it ached. "I'm sorry I couldn't give you the answer you wanted," she said, blinking slowly as more tears dripped from her lashes.

"Isla, love," he said, catching them with his finger as they fell, the corners of his mouth pulling upward in a soft smile. "It will all work out. Have a little faith in us, yes?"

She wasn't sure how he could be so confident, but she nodded anyway as he took her hand and led her back to the others.

Before she knew it, she, Rynn, Jade, and Bri had mounted their horses and set off on the day-and-a-half journey to Lockhurt. The pieces of her heart that she'd left behind were a throbbing wound in her chest. But...the others had each left pieces with her, as well, that slowly worked to soothe the rough edges, reminding her that even when apart, the love and friendship she'd found meant she would never be truly alone again.

Day quickly bled into night, and they stayed at an inn about half a day from Lockhurt. Isla barely slept with the anticipation of being *home* again, of seeing her papa and sleeping in her own bed and wandering the streets she'd grown up in.

The next morning, they were on the road once more, each passing moment causing excitement to mount in her chest. They emerged from the forest, now turning vibrant and green with the dawn of spring, and the village of Lockhurt opened before them.

Deep red and brown brick buildings loomed over cobblestone streets. Bushes and fruit trees dotted the fields beyond the town square, where homemakers and business owners were busy with their daily tasks, as normal as the day Isla had left. Nostalgia flooded her as they drew nearer: the Bear's Head tavern, where she and Bri had spent many nights dancing and laughing their cares away. The bakery several doors down, where the owner had let her and her mother bake pies for the fall festival, the crisp scent of apples and pumpkin and cinnamon still vivid in her mind. All of the many hiding spots she, Arden, and the boys had found throughout the years as children, the trees in the far eastern forest where she'd made her first kill, the corner where her mama had scolded her for stealing a piece of candy from the market.

She would have time to stroll the streets of her memories later. Now, there was only one place she needed to be.

They reached the start of the neighborhoods, and she was met with the sight of familiar wooden cottages, moss-covered roofs, and towering trees ripe with fresh fruits and nuts swaying in the cool breeze. Her heart jumped to her throat as she squeezed her calves against her mare and broke into a gallop. Wind whipped through her braid. Her stomach churned with nerves and excitement and feverish exhilaration, unable to stop her lips from curving. She turned down the last street, looking for the red brick chimney that marked her home—

There he was.

Her father stood in their front yard with an ax in his hand, a pile of wood resting to the side of a chopping block, the sleeves of his loose, tan tunic rolled up to his elbows. His light brown and gray beard was longer and scruffier than Isla had ever seen it, but other than that, he hadn't changed a bit.

She brought the horse to a halt in front of the house, then carefully dismounted.

"I'm done taking orders for the week," her papa said, not looking up as he swung the ax down on another piece of firewood. "You can come back next week. I'll have more spots open then."

Isla bit down on her lip, tears welling as she drank in the sight of him. "I'm not here to place an order," she said quietly.

He stumbled, the ax dropping from his hand with a thud. When he looked up at her, his brow furrowed, his mouth falling open wordlessly as his chest heaved.

"Isla?" he asked hesitantly, as if he didn't want to believe his eyes.

She nodded and sucked in a breath, letting go of the reins and breaking into a sprint. Her papa walked toward her with outstretched arms, but he fell to his knees, his features screwed tightly and overcome with emotion. Isla met him where he knelt and dropped to the soft grass, throwing herself into his open arms.

He whispered her name over and over while she sobbed into his shirt, clinging to her heart, her soul, her papa.

She was finally home.

CHAPTER FIFTY-SIX

Isla

Two Months Later

Isla fell back into the motions of her previous life with ease: helping Papa with the housework, weekly trips to the crowded market, and making weapons and tools for their many paying customers. Orders had more than doubled since she got back, now that there were two sets of hands able to carry out the work, and the townsfolk were ecstatic to have their little Isla back home.

It had been no easy feat to explain to an entire village how Isla had seemingly come back from the dead, but they were eventually convinced she'd been seeking the expert care of healers in Ara Mir after contracting a deadly disease, and had returned good as new.

Her papa hadn't let her out of his sight for the first couple of weeks, but she didn't mind. She was thankful for the time with him, and even more thankful they had one another to lean on while the shadows of the last few months continued to creep up on them, lurking around the corner of every happy memory. They managed to steal pockets of joy for themselves, tucking them away with small smiles as they rebuilt their life together piece by piece, moment by moment.

Bri had left on a grand, whirlwind adventure after a month. Isla hadn't been surprised; she knew the instant her best friend got a taste of what awaited outside this small town, she'd be hard pressed to stop her from wanting more.

She'd received two letters so far, each detailing her wild stories of hitching a ride across the Strait of Pyr on a sailboat in the middle of a hurricane, trekking through Karstosian jungles, and drinking hard liquor from a stranger's boot.

Kai and Aidan had also written several times, their happiness practically jumping off each page. They'd gone back to Ara Mir and saved up enough money to buy their own small home—not permanent, they were quick to remind Isla, but better than the hovel they'd been renting before, and perfectly fine for raising a child. Isla's favorite part of the letters were when Kai and Aidan would send the latest baby name options: currently, Aidan was pushing for "Draken" if it was a boy, to which Kai absolutely refused.

Rynn had left for Karstos a week after they returned from Iona, and Jade was still in Lockhurt, doing her best to find her purpose. She and Isla crossed paths often. One day at the markets, Isla saw her and a young blonde woman who was introduced as Emilee setting up a booth. Jade and Emilee had been experimenting with herbs and tinctures in the hopes of finding remedies for pain and other chronic illnesses, something the healers in Evonlea had not yet mastered. Their tonics seemed to be selling well. Jade wasn't one to brag or overshare, but Isla could tell she was proud of her work, and she glowed a little brighter every time Isla saw her.

Isla's heart burst at the seams with the joy and fulfillment her friends had found. Their happiness meant the world to her. And being with her father again, laughing in the pub with Hamil and her childhood peers, working with her hands to provide for the town...it was almost enough.

Almost.

Something was still missing. And the longer she tried to ignore it, the more the longing grew.

Of everyone, Sebastian had written to her the most by far. Every week she'd come home to a new letter, sometimes two, even when she knew her last response couldn't have reached him yet. He seemed to keep a running stream of consciousness with his notes to her. He'd write his thoughts down as soon as he thought of them, whether it be recounting the last boring council meeting, sharing a funny story about Rynn and Annalise, telling of his mother's declining health, or just wanting Isla to know he was thinking of her. Some letters were long and eloquent, some were rushed and sloppy, as if he had more important things to do but couldn't wait to pen his thoughts. The ones that made her the most emotional were often the shortest. The last one she'd received a couple of days ago simply said,

I took my mother to watch the stars last night and told her about you. It was the first time she's smiled in months. You bring me new joys every day, without even being here.

Forever yours,

S

He ended each letter the same way. And each time, her chest tightened. She missed him more every day. His ridiculous charm, his smell, how he sounded when he called her "love." Being wrapped in his arms. His smirk. Gods, that smirk. It still made her stomach flip.

She missed having someone to share the nights with, to share her darkest thoughts, to share a smile. The way he would pretend not to care too strongly with others, but behind his mask, she knew his emotions ran as deep as the ocean. He never hid from her, and she missed the freedom that came from being herself with someone, no boundaries, no judgment.

But life in Lockhurt...it was good. Easy, normal, constant. And this was where her father was. How could she leave him again? How could she walk away from all she'd ever known?

She had the same conversation with herself each day, and this one was no different. As she put the family horse, Buttercup, back in his stable and headed to the front door, she was about to get to the part in her inner conflict where she convinced herself to stay home and think of her father's happiness, when he came stomping out of the house.

"What's wrong, Papa?" she asked, tucking her riding gloves into her pocket.

"What are these?" He held out his closed fist. Within his grasp were pages and pages of letters.

Sebastian's letters.

She'd left them out on top of their shared desk the night before, when she'd written her latest response and had fallen asleep before cleaning up.

Her cheeks reddened, her body heating. "Letters from a friend."

Her papa snorted. "A *friend*? Sweet girl, I may be old, but I'm not dead. Or blind." He gave her a knowing look, his expression softening. "Why haven't you told me about this boy?"

Isla sighed and scrubbed at her face. "Because...I don't know, Papa. It's complicated."

Nodding slowly, his wise eyes scanned hers as if he could read beneath the surface. "Complicated, you say." He hummed. "Do you love him?"

A knot formed in her stomach, her heart pounding faster. She'd never said the words aloud, but had known for some time how she felt.

Swallowing, she whispered, "Yes, Papa."

"Then it's not so complicated, after all," he said simply, then turned on his heel to go back inside. "Come on, Isla. It's time we had a talk."

She followed him into their house, feeling like a little girl about to be reprimanded as she twisted her hands together and bit down on her lip. She took a seat on the couch while he disappeared into the kitchen. A few moments later, he returned with two cups of tea. The air sweetened with the scent of honey and spice.

"So, who is this mysterious 'S'?" he asked, taking a sip of his drink.

Her eyes shifted to the letters now resting on the coffee table. She'd thrown away the envelopes they came in, otherwise her papa would've instantly recognized the royal seal of Karstos. To him, "S" could've been any random man from any village. While she'd told her father most of what had happened over the last several months, she'd been careful to leave out some details, such as how closely she'd worked with the king. She wasn't sure how her papa would feel about Sebastian given the last time he'd seen him, the king had kidnapped both him and Arden and leveraged them against Isla.

She pinched her lips together and became very engrossed with the herbs floating in her tea bag. "Well, his name is Sebastian," she said slowly.

A long pause followed, tension in the air as thick as the steam rising from their mugs.

"As in...the king of Karstos," her papa said. It wasn't a question, but she nodded anyway. "I see."

She risked a glance up, finding his face solemn and contemplative, his finger tapping against his cup as he looked out the front window. After a minute, Isla awkwardly shifted in her seat, itching to fill the strange silence, when he said, "Do you want to know why I never told you or Arden of our heritage?"

Her eyes widened and she blinked several times, caught off guard by the change of subject. "I assumed it was because it was so long ago, you didn't think it mattered."

He let out a low chuckle. "Not at all, sweet girl. I feared it mattered *too* much. I was worried if the two of you learned of some far-off kingdom where legends of power and magic ran rampant, you would want to know more. I didn't want either of you to feel as if you didn't belong here. And while I didn't necessarily believe all the legends told in that old Vasileia record book, I knew they came from truth, and I didn't want that kind of world for you.

"It was selfish and short-sighted, to withhold everything from you both, but I never claimed to be perfect. I should have known if the gods wanted you to find it, you would." He leaned forward and covered her hand with his own. "I'm sorry for keeping the truth from you, Isla. It may have been my job once upon a time to decide what was best for you, but it isn't any longer, and hasn't been for some time."

"It's okay, Papa. I understand. You have nothing to be sorry for." She squeezed his hand. "But...what does this have to do with Sebastian?"

He sat back into the couch cushions. "I don't know much about the man. I caught glimpses here and there while Arden and I were being held in his palace, enough to understand that he...wasn't himself. And that was confirmed after everything we witnessed on the beach." He shuddered slightly, his eyes getting the same distant look they always did when he thought about Arden. "I'm sure there's still much for me to figure out. But what I do know, Isla, is that the man who wrote these letters loves you. Very much. I hope you'll forgive me for reading some of them." He grinned sheepishly behind the rim of his cup, and Isla had never seen her father look so bashful.

She shook her head and laughed. "It's fine. I would expect nothing less. You and Arden were always so nosy."

"Yes, well, I may be nosy, but like I said before, it's not my place to tell you what's best for you. And, from the old eyes of someone who hasn't courted a woman in decades, it seems like he desperately wants to be with you." His brow furrowed as he spoke. "What's holding you back, sweet girl?"

Isla took a deep breath and rolled her head so she was staring at the ceiling, her daily argument with herself coming to the surface.

"We *just* got our lives back, Papa. And things here are good. We're finally happy again, and I don't want to leave you or mess everything up."

"How would you being with the man you love mess everything up?"

She pursed her lips. How did he make her fears sound so illogical? "He lives in Karstos, Papa."

"I am well aware that the King of Karstos does, in fact, live in Karstos."

Turning her head, she narrowed her eyes at the humorous expression on his face. "How am I supposed to pick up and move all the way down there? Plus, he's a *king*. I don't—I can't be a—" She couldn't even get the word out. "But it doesn't matter, because I don't want to leave you. Not right now. The fact that you were alone for those months before I got back *killed* me." She held a finger up. "And, before you complain that you're a grown man who can take care of himself, it's not just about that—*I* need *you*, too."

Throughout her speech, his eyebrow raised higher and higher, that same bemused look never leaving his features. "I understand. But did you ever think of asking me one thing?"

"What's that?"

"If I would go with you."

Her heart tripped over itself. "You—what?"

"You don't want to leave *me*, but what about our home? Our village? If I were to say that I didn't need to stay here to be happy, would you go chase after your king?"

She blinked rapidly, her thoughts cloudy. "I wouldn't ask you to do that, Papa. Your entire livelihood is here, your job, your—"

He waved his hand in the air to cut her off. "This was your mother's family business, Isla. I carried it on out of obligation and honor to her and the Belthares, but *you* are more important now. Besides," he said, a smile forming on his lips, "I'm sure those people in Karstos could use a lesson or two from a hunting expert."

Isla's mouth hung open. "You—you're serious?"

Her papa set both of their mugs on the table, then twisted so his knees were touching hers and grasped her hands. "Where you go, I go, sweet girl. For as long as you want your old, soon-to-be senile father around, I'll be there. We can make a life anywhere. You only need to be sure of what you want, and don't let anything hold you back."

Tears flooded her eyes as she nodded, unable to speak. He smiled and pulled her into his embrace, those strong, steady arms as comforting now as they were when she was a child.

He broke away and wiped at her cheeks with his sleeve. "Well, I suppose we have some plans to make, don't we?"

CHAPTER FIFTY-SEVEN

Isla

The Karstos palace in Delarossi was larger than Isla remembered. She'd seen parts of it very briefly when she'd stopped that raging cyclone four months ago, but that quick glimpse hadn't done it justice.

When she stepped out of the carriage and lugged her travel case to the ground, it splashed in a large puddle, spraying her dress with flecks of mud. The clouds overhead had darkened considerably as she journeyed further south, until the skies had opened and pelted the wood and iron with thick, heavy showers. Fierce wind made the rain slant as it fell, bolts of lightning flashing through the sky and lighting the palace ahead of her.

She was dropped off at a wrought iron gate, which opened to an enormous courtyard. The night storm cast everything in shadows, darkening the green grass and turning the stone statuary cold and menacing. Recently formed puddles and rounded bushes dotted the cobblestone path leading to the palace steps. Three towers of marble loomed before her, gray domes topping the stone and gold trim adorning each window and door.

Isla battled through the deluge, unused to the humidity and warmth of this rain as opposed to the icy, dagger-like drops in Evonlea. Her papa was going to love it here when he arrived in a few weeks; he'd always hated the cold. Expecting to find at least a couple of guards stationed in the courtyard, she was surprised when she didn't see a single soul as she dragged her luggage to the bottom of the steep stone staircase.

Before she could go any further, she heard them. Footsteps. From the sound of it, several footsteps.

"This happens every summer when the first storms hit." A woman's familiar voice came from around the corner of the covered entrance. "Lord Perrin already sent *two* messengers complaining about the floodplains up north."

"Yes, well, when it rains, there tends to be water. Tell him to—"

Sebastian stopped mid sentence when they came into view, and Isla forgot how to breathe.

There he was—a white tunic tucked into tight black pants, his navy blue jacket wrinkled as if he'd thrown it on in haste. His blonde hair looked as soft and perfect as ever, a couple of strands hanging over his forehead, like they tended to when he'd been running his fingers through it. When his bright blue eyes met hers, she dropped her bag to the wet ground, unable to move her legs.

He stared down at her from the top of the steps, and behind him, Annalise and their guards halted in their tracks.

"Hi," Isla said weakly, rubbing a hand against her neck, nerves coiling in her gut.

Suddenly, this seemed like a terrible idea. What had she been thinking, catching a ship to Karstos, assuming he'd be okay with her charging into his home with no warning after months of not seeing each other? It was presumptuous and foolish. Her cheeks reddened the longer he looked at her.

"Isla?" He took a step toward her. "What are you doing here?"

"I—well, umm—" She swallowed, internally cursing herself for not preparing for this moment better. He kept moving closer, down the stairs, one hesitant step at a time. "I wanted to see—if it's not too late, that is—"

As she stammered, he reached the last step, the rain already soaking through his jacket and white shirt. He was so close, she could see drops of water falling from his hair onto his cheek, even in the shadows of the night and storm clouds.

"You're wet," she said, her lips saying the first thing she could think of.

He smirked, and it set loose a thousand butterflies in her stomach. "And you're here." He moved a rain-logged curl behind her ear, his skin slick and warm against her own. "Would you like to tell me why?"

She nodded. This was the moment the past months had been leading to. The letters, the restless nights, the constant arguments with herself. All because she couldn't let him go. Because she had never told him the depths of her feelings. And now...here he was, looking at her as if not a single second had passed since their goodbye.

"I love you, Sebastian. I'm sorry it took me so long." The words flowed from her tongue like sweet honey. "I can't imagine my life anywhere but here. With you. If I'm not too late, if you still want—"

He didn't let her finish her request before his hand gripped the back of her neck and his mouth collided with hers. Her heartbeat filled her ears, like a tidal wave breaking through her doubts, his lips on hers the only thing that mattered. The rain continued to fall around them as she curled her fingers in his hair, the warm drops stoking the burning flames at her skin. Her body craved him, her soul sang for him, her heart beat for him.

"Yes," he whispered against her lips, stealing another kiss before cupping her cheek in his hand. "Of course it's not too late. I would have waited my entire life for you." His thumb brushed against her cheek, his eyes so tender and endless, she wanted to drown in them.

He glanced down at her bag. "Does this mean you're staying here?"

She beamed and pressed her lips to his again before burying her head in his shoulder, his arms the only thing keeping her from floating into the heavens.

"I'm not going anywhere. Not ever again."

Above them, the rain lessened and the clouds began to part, giving way to the inky expanse of night. Stars winked down at her, their silver light like a beacon to her soul.

And she knew, beyond a shadow of a doubt, this was where she was meant to be.

EPILOGUE

Isla

One Year Later

"**W**here is she? Gods, you'd think *today* of all days she would actually let someone else do the work, for a change," Kai grumbled, straightening her black dress with one hand while rocking a napping baby in the other.

"Really?" Jade scoffed. "I'm not the least bit surprised."

"I'm sure she's just going over some last minute details with the staff. I'll go check," Isla offered.

"Thanks, Isla. Oh, can you also find Akir and make sure he's still comfortable with taking Amaya? I don't want to ask too much of him." Kai glanced down at her daughter, concern crossing her features. "On second thought, maybe it's better if I stay with her. They don't really need me, right?"

"Kai, relax," Isla said, holding back a chuckle. "He'll only need to watch her for a few minutes. I promise, it'll be fine. I'll check with Akir again, but I bet his answer will be the same as the last three times you asked."

Kai smiled apologetically. "I know, I know. Look at me—I'm turning into you, worrying about everything."

This time, a snort escaped Isla. "I'm going to pretend I didn't hear that. I'll be back," she said, striding from the bathing chambers they'd been getting ready in and making her way to the gardens, then the ballroom, stopping anywhere she thought she might find their missing target.

Finally, she heard her voice coming from the kitchens.

"Remember, please have the main course ready by seven o'clock. My father is allergic to shellfish, so don't let him eat the crab cakes—no matter how much he argues."

Isla opened the kitchen door to the sight of Annalise in a long, white robe, holding a small stack of papers, reviewing each of the details written on them with the head cook. The kindly older woman patiently listened and nodded her head along, even though Isla knew she'd heard these instructions at least twice already.

"Annalise?" Isla called sweetly. "Come on, let's leave Miss O'Connor to do her job. You need to get ready."

Annalise sighed. "I'm sorry. You're right. Thank you, Miss O'Connor. I appreciate everything you've done," she said, before giving the kitchen one final look and following Isla out the door.

"I thought we talked about you taking the day off from your advisor duties," Isla said in a jokingly stern voice as they made their way back to Kai and Jade.

"I don't recall that conversation," Annalise said with a sniff, then groaned. "I don't know how to 'take a day off,' Isla. *Especially* on my wedding day."

"Well, I'm just impressed you're still going through with this—the big, grand ceremony, that is. Rynn would rather tell everyone to leave and go elope on a ship in the middle of the ocean."

Annalise laughed, some of the tension leaving her shoulders. "That's sounding better and better, honestly."

Before they entered the chambers to finish getting ready, Isla turned to face Annalise. "You two really are so good for each other. I'm glad he found you, Annalise."

She smiled, her green eyes bright and swimming with emotion. "I am, too. I have to admit, he wasn't what I expected."

"They never are," Isla said with a wink, then opened the door to a squeal from Kai and a muttered "it's about time" from Jade, who proceeded to smile warmly and scrambled to get Annalise's dress.

The next few hours passed in a blur of gossamer, flowers, and sparkling wine. Before Isla knew it, Annalise's father, Sebastian, and Aidan were knocking on their door, ready to escort the ladies to the garden where the ceremony would take place. Sebastian took Isla's arm and kissed her temple as they walked.

"You look beautiful," he said quietly.

She glanced at him, her eyes roaming over his fitted black pants and crisp shirt, a matching black jacket hugging the muscles of his arms. He caught her lingering gaze and pinched her side.

"If you keep looking at me like that, love, I'm afraid we might miss this wedding altogether," he murmured against her ear, his warm breath sending shivers along her skin.

"What a shame," she hummed.

His eyes heated. "Be good," he said with a growl as he led her to the gardens, and the vision before her made her forget their little game.

The garden was decorated to perfection—unsurprising, since Annalise planned it all. Strands of small orbs holding flickering flames hung from the gates. Tall marble pedestals lined the pathway, each bearing an enormous arrangement of lush greenery with specks of color—a couple of roses here and there, dashes of white carnations and light purple lilies every few feet. Only a few rows of chairs took up the space in front of a white archway, as Rynn and Annalise wanted to keep the event small and intimate. Green vines and garland wrapped around the columns of the arch. Next to each row of chairs were large lanterns filled with candles and rose petals. Three musicians were stationed in the very back, their beautiful, soft music filling the evening air with calm anticipation.

It was a fairytale come to life.

Just as Jade, Kai, and Isla moved to stand on the side of the altar, a loud tapping could be heard over the music, right on the other side of the gardens. Isla craned her neck around the archway and almost burst out laughing at the sight.

There was Bri, all dressed up in a dazzling red gown, her heels clipping against the stone as she sprinted as fast as her dress would allow.

"I'm here! Don't start yet!" she panted, and Isla shook with laughter.

"I didn't think you were going to make it!" she cried as Bri reached the open gate and flung herself into Isla's arms.

"I couldn't miss this!" she said breathlessly. "Gods, I missed you. Oh, and Kai, I can't wait to see the baby!" She pulled Kai in for a hug as the latter came around Isla. "Okay, okay, I guess I should find a seat—sorry, sir," she said, turning to the priest and offering a little bow as she skirted around him, throwing a quick wave back to Isla and hurrying down the aisle.

Rynn emerged from the side of the gardens with his cane and took his spot next to Aidan and the priest. He looked handsome in his black ensemble, his brown hair groomed instead of its normal wild, haphazard state, and the scruff at his chin trimmed and neat. Isla was amused to find he looked *nervous*, an emotion she didn't think she'd ever seen on the man. His fingers tapped at his side and he kept pulling his lip between his teeth, glancing down the aisle every few seconds.

Soon, the music changed to a slow, deep melody, and across the gardens, Annalise appeared. It seemed like every guest exhaled at the sight.

She glided down the aisle with grace and beauty, her bronze skin gleaming against the ivory lace of her dress. Delicate mahogany curls swayed down her back, a crown of white flowers, vines, and pearls resting atop her head. The smile that broke out on her face when she caught Rynn's eyes took Isla's breath away.

The ceremony was simple yet powerful, the two of them exchanging heart-felt vows that had Kai, Isla, and even Jade sniffing into their handkerchiefs. All too soon, it was over, the bride and groom beaming at one another as the entire world melted into laughter and cheers, Isla's heart lighter than it had been in months.

To both Annalise and Rynn's chagrin, Sebastian had pulled rank as king and planned a lively ball teeming with members of court and what seemed like every citizen of Delarossi. When their group entered the ballroom following the ceremony, the space erupted into applause and swept Rynn and Annalise into conversation and congratulations. Sebastian merely chuckled and tipped his glass of sparkling wine at Annalise when she shot daggers at him.

"I still can't believe you did this," Isla said with a laugh as they danced through dozens and dozens of couples. "You *knew* they would hate it."

"They can leave whenever they please, and I told them as much. I have a private carriage outside and a ship waiting at Callum's Port, ready to take them anywhere they want." He smiled down at her and kissed her forehead. "This isn't for them, anyway. I like to take any chance I can to give my people something joyful to celebrate. What better reason than my best friend finding the love of her life?"

The two of them danced their way closer to Kai and Aidan, the latter of which had already abandoned his jacket and rolled up the sleeves of his shirt, looking casual and comfortable as he twirled his wife across the dance floor. To the side, Akir and Eliza waved at them, little Amaya cooing in Eliza's arms. Kai was never more than a few steps away from her daughter, but Isla was happy to see her relaxing and having fun.

"Come with me," Sebastian suddenly said, and Isla gave him a questioning look. He merely shrugged, as if to say, "you'll have to come to find out," and took her hand. Leading her out of the ballroom, they ventured down the hallway and back through the entrance to the gardens.

The sun had fully set, and the stars twinkled with delight in the deep blue and black sky, swirled together like paint strokes on a canvas. To the far right of the ceremony site was a wooden gazebo, now aglow with candles lining the steps and along the railing. The ballroom was close enough that they could still hear notes of music drifting through the night, a quiet backdrop to the sounds of insects buzzing and wind whistling through the grass.

They walked up the steps to the gazebo and he held out his hand. When Isla took it, he pulled her flush to his chest, swaying back and forth to the echoes of the music.

"What does this remind you of?" he asked.

She gave an involuntary shudder. "The night of the ball in Iona." She hated to think of that night over a year ago, how she'd been ready to throw everything away. The heartbreak of her words still splintered through her.

"That wasn't how I expected that night to go, I admit. I'd planned to give some grand profession of my love and dramatically ask you to run away with me," he said, winking.

She snorted. "I wouldn't have said yes, even if I didn't think I was about to die. That would have been way too fast."

He lifted her hand to his chest and clutched at it, faking a hurt expression. "You wound my poor, fragile heart."

Kissing the back of his hand, she said, "Well, I'm here now. So I suppose your plan worked."

"Not quite, but there's still time."

Furrowing her brow, she opened her mouth to ask him what he meant, but he pressed a kiss to her lips instead. She sighed into him, her mind buzzing with contentment as it did every time he touched her.

"I love you," he whispered against her lips. "I know it's my best friend's wedding, and this is terrible etiquette. But I can't stand one more second without the world knowing you're mine."

"I've always been yours, Sebastian," she said, running her fingers through his hair and kissing his nose, then his cheek.

"Then marry me, Isla Vasileia. Be my queen, my wife, my equal in every way." He pulled away from her quickly, his blue eyes boring into hers.

Her lips parted in a silent exhale. It wasn't as if they hadn't discussed this over the last year. She'd known exactly what she was stepping into when she moved her and her father to Karstos. But she still couldn't believe this was *real*.

He cupped her cheek with one hand and held her waist tightly with the other, pulling her close enough to feel his warm breath fanning over her cheeks. "You are everything I could ever hope to be, Isla. Every good and beautiful piece. I was broken when you found me, but I have never felt so whole as when you're by my side." Isla closed her eyes as a tear dropped from her lashes.

"Marry me, my love. Stay with me, and I promise you, I will love you until my dying breath."

She looked up at him, her heart and mind made up long before he asked.

"Yes," she said with a shaky breath. "You're my forever, Sebastian."

His answering smile shattered her world, and he sealed her promise with a kiss.

"Forever," he said, humming. "I like the sound of that."

The End

ACKNOWLEDGEMENTS

There is an undeniable thrill that follows each time I finish a book; a moment where the world seems to pause and my fingers shake over the keyboard, my mind racing to catch up with what just happened—did I actually *finish* this? Is this real? And then comes the satisfaction, the relief, the pride. Later, the doubts and fears and imposter syndrome. But finishing this one was different from last time, because it's the *end*. My first completed duology. Saying goodbye to these characters was like saying goodbye to a dear friend. Writing their story and watching readers connect with them has been one of the most fulfilling, heart-warming experiences of my life. I am so very thankful to you for taking a chance on Isla and the gang, and loving them in all their broken glory.

First and foremost, all thanks and praise be to God for giving me this opportunity and blessing me each and every day with the ability, support, and love to pursue this dream.

To Taylor—thanks for not saying I was crazy two years ago when I said I wanted to publish a book. Thank you for giving me the space and freedom to write and work on the neverending to-do list that comes with self-publishing. I need your positivity when the days are hard, your excitement when my constant doubts arise, your easy-going nature when my mind begins to spiral. I love you and don't know what I would do without you.

To my family—some of the very first people to buy, read, and recommend my books to everyone you met. Your faith and pride in me throughout this entire journey has lifted me up and kept me going. You have never doubted me or questioned my decision to dedicate so much of my time to this dream of mine, and I'm so incredibly grateful to have your support and love.

To my alpha and beta readers—Haley, Kaitlyn, Natalia, Peyton. Thank you for taking time and energy to read this draft and help shape it into the best version. Your feedback and love for this story means the world to me, and I can't thank you enough for the attentive care you gave to making sure this finale was everything it could be. Thank you for being on this epic adventure with me from the beginning.

To my editor, Amanda—once again, I am incredibly thankful for your eagle eye and your devotion to fine-tuning each aspect of this book. I'm so glad I found you over a year ago, and I hope you know you're officially stuck with me. Are you ready to leave the elementals and follow me to Veridia City?

To the bookmasters—Alice, Brit, Cris, Katie, and Melissa. You are my sisters, my shoulders to cry on, my writing buddies, my constant support, my best friends. I would have given up so many times if it weren't for you. Having this group as we each go through our writing journeys has been such a joy. I'm so proud of every single one of us, and I'm counting down the days till I can squeeze you.

To the coven—you know who you are. I never thought joining a random Discord group one day would lead to some of the best friendships I could ever ask for. Thank you for cheering me on in the good days, letting me complain on the bad, lifting me up when this gig threatens to drown me, and giving me some of the best laughs of my life. I can't imagine a time when I didn't have you all by my side, and I hope I never have to. Let's just keep postponing that falling out, yeah? :bessieflower:

To my street team—thank you for cheering me on and hyping me up and loving these characters so completely! Having you guys at my back and helping get the word out about these books has been incredible. You showed up time and time again, screaming from the rooftops to recommend me and my little books. It means everything to have you in my corner!

To my readers—words cannot express how much I appreciate the overwhelming support I've had with this duology. Every kind word, every review, every message, every comment. It fills my heart and makes the hard days worth it. Even though the elementals and their stories are over, I hope you'll stick around for what's next. Thank you from the bottom of my heart, friends.

While these characters and this world may be ending, I have so much more in store.

This is just the beginning.

About the Author

V.B. Lacey is an office manager by day and an avid reader-turned-writer by night. She grew up on stories of magic, love, and sarcasm, and equips her writing with all three. She lives in Texas with her supportive husband and two rambunctious dogs. When she's not writing about morally grey characters and far-off kingdoms, you can find her reading (mostly fantasy and contemporary romance), playing board games, or spending time with friends.

Visit her online at www.vblaceybooks.com, or follow her on Instagram and TikTok: @vblacey.books.

Made in the USA
Las Vegas, NV
25 November 2024

12577575R00286